PRAISE FOR
180 DAYS

"Screenwriter Alfredo Botello's action-packed novel—part Bay Area love story, part punk rock anthem—is a race-against-the-clock tale that will remind readers of the profound power of redemption and second chances."

—Elaine Szewczyk, Author of *I'm with Stupid*

"A love letter to art, architecture, music, dreams lost and found, innovative plumbing, and, finally, love itself, *180 Days* is smart, funny, and fearlessly romantic.... The novel's characters may be running out of time, but Alfredo Botello's boundless talent is just getting started."

—Liam Callanan, Author of *When in Rome*

"It's always the voice on the page that keeps me reading, and what a deep and abiding pleasure to find in Alfredo Botello's debut novel, *180 Days*, a fresh voice to love. In this story of a marriage on the rocks and the wild, desperate, at times funny struggle to save it, Botello has created a real page-turner. His characters are human beings, complicated, quirky, honestly searching for meaning and love. And the form which the author has chosen to tell this story—an examination of days in the countdown until, by California law, the divorce is final—is elegant, energetic, and surprising. Highly recommend! *180 Days* is a novel to savor."

—Murray Silverstein, Award-Winning Poet of *Any Old Wolf*, Coauthor of *A Pattern Language*

"Loved it. *180 Days* reads like coffee or drinks with an old friend. Smart, funny, emotional, and naughty. Filled with musical Easter eggs and authentic Bay Area details offered up in spades. It's a painfully relatable love story that poses so many questions—and so many answers—in vivid and raw detail. Hella yes!"

—Mike Dirnt, Bassist, Cofounder of Green Day

"Alfredo Botello's debut novel delves into themes of self, uncertainty, passion, loss, and the overwhelming need for each of us to redeem ourselves, to surmount past mistakes and reclaim who and what we really are. With an intensity that mirrors the depth of these themes, Botello's story floats lyrically, carried by characters—Tomas and Naomi—who are memorable, vulnerable, complex, and very, very human. An outstanding and moving piece of writing that merits a spot on any library's top shelf."

—Greg Fields, Author of *Through the Waters and the Wild*, 2022 Winner of the Independent Press Award for Literary Fiction

"A compelling and deeply insightful exploration of love, forgiveness, and self-discovery, Botello's *180 Days* skillfully delves into the complexities of human relationships, offering a raw and authentic portrayal of the challenges faced by many, making it a truly remarkable and thought-provoking read."

—Ted Kissel, Author of *Betrayal in the Casbah*

"In this novel about broken love and coming to terms with our sense of self, Alfredo Botello deals wonderfully with the concepts of limitations, expectations, and ultimately, the realizations one comes to when dealing with a marriage at a crossroads. Actions have very real consequences, and the fallout after infidelity is portrayed with an honest and tender pen in this compelling narrative. Original, funny, and wise, Botello's *180 Days* is a beautifully delineated tale of love, hurt, hope, and our search for personal validation."

—Fionn Mac Meldrum, *The Shadow of Banshee Hill*

"*180 Days* is a timely, nerdy love letter to the Bay Area, long-lost-love-filled vacations staring at buildings in Barcelona, growing older, and the crushing realization that love takes work. A must-read for fans of *99 Percent Invisible* and second chances."

—Brian Krans, Award-Winning Bay Area Journalist, Author of *Assault Rifles and Pedophiles: An American Love Story*

"*180 Days* is a beautiful and undulating sprint of a love story that is so enthralling, I couldn't wait to find out how it would end. In deftly shifting points of view, Botello creates an exquisitely dynamic dialogue with a genuine intimacy that is nothing less than genius. His prose is indeed electric, erudite, inspired, and often poetic. I loved this book. Bravo!"

—Michael J. Cooper, Award-Winning Author of *Wages of Empire*

180 Days
by Alfredo Botello

© Copyright 2023 Alfredo Botello

ISBN 979-8-88824-183-7

All rights reserved. No part of this publication may be reproduced, stored in a retrieval system, or transmitted in any form or by any means—electronic, mechanical, photocopy, recording, or any other—except for brief quotations in printed reviews, without the prior written permission of the author.

This is a work of fiction. All the characters in this book are fictitious, and any resemblance to actual persons, living or dead, is purely coincidental. The names, incidents, dialogue, and opinions expressed are products of the author's imagination and are not to be construed as real.

Published by

3705 Shore Drive
Virginia Beach, VA 23455
800-435-4811
www.koehlerbooks.com

180 DAYS

A NOVEL

ALFREDO BOTELLO

VIRGINIA BEACH
CAPE CHARLES

Under Section 2339(a) of the California Family Code, spouses cannot finalize their divorce until six months after, "the date of service of a copy of [the] summons and petition or the date of appearance of the respondent, whichever occurs first."

PROLOGUE
DAY MINUS 4743

CLUTCHING WATER WAS A HOPELESS TASK, of course, but he had to try. Tomas Araeta returned to the Barcelona Pavilion for one more look. He was afraid that the visit he and his girlfriend Naomi Curran had made only hours before to the Modernist architectural jewel was not enough. He worried, he fretted—no, he was certain now—that the views he had taken in, the feelings, the sensations he had experienced of walking through a building he had until this trip only admired in still photographs, would be too fleeting.

Yes, of course he would look at the dozens of pictures and the video he had taken when he and Naomi returned home to the States, but it would not be the same. Not for Tomas. Anyone who has ever been to a concert, a museum, a sports event, or any other religious gathering, he felt, understood this. Enjoying a high-quality print of a Rothko is in no way comparable to the transcendent experience of sitting before a genuine Rothko, something Tomas had done at least a dozen times at the San Francisco Museum of Modern Art, which enshrined Rothko's orange and blue *Number 14.*

Was it not true of all the arts? For Tomas, listening to a recording by X or the Libertines was not the same as seeing the louche body language of front men John Doe and Carl Barat as they performed on stage, not the same as being crammed ass to crotch with strangers in a hot, humid venue that reeked of weed, not the same as dissolving into the mass of worshipful fans in the sweaty crowd, not the same as going slack and trusting one's newly appointed navigator: the moment.

And then there were the experiences that transcended the transcendent. Not just the Barcelona Pavilion. Or Schindler's Kings Road House. Or Rothko's Seagram Murals. Tomas and Naomi were some of only a handful of people to have seen iconic punk band The Pill Splitters live before they broke up. Tomas had seen a genuine shaman—front man Evo Korman—work his magic, mesmerize the crowd. And the kicker was, Korman didn't have to try. His interior and exterior lives seemed to be in complete harmony. He just *was*. About this he and Naomi were in complete agreement. When Tomas told the story of the show now to anyone who knew anything of The Pill Splitters, they would listen, rapt. Like he was telling an anecdote about holding hands with Neil Armstrong on the moon or helping women and children into lifeboats as the Titanic sank. The things we will one day tell ungrateful, disinterested grandchildren.

So Tomas intended to return, alone, to the Pavilion. Naomi, tired, not wanting to force another look at the building, not wanting to force *anything*, not wanting to risk sullying the memory of their visit just four hours before, stayed behind in the Pension Estrella in their small, hot room, with a shared bathroom in the hallway. The Pavilion had gobsmacked her too, of course, but why risk tarnishing that, now that her energy was depleted, the heat of the day climbing?

"How can you go to Spain and not want to siesta?" she asked Tomas.

"We're only here for a few days, I don't want to waste my time."

"Are you saying I'm wasting my time?"

"Yeah, that's exactly what I'm saying, Nomes, it's the Barcelona. Freaking. Pavilion."

"Yes. I know. And I saw it, too, Tomas. And I loved it. And *now*?

Now I'm going to enjoy something maybe even more beautiful than a nice building—a nap, a leisurely rest—in Spain. I shouldn't have to say this, but vacations are *for* wasting time."

"A tornado could take the Pavilion from us tomorrow," said Tomas.

"Do they have tornadoes in Spain?" mused Naomi.

"They have catastrophes," said Tomas. "Every place has catastrophes."

"Enjoy," said Naomi, shutting her eyes, ready to take in the sounds and smells of Spain from their open fourth story window once Tomas left her in peace.

Two months into their postgraduation Eurail tour through Europe to see the "great buildings" in person—from St. Peter's Cathedral in Rome to Hundertwasser's wavy gravy hippie apartment buildings in Vienna, to Santa Maria Novella in Florence, to the Centre Pompidou in Paris, to Gunter Behnisch's Postal Museum in Frankfurt, to countless other cathedrals and secular gems throughout the continent—Naomi was burned out. By the time they arrived in Spain, she had proclaimed unequivocally, "I'm tired of buildings."

Tomas had stopped and stared at her as they wound their way through narrow streets looking for the one-star pension.

"My *architecture* TA, my mentor, my dearest friend, my girlfriend, my life partner, the sun to my orbiting moon, my fuck buddy nonpareil, is saying, out loud, unambiguously, that she is— Lord, if you exist, forgive me for letting these heretical words pass my tongue—*tired*—of beautiful buildings."

"Good. You get it. So—let's just focus on food and people and doing nothing we're supposed to do just because we went to architecture school. Seriously, babe, don't you ever get monument fatigue?"

Apparently he didn't.

Back in their tiny room, she opened her eyes and glanced at him— he was looking out the window—portrait of the intense young man pensively contemplating . . . *something?* Hopefully not architecture.

"You're right," said Tomas. "As usual." He sighed and arched his eyebrows, adding a flourish of begrudging cheer to his capitulation. It had to be said, Naomi was always right on those things in life that comprise the big-ticket items. "And honestly, the pictures I take aren't a fraction as good as what I can get in a cheap Rizzoli paperback."

"Good. Come. Siesta with me. It's too hot out anyway."

"I will. Give me like an hour. I have an errand to run."

"An *errand*? Going to Safeway for Peet's coffee?" She tried to shoot him a disapproving glance, but he was already out the door. In the hallway he froze a moment and shook his head.

Shit. His little white lie could dampen her libido and make for a night of no sex. And he, at twenty-two, and she, at twenty-five, should—and did—have animal lust to spare. *"I have an errand to run."* That was the best he could do? He only had an hour to get back to the Pavilion and then return with the bogus result of whatever "errand" he would invent.

He quick stepped down the stairs out of the pension. Why didn't he just stand his ground and tell her he was going back to the Pavilion? Why lie? She wouldn't really be mad. Silly. He promised himself he would never lie to her again, about things big or, in this case, shamefully small. He was above it. She was above it. *They* were above it. Naomi had loved the building, too. From its overall gestalt and siting to the gorgeous natural patterns on the red onyx and travertine walls to the slender cruciform columns to architect Mies van der Rohe's iconic chrome and black leather chairs, she, too, had found the building sublime. But she was also burned-out. One cathedral bled into the next. One stone farmhouse as picturesque as another. One Modernist masterpiece as restrained and elegant as the next.

They both had noticed something right away when they reached the Pavilion. The pictures they saw in school never revealed that the Pavilion was at the base of a prominent hill in Barcelona—Montjuic—crowned by a seventeenth century castle that overlooked the city, with stepped waterfalls, large domes, massive columns—a grand, ornate, imposing structure—the fare one would expect from an impressive monument. But the books didn't include the castle, or make mention of it, as it hadn't become the holy site for architects and design enthusiasts the Barcelona Pavilion had become.

The massive castle was fine. Mies van der Rohe's tiny Pavilion, however, built for the 1929 International Exhibition, transcended the transcendent.

The little flat-roofed building was intended to exist only temporarily, as part of the exhibition, and so was torn down in 1930, one year after its creation. But in the mid-1980s—by popular demand, and belated outrage—it was rebuilt to Mies's exacting specifications. Now everyone—Tomas Araeta and Naomi Curran included—could make the pilgrimage and let its effects wash over them.

And so Tomas returned to make sure he was thoroughly soaked in Mies's genius. He was hoping to indwell to the point of being bored. But boredom never came. Mies was one of the great men whose work never became tiresome.

For Tomas it was an ongoing epiphany: great art bears more, not less, fruit upon repeated viewing. He had once discovered a 1966 black-and-white YouTube clip of Tina Turner singing "River Deep, Mountain High" in what appeared to be the hollowed-out fuselage of an airplane, or perhaps just a low-ceilinged basement. Every time he watched the video, he could detect Tina shredding a different part of her vocal chords as she blew apart the word "baby," all the while dancing in an extremely well-cut and sexy white pantsuit—*white pantsuit*—her backup dancers smiling joyfully in the presence of this powerhouse. It was all so simple and captivating and never tiresome. Like The Pill Splitters. Or a low, orange moon. Or Mies.

Mies was known for his rigorously pure and simple designs: the perfect square or rectangle, divided and supported by a rational structural grid. Elegant detailing. No half measures: a wall was either an opaque wall or it was a pane of glass. There weren't cute windows with shelves for flowerpots in a Mies building. In the Seagram's

Building in New York, an office skyscraper, he designed window shades that could only be adjusted in three positions: fully open, half open, fully closed. So that, to the passerby across the street, there would still remain a semblance of intentionality, of order. Nothing arbitrary or capricious. To let some human being adjust the shades willy-nilly would be an insult to his work. Allowing them to be adjusted *at all* was already a gutting compromise to Mies. But people would cook in the Manhattan summer heat. So he allowed the three-position window shades.

He built not for the executive or secretary, but for eternity.

But with this project, the Barcelona Pavilion, forty-three-year-old Mies had for some reason loosened up: the columns and hovering roof which they supported *were* on a regular grid, and marched along rationally, but then, breaking his own internal logic, walls slipped one past the other; a wall that began "inside" the open pavilion extended "outside" into the quiet, meditative water basin upon which the sculpture of a woman seemed to be floating. The smoked glass walls were neither opaque nor clear.

The result was—and let's be cautious not to throw the word around too lightly—genius. Whether by intention or instinct, or an unequaled admixture of the two, Mies had designed a perfect building.

Tomas slowly walked through the Pavilion again, feeling transported, taking in something still photographs could never convey: architecture as a fluid, not static, art, where one needed to move through a building, to cast about one's gaze, to feel the progression of light and shadow, to love or hate it fully.

But of course hate was not a consideration here.

Hell, even the *chair* Mies designed for the Pavilion—"the Barcelona Chair"—had become iconic. It was a must-have for any office building or midcentury home. It had become shorthand—a signifier—that the owner had good and expensive taste. The wealthy tech and hedge fund folks who bought midcentury homes today knew they better have a Barcelona or Eames chair or Corbu lounge in their living room if they wanted to appropriately honor the spirit of the buildings in which they were fortunate enough to eat, sleep, fuck, and shit.

Had Mies never designed the Pavilion, had he only designed the Barcelona Chair, he still would've made the cut into Tomas's private pantheon, the exclusive residence in his mind and heart of the great men and women designers of the world.

Stepping back into the dipping Catalan sunlight, standing atop the Pavilion's long travertine plinth, glancing up again at what he considered the "clunky" castle atop Montjuic, Tomas felt sick. He felt the sudden urge to leave. Something in the back of his mind, something he had sublimated, an overfilled suitcase he could sit on and zip close most days, had burst open, yanked out from under him by returning to the building: the horrifying realization that, if he had a thousand lifetimes, he would never create something half as beautiful as the Barcelona Pavilion.

Naomi was right. Coming back was a mistake.

"I thought you were siesta-ing," said Tomas as he quietly opened the door to room 4-B of the Pension Estrella.

"Huh? No," answered Naomi distractedly. She was sitting up in bed, in shorts and a T-shirt. Tomas took in a sight that never grew old, a sight that was, in its way, as sublime as Mies's masterwork—the soft, smooth skin and lovely curve of the underside of her thighs. And her knees. Those glorious, perfectly formed knees.

"Listen to this," said Naomi, reading. "*She hurled herself into his arms. 'It's so good to see you! You look fantastic. For a guy who spends his life screwin'*—yes, she said screwin', Tomas, not screw-*ing*, *'spends his life screwin' around, I don't know how you do it.'*" Naomi lightly touched the skin above her breasts and read breathlessly, "'*I love you madly, Lennie Golden. Welcome back.*'" Naomi dropped her voice low, adopting that charmer's Lennie's voice as she read the next line. "'*I love you too, monkey face.*'" Naomi finally looked up at Tomas. "Is this not *wonderful*?"

"It's breathtaking," said Tomas. "I feel like I've failed you. 'Nomes' is about as uncreative a pet name as there is. *Monkeyface?* Good god, the bar's been set high."

She put down the dog-eared copy of Jackie Collins's 1985 novel *Lucky*, which she had found in the pension's "take one-leave one" library.

"What is that?" she asked, taking note of the greasy paper bag Tomas was clutching.

"Bocadillos with jamon serrano and manchego, some cheap table wine, and some fresh basil I bought to throw on the bocadillos——and some kind of candy that I'm hoping is not that disgusting almond stuff but looked so pretty—little pineapples—I had to get it."

Naomi tilted her head, perplexed.

"Wow. I was sure you were going straight back to the Pavilion to torture yourself some more."

No more lies, not even the teensiest of ones.

"Oh, I did that, too. But I needed cover, so I got this."

Naomi stood up, walked to Tomas, and put her arms around his neck.

"Of course you went back. You're sick like that. But you turn me on just the same."

"You're just excited about the greasy ham."

"Of course."

"So we eat?"

"Absolutely. Right after we fuck."

"When we get home," said Tomas, pursing his lips thoughtfully, "I'm buying a whole pig and every Jackie Collins book ever written." Naomi began lifting his T-shirt over his head. He helped her by raising his arms. With the shirt covering his face, he mumbled, "Sex before dinner. Very cool."

"And probably after," said Naomi. "No, *definitely* after."

In a frantic rush to finish undressing, they sat down on the thin, sagging mattress and fucked themselves nearly blind, as only new lovers or twenty-somethings can do.

Afterward, liquid exhaustion setting in, Tomas spooned Naomi, waited for her to begin snoring, a soft, deep breathing punctuated by violent snorts—a sound he had come to love—and thought no more of the demoralizing perfection of the Pavilion.

DAY 1

NAOMI DROVE. ROUNDING OAKLAND'S LAKE MERRITT, the Alameda County Courthouse came into view. Tomas was in the passenger seat. Naomi parked at the first available street spot she could find.

"Please don't fight me on this."

"What are we doing?"

"Don't play dumb, it's on the second floor."

"I'm not. This is where we got our marriage license."

Before exiting the car, Naomi clasped Tomas's hands tightly, wrapping hers around his.

"I remember everything, Tomas. And I don't want to talk right now. Let's just do this. That is my ask."

She climbed out of the car, and, without looking to see if Tomas was following her, trotted up the stairs toward the courthouse entrance. Tomas got out of the car, but stayed behind, staring at Naomi, wondering how long this charade would last.

"You can't be serious," he called after her.

"I am." She didn't break stride. Tomas skipped up the stairs after her.

"You're pissed, you're furious, I get it. But, Jesus, give it a week, even three *days*. This is crazy!" If it is possible to skip up steps in a pleading manner, Tomas found it. "I don't wanna divorce, Naomi."

Tomas suddenly stopped and sat down. Everything seemed distant and cruel: the cars driving along 12th Street, the colors of the sky, buildings, the sound of people speaking on their phones. What was their goddamn problem? And what was happening here? This was absurd. This was rash. This was beyond unreasonable. This was not the Naomi he had known for seventeen years.

Naomi could hear that he was no longer following her. She turned around to look at him. The first thing she noticed was the cowlick of his dirty blond hair. Even his stupid little cowlick was annoying. He was sitting on the granite steps, facing the street, holding his head in his hands, as if the damn thing weighed two hundred pounds.

"Tomas, please, I don't *need* you to go into that building with me, but it would make it easier if you did. I can hire someone to serve you papers, but that's a hassle."

"Fine. Good. Let's hassle. I don't care." He didn't turn around. From her vantage point, he just seemed to be calmly watching the cars passing back and forth.

"Tomas. I've made up my mind. Let's not fight about this. Can we at least go out on a dignified note?"

"Marivel. Marivel talked you into this, didn't she? She's always hated me, and your mother's a spinning weathervane. She just does whatever Marivel says."

"Good god, Tomas, are you really trying to deflect this onto my mother's partner?"

Strangers ascending the steps took notice of a conversation in which a young man spoke into the air rather than turning to face the woman he was addressing.

"You're mad, Nomes. You're in shock. You're pissed."

"Don't tell me what I'm feeling."

"Okay. Whatever you're feeling, and I'm just telling you what I think is happening here, *right now*, and it feels really drastic and really... sudden... *to me*. And I just—you know, why don't we sit on this thing a week and then come back. Courthouse will still be here; it's not going anywhere. You can always serve papers on me then. And, I promise—I *promise*—I won't resist. I will walk in there with you and sign whatever you want me to sign. Just not today."

"You're an ass."

Naomi slowly walked down a few steps, forced herself to exhale, and sat next to Tomas.

"Please look at me," she said. He turned to her. Whether it was pity, muted anger, or sympathy in her eyes, he did not know.

"Tomas, I don't want to wait a week. I don't want to not remember exactly how I've felt since two nights ago. I don't want to drive around on three tires and pretend everything is okay. So—please—come with me now and let's fill out these forms and move on with our lives. We have no kids yet, thank God. We're not young, but we're not old. We can each still find happiness maybe. Think about it. Really."

She stood back up, and with no great haste but all deliberation, walked toward the heavy front doors of the courthouse. The pressure behind Tomas's eyes was enormous, and his throat was clutched like a vise. He stood and quietly followed Naomi into the building.

They entered the Family Law Unit on the second floor. The office looked like any other neglected government office: scuffed vinyl tile floor, dropped ceiling with fluorescent lights, people milling about, spinning metal racks with dozens of forms, bored clerks.

Such a dignified neoclassical building from the outside, so unremarkable inside.

"I just want to make sure we get the right forms," said Naomi, getting in line. She glanced back. Tomas was mindlessly spinning a rack, perusing the dozen or so forms that helped facilitate the end of a marriage.

Just three days ago he had been perusing greeting cards that were to accompany flowers.

"Tomas."

It was their turn. Tomas joined Naomi at the counter in front of the clerk.

"Hello," said Naomi. "We want the form that allows us to divorce without hiring a lawyer—we have no kids, no prenup—the simplest one."

The clerk handed Naomi several blank forms.

"Fill out the FL-100—one of you will be the petitioner and that person will serve it on the respondent. If you're both in agreement, it doesn't matter who the petitioner or respondent is. And each of you also needs to fill out an FL-142 and an FL-150."

Tomas had kept his cool for the last fifteen minutes, but now, here, with this official-looking piece of paper in front of him—FL this, FL that—he no longer could deny that a house was on fire. And it was his job to put out the flames.

"What if we're not in agreement?"

Naomi shot him a look: not now, not here, not ever.

"Then one of you will serve the other one."

"What if one of the parties isn't thinking clearly?" asked Tomas.

"Tomas, no."

"What if, tomorrow, or a week from tomorrow, or two weeks from tomorrow, she—or he—but really, she—wakes up and thinks, maybe I rushed into this. Maybe I want to think about it some more?"

"This is how you respect my wishes?" said Naomi. "Are you *trying* to prove how right I am in coming here today, because you're doing a spectacular job of just that."

With grim satisfaction, Tomas imagined that his little protest—*what if we're not in agreement*—must've shocked the clerk. He wasn't going to go down without a fight—yes, sure, perhaps an impotent protest—but *something*. He wasn't yelling, wasn't really causing a scene, but at least he had the good sense to speak his piece in earshot of a neutral party.

But the clerk said nothing. Was his sympathetic witness betraying him? She just looked bored and impatient. Tomas suddenly realized she must see a dozen scenes like this, and worse, every day, and that his well-behaved, middle-class hostile "chat" with his wife wouldn't even qualify as table stakes in here. The woman just wanted to do her job, shorten the line, wrap up, go home. That's it.

"Are there any other forms we need?" Naomi asked the clerk.

"No," said the clerk, her eyes on Tomas, who was mumbling silently to himself. "You don't have to," added the clerk, "but a lot of people have lawyers help fill them out."

A lot of people? Why state something so obvious? And why take sides? Who was she, thought Tomas, to express even a sliver of sympathy for Naomi? She knew nothing of their situation, knew nothing of the intricacies, the give and take of their relationship, let alone the foibles and virtues of their characters? And after all, what are we really talking about here, besides human foible and folly? The woman absolutely had no right to suggest the engagement of attorneys.

"Hoping to avoid that," said Naomi, "but it's kind of not up to me." Naomi let her words trail off. She could see the clerk understood her just fine. Just another cheating, rationalizing, pleading, begging, moody, indignant, lying, selfish, childish, worm of a philanderer voicing some silly little objection only because he'd been caught, only because he feared division of assets, some family embarrassment perhaps. Here was just another little pimple who, since time immemorial, attempted to have his cake and eat it too.

Tomas could feel Naomi's hate radiating from her body, could see, in profile, her jaw tightening. What was happening here? So many expressions, so many sounds, coming from Naomi Curran, sounds and faces that, in seven years of dating, and ten years of marriage, he had never seen or heard. True, her anger was justified, but what of this show? Was she *trying* to conjure looks of contempt and sorrow? For what audience? Had she practiced in front of a mirror? It had been three days—seventy-two hours, *seventy-two measly hours*—since he'd made his mistake.

Well, seventy-two hours since she had become aware of it.

So be it: he would have to be the voice of reason, of measure. This was absurd. He gathered himself and spoke calmly.

"Okay. Okay. Let's take half a breath here," he said, addressing the clerk. "It's not impossible that someone could change their mind. And obviously it's possible Naomi *won't* change hers. That's fine. I get it. But before we put official stamps and case numbers and god knows what else onto these ugly pieces of paper—"

"Fuck you!" yelled Naomi. Ah, yes, here it was. The actual scene. Fine. Let's get it out, let's air it *all* out.

"There will be time to change your mind," said the clerk, her voice no softer or louder than it had been since they reached the counter.

"*What*?" asked Tomas.

"Neither of you will be single until six months and one day after the Respondent is served."

Tomas swiveled his head to face Naomi before snapping it back to face the clerk. "Explain. Please."

Naomi glanced at him, hating the eager schoolboy's tone with which he asked the question, loathing the smug expression on that handsome, wretched face, a face—and defective mind—which wanted—now, suddenly—to hear *exactly* what the clerk had to say, and no doubt in excruciating and unnecessary detail.

"It's called the 'cooling off' period. Six months. One hundred and eighty days. It's there in case couples patch up and don't want to have to undo a bunch of legal papers."

"A cooling off period?" parroted Tomas. God, the irritating little pedant. He understood her just fine, she was not speaking Cyrillic, he just wanted to savor this false victory. What a little cocksucker. Naomi realized she was wrong. She thought her husband was capable of some small flicker of shame. Clearly he was not. Oh good lord, he was opening his mouth again—was he really going to draw this out further?

"So if I'm understanding correctly, over the next six months, if we change our minds, none of this matters?"

"You can file today, but the court won't look at it for a hundred and eighty days, correct."

Tomas glanced at Naomi, who—it struck him—now wore on her face the kind of smile she normally reserved for greeting bank tellers and strangers in line at the supermarket.

"Awesome. Can I also get a set of those forms?" he asked.

The clerk turned to retrieve a set for Tomas.

Through clenched teeth which weren't actually clenched, but still could turn coal into diamond, Naomi said, "Tomas, your little performance here today is cute—but you know you're full of shit. I said no to your marriage proposal twice, and I told you that if we did get hitched, all you had to do was talk to me first if something was bothering you. But you didn't. So kudos to you—but, if you have any honor or dignity left, try—*try*—to summon just an iota of it."

"I've done nothing undignified here today. I'm educating myself."

As the clerk returned, Tomas asked her, "Excuse me, ma'am? Have I caused a scene? Have I embarrassed you? Or us? My wife seems to think so."

The clerk looked briefly at Naomi, enough to express her shared disgust of the unctuous, entitled little toad standing next to her, and said nothing as she handed Tomas the forms.

"The founding fathers were geniuses!" blurted out Tomas. "They understood human nature." Naomi wouldn't look at him. Fine. No matter. He had legal forms, he had history, had *human nature,* on his side. "They literally baked in six months because this kind of shit probably happens every day,"

Naomi left. For a moment, Tomas was startled. Clearly she did not want Tomas to chase after her, but chase he did, and why? Because, in the grand scheme of this laughably pedestrian transgression, the very marrow of soap operas and novels, a chase was—as his father Tomas Araeta Sr. might say—*appropriate.*

Lord the woman could walk quickly. Outside the building, he watched as Naomi descended the steps. She was fleet of foot and moved gracefully. He had known that since the first day he set eyes on her in Wurster Hall. It was very sexy, very appealing. There was just a certain forward momentum, drive, and, really, *elegance* about her gait.

Tomas yelled, "Wait up!"

Naomi stopped. Something in her enjoyed—well, what she felt wasn't really enjoyment, no, it was more a curiosity she felt watching this deluded animal writhing that compelled her to turn and face him. She smiled. He just looked so . . . obliviously confident. The poor little thing. He was right about one thing: Marivel did not care for him. She saw through him like the flimsy palimpsest of a man he was.

"Yes?"

"Let's talk. You know, really talk. I mean, we've got six months anyway. It doesn't have to be now, but let's talk. I am here. To listen."

"Oh, I think my heart just skipped a beat. I am so *grateful*. Thank you." She paused and smiled wider than before, adding, "I'm filing the papers. I'm done, Tomas. Done."

Oh how the fevered mind can collapse in an instant. Exhaustion—physical, mental, emotional—overtook Tomas. He considered saying something to the effect that what she thought today she might not think tomorrow, but he knew he had already exhausted her reserves of patience. Plus there was no need to expend any more energy today—he had the law on his side. And *time*. The wisdom of dispassionate, thoughtful people who understood the anger and recklessness of the moment—would carry the day. Not *this* day, perhaps. But a day.

"I don't care about some one-hundred-and-eighty-day loophole, Tomas. I don't want to say it again: please don't fight me on this."

She tossed him the keys to their car. "You're probably already late for work."

As she did five days a week, she would take the subway, BART, into the city, San Francisco, for her job at Macy's.

"Whatever you think of me," said Tomas, "it's literally a law." Then it hit him. "Ohmygod, wait. You hear this from Marivel all the time. I've heard her say it a shit ton of times. 'Strike while the iron is cold.' She's a therapist, Nomes. *Strike while the iron is cold.* We talk when we've cooled down. Duh."

"Do you really think I haven't thought of her, and those exact words?"

"Apparently not, because she *knows* this stuff. God I love that woman."

Naomi gathered herself, took a moment, and said with icy certainty.

"Today, six months, six years—you won't change."

Tomas's confidence was undiminished. He could change. *Of course* he could change. In fact, he mostly didn't need to change. It was a tiny corner of his being that needed a tweak. Minor stuff. One doesn't just start with open heart surgery. There are blood thinners, stents, changes in diet, to be tried first. One proceeds cautiously, as noninvasively, as possible. One diagnoses the problem, and *then* proposes a remedy. Naomi was proceeding backward. Now wasn't the moment to point this out to her, but, when the iron had cooled, yes, then this—whatever this thing was—could be handled *appropriately.*

"Right, exactly, you tell me when and only when you're really ready to talk," he added.

She shook her head. The contempt she felt was palpable to Tomas. Yes, better words failed him right now, but he would find them later. He would. He had to. He wasn't there yet, but he would be. He could fix this. He would fix this. He had time.

This was one conversation, an aberration in some crazy overheated hothouse called family court, among many others they would surely have. He could take all the barbs she needed to throw. She could riddle him with more arrows than St. Sebastian and he wouldn't blink. He deserved them all—absolutely. Fire away! This is good. This is *good.* Healthy. Let her kick my ass until she can't lift her foot.

Naomi descended the stairs and turned left on the sidewalk toward the Lake Merritt BART subway station. Tomas ran after her one more time, unable to tamp down the frenzied optimism he now felt.

"This is not over, Naomi."

"In a hundred and eighty-one days it will be."

DAY 94

IN THE WANING SUNLIGHT of a desolate stretch of Interstate 5 in California's Central Valley, Tomas thought for a moment of Edward Hopper's famous painting, *Nighthawks*. A couple of lonely souls drinking coffee at a late-night diner. Nothing so romantic or melancholy here on the interstate. Just an offramp that promised fast food and lodging. But there were the gas stations with their bright bands of rooftop neon beckoning drivers. So, yes, some bastardized version of *Nighthawks*, if one squinted hard enough and ignored the families filling minivans with gas and eating Taco Bell, could be had. Hopper was not in Tomas's pantheon, although he greatly respected the man's work—his portraits of solo persons alone in nondescript rooms *were* haunting and deserved their accolades—but right now it was *Nighthawks* that came to mind.

Tomas left his car in the Comfort Inn parking lot and walked across a concrete and grass median on his way to one such gas station minimart, where, to his relief, beer was sold. Not all of them sold alcohol. He bought a tall can of Pabst and took it back to his room. Leaving the TV on the first channel that happened to come up, he quickly finished his beer—it was only 7:32 p.m. Christ, he had driven three hours to eat time in the hopes of breaking the unrelenting loop of rumination that had tortured him for months. Add to that the stroll to the minimart and he had managed to kill a whopping forty minutes since his arrival. Lovely. Didn't someone once say, "It's not one day at a time, it's one *minute* at a time"? Well, if they didn't, they should have. Tomas had two hundred fifty or so more minutes to kill in this town—was it the Buttonwillow exit he had taken?—he wasn't sure now—before he could hope for fatigue, beer, and weeks of vigilant yet unfocused tension to overtake him and bless him with sleep. His leg itched. The duct tape he'd pulled off his thigh hours ago had taken off hair. He scratched at the irritated, reddened skin.

He had to get out. Maybe find some bar without the horrific buzzing fluorescent light of the gas station minimart. Everyone needs to have a drink now and again with other human beings nearby, even if you are so consumed by your thoughts that you don't so much as say hello. Just being with people. Or—if you prefer—not being alone—might help. That was the point. Nighthawks. Just knowing someone else's heart was beating near yours. He had to kill time. And beer and television weren't getting the job done.

Beyond the gas stations and fast-food franchises along the branch road feeding onto the interstate, fate obliged Tomas. Looking out his window, he saw the sign: La Frontera Bar and Grill. The cheap box sign lacked the retro romance of the signage in any of Hopper's paintings—but by god, it called to him like a siren.

Tomas left his room, walked along the branch road, and entered the bar.

Most of La Frontera's clientele—most of them men—wore cowboy hats and shirts, but they weren't good ole boys. Most were, it was fair to guess, Mexican and South American farm workers. Tomas felt a pang of admiration for them. He had seen them working the endless rows of lettuce and fruit trees as he drove down I-5, men and women stooped over pulling the plants out of the ground, some with heavy burlap sacks on their backs to carry their haul. He hazarded another guess that the men enjoying their beers at La Frontera did not go to chiropractors after spending ten, twelve hours of grueling work. No, they probably grabbed a shower, put on their finest Western shirts with glittery floral shoulder designs, had a shot of tequila and a Tecate or two, and relaxed for a few hours before getting up and doing it all over again.

For a moment, Tomas wondered if his assumptions, the little scenarios he concocted, were just the tired, clichéd byproducts of White middle-class guilt, some kind of cringe-worthy romanticization of "the immigrant working poor." Tomas banished the thought. Why should he care? He had much bigger questions to probe and dissect. This was just one human being looking at another human being and feeling something. Any other thoughts reminded Tomas of what a building contractor had once told him when his specs called for three coats of gloss oil paint on a stair handrail.

"You're just stacking coats," the builder had said. "There's no point."

He was stacking thoughts now, looping them over and over. There was, as the builder had said, "no point."

Or, as Naomi had put in when she was his TA seventeen years ago, "Paralysis by analysis." She could see her comment left him a bit crestfallen in the moment, so she'd added, "When that deadline is screaming in your ear, you just commit and execute. And if you have the chops, and if your big idea isn't fundamentally flawed, you just might make something beautiful." Then she'd smiled breezily at her student, Tomas Araeta Jr.

How had this wonderful, kind, sweet person read him so thoroughly? How did she know exactly what to say to take him from crestfallen to inspired? Tomas stared intently at the red and gold floral pattern on the shoulder of a patron's shirt. How had he lost her? How had he played Russian roulette with their relationship? Never mind. Don't overthink. Just appreciate the moment. Sabotaging oneself is only one option among many. And it may not even be the best one.

But it was the most convenient. He considered himself a hack. Tomas didn't fully accept Naomi's thoughts on "just commit and execute" until they had gone to Rome six years later—as a couple—and seen the three versions of Michelangelo's *Pietà*. Tomas didn't know that Michelangelo had sculpted three distinct versions of the statue. He knew of the one most people were familiar with: the *Vatican Pietà*, which the artist had sculpted at the age of twenty-three. *Twenty-three!* Were he alive today, Michelangelo would have had his first legal drink two years before, he may still have had some pimples, and he might be a barista biding time before grad school. The second one, the *Bandini Pietà*, he sculpted when he was seventy-two, and the final pietà, the *Randanini Pietà*, was incomplete at the time of his death when he was seventy-eight.

It was baffling and shattering to Tomas. The Vatican Pietà—one must objectively admit, unless one was being willfully contrarian—was the most beautiful and moving of the three. How could this be? Where did a twenty-three-year-old find the depth of emotion to convey as no other had the sorrow of a mother cradling her dead son? Had he simply won the talent lottery, something that could never be taught or learned, ten thousand hours of practice be damned? Had the gods, for whatever reason, chosen to anoint him as their earthly vehicle to capture the divine and the perfect? Fifty years of life's vicissitudes later Michelangelo would again tackle the same theme but the work—again objectively—would show no greater understanding of the human condition than the work he had created as a baby-faced twenty-three-year-old. The emaciated body of a dead carpenter was draped so gently in the lap of his grieving mother, that tears were the only appropriate human response. For Naomi, who also favored the Vatican Pietà, she too was baffled. How could Michelangelo evoke such empathy and tenderness from a mute slab of marble? But in her eyes, Jesus's mother wasn't solely grieving. There was something placid about her expression. Yes, the grief was there, but so was an appreciation that she had been privileged to have known her son for the short time he was here.

And Michelangelo, young or old, with no room for error in a medium as unforgiving as stone, just cut and hammered and chiseled until he took what his mind's eye saw and concretized it, sanctified it. Naomi was right. Commit and execute. But first make sure your big idea is sound, make sure you have *something to say*. Michelangelo did. Tomas stared without focus at the back bar. He would never have something of substance to say, not at twenty-three, not at seventy-two, not at seventy-eight.

"What can I get you?"

The bartender working at La Frontera stood in front of Tomas. She was pretty, young, Latina, maybe twenty-five. Tomas noticed an older man in the kitchen visible through an opening in the backbar wall, slicing carrots, his head slicked back with pomade, covered by a hair net.

"How about something tequila?" asked Tomas listlessly.

"We have forty-eight tequilas," answered the bartender. Annoyed? No. Just a little tired of people who didn't know what they wanted.

"Oh. Okay. Well, you pick, but maybe you can mix it with something? But I'm not a margarita person."

"We make the best margaritas in the valley." She spoke mechanically. Perhaps she was—now—becoming annoyed. Tomas would just keep it simple.

"Oh, okay, well let's do a margarita."

"Classic, Cadillac, or strawberry?"

Strawberry sounded too sweet.

"Cadillac."

She stepped away to make his drink. Tomas turned and saw a small parquet dance floor between the bar stools and pool table. Someone played "Me and Baby Brother" by War on an old CD jukebox. No one was dancing just yet, but it was early.

Tomas thought of Paul Weller and The Jam, one of his favorite power pop bands, nothing at the level of The Pill Splitters, mind you, but certainly a band deserving of a spot in the pantheon. At twenty-two, *age twenty-two*, one year younger than Michelangelo, Paul Weller had written "Life From A Window." How did this child understand the quiet despair of a man who could see the world, but felt detached from it? That's the stuff—a piece of it anyway—of midlife, no? Something a forty-year-old might stack coats on. Twenty-two-year-olds should be doing keg stands and fucking girls and boys whose last names they will never learn, unworried about the past or the future. Musical polymath Prince (he was said to be able to play twenty-seven instruments) wrote "I Wanna Be Your Lover" when he was twenty-one. At the same age Poly Styrene of the X-Ray Spex wrote both "Germ Free Adolescents" *and* "Oh Bondage! Up Yours!" The range of feeling and sentiment in those two songs alone! Green Day's Billie Joe Armstrong penned "Christie Road" at nineteen, a song with the finessed, polished build-up and release of anything by The Who. He hadn't yet rounded out his second decade on the planet. At seventeen—*seventeen*—Carole King wrote her first number one hit, "Will You Love Me Tomorrow?" for The Shirelles. Tomas was thirty-six. At twenty-three—the same age as Michelangelo when he created the first Pietà – Evo Korman had defined the apotheosis of punk rock with the song "Blistered Eye." What had Tomas done of note besides ruin a marriage?

The bartender returned with his margarita, placed it on a square napkin, and left to attend to the small handful of other customers at the bar.

Jesus fucking Christ, thought Tomas as he took his first sip of the margarita, returning to memories of Rome. The Pietà was stunning and beautiful, but no more beautiful, no more moving, than sitting on marble steps near the Tiber river with Naomi and eating a cheap roast chicken bought from a corner store, washed down with a Peroni beer. Finding a spot of shade in the unforgiving midday sun. That pedestrian, fleeting experience held more meaning for Tomas now than he ever realized. And it had nothing to do with Michelangelo's *Pietà* or Salvi's Fountain of Trevi. It had everything to do with sharing a cold beer, exhausted, cheeks flushed red, next to the most important person in his world.

He put a five-dollar bill on the bar and left.

Outside the stars were beginning to make their appearance. Tomas felt buzzed. It felt good. The tightness was slackening just a bit. He stopped again at the minimart and bought a pint bottle of tequila and some ginger ale and went back to his room. He flipped through the channels. Even out here, at the Comfort Inn in Buttonwillow, there were adult movies for purchase (the note on the bottom of the screen assured him that "specific titles will not appear on your bill"). Did anyone with a laptop or smart phone really still need to order porn at a commuter hotel?

He turned off the TV.

He felt no desire to masturbate. One hundred days ago masturbation would have solved everything, would've switched the train onto a separate track just in time to avoid the head on collision. All men knew it from experience. Even boys of twelve or thirteen understood it: the moment the itch is scratched, *that very moment*, the instant one had ejaculated into bedside tissues, the distracting urge which had nagged one all day, which had consumed every thought and inchoate feeling, which had turned every girl over fifteen into an object of lust, would vanish. Gone. A quick jerk and the seemingly unquenchable desire evaporated as if it had never existed.

At least for a few hours.

Tomas took out his phone and looked through a few of the more recent pics of him and Naomi. The selfie he took ("you have longer arms" she reasonably pointed out) of them in front of the stagecoach diorama at the Oakland Museum of California; Naomi dancing for a moment on the black bar top at Radio, a long shoe box of a bar with a tall ceiling in downtown; a shot of them with Oakland's shipping container cranes—which bore an eerie semblance to giant camels or horses—visible in the background, taken by a passing stranger.

He then scrolled without purpose through his contacts. But soon he was in the "N's," and there she was. *Naomi.* He wanted to scroll her name away, but he touched her contact by accident and with a little too much pressure—*shit!*—his fingers were just gliding and scrolling, tequila was at play here—he didn't *think* he meant to call her, not consciously, anyway—well, intentional or not, the screen showed him that he was, in fact, calling Naomi.

It rang once, and he immediately hung up.

Jesus. What was he thinking? A margarita and a beer and he was calling her? Yes, he had hung up the moment he caught his mistake. But she would see a missed call from him. What would she make of that? If he actually *knew* what to say, had something *of value* to say, had just the tiniest clipped fingernail of Mark Rothko's or Tina Turner's or Mies van der Rohe's insight into life, maybe he would've let the phone continue to ring, at least giving her a chance to answer if she wanted to. But he didn't know what to say, he just touched her name. Maybe he just wanted to hear her voice? Could that be it? But maybe, just maybe, a little drunk, he would've accidentally said *exactly* the right thing? Maybe that's what was going on. Maybe, like Evo Korman, his interior and exterior lives would align for once. Or—more likely—maybe not. More than likely she wouldn't have picked up anyway if he had let it ring. And then he would've spent the night torturing himself, ruminating as to why, *specifically*, she didn't pick up.

He ruminated anyway. He left the small plastic bottle of cheap tequila unfinished on the bedside table and dozed off around 4 a.m. His sleep was fitful and unsatisfying. He woke up feeling nothing but fatigue and anxiety. "Wired and tired," was what he used to tell Naomi when he woke up irritable and snappy.

"Get up on the wrong side of life again?" she'd ask.

He needed coffee. Pacoima was still a three hour drive away.

DAY 76

NAOMI STOOD OVER THE TORN LAUTNER SKETCH. Had she really just smashed one of Tomas's prized possessions? The sketch was fragile, the thin trace paper on which it had been drawn sixty years ago could easily tear if one just tried to remove it from its frame. Shards of broken glass and a cracked black lacquer frame lay on the ground along with the shreds of a perspective sketch drawn by the hand of Frank Lloyd Wright pupil John Lautner. It was an early perspective view of the living room of the Sheats-Goldstein house in Los Angeles. Naomi looked confused for a moment, as if a stranger—not she—had destroyed the beautiful graphite drawing. She was horrified and confused. She loved Lautner, too. He took the integrated and soft-yet-hard approach to design of his master—the built-in furniture, the balance of concrete and wood, the hard and the soft, but invented his own idiom of sensual forms. His designs of the early sixties—the dramatic curves, the impossible cantilevers, the disdain for the ninety-degree angle—exuded optimism, playfulness, a hopeful new language, one man's bulwark against the threat of nuclear annihilation. Tomas had pronounced Lautner one of "the greats," and had included him in his "pantheon," deservedly so.

The sketch belonged to Tomas, but the work belonged to the ages. Naomi could practically hear her husband saying those very words. Was she not above this? Was this not just the hipster version of the jilted wife smashing plates or throwing clothes out a bedroom window? She thought she had moved past this "phase." That was perhaps the most aggravating thing about it all. This sudden bout of rage and desire to hurt Tomas in some way, nearly three months after the fact, caught her off guard. Time had passed. She was better than Tomas Araeta, so why had she done something so petty and, to her mind, so off the mark?

Because it felt *so fucking good*. That's why. It was glorious. It hit him where it counted, even if he wasn't there to see it. He treated that drawing with more respect than he did his life partner.

And then it was done.

The release lasted a millisecond. It vanished the moment the glass and frame shattered. She knew already she would try to tape the sketch back together.

The house was blessedly empty. Wherever Tomas was these days, it wasn't here.

No, on second thought—not even a thought really, just a white-hot impulse—she would not tape the sketch back together. Screw it. That was in the past, and the past was unalterable. What did remain in her control, though, if she could get there, was her attitude, her feelings, *about* the past. Seconds ago Tomas—the past—had dictated her behavior. No more.

She wasn't going to let him define her life a moment longer. This she vowed.

DAY 8

AT STUDIO ARAETA, before checking his work emails or continuing to address the building department's red lines for his remodel of the Norman's kitchen, Tomas found himself idly clicking on image galleries of buildings he knew well by the Japanese architect Tadao Ando and, of course, Mies. He never tired of their work. Mies found his voice in the rectangle and spent a lifetime refining it. Ando, too, was chaste and unflinching in his geometry. One theme, one obsession. Ah, and Louis Kahn! Kahn *must* be included in the conversation of the Platonists. He too held a special place in Tomas's pantheon. There were plenty of other architects—Jeanne Gang, Mario Botta, Snowhetta, Herzog and de Meuron, Hadid, Lu Wenyu, especially, the list went on of people whose work he admired, but the confident purity of Ando and Mies and Kahn soothed him like no other.

And if he could find anything that did soothe him—how *does* one find OxyContin these days?—he needed it in bulk. Could he claim a back problem and get some? Does yoga really help? Should he take a few days off and just start driving—somewhere, anywhere? A masseuse? A chiropractor? Getting blind drunk was always an option. Naomi was no longer responding to his texts or picking up the phone. So for now he turned to the only religion he knew that might bring him distraction and solace: architecture.

When he went out on his own eighteen months ago and started Studio Araeta, Tomas had rented space in a Jingletown warehouse, which he shared with a weed grower and jewelry maker and a fourth tenant who rarely came out of the plywood shanty he had built for himself in the corner of the 11,000 square foot space. It was never clear to Tomas what the fourth tenant "did." Occasional muttering, the screech of a hammer pulling out a recalcitrant nail, and some type of gurgling noise were the only sounds he could ever discern. The weed grower was quiet, but for two months prior to the harvest, the smell could be overpowering. He had no issue when Billy, without asking, bought two strong fans to divert the scent from themselves and clients, and presented Tomas with a receipt for reimbursement. Most clients found the jewelry maker—her tats, her layered thrift-store clothing, the occasional knocking of her forming hammer—charming. It was all part of the frisson of coming to the funky warehouse "office" of a cool young architect. Even the one-story ride up the old, noisy service elevator felt slightly illicit.

Fuck it. One more text. What did it matter? He couldn't make things worse. Well, that's not true—if anyone could find a way to make bad worse, it was he.

He typed, "I'm not staying at the house anymore." And hit send.

He returned to Ando.

He looked at a photo of the interior of Ando's Church of Light, in the city of Ibaraki, Japan, a stark concrete box, the altar's crucifix composed not of a statue of Christ on the cross, but of *nothing*, of light—a crosscut into the concrete wall behind the altar that let daylight in. The longer he stared at the photo, the more he felt drawn into it, as if he were getting closer and closer to the light. It was so bright in contrast to the heavy, windowless concrete in the rest of the room that he found himself squinting at the image, as if he was staring at the sun.

A destroyed retina was a small price to pay for the experience.

"Do you ever porn-surf architects who aren't a hundred years old or dead?" asked Billy, peering over Tomas's shoulder. Tomas's assistant William Sugarman—Billy—was no stranger to Tomas's love of Mies, Ando, Kahn, and the other stark minimalists.

"Do you ever porn-surf architects who are *good?*" replied Tomas.

"No, when I surf porn, it's for *porn*. Usually guy-girl, sometimes group, sometimes weird Japanese game shows where they do awesome glory hole contests, but still blur out the privates. Boring cis-male stuff, I know. Sucks. I was just born this way." Billy thought for a few more moments. "I wonder if Ando looks at Japanese porn without blurred-out cocks and pussies—maybe he gets special access to unfiltered bush and scrote because he's a big dog."

Tomas scanned a few other images. This time Louis Kahn's Exeter Academy Library in New Hampshire—on the outside a brick box with truncated corners, on the inside an open atrium of prominent wooden railings framed by large concrete circles. "It's so crazy. It's all the simplest shapes—square, circle, triangle, rectangle, but if you're one of the greats, what you do with those forms is profound."

In a sing-song voice, his twenty-five-year-old assistant said, "Sounds like someone wants to be a starchitect!" Tomas turned to his, well, he at first thought he was hiring a protégé, but had come to make peace with the idea that he had hired, and maybe even needed, a pest.

"Don't you? What, your generation shoots for mediocrity?"

"Oh god, please no more Gen Z jabs. They are so tired and off point, and, really, in the end, diminish you more than me."

"You know what it is," said Tomas, looking now at a picture of Kahn's Kimbell Museum. "This work is both of its time and timeless. That's not easy to pull off."

"Thanks for the middle-school definition of 'great art.' I'll give you this, though: Ando's Church of Light is pretty amazing."

"Duh."

"No, I mean I checked it out once when I was in Japan looking for one of those used-panty vending machines."

"Wait, *what*? You saw it in *person*? And you never told me?"

"I don't ask you about every building you've been in."

"This is different." Tomas stared expectantly at Billy. "Well?"

Billy leaned over Tomas's shoulder, and back clicked to an image of Ando's church. "It was, I dunno, I'm not religious, but I cried a little bit. I'm not even sure why. I was in there maybe ten, fifteen minutes tops. I was waiting to get one second alone without some other lame-ass pilgrim killing the vibe. And I finally got it, and I thought, 'Man, if this doesn't move you, you're a bona fide sociopath. You for sure kill puppies in your spare time.' You should go and see it, boss man. Life is short, and pictures don't do it justice."

"Does your generation still say 'FOMO,' because that's what I have right now, hearing about a philistine like you inside a cathedral like that."

"Okay. Let's say it together, right now."

"What?"

"Repeat after me. I, Tomas Araeta, promise myself that I will visit the Church of Light, within the next year. And while I am gone, I give William Sugarman complete authority and latitude to improve my design work, which is an extremely low bar, but that's just editorializing. Oh, and I will shut up about Ando once I actually see an Ando."

Tomas repeated the words.

He then opened the Norman's drawings the city had returned, making notes for how he wanted Billy to execute the required red line changes. Billy took the blueprints to his desk, which stood back-to-back with Tomas's.

A few minutes later his protégé piped up again.

"A little secret, Tommy Boy?"

"Hmm." Tomas grunted without looking up.

"I probably wouldn't be here if you *weren't* shooting to be one of the greats. Delusionally trying, but at least *trying*, to be a starchitect. Not all Gen Z-ers have no ambition and believe the world to be preruined by you millennials, Gen X, and the boomers." Tomas, his eyes suddenly welling, swiveled in his chair to gauge just how sarcastic his pest and protégé was being. Billy hadn't turned around, but even just looking at his hunched back and shoulders, Tomas found no sarcasm. "You'll probably never get there," clarified Billy, still not turning to face Tomas, "but I appreciate that you're trying."

Billy could never know how much his words meant to Tomas, here, now, this day. Tomas had to refrain from rolling his chair over two feet and hugging him.

"Hey, just a head's up, I'll be staying here for the unforeseeable future. Whore baths, all that, but I'll be up and hair combed before you even get here."

Billy instantly knew what his boss meant.

"Yeah. Okay."

DAY 42

NAOMI HAD PUT IN A FULL DAY of work at Macy's. The faceted swizzle sticks made of frosted acrylic she was arranging in the display windows, still hidden from the public by swaths of butcher paper—were taking shape—a forest of sweetness. The large crystals jutting this way and that out of the floor, underlit in soft LED pinks, yellows, greens, and blues, evoked both childhood and other worlds, realms of retro-futuristic fantasy. The work was good. Naomi knew it. She needed no one to tell her. It brought her a sense of serendipity and joy—two of the most important metrics to her in deciding whether something, anything—food, people, architecture—were good. "Rightness" was another, but too airy-fairy in her mind to attempt to describe to others. Naomi wiped her brow, then wiped the sweat from her fingers onto the faded T-shirt she wore.

She stood back, hands on her hips, and looked. The wave hit her—yes, this was definitely "right" for this year's Christmas display window. She couldn't explain or defend it. You either agreed with her or you didn't. You prefer chocolate or vanilla, red or blue, and either response is fine and is not subject to judgment or explanation (but really, for Naomi, how could you *actually* prefer vanilla to chocolate)?

Then another wave hit her: a spike of euphoria, and it had nothing to do with the work in progress before her. She and Tomas were grown-ups. They were *supposed* to be able to talk through their wants, their hurts, their desires. Being able to have difficult conversations was one of the hallmarks of a healthy relationship. And he had failed. The poor child. In some moments she could flick the little mosquito off her skin before it could take so much as a drop of blood. In some moments, the best ones, she hovered 10,000 feet above it all, shook her head, smiled with pity. In the grand scheme, this common little man, who did have virtues, could be forgiven. Or not. Who cares?

She couldn't know it, but there was one novel thing both she and Tomas were experiencing at the same time: the discovery that what she had previously considered the outer limits of her emotional life were no more than their visible spectrum. She was now living in the uncertain world of X-rays, gamma rays, and other bits of minuscule, absurdly strong energy. And that world, it had to be said, was a place of pain, not euphoria, leaving her feeling panicky, angry, anxious, and without purpose. She was not hovering at 10,000 feet anymore. Unlike Tomas, though, she didn't deserve this unwanted discovery. But, perhaps because of her father Bruce's visit, perhaps because of some inexplicable tic of one or other chemicals in her body, perhaps for no good reason at all, today, as she stepped forward and adjusted one giant acrylic crystal just so, she was okay.

Okay enough. On balance. Sometimes.

And then as quickly as the euphoria had spiked, it vanished. Another wave came crashing down, heavy with anger and grief, and left her gasping for air in the whitewash. A veil now hung before her. Her critical eye became useless. Whether her ideas were "right" or not, whether it was better or worse if she moved another crystal or adjusted the angle of a light just so, she no longer could say.

She took the next two days off—her boss, Garrett Turner, Macy's San Francisco vice president of retail operations, would understand. He *always* understood, and she knew in her heart she wasn't being manipulative, wasn't using his crush to her benefit. He knew her hurt was real, as, unfortunately, did she.

A grand plan took shape: she would walk around Lake Merritt in the early evening, eat macaroni and cheese with bacon bits at Homeroom restaurant, and read. Or maybe nap. Or watch TV. Or visit her mother and Marivel. They would love the visit. But she couldn't stand the thought of their questions about how she was doing, their sincere concern for her feelings. Their sympathy was smothering. Forget the visit. Just focus on the macaroni for now. The rest could be played by ear.

She let Garrett know she would be back in a day or two, and in any case would make her deadline. He nodded and said, "Okay."

DAY 116

NAOMI SAT BACK DOWN ON THE SOFA, opened her laptop, and there it was. The latest email from Love Without Limits. She inhaled sharply, struggled to catch her breath. She reread the first lines of the email several times, shut her eyes tight, turned her head to the side, exhaled with careful and thorough deliberation, eyes still shut, then turned back, opened her eyes, and read the email once more. No, she hadn't misread anything. She and Tomas had moved to number nineteen on the list. The email advised them to have their travel documents in order, Covid protocols and timely test results included, for the in-person interview in two months in Sucre, Bolivia. The "baby brokers," as she and Tomas had nicknamed the nongovernmental organization, acted as the liaison between the Bolivian government and anxious couples from the West trying to adopt.

Naomi remembered the day when guarded hope turned to jittery excitement.

She and Tomas had been languishing for a year in the 200s. But this day was different.

"Are you kidding, we're number ninety-two? This better not to be a typo!" said Tomas, checking his emails.

"No, it's legit," said Naomi, speaking double speed. *Slate* had a piece on this new cabinet minister who wants to thaw things out with the US, and because she's spearheading, the president can dip into the shadows on this and save face. All I know is—"

"We've jumped to ninety-two? Ninety-fucking-two!"

"Tomas, if this keeps up, or even goes at half speed, we're parents in like, ten, eleven months."

"Holy shit. Holy shit. I need more time to get ready! Time, I need time."

"I'm so scared!" yelled Naomi happily. They fell in each other's arms, laughing, gasping.

A battle with leukemia in her teens had left Naomi infertile. She had been cancer-free since nineteen, but the unforgiving treatment, the chemo and radiation, had taken its pound of flesh. She and Tomas had both quickly considered—and ruled out—long-shot attempts that IVF clinics offered. It wasn't the bad odds or expense—this was one of the few times Tomas had said he would be willing to approach his father for money. It was that both of them, Naomi especially, had learned to heed Epictetus's two-thousand-year-old advice: "Man is not affected by things, but by his thoughts about things" (the quote was something Naomi had found in a four-by-four coffee table book, *Daily Pearls Of Wisdom*, that her mother Abigail brought home from the discount table at Barnes and Noble years ago). So she was infertile. So what. She could let it crush her or not. Infertility didn't matter. How she and Tomas felt about it did.

Now it was just a matter of patience and process. And suddenly, today, all of the waiting, the tamping down of expectation, all the redundant and intricate paperwork, had paid off. They were ninety-two.

"I'll let you pick the doorknobs for the nursery," said Naomi.

Tomas's heart was pounding.

"No oil-rubbed bronze; I promise!" He suddenly became somber. "Do we still like Marco for a boy and Daisy for a girl?"

"I think so," said Naomi, adding, "But I swear, I overheard two women today—*two*—call their daughter 'Daisy.'"

"Um . . . how about Violet, or Rose? You hate them? I love them."

"I love Violet and Rose!" said Naomi. "But what's with the flower names?"

"I don't know, I don't know, I know nothing, don't listen to me. I need time, ohmygod, ohmygod, this is gonna happen!"

"Are you going to the store later?" Naomi wasn't often passive-aggressive, and she did it with such coquettish charm that Tomas didn't care.

"What do you need babe?"

She wanted another glass of wine, and they were out.

"You got it."

In a gleeful panic, Tomas slammed the front door shut behind him.

They were ideal candidates for adoption: no felony criminal records; modest but steady incomes; a ten-year, stable marriage. They were about to become parents.

And then Tomas had done what he did and blew up their lives. They were about to become three. They had love to spare for a young baby or child. He took that away from her— destroying the stupid Lautner sketch was excessively *nice* of her—but wait—*had* he ruined the prospect of parenthood?

She could still be an excellent mother. Why not? Her adrenaline skyrocketed; her thoughts came in a torrent. She tried to catch her breath again, tried to slow down. Breathe. Life happens. Things *change*. That is the essence of everything—change. Cliché to say, but vital to feel and integrate. Okay, okay. "Hasten slowly," as the Roman emperor Augustus wisely advised. She would never make fun of *Daily Pearls of Wisdom* again! She was on a first-name basis with their primary contact at Love Without Limits, Cecilia Duran. They'd had several Zoom calls with Cecilia, sent letters. Cecilia knew them, knew her. Naomi would inform Cecilia of a recent change in their lives, one that had no bearing on her enthusiasm about motherhood. It was a significant change, yes, but it was hardly a mortal wound. And if need be, Naomi could easily have additional character-reference letters written on her sole behalf as well—from

Garrett, from old professors she could look up. If needed, her father Bruce would certainly sign a letter of shared financial obligation. No, she would be a great single mom. For God's sake, her own mother had left her father to be with another woman, and they were both still wonderful parents.

No, the truly negative change, she thought, remembering the cold, stilted interactions she had with Tomas's parents, and his stories about their brittle horror show of a marriage, would be to subject a child to a frosty relationship full of unsheathed daggers and resentments simmering just below the surface—the tense, silent dinners, the small talk to avoid the large talk, the snide asides. If she and Tomas did give it another shot, and it failed, or worse, half-failed, and just limped along, became drawn out, that poor child would end up in an ice cave. Modeling that type of a relationship, letting a child grow up thinking such an excruciating marriage was the norm, would be the real tragedy. Having a wonderful, loving, competent, grown-up for a parent who loved you to pieces—that hadn't changed. It had just gone from two to one.

She had always thought she wanted a partner in the picture when it came to raising a child, it's true, and six months ago she had no doubt that Tomas was the guy. But that was six months ago.

She began composing a letter to Cecilia. She felt strong. She could say without reservation that she embodied the name of the organization, Love Without Limits.

DAY THREE

NAOMI FORCED HERSELF TO GO TO WORK. Of course she would allow herself time to feel the pain, she would, it would be unhealthy not to, but the fucker had an erratic work schedule. Ever since opening Studio Araeta eighteen months ago, he could come and go as he pleased. He was a one-man shop (could that really even be considered a "studio"? Either her husband was a pretentious prick, or really had outsized ambitions) with one assistant, Billy, who was an employee, not an equal. Kudos that he took the risk to leave the soul-deadening security of Bennett helping to lay out parking lots, but now this left her vulnerable. Without a boss to answer to, or a schedule to adhere to, he was his own man. And after hearing of this ridiculous six-month loophole, surely Tomas would be waiting for her at home.

And he was. Their car was in the driveway. She was ready to turn on her heels, but she hesitated. If she did turn and leave, he would win.

She unlocked the door and entered the modest two-bedroom clapboard bungalow they owned in Oakland's Clinton neighborhood. How ecstatic they had been when they found matchstick wood flooring beneath puce 1970s carpeting. Thank God for bad trends. The decision to carpet over the gorgeous floor had preserved it for thirty years. And then the built-in cabinet for dishes separating the small kitchen from the small dining room? The single pane windows with thin mullions? Since 1934, outside of coats of paint that came and went with the fad of the day and that glorious carpeting, the bungalow was nearly untouched. They had bought it, with family help—the one time Tomas accepted anything from his father—eight years ago, for $395,000. Today the modest cottage designed for the working class of Oakland would fetch, at minimum, $1.2 million.

They could never afford to buy this house again.

"Tomas?" she called out.

"Yup," he answered. "In the kitchen." She entered the kitchen to find that he wasn't scrubbing dishes—*that* he had already done, as he was surrounded by stacks of clean dishes—now he was wiping down the cabinet shelves with diluted Pine Sol and water, removing any bit of stickiness or cooking grease that had settled over the years.

"What are you doing, Tomas?"

"Don't worry. I ordered Thai—this is a work in progress—I'll have it back to normal by tomorrow."

"Mmm."

"Thai okay?"

"I'm not very hungry." She disappeared into the bedroom. He wanted to follow her and interrogate her about her lack of appetite, to find any toehold, any on-ramp, however flimsy, to talk.

Minutes later she emerged with a packed travel suitcase.

"What's that?"

"My suitcase."

"I know. I mean, what are you doing with it?"

She shot him a disbelieving look before dropping her exhausted body on the couch. She looked around at their home; at the knock-off Craftsman hutch they had found at the Laney College flea market; at the "frame worthy" photos of themselves and family and Tomas's old cat "Dasher," may God rest his soul, on the walls; at the midcentury chrome and Formica dinette set they had found on eBay; at the fake chrome chandelier with its three angular arms. Tomas watched her eyeline carefully.

"Remember where we found the eighties coke dealer chandelier?" he asked.

"Ross, I think."

"Their buyers are second to none. Not even Target's knickknacks come close," said Tomas. Naomi nodded half heartedly. Their taste was eclectic and funky—they couldn't afford otherwise.

"You asked about the suitcase."

"I did."

"I don't want to stay in the same space as you, Tomas. I can elaborate as to why, but I'm pretty sure you don't want to hear what I have to say."

"Actually," said Tomas, "I do." Did she just hear a tinge of self-righteousness in his voice, as if he had the right to question or demand anything? "Yes, I fucked up, and I'm sorry," he continued, "and it may take forever for you to see I mean that, but I know you will."

The gall.

"I'll give you the bullet points, Tomas. You're not the man I thought you were. If you love me, how could you hurt me like this? I feel like a fool. Like I've wasted seventeen years of my life, my youth, some of my best years, being duped. I have so many questions about you and Marie, but I don't really want to know, because all I can imagine is your penis in her vagina, and the look on your face when you cum. That's *my* look. Or it was supposed to be."

"You and I talked about the possibility of opening things up. More than once."

"*No*. We talked about the possibility of trying whatever, but of talking *first*. Being grown-ups. I told you this the first time you asked me to marry you, the second time, and by the time I said yes I was sick of hearing my own voice on the topic. I knew you were antsy. About everything."

"So you're basically saying you understand why I did what I did?"

"No. I'm not. Why do you think I turned you down twice? You were supposed to sow your wild oats, live in an ashram if you wanted, sketch the Acropolis all day and night, fuck anything that moved, I didn't care. All I cared about was that, when I said yes and we did decide to marry, that we come to each other with our thoughts and desires, no matter what they were."

"You're right. I should've asked. We should've talked. But it wasn't planned. I would literally have had to call you just when—"

"Tomas."

He said nothing.

"I'm very tired. I'm moving out."

"What? No. You stay, I go. You shouldn't be inconvenienced."

She looked at him with disbelief. "You using the word 'inconvenienced' after what you just did is *exactly* why I can't stand to be around you. Goodbye." She stood up and began pulling her bag toward the front door. God how those little plastic wheels screeched.

"Would you have said yes?"

She turned back. "You'll never know, will you, because you didn't do the right thing and ask. I'm taking the car." The horrific sound of the rolling suitcase rang in his ears for the next hour, even as he dusted baseboards and swept and mopped the precious matchstick flooring.

Naomi drove their car, a 2014 Hyundai Elantra, around the corner and parked. She dialed the number. Her mother still had a land line phone, and still answered it. Marivel picked up.

"What's wrong, chica?" she asked after what Naomi thought was a cool and collected "It's me, Marivel." This was the problem with her mother having a good therapist as a partner—she could read you over the phone with three innocuous words.

"Is Mom there?"

She could hear Marivel yelling, "Abbie! The phone!"

Great. Already Marivel was ramping it up with this urgent scream. It's not that Marivel didn't scream on occasion, it's that she had a master craftsman's control over her timbre. And this timbre said, "Get your ass over here—Naomi's hurting." Maybe she had wanted to talk to Marivel, too. She could just as easily have called her mother's cell number.

"Honey, hi, what is it?" asked Abigail nervously.

"Hi Mom. Um, is it okay if I come over?"

"Of course. Why are you even asking? There's no need to ask. That's strange. I'm your mom. You never have to ask. Are you okay? Why did you ask? Where are you?"

"I'm fine. I'm in the car."

"Do you need us to come get you?"

"No. I just said I'm in the *car*. I'm fine, I just wanted to talk—I'll be over soon."

"We can pick you up."

"No, Mom, I'm already driving."

"Are you driving safely?"

"Jesus, Mom, I'm hanging up now."

She hung up. Was she gritting her teeth? Maybe. She loved Abbie, she did. It's just, everything the woman did irked her. She could breathe or blink the wrong way and it would set Naomi off. After the first twinge of annoyance came the predictable second twinge of guilt. Naomi put the car in drive and headed off.

Abbie and Marivel were both waiting just inside the front door of the bungalow they shared in Oakland's tony, shabby-chic Rockridge neighborhood. It was, literally, as if Tomas and Naomi owned the toy version of her mother and Marivel's home. The only funkiness in her mother's home came in the form of a surfeit of colorful blankets draped over every couch and chair, a dark-stained wood display case with small souvenir spoons from around the world that Nana Riva had gifted her daughter Abbie, and an oversized poster from Oakland's "Occupy" protest movement of 2011 that Marivel had torn down from a telephone pole and preserved. Otherwise, from light fixtures to doorknob escutcheons, the home was tastefully and consistently furnished with Craftsman pieces, some of them genuine Stickleys.

"What happened?" were the first words out of Abigail's mouth.

The look on Naomi's face told Marivel everything she needed

to know. "Dump him." She hugged Naomi. "I'm in the kitchen if you need anything," she said before disappearing to leave mother and daughter alone.

Naomi headed straight for their bedroom and fell on the bed crying.

"Honey, what happened? Please. Tell me!"

"Exactly what you think happened!" yelled Naomi. Naomi *did* need to talk to her mother. She also needed someone at whom she could lash out, someone who could take the punch but not take it personally. Abigail sat down on the bed and began gently stroking her daughter's back, something which had always helped calm her. At least thirty-five years ago it had.

"We're a few months away from a fucking baby, and he does this."

"He cheated on you."

"Yes," said Naomi. "Bravo, you figured it out. What gave it away? Me calling? Crying my eyes out?"

"When did you find out?"

"Three days ago."

"I'm sorry, I'm so so sorry," murmured Abigail.

"Don't apologize. You're always apologizing."

"Sorry—shit!"

In spite of herself, Naomi laughed, giving her mother license to do the same.

"I guess I should thank God we still *are* a few months away," said Naomi, a thin razor cutting into the shock and pain. "Makes it easier. We're over. No kids, no problem."

Abigail said nothing.

"What?"

"Nothing honey," said Abigail as she locked her daughter's fingers in her own.

"You think I shouldn't leave him?"

"No. I didn't say that."

"You didn't have to."

"Honey, I think you should think about whatever it is you're going to do. Leave him, kick him in the balls, stay, whatever, but just talk to somebody. Marivel can recommend someone. It's only been a few days. I know how raw it is."

"Can you please get off the goddamn fence for once?" Naomi spat back.

"You know your father and I have been where you are—"

"Yes, I have some awareness that you came out of the closet and cheated on him."

To Naomi's great shock, the barb didn't appear to land. The woman whose skin was thinner than an onion's suddenly seemed to be wearing a suit of armor.

Her mother continued, "Naomi, for your sake, for your peace of mind, *not his*, it will not hurt to talk to someone. I'm speaking from experience."

"Sorry, I've been eavesdropping." Marivel stood in the doorway. "I *can* recommend someone, but I won't. Your future ex-husband spends more on his haircuts than you do. Dump him."

"Thank you!" exclaimed Naomi. Marivel nodded quickly, then turned and disappeared.

This was one of the things that had exasperated Naomi ever since her mother came out of the closet: nuance. Everything was shades of gray to this woman. She didn't see both sides of an issue, she saw all fifty-six. And it left her paralyzed to act, or even speak, with any degree of certainty or conviction. Naomi saw the tears welling in her mother's eyes. Shit. Could one blame her? She had lived a life of denial and shame and untruth for decades before finding the courage to admit to herself who she was. Lord knows she'd probably already spent half of Naomi's meager inheritance on therapists. But for God's sake, this nuanced, mealy-mouthed fence sitter—whose side was she on in a case as clear cut as this one?

"I mean, only if and when you're ready," added Abigail. "And maybe you won't be. Maybe Marivel's right, maybe it won't be the right way for you; I don't know. I just want to do or say anything to help you."

"Mom, he fucked a client, then came home and made dinner. He was distracted. When I asked him about it, he said it was nerves about the adoption. *He used the baby as a shield.* Where is there a fucking square inch of room to hesitate? There are not two sides here."

"Honey, of course I will support whatever decision you make."

"I don't want your support. I want you to say the guy is a fucking creep asswipe who doesn't deserve me! That's what I want." Abigail parroted the words back.

"He's a fucking creep asshole who doesn't deserve you."

"Ass*wipe*," said Naomi.

"Asswipe, sorry."

Naomi bit her tongue but rolled her eyes at the reflexive apology. "Are you staying the night?"

"Can I?"

"Oh honey, please don't ask."

Abigail fetched some blankets from the backs of chairs and couches. From a closet she grabbed sheets. Last, also from the closet, not the back of a couch, she pulled out a small, crocheted blanket that Riva had made when Naomi was born. She gave it to Naomi now.

"Thanks," said Naomi quietly. She tucked it under her neck. She spent the next few hours lying curled on the couch flicking blindly through television channels, thumbing through *People* magazines (one of her mother's guilty pleasures), and throughout, fought tooth and nail to push back the heavy lump in her clenched throat and stop the hot tears from cresting her eyelids. She had no problem crying, but she was afraid of upsetting her mother further.

DAY 1

TOMAS HADN'T SLEPT, EITHER. There was too much to clean. Naomi had left, taken the car. For the first half hour, he clutched his cell phone, stared at it, unsuccessfully willing her to call or text him. Screw it. If she was going to call, she'd call. And if she wasn't, no amount of staring at this awful little machine would help. Best to return to cleaning. He turned the ringer volume on his phone to high, left it centrally located on the dining room table, grabbed the sponges and cleansers from under the kitchen sink, and began his attack on the bathroom.

"I don't do it often, but when I *do* do it, it's an A-plus job" was Tomas's standard line to Naomi whenever the urge seized him, and he tackled some of the housework. Naomi had a standard response of her own.

"No one likes a grind; they suck the joy out of the room."

Their stupid little banter. He'd thrown it all away, *why?* To fuck some bored rich housewife who probably threw the word "genius" around whether she was talking about mediocre architects or a good street taco.

Tomas thought of how Naomi made the bed. She would pull up the crumpled sheets and blankets so that the sheet was left longer than the blanket, and declare her work done. Time elapsed: fifty-two seconds. When Tomas made the bed, he would strip off all the bedding and begin by pulling the fitted sheet tight around all the corners, then carefully aligning the top sheet and blankets, and tucking them all in at the foot of the bed—he loved the feeling of his feet being constrained. Finally he would pull the pillowcases high and tight on the pillows and place them with the open ends facing the outside edges of the bed before considering the job adequately done.

Jesus, I am a grind, aren't I? he thought now as he carefully cleaned the mirror and medicine cabinet.

The toilet, which most people abhorred, was, to Tomas, the easiest thing of all to clean in a bathroom. Any abrasive cleanser, a standard brush designed solely for this purpose, which kept one's hand a foot or so away from the real ickiness, and a few dampened paper towels for the porcelain body, was all one needed. Tomas stood up, knees damp. At least Naomi would be coming home to a clean house—when she came home. Tomas stopped. He surveyed the bathroom. Something wasn't right, but it had nothing to do with any flecks of dust or rust he may have missed around the bolts that kept the toilet secured to the floor.

He despaired for a moment, and unlike the thousands of moments that had passed since Naomi discovered his indiscretion, this one wasn't spent ruminating about what he had done. This moment he spent ruminating over something else.

The greats didn't grind, the greats didn't sweat over whether a sheet was evenly laid on a bed or not, or whether any motes of dust around a toilet had been missed. The greats tilted their heads to the heavens, not the earth. And the results came naturally. No doubt they put in some arduous training in their youth to develop the basics, but then, afterward, they, they who had been gifted by the gods with that unteachable X-factor, for them, the work came without excessive peristalsis. It reminded him of something Naomi had once said.

"All you have to do to be happy, hon, is *be happy.*"

"What coffee-table book of 'uplifting' sayings did you get that from?" Tomas replied.

"You've seen my mom's coffee table—take your pick," said Naomi, then added, "but I am right." And she was. Maybe if he didn't try to so damn hard all the time, he might find his way to some form of grace.

In his better moments, the moodiness faded, the envy of the greats faded, and he learned from Naomi Curran. They were in line once at the grocery store on a busy weekend shopping morning, and Tomas was irritated at how slow their line was moving. The line next to theirs shortened—perhaps the cashier was a little quicker, perhaps the person in his line was fumbling for a payment method. He abruptly began to turn their cart to hop lines.

Naomi had gently put her hand on the front of the cart, stopping him. "I like being in line with you. What I don't like is letting an extra minute or two or three get to me. Does it really matter?"

She was right. The joke was on him. No one—not the other customers, not the cashier—cared that he was irritated. His mind drifted from the crowded grocery store aisle back to the present and the thought hit him like a runaway truck: *She*—not he—was the natural great! The savant! She didn't have to try, and the scope of what mattered to her, the things that gave her life meaning and a sense of purpose, were so much more expansive than his. It was shameful. Her eyes were not on bedsheets or checkout aisles or who made the cut on Builders's Booksource's "new releases" shelf; they were on quality of experience, on the hue of an emotion, on internal contentment and fullness of feeling.

No, thought Tomas bitterly, Naomi's eyes and heart, her aspirations, were focused on the right things, on the heavens: contentment, sharing a life raising a child, enjoying a breeze or the view from a BART train, or crying at a corny sitcom. Yes, she enjoyed her design work, but she had the smarts—no, *the wisdom*—not to ruin her day, or her sense of self, by constant comparison. She enjoyed, but did not envy, looking at the works in the glossy architecture books; she could laze away a hot afternoon in a cheap Spanish pension without feeling she was missing something or not maximizing her time. Had he actually chided her about not maximizing her time? More than once. He had used that word—"maximize."

She just laughed.

"What?" he asked, annoyed.

"You 'maximize' tax deductions, babe, not life."

She embraced the whole of life without becoming overly consumed by any one thing. But she wasn't detached or aloof, either. On the contrary, she felt everything, she was in the moment. All of this, thought Tomas, made her a great. And unlike him, she would no doubt have had the stones to have hard talks before taking cowardly actions. Not just cowardly. *Sneaky.* Yes, sneaky.

Such an ugly, apt word: sneaky. Tomas had slunk around the last seventy-two hours, and the twenty-four hours before that, being sneaky.

He went on to mop the living room and bedroom floors. He pulled a few things off the closet floor—a duffel bag, a cardboard box containing HDMI cables and other accessories that had come with the TV, and other gizmos, preparing to mop those bits of floor as well.

And then he stopped.

He let the mop fall to the floor, and pushed his palms hard against his closed eyes, until specs floated in this nonspace.

He tried desperately to think of one negative thing about his wife. He needed to. She would never claim to be a *bodhisattva* or saint or any such thing. Never. She didn't fight well. She was harshly critical in her own way of others. Judgmental. She was a beautiful person, but the contempt she could conjure in a glance? The disgust she could convey with the upturn of a lip? No one else saw it. But he did. She could be emotionally mercurial, leaving him walking on eggshells sometimes. Yes! It was true. Her response to immediately file for divorce after his indiscretion without talking *even a little?*

Wait, here was something. Something maybe of substance.

She literally contradicted herself about "having hard convos before doing something you can't undo." She *did not* have the hard conversation about separation, wouldn't even agree to one therapy session. This after calling Marivel's work "God's work." One could call that hypocritical. Not him, of course, he had forfeited that right, but a judge or umpire or man or woman on the street—a stranger—could reasonably point out the hypocrisy.

Ah, money! Wasn't money one of the "biggies" on the list of serious issues in a relationship? They had fought recently about money. As soon as they became serious about adopting a child, Tomas wanted to make sure to start putting aside enough for the biggest thing parents fret about: schools. Their neighborhood was a fine place for adults to live in, but the public schools in Clinton had low test scores, so Tomas wanted to start saving for private school. Naomi felt they were buying into the rat race, that the child would do fine in public school. Tomas disagreed and wanted to hash it out. Talk about the pros and cons. Naomi wouldn't. When she thought she was right about something, she didn't allow for a good healthy argument, the very thing she continually advocated for. She would clam up, become distant, and after two or three days, maybe, *maybe* say something.

When he first brought up the possibility of saving for private school, she flatly answered, "We're house poor. It's a waste. The kid will be fine."

"But shouldn't we give them as many options as we can?"

"We can spend our money on better things."

Her body language made clear that the topic was closed, at least for now. Naomi bringing *money* into a discussion of education for their child? She couldn't have meant it. That was not the Naomi he knew.

Two days later, as they were washing dishes after dinner—he washed and she dried—she'd abruptly said, "I just think you're wrong about the school thing. I went to a shitty public school, and I came out okay. I got into Berkeley same as you, I taught you, for Chrissake. Not that it matters, but I got better grades than you."

"And that's great, and you're great," replied Tomas evenly, "but why take the chance? What if our kid doesn't have your brains and is vulnerable to falling in with the wrong crowd?"

"That sounds bourgeoise," said Naomi.

"That's not an answer to what I just asked," replied Tomas. And he was right. He knew it and he knew she knew it.

"You went to private school, so you're just going with the familiar. If you want to jump in with the other Biff's and Buffy's and spend fifty, sixty thousand a year on Head-Royce or Saint Ignatius or wherever, do it, but find a different mom."

Where was this spleen coming from?

"Sorry, are we having a robust chat about schooling our child or are you threatening to leave me if I don't go along with you, and, while you're at it, throwing in some side 'Biff' jab because my parents sent me to Head-Royce?"

"Don't make this about you."

"I'm not, you are. This is about opening as many doors as possible for our kid."

"What if they just want to be an electrician or gardener or whatever?"

"As long as they're content? I'd be ecstatic. But I don't want to look back when we're grandparents and think, 'We limited them.'"

"You're snobby, Tomas. I'm not saying it's your fault—I know your folks—but you can be better than this."

"Sorry, did you say we were—or were not—making this about me?"

She shook her head. This was one of the few times he was certain he had the moral high ground to do any head shaking. But he didn't. He wouldn't take the bait. This topic was too important.

"Look, Nomes, a good school is just like those bumpers in a bowling alley. They put them there so kids and uncoordinated goofs like me don't throw a gutter ball every time."

"It's a waste of money. The kid will have us as his or her guard rails."

"You joking? After they hit twelve or thirteen, we'll just be wallpaper to them, a place with a refrigerator and a bed to sleep in.

They'll do whatever they want."

"If you wanted all that kind of middle-class stuff, you should never have left Bennett"

Tomas was speechless. She had always said she supported him hanging out his own shingle, had always said money didn't matter to her. And hanging an argument over schooling on money? Yes, *he* might be so vulgar and disjointed, but she?

They had finished washing the dishes in silence.

Tomas was exhausted. He left the mop on the floor. What had he accomplished by scouring his memory to find shortcomings in his wife? Proven to his satisfaction that she, too, had flaws, or could be mean? Fine. So what? Was this connected in any meaningful way to his cheating? Did it excuse it? No. It just confirmed what was true of any couple: no one is perfect, even if one of the two is wrongheadedly striving for perfection.

DAY 22

NAOMI LOOKED INTO THE MEDICINE CABINET MIRROR at her mother's house. After Tomas's text about not staying at their home, she had returned to their bungalow, but on some nights she just wanted to stay at her mom's. She pulled at the underlids of her eyes. The dark circles were becoming a permanent fixture, a tattoo of pain. She washed her face, showered, and was applying light makeup when she heard a gentle knock at the door.

"Naomi, everything okay?"

Naomi opened the door. Abigail stood there. "What do you need?"

"Sorry, didn't mean to interrupt."

"Well, you have, so—" Naomi caught herself. This whole thing, the pain, anger, the lack of sleep, was bringing out a snippiness in her that she hated. She remembered how poorly she had behaved when Tomas brought up the subject of schooling. She had always regretted not apologizing and reengaging on the subject, but now? Fuck it. "Hey, Mom, I'm here. What's on your mind?"

Naomi waited for whatever it was her mother had to say. Abbie chewed on her lower lip, one of her tells that she was feeling more insecure and anxious than usual. Naomi waited to hear whatever little bomb her mother was fretting over dropping.

"If you think it would help, Marivel can still make a recommendation."

"She was pretty clear about doing exactly *not* that."

"I begged her."

"Why? Mom, don't assume I want to see anybody. Don't assume anything. Don't push your shit on me! I can't think about that right now. I just—I'm going to work."

"Okay, honey, just a thought."

Just a thought. One of her mother's little throwaways to try to back away from what she really felt. The way people can have entire conversations, and not until they're about to depart someone finally says, "Oh, by the way . . ." and gets to what they really wanted to talk about all along.

At Macy's, Naomi rearranged the rock candy crystals over and over, never satisfied. It took all the energy she had to rearrange the crystals at all. She *wanted* to care. Wanted to access that calm sensibility in her that could revise a design vertically, not just horizontally. Better, not just different. She thought she had found that space again, but—today at least—she hadn't.

Naomi's phone chirped. Viola. A dear friend. Not her best friend, but one whose boyfriend had cheated on her. An hour earlier Naomi had found her contact info and texted her: *Viola, it's me, Naomi. I really need to see you.*

As Naomi now answered the phone, it happened. Anger crumbled for a moment and gave wide berth to a much more difficult emotion: sadness. She could barely speak.

"Naomi? Naomi? Are you okay, what's happening?"

"Do you have time for a drink today, after work?"

"Of course. Is everyone okay?" Viola asked, imagining a diagnosis of stage IV pancreatic cancer or a horrific car accident behind Naomi's voice.

"No. I'm not. Mockingbird at six?"

"Wherever you want. Just—that's two hours from now—I can't take it—tell me, is someone dead?"

"No." Naomi's voice was low, quiet.

"I'll see you soon," said Viola, gray, somber, guessing correctly now at what had happened.

DAY MINUS 3

IN HIS SHOULDER BAG Tomas carried his sketch pad, small wooden stakes, a spool of string, and a tape measure. He stood a moment in front of the imposing ten-foot door, then lifted the heavy brass lion's-head knocker. He knocked and waited. His heart was pounding. God, he was being silly. He knocked again, and after a few more moments, she answered.

"Sorry, didn't hear you, Tomas, I was in the back. Come in, come in."

He gave Marie Partridge a curt hug—something most of his female clients signaled as desired and appropriate. Normal for a small office working on small, personal projects. Bennett clients didn't hug.

Tomas followed Marie through the home's three enfilade first-level rooms to the garden. When the large glass doors between the rooms were open, one could see clear from the front room through to the backyard.

"A shotgun house," Tomas commented on his first visit. That was the Southern phrase for this type of layout, and both Marie and her husband Cole laughed about it. In subsequent meetings, they told Tomas that they had told their friends that they owned a "shotgun house."

"Did I even do it right?" asked Marie as they stepped into the backyard. Tomas looked over a rectangle of string she had staked out, indicating the outline of the future hovering pop-out above—

something he dubbed "the treehouse."

How had he ever sold that?

Simple. He had *found himself.* Sixteen days ago he had taken a chance and decided to bet on himself. Decided to align his inner and outer selves, consequences be damned. Better to regret the things we try than to regret the things we don't try.

On that day, Thursday, October 13, 2022, there would not be three options for the clients to look over, and his one and only proposal would not look like it had "always been part of the house," something Cole Partridge had asked for at their initial meeting. This was not a refinement to the preferred Alt. B that Tomas had promised the Partridges at the end of their last meeting. No, this was a complete rethink.

He had gone rogue, had done what a great designer like John Lautner or Gabriela Carrillo or Alvar Aalto might have done: which was not to interpret a client's *wants,* but to divine their *needs,* the things they deeply desired that they didn't even know they desired. Tomas was to be midwife, oracle and egomaniac, helping them birth the child they never had expected, but always pined for. Today? Today was Alt. D day. A whole new concept, and Tomas had brought along no safety net of other alternatives—he had, as he told Billy, who accompanied him today, one shot.

The itch in his brain, his heart, had set in a week ago. Tomas had been inspired while porn-surfing the Guggenheim Museum—not Frank Gehry's in Bilbao, but Wright's earlier spiral in Manhattan. An iconic building. This was no deep cut by The Pill Splitters. No B-side for the "true fans." Everyone knew Wright's building. And some—perhaps most—knew that a spiral was an impractical way to hang, or view, art. The Guggenheim family had asked for a building to showcase art. That was their want. What they didn't realize, what the great man understood, was the note behind the note: the Guggenheims *needed* to feel that they, too, were artists. Needed a building that would itself be a piece of art, whether anything could be displayed in it or not. Wright intuited this—his wildly outsized ego knew no hesitation—and he had hit it out of the park.

Now it was Tomas Araeta Jr.'s turn.

The "loft-kitchen"—a second story kitchen that cantilevered over the backyard garden, creating a covered porch below for outdoor eating—was his Guggenheim. Would it be a hassle to walk up and down a staircase to prepare and serve a meal? Absolutely. Was it strange to put a public space onto a second floor consisting mostly of private spaces—bedrooms and bathrooms? Yes. Did this cantilevered jutting box fit in with the existing architecture? No.

But Tomas felt he had something here. Something inspired. "Anyway, what's the worst that could happen?" he had nervously asked Billy as they walked up the old wooden steps to the front door of the Victorian home.

"They could shoot you a look of bewilderment and betrayal, fire you, not pay their final bill, I dunno, stuff like that," offered Billy.

"Excellent hype man, thank you," said Tomas.

"You asked. Hey, if you want me to keep my mouth shut in there, just say so."

"No, I just mean, let me take the lead on talking. Of course you can chime in. Appropriately."

"That's a soft no. I can handle the direct approach. We're not all snowflakes."

Enough. The Partridges were waiting.

Fifteen minutes later, everyone gathered in the dining room, Tomas, eyes alight, stood up from the heavy oak dinner table, and looked away from the freehand sketches and rough chipboard model of what he called "the treehouse."

"We've talked about all the reasons this doesn't make sense," he said calmly. Marie looked bewildered, Cole too. Or did they? Tomas couldn't read their expressions. Even Billy's expression gave away nothing. Had the presentation gone well or not? He didn't know.

Push through or walk out. Don't waffle.

"Now let's talk about why this is the best—the only—solution for you. A, I'm willing to bet cash money Claire would love eating in a glass box overlooking your garden." Claire was the Partridge's seven-year-old daughter.

"Well, sure. But she doesn't cook yet, and she's not paying for it," said Cole, his tone revealing some understandable reservation, but certainly not entirely shutting Tomas down, either. The comment seemed, well, jokey to Tomas, like his pitch hadn't put Cole Partridge in ill humor. *That* was something. Tomas glanced at Marie, hoping for her to chime in sympathetically. She said nothing.

"Preparing meals is about sharing, about shared experience," continued Tomas. "It's about giving—feeding a hungry person, showing you care through your action. It's about being in the moment. The taste of fresh burrata, the first sip of a decent cab franc. Like music commandeering your senses, food puts you in the moment, the now. Sharing, giving, being present—in the past people would do this in places of worship—a church, a mountaintop, a sports arena. So why am I blathering on so pretentiously? I don't even really know what cab franc *is*. Here's why: the procession up the stairs to the kitchen—that very act of *transition*—of sensing you are about to enter a special realm, and then delivering with this glass and steel box, impossibly suspended into and over the garden—will delight. Yes it's a kitchen, but it's also a chapel—actually I call it a treehouse—and I think you will find it as joyful as the things we climbed as children for no other reason than exhilaration and happiness."

Marie gently bit her lower lip, looked to her husband, his fingertips supporting him on the table as he knelt down to look over the model at eye level.

"Plus," said Billy brightly, "you never have to worry about your friends and neighbors *not* talking mess—good or bad—about you behind your back when they see this. They will have an *opinion*." Tomas shot Billy an approving glance at this bit of unapproved ad lib.

"Definitely does not fit in," said Cole. "And walking up stairs to prepare a meal? Carrying dishes downstairs if we want to eat in front of the TV? It's a lot," he said. Yet it still didn't feel like a no. Not yet. Perhaps the set-up to a gently delivered no, but it certainly wasn't a hard no—not yet. In the end, thought Tomas, they could always go back to some version of Alts. A—C. It wouldn't be the end of the world. Marie had said they were all great, and Cole had said he liked B.

"This business about a 'chapel,' a 'treehouse?' I'm about as secular as you get," continued Cole, standing back up. "I love beautiful architecture, and when I go to some avant-garde museum or restaurant, I expect to be wowed by the building. But this is *our home*, the place where we relax." Cole turned to his wife. "Marie, you've been quiet?"

"Okay," said Marie, her voice clipped, cool. "It's—I don't know what you were thinking, maybe 'thought' wasn't involved at all, I dunno. Cole's right: it doesn't fit in, it's 'impractical' if that's how you're thinking about architecture. It's a pain in the ass." She glanced at Tomas and Billy, then nervously at Cole. "And what I want to say is . . . I don't care. You are a genius. This, *this*, is why I knew you were our guy." She looked at her husband. "That, honey, is what I think."

Billy cocked a skeptical eyebrow. Tomas said nothing—he double-checked himself: yes, she had said the G-word. No doubt about it. And Marie was no ditzy trophy wife. Tomas had gleaned over the course of several meetings that she had a master's from the University of Chicago. And she was not prone to hyperbole. Everything wasn't *incredible*, or *amazing*, or *awesome*.

Cole frowned. But even if he was shot down, Tomas's victory was not Pyrrhic.

Marie Partridge, this ebullient, beautiful, discerning woman had seen the risk Tomas had taken, had understood the spark not just of the initial cocktail napkin idea, but of the sketches and model of how this beautiful gesture, this ode to family, community, sharing—could be executed, could be *elevated*, and had proclaimed him a genius.

Tomas thought bitterly of the moment seventeen years ago when his TA, Naomi Curran, a woman he had been falling in love with ever since she had spoken of her love for The Pill Splitters, ever since she had spoken so knowledgably and *emotionally* of what great architecture was, ever since she had shot him a look, subtly rolling her eyes, over guest critic Gunter Olsted's description of a student's work as "Brechtian," now stood at his desk, raising a leg and turning her foot at the ankle to relieve some fatigue (god the woman's ankles and knees alone could, and should, start wars) as she looked over his sketches. She had smelled so good. When she spoke, giving him feedback for that semester's main design project, a fire station, she had said, "I see an idea, but I don't yet see a building. It's easy to fall in love with the napkin sketch, but it's like writing a song and thinking one note is enough."

"But if the sketch is already bad, then no amount of polishing the turd is gonna help."

"Ouch. Who called your sketch a turd?"

"No, I mean, well," and here Tomas had thought for a second. Naomi was smiling. This was all light and silly to her, it seemed to Tomas, and he didn't want to come across as petulant or humorless. "Well, you didn't say it was the next Guggenheim, either."

"Do you think it is?" asked Naomi.

"I'm deluded, but not that deluded."

She had smiled again—god her smile had transported him.

"Your sketch is good, Tomas. But don't stop there. I've seen a lot of students think they're done when they're only just beginning."

"But is this beginning worth it?"

"It is. It's a good sketch."

Good. It was a *good* sketch. An edible meal is good. Nice weather is good. Not being hit by a car today is good.

"Thanks. I'll keep at it."

"You should."

Tomas grew to hate that word: *good*. It was just a synonym for the word that did him the gravest injury: mediocre.

What Naomi had told him all those years ago about falling in love with an idea and then not following through on its execution—well, Tomas had just rectified that with the treehouse. More than that, he had achieved Naomi's lofty goal of "unexpected joy" as her criterion for good architecture. Naomi may not have had much faith in him as a nascent great man, but as a certain Marie Partridge had just said, his work was "genius." Marie could barely get the words out fast enough. Cole's expression gave away nothing. Until it did.

"I defer to Marie on this," said Cole. "I'm a little more conservative by nature, but it is fair—with my travel schedule—to say she spends more time in the kitchen than I do—although I always do the dishes and I'd say a decent job of ordering out when I'm home."

"You order Indian like nobody can," added Marie.

"But I see she loves it, which means I will come to love it. I mean, don't get me wrong, it's amazing, awesome, etcetera, it's just not what I was prepped to see, but, hey, no risk, no reward right? And yes, Claire will lose her shit over it." Cole looked at his wife, then Billy, and finally at Tomas, and smiled. "Nice work."

As they left the Partridge home, Marie touched Tomas lightly on the arm, and shot him a conspiratorial glance which said, "I wanted to shout 'Genius!' the moment I saw that model, but I had to walk Cole into it, give him his time, his due."

"She totally wants to fuck you," said Billy when they got back into Tomas's car.

"Ha ha," responded Tomas dryly.

"No, that touch on the elbow. Even you have to know what flirtation looks like."

"She said it was genius."

"Right. Which is why she wants to smash." A moment of silence passed as Tomas pulled into traffic. Billy spoke again. "It's a wow-wow awesome design. And your balls should be bursting with jizzy pride over taking that risk. I'd probably do it, but you? Color me surprised."

It had been nine months, and Tomas was still not sure whether his sole employee liked his work or hated it, or merely needed the job and experience. Now he knew. Knew Billy admired his talent. Knew that, even if Naomi didn't see it, he had *IT.* Capital I, capital T. Touched by the gods. Genius *was* there. He *had* been his own worst enemy. The days of placing stumbling blocks in his own way were over.

Like the great men, he would now chart his own course, unfettered by the small man's worries, the concerns that, on our death bed, we chide ourselves—too late—for having spent so much time fretting over. But for Tomas, it was not too late. He was thirty-six. Frank Lloyd Wright designed the most famous home in America—Fallingwater—more famous even than Mies's Farnsworth House, when he was sixty-seven. Frank Gehry—the only true new form-giver of the last half century—designed the Guggenheim in Bilbao, Spain, when he was a year older than that. He could've been on Medicare and collecting social security during the ribbon cutting. On this count, architecture was *not* like power pop or punk.

Tomas Araeta still had time.

DAY 39

NAOMI PICKED DISINTERESTEDLY AT HER BOWL of Mockingbird brussels sprouts. Viola looked on while waiting for their drinks and her entrée of pomegranate lamb to arrive.

"How long does it take to make two fucking cucumber martinis?" Viola asked, glancing at the bartender.

"I can wait," said Naomi.

"I can't," Viola replied. "You gonna eat any of those?"

"Yeah but help yourself."

Viola stabbed a brussels sprout with her fork.

"I know it doesn't really matter," said Naomi, "because every relationship is different, the truth behind closed doors and all that—and please tell me to shut up—but I wanted to ask you about something . . . and maybe talking about it is too difficult—"

"Naomi?"

"Yeah?"

"Shut up. You're babbling. Ask or say anything you want." Naomi remembered the details Viola had shared with her when she caught Edgar cheating.

"Do you think he left his emails up on purpose?" Naomi asked. "Like, you can't be that stupid to leave a cheating email open on a shared computer and think your girlfriend might not find it."

"Oh no, he was just stupid. I don't know what it is, but I've known so many guys who just do clueless shit like that. Not flushing the toilet. Leaving price tags on gifts. Leaving open incriminating emails. Just dumb."

"Oh." Naomi sounded almost crestfallen.

"What?"

"I guess, in my mind, I pictured that he did it on purpose, wanting to get caught."

"That would make it better?"

"Maybe. I don't know. I just—the sneakiness, the lying—I almost feel like self-sabotage is better than trying to spin and weasel out of it."

The bartender brought over two large martini glasses, filled to the rim, bits of muddled cucumber floating inside, the whole concoction a vivid light green.

"Yeah, the damage control garbage is the worst," agreed Viola, bringing her head down to the lip of the overfull glass and slurping. "Cheers."

"Not sure what we're cheers-ing," said Naomi.

"Bad luck not to cheers." Viola took another sip, then lifted her head back up. "Oh. Oh. Oh *yes*." She sipped again. "Worth the wait, no?"

Naomi sipped, too, also bringing her lips to the rim of the glass. "Absolutely. Ohmygod."

"Next time he passes by I'm ordering another round. My impatience level skyrockets after my first drink." Another server brought the pomegranate lamb to the table. Viola cut herself a bite and, chewing, continued, "You were hoping Tomas wanted to blow stuff up on purpose by being stupid about his cell phone?"

"I guess. I'm not sure. With Edgar, I thought he was afraid to say something, and so, in some boneheaded way, he was trying to send you a signal that the relationship needed work."

"The signal? Oh the signal was clear. *Crystal* clear. The relationship was over. That was the signal. He made me feel like an idiot and a fool."

Naomi was confused.

"Then why did you stay with him?"

"That's the question, isn't it?" mused Viola, ordering that second round. "We really should have at least two or three more of these right now."

"I don't think booze will help."

"Of course not. Not for real. But shit, take the win for the next hour." Viola started rummaging through her purse. "I have a Norco or Vicodin in here somewhere, hang on." She kept looking. "Shit, I swear I brought one for you, too. Already had mine. Sorry."

"It's okay."

"Fuck. Okay. What were you saying? Right. Why did I stay with Edgar Philip Blatz after I caught him fucking someone else?"

Naomi nodded, staring at Viola.

"Because, in the end, I believe he didn't love her. I believed—*believes*—he loves me."

"How could you forgive him? I don't remember you saying the relationship was over back then, I thought maybe there was some crazy, y'know, mitigating factor, I didn't know about that let you forgive him. Like the on-purpose laptop thing, or maybe stress or drugs or . . . I don't know."

"Nope. It's love. Love is the mitigating factor."

Naomi looked disappointed.

"Yeah, it wasn't like he banged Charlize Theron, or he had been drugged—that would've been instantly forgivable," Viola said.

"So then?"

Viola put down her fork, drained the last drop from her already empty second martini glass, before she spoke again.

"Because—and first of all, let me say, I *was* going to leave his lying cheating ass, but I honestly—and this is how crazy I was—I wanted to stay together at least for, I dunno, four or five months, so he could really *really* suffer for a while—and *then* I'd break it off. If I just let him go right away, he might skulk off and get over it too quick. Find a new girlfriend. He needed to *pay* for a while. I needed him to suffer first. Then kick him out. That was the plan."

"And something happened in those four or five months?"

"And the thing is, I still dunno if taking that time to punish him was the best thing I've ever done for myself—or the worst—and I may never know. But in those months some of the anger—like the top layer, the crust of it—cooled, and I saw how he behaved, and what he said, and I hate to say it, but I think the fucker really regretted what he did—not just regretted *getting caught*."

"I fucking hate that!" blurted out Naomi.

"Oh yeah, it's the worst. But—this is the thing—I think Edgar also regretted *what he did*. Least I hope so. Otherwise I'm a jackass for being with him now. He needed to grow up. I told him flat out, 'That's the deal. Saying yes to one thing means saying no to another. And if you can't handle that, get the hell out.'"

The third round of martinis arrived. Naomi took her first sip then quickly took another.

"You are so right—this hour *is* improving." Naomi then quickly tossed in, "And it's not just the booze!"

"Shit, I don't care what it is. If chatting with Ted Bundy over martinis helps for a moment, I'm all about it."

"So, love. You fell back in love?"

"I don't think I ever fell out of love. I was just really, really hurt. And angry. For a while, I mean a *while*, we were just roommates. Even now we only have sex once every, like, three, four months. And the sad thing is, I'm okay with that. And I think he is, too. Probably jerks to porn or whatever, but that's cool."

"We boinked once or twice month."

"Animals! Damn! Good on you. I don't know any couple, especially married couples—especially after, I dunno, five years, say, who aren't basically civil roommates who, if dinner is perfect, and the wine is good, and all the stars in the world align, maybe they screw three or four times a year."

"And you. You're really okay with that?"

"Yeah. I dunno, maybe I should get my hormone levels checked. Serious blood work, y'know. But the wild thing is, the bastard has me believing that—and this is the real insanity, I know—that people can change."

Naomi nodded, sipped again. A warm liquid feeling suffused her entire body. Her bones, her mind, softened, and for a few moments, the pain faded, just a little.

"You guys—am I prying, ah who cares?" said Viola, "I thought you guys had some kind of 'open thing?'"

"No. We had an honesty thing." Now it was Viola who looked a little confused. "I told him, 'you want to try something—sleep with someone else, take a break, do something a little kinky, whatever'— just, let's talk about it first."

"So in a perfect world, he would've come to you and said, 'hey, I think I'd like to have sex with my client, is that okay?'"

"Yeah."

Viola held a forkful of lamb in the air. "Would you have said yes?" The lamb hung suspended.

Naomi took another sip. "Depends. Maybe. I probably would've said yes, *if . . . if,* I believed that it wasn't a threat to our relationship."

"Then he should've asked you. You practically gave him a goddamn paint-by-numbers book on how to do this."

"Yes. He should've. But also, she's married with a kid."

"Oh."

"Yeah. Actually, it would've been a hard no."

Viola chewed and mumbled as she spoke.

"Honestly, I can rattle off a couple bullet points—that I never fell out of love, that I think he genuinely felt bad, that he changed, that he loves me, blah, blah, blah, but after that? But—and here's where I *can't* help you—yeah, I have the bullet points, but at the end of the day? Someone else with that same list could easily say, 'nope, not good enough.' It's too damn personal, and then you add in personal baggage *plus* couple baggage? It's gut and heart at the end of the day."

"You suck at advice."

"I know, right?"

God that martini was magic. Not only had the pain subsided, but a hint of giddy euphoria flowed through Naomi's body. "Are you guys happy now?" she asked.

"I am. We are."

"That's amazing." Naomi smiled at her friend with buzzed envy.

And then the buzz faded as quickly as it had come on. Midway through her third martini, Naomi was exhausted and felt a splitting headache coming on. The emotional tension of the last thirty-nine days, on top of the alcohol, had come to collect its tab.

"I wish I did have better advice to give you, but honestly? All this shit is case specific."

Naomi reached into her back pocket.

"He sent me this, along with others. It's the only one I opened. Not sure why."

Naomi handed Viola a handwritten letter. She unfolded it and read aloud, "*You, Naomi, are kind, generous, easygoing, funny, and smart.* Okay, stating the obvious, but not a *horrible* opening," said Viola. She continued, "*That, anybody can see, and it's why you are loved and admired by so many. But when it comes to you and me—to us—something happens that I can't put into a list, or find quite the right words for, or even really understand.*" Viola looked up, put the letter down on the bar. "Son, if you're going to write a letter, you might try a little harder to find the 'right' words. That's what a letter *is*. Otherwise shut up or send flowers or something."

"He did that, too," added Naomi.

Viola continued reading. "*It is a feeling—of care and warmth and desire—that is like kryptonite. Good kryptonite. It stops me in my tracks, and time goes away.* Superman reference? I'm not pleased, but I will hold my tongue for a moment." Viola looked at Naomi, and quickly snapped, "but not forever. *It's everywhere: the sound of your laugh, the way you lift one foot up and turn it when you're tired,* when you say 'I never make snap judgments' and then disembowel people (remember backward-baseball-cap-dude at Ruby Room?)—Okay. Specifics. Better. God that place if filthy. I love it. Think I once wore open-toed shoes in there and caught a couple things in the bathroom. Not that you can see a damn thing it's so dark. God we all look better in there."

Naomi shot her a look—"Are we going to reminisce about how squalid and wonderful the Ruby Room is, or are we going to talk about the car crash that is my life?"

Viola continued reading. "*The way you go about living your life. You have an ease about you, you know who you are. It's grace, plain and simple. Point is, all of you still makes my heart leap. I have never felt that for anyone else, and I came to take it for granted. When you sleep and I'm still awake I perv out and just watch you—your cheeks flush pink like a baby's—and I listen to you breathe. Your snore rattles my ribs, and I love it. The way you actually jump onto the couch and land cross-legged when you're in a good mood? That kills me. If you feel even half—a quarter—this way toward me, let's give it another chance before we say fuck it. Jump on the couch with me. What do you say? PS – I will send other letters detailing what a shitbag I've been—stuff you already know, of course. But I want you to know that I know it, too.*"

Viola put the letter back down on the bar.

"Well, whaddya think?" asked Naomi.

"It's a decent letter. Maybe tilting toward good."

"Yup." Naomi drained the last of her third martini, then folded the letter back up before saying, "But words are easy."

Viola nodded. She looked a little perplexed. "So you really can't stand guys who wear their baseball caps backward?"

"Deplore them."

"Edgar wears his backward sometimes."

"I know," said Naomi.

DAY MINUS 3

NAOMI STARED AT TOMAS'S PHONE A MOMENT, then looked at him as he spat out his toothpaste.

"So you had a great afternoon?"

"Hmm?"

"You got a text. From M. Partridge: *thanks for a great afternoon.*"

"Oh, here, lemme see." He emerged from the bathroom, took the phone and looked at it. It was all happening so fast. Jesus, what about *today never happened*—he hadn't erased that text, he hadn't erased anything—had Naomi scrolled up just a little and seen it? He didn't know. Tomas took the phone, instantly regretted it. He should've let Naomi hang onto it. They were a couple who said to each other if they were busy holding a pan over the stove or deep into writing an email, "Can you tell me who texted?" There were no secrets. It wasn't uncommon for each of them to ask the other who had texted if they were busy, sometimes even asking the other to read the text aloud.

"A great afternoon?" repeated Naomi quizzically.

"Oh yeah, I killed it at the meeting. They were both getting nervous about the 'treehouse,' so I needed to talk them off the ledge."

"They were both at the meeting?"

Naomi never asked about who was present at client meetings unless they were having a longer chat about their workdays.

"No, just her." Did his voice sound as casual as he intended?

Yes. Yes, it did. He was sure of it. In the nanosecond it took him to answer his wife's question, he knew anything besides the truth—for this little part of it anyway—would quickly unravel. *Thanks for a great afternoon* is not a message sent by a couple, or even one person speaking for the couple. *Thanks for the great advice*, maybe. *A great meeting*, perhaps. But not *thanks for a great afternoon*. No, to simply answer the question truthfully was the right move. It fit the text. It sounded like what it was—someone was nervous and just wanted to share their worries privately, and, after being comforted, thanked the person informally for keeping their little confidence.

"What is she thanking you for?" The tone in Naomi's voice had shifted, but it wasn't yet the outright shock and horror of betrayal. And she wasn't just toying with Tomas, either, forcing him to squirm. She desperately wanted to hear the most plausible, perfect explanation that would clarify everything. She was giving him a little rope and praying he could tie something other than a noose with it.

"Well, I just talked her down, is all. She's pretty afraid of her husband and feels like she's spending his money, and he's iffy on the whole thing anyway. I had to convince her he'd be happy with the end result."

Naomi stared at Tomas. *Afraid of her husband. Feels like she's spending his money.* It's not that the statement could not be true; it's that if it was true, and if it was anything other than Tomas exaggerating a bit and being gossipy, then it meant that she had shared something intimate with him about her relationship with her husband.

"She told you that? That she's afraid of her husband and feels bad about spending his money?" asked Naomi.

"Yeah. I mean, don't quote me, but that's the gist."

"You don't remember what she said?"

"Not word for word."

Naomi tried to keep her voice steady.

"What happened today, Tomas?"

Now he could see the anxiety building in her eyes and brow, the wave massing, heading inexorably toward him.

"Nothing. What do you mean?"

"Can I see your phone again, please?"

"Sure."

What else could he do? He handed it over. The wave was cresting. Naomi read aloud, speaking evenly, coolly.

I'm in a really good mood, just wanted you to know.

Me too.

Claire is back. Back to reality. Xo, M

Naomi handed the phone back to Tomas, trying now unsuccessfully to repress the urgency in her voice.

"How long has this been going on?"

Tomas searched his mind for any possible explanation that didn't involve fucking a client while her husband was away on business and their child was on a playdate. Nothing. Nothing came to mind.

"Today. Just today."

"Did you fuck her?"

"Yes." Tomas answered with clipped precision, like someone being deposed.

"You're saying today was the first and only time you had sex with her?"

"Yes."

"If I ask her that question, she'll say the same thing?"

"Yes . . . but I'd prefer if you didn't ask her."

And here—unbidden—sudden rage entered Naomi's voice.

"Of course you don't want me to ask, you fucking coward, her husband would kill you!"

Tomas said nothing.

Something occurred to Naomi. "Dinner. That's what dinner was all about. The nice dinner. The toasted pecans on the salad, ohmygod." Naomi ran into the bathroom. Tomas could hear the water running and the toilet flushing. By the time she returned, he could only look at her, mouth slightly open, unsure of what to say next, or whether to say anything at all.

"She came on to me."

Naomi stared at him, billowing shock and grief now mixed with the deepest contempt. "The first thought to come into your head isn't 'I'm sorry, and I can't believe what I just did to you,' but to throw this woman under the bus? You *are* a coward, Tomas."

"I'm not in love with her. I made a mistake."

"Fuck you. Besides, you did nothing wrong, right? You just said it was her fault, coming on to you and all."

"No. It's my fault, too. I wanted it to happen. I let it happen."

"Mmm hmm," said Naomi, before adding, "I don't care where you sleep from now on, just not our bed."

He backed up awkwardly until he was just past the door threshold, then she slammed the door shut. Standing alone in the dark, suddenly the image of Marie came to mind. He pictured her, but now, she didn't seem quite so pretty. Ugly. Everything about it was ugly. She wasn't so beautiful, and he didn't need a mirror to know how horrific he looked to anyone with a discerning eye.

Fuck. Fuck, fuck, fuck.

Over the next few hours, sitting rigidly, back straight, on the couch, he agonized over whether to erase or preserve Marie's text messages. Naomi had seen them already, yes, but what if she wanted to see them again when she cooled down? She might want to check her memory. She might want to make sure she had scrolled up and down through any and all messages, checked time stamps. No, leave them. That was the right thing to do. Details must be preserved, no matter what the fallout. The old saying: the coverup is always worse than the crime—that much had been painfully demonstrated to him.

Oh who was he kidding? *Worse* than the crime? He had no right to guess at Naomi's feelings, to weigh what part of his betrayal was the most egregious. Better to simply admit, he had fucked up in every way and in every detail. There's not a bad decision he hadn't made.

At every fork in the road, he had chosen the wrong path. But there had been a sliver of honesty. Surely she believed him when he said this had never happened before. It was an anomaly, not a pattern. That's good. That has to help, right?

DAY MINUS 3—EARLIER

STANDING IN THE terraced backyard garden of the Partridge home, a cool oasis shaded by the walls of adjacent homes on all three sides, Tomas held his chin with thumb and forefinger and critically surveyed Marie Partridge's staked off lines.

"The control point is actually on the second floor, aligned with the main hallway. Hang on." He reached in his bag for the string and tape measure.

"Where are my manners. I haven't even offered you a drink. White wine okay?"

Her voice was quick, distracted, as if this was just the typical nicety she offered tradespeople who came to the house. But wine had never been on offer before. Was she about to put out a small plate of cheese and olives next?

Where was little Claire? From what Tomas had seen, she normally came down from her room when a visitor arrived.

"I definitely shouldn't, but maybe just a little," said Tomas, "but it's your fault if my lines come out crooked." She smiled, giggled. He noticed the half empty wine glass on top of the kitchen counter. How much had she had already?

Tomas thought of his college critiques, of the cheap wine served in plastic cups, when a semester's worth of work—drawings, models—was presented and then left naked to be judged by students, faculty, and guest architects. Wine and architecture were not such an unusual pairing. Novel for Marie Partridge, maybe, but not for practitioners and critics of what Goethe called "frozen music." The great generalist understood the sensuality and emotional journey of good architecture. And artists, and architects, and mothers can have a little wine in the middle of the day if they want to.

She led him back into the house into the small kitchen, which he would soon jettison and transfigure into an inspired riff of frozen music. "It's quiet today," he said. "Where's Claire?"

"Playdate. Thank God. She doesn't need to see her mother in a tizzy over string." Marie refilled her glass and poured Tomas more than a little. She raised hers. "To panicky bourgeois housewives." There was something in her voice. She was calmer now. Her smiling eyes looked at his.

"Hey, cheers to them, they keep hacks like me employed."

"Only a real talent would joke like that. I just need you to tell me everything's gonna be great."

"Everything's gonna be great," said Tomas with no sincerity. She shot him a playful scolding glance. He continued, "So—let's take a look at this disastrous decision of yours to hire me." For a moment, she took his hand—then immediately let it go—before leading him back into the backyard. She was wearing flip-flops and a light white blouse. He could just make out her nipples underneath the thin fabric. She was not wearing a bra. But it was a casual weekday, and this was no formal meeting. She was just dressed comfortably, casually. It was hard to tell, but Tomas thought her nipples were a deep warm brown. Could she see *his* shirt rising and falling arrhythmically over his heart?

Was this how Dr. Edith Farnsworth had greeted Mies van der Rohe on site visits to her isolated home under construction in the woods of Plano, Illinois? What would be the 1947 version of a sheer blouse teasing the color of perfectly formed nipples? Dr. Farnsworth had sued Mies after he broke off his alleged affair with her. That she was infatuated with him was an open secret. He is said to have later quipped, "The lady expected the architect to go along with the house." It had a leaky roof. Water came through in a torrent. And the impracticality of the design—there was no suitable place, she complained during the lawsuit, to put a kitchen trash can. When they were sleeping together, she didn't mind a little water or a house so transparent that it didn't accommodate an unsightly trash can. When they weren't, she did. She lost the lawsuit. Of course she did. You don't need Vegas oddsmakers to tell you what will happen when a mortal and a god collide. Dr. Farnsworth and Mies are long dead. Their legal skirmishes, their dalliance, their collaboration—very few will know or care about. If Mies wants to have an affair, Mies will have an affair. If his roof leaks, it leaks. Go ahead. Sue him. And in the end, the Farnsworth House in Plano, Illinois is an international treasure, and will be an architectural holy site for centuries. You don't sue Mies for leaks and expect to win. Take Mother Nature to court if it makes you happy.

As Tomas contemplated Marie's nipples, twenty-four blocks away, in a cramped window storefront, another beautiful woman was contemplating how to elevate design into frozen music. She smiled and shook her head. Some private thought. Nothing heavy, Garret could tell. He stole another glance at Naomi, caught another private smile.

"It's uncanny, even a little creepy, Naomi," said Garrett as he looked over the progress of her holiday window display, "but you seem to enjoy your job. I'm worried about you."

Naomi turned to face him. He could be charming. No, he *was* charming. She decided his affect wasn't an affectation. She found it flattering and fun, livening and harmless, that he flirted with her. That he didn't seem to be trying that hard made his little salvos all the more charming.

It fell on him to oversee the shop windows, to find designers who were both edgy, yet familiar, comforting yet challenging, and, above all, provocative but not off-putting. He had found that person in

Naomi Curran. This was her third tour of duty. The holiday season was two weeks away, and this was when Macy's put—literally—puppies in their shop windows, allowed vendors to set up hot dog and roast chestnut carts on the sidewalk outside the store, and it was the time when Garrett encouraged Naomi to really cut loose, to sprint all out to the finish line. He trusted and respected her. This perhaps, was the true wellspring of his charm.

"I'm worried, too," she answered. "You know how people say, 'Do what you like, and you won't work another day in your life'?"

"Yeah."

"*Those* are the people you should worry about, Garrett. That's why they invented two different words: 'work,' and 'play.' Y'know, to avoid confusion. No paycheck for Naomi? Naomi doesn't show up. But yeah, you're not wrong, I like what I do."

"You're not fooling me," responded Garrett. "You're happy."

After a moment, she smiled and said,

"Yeah, I am."

"Will it be too dark and cold when you're standing underneath the treehouse?" asked Marie as they stood in the backyard. She swirled her wine.

"It's San Francisco. If it isn't dark and cold in your backyard, I'd be worried." The wine was settling in—that beautiful first-drink buzz.

"I wanted to move to New Orleans at one point—warm, *fun*—but, not really home, not a place to have a family," said Marie. Her eyes were unfocused. Wistfully, she raised her glass and said, "Then I grew up."

"Still trying to put that off myself," said Tomas.

She smiled at him.

"So here's the thing, Marie. The way the sun moves over the course of the day? And the seasons? What you're gonna get is this great variety of sensory experience—some days, when the sun is high, it will be so bright and warm you'll be sweating. Other days you'll want a thick blanket and fire pit. It will change. And remember, too, on the days when rain is pounding, coming in sideways, you'll be upstairs in the kitchen, perched over these terraces, cozy and protected even though you'll feel—visually—exposed and vulnerable. It's like that old Jewish saying, 'If the house is strong, the storm is good.'"

Marie looked at him, her cheeks flushed, as if he had just spontaneously come up with "Ode on a Grecian Urn."

"And that's why I needed you here today," she said, "to remind me of why I love your idea. I can't wait to break ground."

At this moment, thought Tomas, *Naomi is probably hunched over in a narrow display window, talking to Garrett, not realizing the poor sap is probably flirting with her.* He had met her at work several times, had seen how Garrett's body language stiffened, how his voice became a little too officious, when he saw Tomas.

Marie fetched an expensive candy bar from an upper cabinet shelf, tore open the delicate gold foil encasing the dark chocolate.

"It's my secret stash. If I don't see it every second, I figure I won't be tempted to devour it every second. Also I can't tell Claire 'no sugar' then have this lying around for her to find. You've gotta try this."

"Okay, weird. If I had a secret stash," said Tomas, "it would be for the opposite reason: no one else knows it's there, right? So I can have it all to myself. No sharing. Pure selfishness."

"Here, taste."

Points of no return. The great men skipped past them. Life was so short, and there were so few things that meant anything. Yes, of course one's calling was important, and for Tomas it was architecture, but that was a luxury, something one could contemplate only after our primal needs were sated: sex, food, sleep, shelter, emptying our bladder and bowels. *These* were the universal things that everyone in every culture understood, the things that motivated men to get out of bed in the morning.

At that moment Tomas could've pulled his head back just an inch and taken the square of chocolate from Marie's hand by his thumb and forefinger. Instead, he leaned his head forward, opened his mouth and let her feed him. Points of no return.

Instantly the urge to defecate washed over him. Tomas's bowels churned. Marie had given him the rich chocolate, placed it in his mouth, and he'd accepted it. The look in her eyes: the next move would have to be his. But even if he quickly gathered up his things and left, they had crossed a line. The nerves in his stomach still danced, but he forced himself to ignore them.

He would kiss her. He would need to finish eating his bite, but he would kiss her.

"At least we both have chocolate breath," he said as he leaned in. She leaned forward too, and they kissed. It was a long, deep, slow kiss, and then he stopped. He pulled back and just stared at her.

"What's wrong?" she asked. He stammered before saying, "nothing."

Great men didn't apologize. Great men acted, seized the moment, didn't hesitate. At forty-two, Frank Lloyd Wright left his wife and six children and ran off to Europe with Mamah Cheney, the wife of one of his clients. A scandal. The house left in the aftermath of the scandal, though, the Cheney house in Oak Park, Illinois, is still a masterpiece, one of Wright's iconic, groundbreaking prairie houses. If something as pedestrian as an affair or family abandonment leaves behind a masterpiece like the Cheney House or the Farnsworth House, well, it's just the cost of doing business with a genius.

"I just want to stare at you for a minute," said Tomas.

"Don't," she said, but there was nothing in it, only a game, a coquettish, false hint of self-consciousness.

"Okay, I don't need a minute," he said quickly. He kissed her again. He ran his hands lightly over her hips and torso, let his fingers gently brush over her breasts.

"I want you inside me," she whispered.

"Me too." He knew the house. Knew where the bedroom was.

As she untucked his shirt, he softly blurted out, "Today never happened, okay?" He had spent a few seconds agonizing over whether to say this or, indeed, another word at all. But even if it meant killing a moment that would never return, he needed to know that she, like him, could put this experience in a small lockbox and throw away the key. Why she was willing to do this at all, he did not know and did not want to know. More information meant more intimacy. In Tomas's mind, a fuck without a lot of intimacy was something he could live with, something he could put in a lockbox, something which would not compromise his relationship with Naomi. Perhaps he shouldn't have said anything. Did this note of caution he'd sounded shatter the moment for Marie?

Marie reached into a side table and pulled out one of Cole's condoms. Tomas's face must've shown a little surprise.

"The pill makes me a moody bitch. Don't worry. Doubt he counts them," she said. Tomas managed a small, worried smile. "And yeah, this never happened," she added mischievously.

As he hurried to open the condom and orient the reservoir end correctly, he feared the worst: that this break in momentum, this reveal of the machinery behind the magic, would lead to him losing his erection. He knew his expression was intense, focused, too intense, too focused, as he fumbled with the condom. How unsexy he must look. As if she could read his mind, she gently stroked his cock while he struggled with the condom wrapper and struggled with the condom itself. He and Naomi did not use condoms. There was no reason to. She could not conceive.

There. It was on. And he was still hard.

As she guided him inside her, Tomas resumed his thought: not only would this not hurt his relationship with Naomi, it might actually *improve it*. He would return home a different man, bolstered by a surfeit of confidence to fuel the next chapter of their married sex life.

It was good with Marie. Very good. It was electric. The awkwardness of first-time sex wasn't there. Maybe it was the wine. Maybe it was their age. Whatever it was, it was great.

So it came as a surprise to Tomas that he threw up on the drive home. Accelerating at a green light, a wave of nausea overtook him, and he was barely able to pull over in time to fling open the door and hurl what remained of a sandwich and the chocolate and wine onto the asphalt. He parked and found the nearest drugstore where he could buy water and a travel-size bottle of mouthwash. In the store he felt jittery—it wasn't just the vomiting—he felt as if everyone was staring at him, and he thought he looked especially suspicious when he caught himself in the monitor of the store's security camera. He couldn't ignore the pressing need to shit any longer. He found the drugstore bathroom. What was happening? Did Mies feel his bowels churn when he'd fucked Edith Farnsworth? Did Frank Lloyd Wright need to stop urgently at a bathroom when he'd abandoned his family in Oak Park? Did Louis Kahn have GI trouble when visiting his secret second family? *Weakling.* That's the word that came to Tomas's mind as he sat on the drugstore toilet.

Outside, the streets were busy as ever and no one took notice of the pale, pasty man resting his head against the rough stucco wall of a CVS drugstore.

Twenty-four blocks. Right now Naomi was working twenty-four blocks away.

Tomas felt sick again but did not puke. The adrenaline was beginning to subside. His arms felt leaden. And then his phone buzzed. Once. An incoming text message. His stomach leaped.

He looked at the display. It was the office. Billy. Tomas's arms felt impossibly heavy now. He could barely hold up the phone to look at the screen.

Planning department hearing 11.4, 7 pm, we're ninth on agenda.

With jittery fingers, Tomas typed back,

Good. They'll be tired by the time we're up; they'll want to go home. We'll sail through.

No sooner had he finished pressing send than his phone chirped again.

I'm in a really good mood, just wanted you to know.

Tomas thought for a full five minutes before deciding whether he would reply. His initial reaction to Marie Partridge's text wasn't nausea—that was already there—it was a terrifying mix of fear and elation.

Today never happened.

What happened to that? This was an explicit agreement they had made. Marie had signed on. She hadn't protested, the mood hadn't cooled. She'd said yes, then got the condom. So what was this text? This text violated their agreement. This text was giving more life to the experience, not putting it in a lockbox. To comment on an illicit moment was to prolong it, to give it weight, to give it perhaps the weight it'd had all along, despite Tomas's efforts to let it suffocate in an airtight container.

I'm in a really good mood, just wanted you to know.

With eleven words, Marie had punched breathing holes into that container.

Today never happened. Perhaps that's the note he should send back. Put it in writing. A simple reiteration of what they had already verbally agreed to. But even as he considered this, he knew the only response that had a chance of resealing the moment, of encasing it in amber, was no response at all. This is what you did when you wanted no further contact with someone: you simply didn't respond.

Yes, in a few days, perhaps a week, he or Billy would call to arrange a meeting to review the revised drawings that Tomas would have prepared, and of course Cole would also be there. Enough time would've passed that the inflammation of what had just happened would have cooled, and his flagship project could go forward.

Considering all this and wanting to be *responsive* to the problem and not merely *reactive*, he took the time again to think carefully and decide with certainty that the only right move was not to respond.

And so Tomas typed *Me too*, hit send, and climbed back in his car. He didn't think to erase the last two messages—he did not consider himself the type of man who would behave in such a way that he would ever *have* to think about erasing messages. That belonged to the world of calculating, planning adulterers. And that's not what he was. He was a great man—nascent, perhaps—but surely, eventually, one of the greats, and fretting over everyman attempts to cover tracks would have debased him, Marie, *and* Naomi. And good god, such a small, common transgression, and really, for all the right reasons. Here was a woman who understood and acknowledged his talent. Of course he was attracted. What was the harm in giving in to a little animal instinct? Getting it out of his system? This was hardly a serious threat to a good marriage.

Soon he would be a father. He and Naomi loved each other. He had done what he had heard many guys had done, say, at their bachelor parties. He just did it a little out of sequence.

His phone chirped again.

Claire is back. Back to reality. Xo, M

"Back to *reality*." The relief Tomas felt was overwhelming. He could lift his arms again. He and Marie *were* on the same page. What happened was just a moment of frenzy, lust, curiosity. The closing "xo" made him a bit uncomfortable, but hell, that's how Billy ended most of his texts. That or *FYVM*, short for "fuck you very much."

A liquid feeling of serenity slowly came over Tomas. He had come into his own, as a designer and as a man. This must be how Mies and Frank and Louis and countless other greats—men and women—felt. And it was wonderful. He was now free, too, free of the *petit bourgeoise* constraints which had hobbled him, which had prevented him from becoming the man he was destined to become. Marie understood that what had happened belonged to the realm of *unreality*, a wonderful moment that came and went. They would now return to their personal realities, rejuvenated, perhaps enjoying the private reminiscence every now and then of their little transgression, but it was over.

"So how'd it go—bored housewife hit on you or not?" asked Billy when Tomas returned to the office. The nausea had settled. Tomas's bowels were empty. It truly was over.

"Yeah, it was unreal: I did her on the kitchen counter."

"A little eighties-sex-thriller cliché, but nothing to be ashamed of."

"Baby steps."

"Hey man, I know I'm supposed to also be like the accountant for this place, but I've sent out three reminder bills for the Normans, and I'm not hearing anything back. Should I show up at their house with a baseball bat or what?"

"I want you to make that decision, Billy, and it's best if I know as little as possible."

Good. Good. The oily sheen of guilt and anxiety that Tomas was sure a perceptive young man like Billy would see apparently didn't exist anywhere else than in his distracted mind.

The rest of the afternoon at work passed uneventfully, save for Tomas being a little less focused on both the work at hand and his inadequacies as an architect. Today there would be no surfing the web to see the latest conceptual drawings by Daniel Libeskind, Bjarke Ingels, Jeanne Gang, or David Adjaye. Today he just needed to make it to a respectable hour—five o'clock—and go home.

"You're leaving before me?" said Billy as Tomas packed up around four-thirty.

"Yeah," said Tomas.

"Ohmygod, that is so awesome. This is going in the bank for

when I need to bail early."

"You bail early most days, Billy."

"Yes, but on one of those days, I will now have the moral high ground."

"Doubtful."

"Big plans?"

"Hmm?"

"You leaving before me?"

"Actually, I'm surprising Naomi with a nice dinner. I'll buy most of it predone from the deli at Andronico's, but I'll toast the pecans—she loves that—for the salad."

"Ah, yes, the fumes."

Something in Billy's smug tone. Tomas stopped, irritated.

"What do you mean, 'the fumes'?"

"Y'know, the fumes—like fluffers in porn. Prep work. Get the motor revving. Marie Partridge is hot and she's crushing on you. Take that shit home and hump your wife."

"She didn't flirt with me, Billy," snapped Tomas.

"Oh. Sorry. Well, whether you admit it or not, I saw her flirt with you, and you flirted back, and I'm sure she did it again, and now you will carefully transport those juices home, like donated kidneys in a picnic cooler, and apply them to a nice night with your lady."

"Y'know, Billy, you are my underling, an at-will employee without a contract, someone who I could let go tomorrow."

"Duh, I know that. My brother's a lawyer. But when you hired me, you said you weren't looking for a draftsman, you were looking for a *co-lab-o-ra-tor*." Tomas was about to leave without saying anything else, then thought better of it. Every move seemed fraught. Every move had to preserve the veneer of innocence.

"See you tomorrow, collaborator."

Tomas drove straight to Andronico's Market to pick up the ingredients for a "nice" dinner. He filled several takeout containers with Vietnamese and Lemon Garlic drumettes, "hipster hot wings," as he and Naomi called them. He packed up mashed potatoes and grabbed a plastic box of supposedly triple washed (he was always skeptical of this claim) organic mixed spring salad. He bought pecans and feta cheese to garnish the salad, and, in a moment of inspiration, decided on a raspberry vinaigrette dressing. The vinaigrette was an exception: neither he nor Naomi were foodies, and quite proud of the fact. It was one of the few things they could claim, along with a decent collection of old punk CDs and vinyl records, which distinguished them from the rest of the yuppies in their up-and-coming neighborhood. How horrified they would be to find out how many of their "stiff" neighbors *also* loved Jane's Addiction, Operation Ivy, LCD Soundsystem—maybe even the The Pill Splitters—and how many of them raided the chafing dishes at the Andronico's deli for "nice" dinners.

"Toasted pecans? My birthday's not for another three months," said Naomi at the dinette table.

"They completely elevate the salad, and really, they're easy to do."

"Wine's not bad, either."

"I looked at the least expensive bottle they had, then went up three steps from there."

"Wow, what's with all the decadence? Must be that we're . . . *number thirty-two!*"

Tomas froze.

"Are you kidding me?" he said.

"Yes. My idea of 'funny' is joking about us becoming parents. No, you moron, we're the benefactors of geopolitical insanity. Pour me more wine!"

He did. Naomi caught Tomas staring at her.

"You knew, didn't you?" she said. "I know you barely check your emails, but you saw it already, didn't you?"

Tomas paused, smiled, lied.

"Maybe I peeked."

"Thirty-two. *Thirty-two.* It's happening, Tomas, it's *happening.*"

"I know. I feel sick. I'm not ready. I am. I am ready, *of course I am*, but you know, I'm not ready."

"Aw, you'll be a great dad."

Tomas raised a glass and they toasted.

"To the hottest future mom I know."

"I accept that." Naomi smiled. "To the man I'm sharing my life with. And to our little growing family." They kissed. "Nice salad dressing, by the way." For a moment, neither said a thing. Tomas—and Naomi—both wanted the moment to just hang suspended in the warm, reassuring glow of the beautiful present and a future where any quotidian anxiety was trampled by the luminous prospect of becoming parents. Life was good. They were blessed.

Eventually Naomi broke the lovely silence.

"How was work?" Naomi didn't ask the question regularly—they both simply shared whatever they wanted to share about their workday only if they wanted to unburden—but they would both ask it perfunctorily from time to time. But tonight, in this moment, this unutterably beautiful moment, there was genuine warmth and curiosity in her voice. Like she was really thinking about, wondering about, how Tomas felt *that day*, how the man she loved was doing. He had seen the same email she did. What was his day like as they raced up the baby escalator?

"Okay. You?"

"Actually, pretty great. I waited for it to get a little dark and did a test of this, well, I've gone more jagged, almost aggressive, I guess, with the crystal shapes, more haphazard. And I lit them, and they looked like . . . childhood."

"Pics?"

"Not yet. Not until I think you'll be proud of them."

Tomas felt his throat constricting. He fought back tears. "Man, life," he said.

She took another bite of the salad. "First pecans, now this . . . raspberry vinaigrette?" He nodded and smiled. "You *are* inspired tonight." Under the table, she lifted her leg and brushed his shin with her toe. His phone buzzed. A text. Normally, even at the table, he would at least glance at it just in case it was work. But he didn't.

"Who is it?"

"Spam's been ramping up, and it's pecan time. If someone wants me to clean up the environment or extend our car warranty they can wait."

"I swear, we should just get burner phones and call it."

It buzzed again. Tomas knew he should look. It would seem odd if he didn't. Not after two buzzes. Would it be odd not to look? It would.

He glanced at the caller ID. It was Marie.

Just a hello. Am I the lamest texter ever? Tomas had a split second to decide what to say to Naomi. He knew the expression on his face had to synch with what he just saw, and yet, no matter what his reaction, he'd be play acting. But it would be out of character for him not to say something casually about who was calling. A simple "It's Billy," for example, would suffice. But something in him intuited that even a small lie would not play in this moment. He had something to hide, true, but Naomi had no reason to suspect anything. Just be cool. Finesse it. Be real.

"Partridge. Already fretting over cabinet knob finishes. I always tell them, when in doubt, oil-rubbed bronze." He had, in fact, told them this—as he did most of his clients—oil-rubbed bronze almost never doesn't work, no matter what the cabinet material—and, most importantly, Naomi knew this was one of Tomas's go-to comments.

"Her or him?"

"He couldn't care less. This is her baby."

"You're not even done with schematics and she's sweating hardware finish, good lord."

"Hard to predict when they'll hit the panic button."

Again he knew Naomi would know what he meant.

"It's always the rich ones who obsess worse than the ones who can barely afford it," said Naomi.

"Textbook case of boredom," said Tomas.

"Enjoy the boredom, babe," said Naomi. "'cause in a few months, you'll wish you had more of it." She smiled at him. "Thirty-freaking-two!"

The phone buzzed again, and again, Tomas glanced at the text: *Moments that never happen are sometimes the best.*

Did she really write that? Yes, of course she did. Okay, so she was still in the afterglow of the excitement. It would pass. Naomi didn't even ask about the sender or content of the second message.

"'The Good Place' tonight?"

"Hmmm?" asked Tomas.

"Let's take a break from 'Squid Game.' I'm feeling comfort food-y. Let's rewatch a few 'Good Places'?"

"That. Sounds. *Great.*"

They cleared the table and loaded the dishwasher. Tonight Tomas's—to Naomi's mind—uptight "clean as you go" approach didn't bother her. Tonight everything was good. Naomi climbed into sweatpants, and they settled in to watch a few episodes. Tomas hated popcorn; Naomi loved it. For a split second he thought of getting up and making her a bowl but caught himself. It would be a dead giveaway. When she wanted popcorn, she made it. Always. On top of the pecans and the vinaigrette and the chatter about parenting? It would be too much.

After putting a bowl of fresh popcorn within arm's reach on their coffee table, she lay with him on the sofa, her head on his chest, one leg draped over his.

They watched two episodes, he listened to the words spoken by the characters, followed the sequence of events depicted, but by the closing credits, he couldn't tell you a damn thing about what he had just seen.

"You okay?" asked Naomi as she turned off the TV. The room was now dark.

"Yeah, why?"

"You just seem quiet, that's all."

"Oh, it's just, number thirty-two and all. I have to shift gears, from 'keep cool and just wait,' to 'ohmygod it's happening.' What are we going to do about the nursery, blah, blah, blah, I haven't really let myself think about it."

"Oil-rubbed bronze, right? Goes with everything."

She squeezed him tighter.

That clever little lie—a man blaming his distraction on an impending adoption—a salty red herring so perfect that Naomi would have no choice to but to swallow it whole, was in itself as damaging as what happened next.

Over the next hours and weeks, Tomas would replay the scene countless times in his head. They were getting ready for bed. He had gone into the bathroom to brush his teeth, and Naomi was grabbing her sleeping T-shirt from under her pillow. His pants were on the ground next to her, and she could hear his phone vibrating. In the past, they had sometimes picked up each other's cell phones. Just a glance to let the other person—who might be busying composing an email or brushing their teeth—know if it was important. Not a big deal.

She pulled his phone out of his pocket and saw the message. He hadn't set his phone—hadn't had *reason* to set his phone—so that incoming messages would be hidden.

Thanks for a great afternoon. He hadn't heard the phone vibrate. Hadn't realized she had picked it up. Hadn't realized she had read the message. At that moment, spitting out toothpaste, he was thinking of another great afternoon.

A light rain fell. Kids shrieked and played. Irritated office workers hurried back from their lunch breaks. A man with a giant soap-bubble paddle hustled for change. Naomi loved them all. Tomas fidgeted on the bench, couldn't get comfortable. They were sitting outside the National Art Gallery in Trafalgar Square in London. They both had just seen Rembrandt's portraits of older men and women, something so moving no camera could ever capture what the master's hand had.

"If I was content with everything, I'd be bored," said Tomas. "Know what I mean?"

"No. If I was content, I'd be content," replied Naomi, looking out dreamily at the gray London streetscape.

DAY 1

AFTER TOMAS HAD SWEPT AND MOPPED the precious matchstick floors and attacked the bathroom until it was spotless, more spotless than it had ever been, cleaner than Naomi would ever care for it to be—"This isn't *Sunset* magazine; we're inviting a filthy little child into our home soon, let's practice for reality"—a sentence began taking shape in his head, and he grasped at it for dear life. It was an epiphany really—his first clear insight into what had happened.

"I fucked an idea, not a person."

The notion came to him unbidden, so it must have a good portion of truth to it. He had fucked an *idea*. Marie wasn't his lover, his next wife, the soulmate he had missed. No, not at all. She was, well, at its crudest level, the embodiment of missed sexual opportunities (all men keep such an invisible ledger, do they not?). But yes, she certainly was more. That much must be admitted. She was validation for his architectural talent, she was an incomparable attaboy—one that he had happened to fuck. That was it. Their little dalliance was a necessary tonic against a corrosive sense of mediocrity, of potential unfulfilled, or, worse, of potential that was never there. It served its purpose, it was done. It certainly wasn't an affair. No, this was childish entitlement, nothing more. And in a certain light, a fair light, truthfully, well, it was practically entrapment. Marie had called him a "genius." A genius! What sentient male wouldn't bend just a little bit, wouldn't indulge himself when his gift was acknowledged properly?

Would it have been better if he had continued to let difficult feelings nag at him, intensify with age, slowly poison his marriage, than it was to have this one stupid encounter and get it out of his system? It was, after all, the great man's prerogative, only he wouldn't make a habit of it. No, unlike them, he was very decent to others in his nonwork life. In this regard he was not a great man, he was just a *good* man who had fucked an idea. Entirely forgivable.

Naomi was smart. She would understand. Really, she was wiser and smarter than he—she would be able to see all this silliness with a certain detachment, the view from 10,000 feet. When she had a moment to cool, or however long she needed—many moments, he didn't care, he could wait—he would calmly and dispassionately, but with all candor and sincerity, explain to her that what unfortunately had happened was that he had made the careless, okay, no, *selfish* (let's take accountability here), the selfish mistake of "fucking an idea." The idea of affirmation, of validation. Earned affirmation. Earned validation.

He might leave the part out about this mistake ultimately being for the best. Not just for him, but for them, their growing family. Best to let her come to that realization on her own.

Feeling completely reenergized, he vigorously resumed his cleaning. He wanted the house spic and span for her. He began dusting the top edge of the interior window and door trims—he should've dusted them before cleaning the floors—he had forgotten the "top to bottom" rule for a moment – dust falls down, not up. But that was an easy fix, a quick remop—when another thought came to him: flowers. Duh! But he immediately second guessed himself. It seemed trivial and cliché to buy flowers for Naomi, so obvious, so expected, and were flowers even the correct proportional response to fucking an idea? One might not think so, but ah, hadn't she always said, "Flowers work every time" when he had bought them for her? She had. She had said that. When he was stuck looking for a creative birthday or Valentine's Day or anniversary gift—"I dunno, surprise and delight me!" she would say playfully when he asked her what she might like—a bouquet of roses, in addition to whatever else he may have come up with, made her smile. And the way she would trim the bottoms of the stems, add the little packet of plant food to the water, find a suitable vase for them, and display them on the bureau in the front hall, was all the proof Tomas needed to know that, indeed, flowers worked every time.

The only local flower shop he knew opened at ten. He still had four hours to kill. He had woken up from two or three fitful hours of sleep at four in the morning. Fine. He would go to the studio—there were a few things that required his attention—then leave Billy in charge while he bought the most beautiful roses he could find. Naomi still slept, or at any rate hadn't opened the bedroom door yet.

He certainly wasn't going to tell anyone about what happened—not yet anyway—so he had to pull it together until he could explain to Naomi what happened, what *really* happened: that he'd fucked an idea, that Marie had tickled his ears with just the right words, that he got caught up in the entitlement of the great man, and that—here was the silver lining—he had successfully exorcised those demons.

When he arrived at Studio Araeta, the first thing he did was turn on the Bluetooth speaker. Forget the melancholy "Another Day" playlist he had been listening to at home to reflect and amplify his grief and pain while cleaning. No, this moment called for "The Pill Splitters' Blistered Eye" on a repeat loop. A two minute and forty-eight second ampoule of adrenaline. An angry yes to life. Not a note could be added or subtracted. The song could neither be a second longer nor a second shorter. It was perfect. Lead singer Evo Korman would never have another take like the one that made it onto that first single. Freeze it. Enshrine it. Appreciate that you were alive *after* it came into existence. Tomas listened to "Blistered Eye" five times before he felt that itch well and truly scratched. And the itch was now gone! Just as it was after he'd fucked Marie. He had an itch, he scratched it, time to move on.

"What do you think, this is a government job?" asked Billy as

Tomas packed his shoulder bag to leave after a whopping two hours of work.

"Gotta new prospect," said Tomas.

"Care to share?" asked Billy.

"No. I've probably already jinxed it."

"You look like shit, by the way," added Billy. "Go eat a hamburger."

"Yeah, probably should."

"Up too late watching porn after Naomi fell asleep?"

"Is it ever *too late* to watch porn?"

"Wow. You actually made a point. A decent one." The jittery euphoria was subsiding, but the optimism remained. Billy intuited nothing. "Yeah, plus playing that damn song a quintillion times," added Billy, "as a 'good morning?'—don't get me wrong, 'Blistered Eye' is a *fine* song, I've conceded that—but too much of a fine thing is *not* fine. It's irr-i-ta-ting. You probably *should* go, now that I think about it."

"I will go, but you're wrong about the song. I pity you. I really do." Billy shrugged. "Pearls before swine," said Tomas as he left.

At the florist, after briefly considering and rejecting stargazer lilies and purple asters, he was certain: a dozen long stem roses and baby's breath would be perfect—timeless, rich, unequivocal.

"Would you like to put in a card?" asked the florist.

"Hmm?"

"They're free." The florist indicated a selection of small cards on a countertop display rack.

"Oh. Sure."

Tomas considered. Should he play it light? Should he say just a few serious words, and leave the rest for their reconciliation conversation? Should he include a card at all? After getting married, Tomas and Naomi promised each other not to have any expectations regarding the giving of cards for special occasions. After all, they would be spending all their Christmases, anniversaries, and birthdays together, in the same room. Would it not be silly to hand each other cards and sit there smiling stupidly, waiting for a reaction? There was no reason to put that kind of pressure on another person—waiting for them to gin up some kind of exaggerated response. What if they weren't feeling it? Standing there in front of the person expectantly waiting for a positive reaction, was, literally, making it about you. If, however, you simply felt it, or perhaps found a good joke card, then fine. Maybe leave it for the other person to find, alone, an Easter egg surprise. But they had agreed: there were to be no expectations as to the giving of cards.

On the plainest card available—a white-on-white embossed flower—no preprinted text—Tomas wrote *I don't deserve you*, then threw it away, not wanting to plant a thought that she certainly must already be having. Next he wrote *I love you*, then folded that card and threw it away. It was fine but lacked a certain specificity necessary for the occasion. *Wow. I fucked up.* was his next attempt. Again, he threw the note into the wastebasket. Too glib.

"It's hard, isn't it?" asked the florist.

Tomas wasn't even aware that she had been watching him.

"Yeah, I just, y'know, don't want to be too corny or too stiff."

"What's the occasion?" asked the florist, "I'm pretty good with this stuff."

Tomas quickly pulled his crumpled prior attempts out of the waste basket and stuffed them in his pocket.

"Just telling my wife I love her."

"Oh, and it's not even Valentine's Day. How sweet. Well, believe me, the flowers alone will probably leave her in tears."

"I'm sure you're right."

Tomas left without filling out a card. After spending a few more unfocused hours at work, he went home. If Naomi had gone to work, he had an hour or so left before her normal arrival time to do a little more cleaning and think about what he would say to her. If she had gone to her mother's, or a friend's, or a hotel, who knows when she might return. But there was always something to clean. Or he could watch TV. Maybe go to church. Take a walk. Options. He had options.

When he turned the corner toward their house, he froze. Their car was in the driveway. She was back. His heart leaped. She was clearly already ready to talk. He quickened his pace toward the house, opened the front door.

Naomi was in the dining room, reading glasses on, looking at her laptop.

"Hi."

Without looking at him, Naomi responded, "Hi Tomas."

"Uh, I didn't have time to mop the kitchen yet. Y'kinda caught me off guard."

Naomi looked up at him. He was smiling. She made no comment about the bouquet of roses in his hand. "Will you go somewhere with me?" she asked.

"Sure."

"Now. Do you have time now?"

"Well, I guess the floors can wait." He threw on his winningest smile.

"Let me put those in water."

Tomas was elated. Naomi's voice—the tone—no sarcasm, no contempt, no pain. All he could hear was patience and reserve. It wasn't her normal tone, to be sure, but it was closer to that of an elementary school teacher or nurse than a scorned woman. Her demeanor was cool, precise. The word *rational* came to mind. She trimmed the ends of the flower stems, added the food packet, and put them in a suitable vase.

"They're beautiful."

"I'm glad you like them."

"And the house smells like Pine Sol dipped in bleach."

"I guess I got on a stupid cleaning jag."

"Not a speck of dust. You went all in."

"Except the kitchen floor."

"That's nice," she added blankly. She shut her laptop and grabbed the keys.

Nice? Tomas's nerves began to tingle, but he was able to stop himself from catastrophizing.

"Where are we going?"

"You'll see."

In the car Tomas asked if he could turn on the radio.

"I don't care." He turned it on. The second song to come up on Little Steven's Underground Garage satellite radio, after Edwin Starr's "Twenty-Five Miles," a tune far superior to his massive hit "War (What Is It Good For?)," was "Blistered Eye." Perfect! What a sign. How they both worshipped this song, how they both had gushed about The Pill Splitters into the wee hours in college in the studios until other students rolled their tired eyes. In the Venn diagrams of their playlists, this one overlapped both circles.

"You know, Nomes, I have no idea where to start—I know this is my baggage—but I just hope it means something that it all began and ended two days ago. I didn't erase that text because I wasn't thinking that way." She nodded. This was wonderful. Wonderful! She already understood what had actually happened. She really was wiser and smarter than he.

"You cheated on me, Tomas, and you lied about it. I know it wasn't a decade's long affair, and I don't think you love the woman, and I think you genuinely regret what you did, but you did it. All I asked of you before we married was that you come to me with your feelings first, and you didn't. That is a very, very small ask, Tomas. You disregarded my wish and acted selfishly."

He stammered a moment, like the cornered, chastised toddler he suddenly felt himself to be.

"I . . . I . . . I know." Naomi wiped a tear from her eye but kept her jaw tight and her eyeline frozen. Tomas felt sick. He wanted to stare at Naomi, to do or say anything to keep another tear from falling, but he was lost now, and merely stared out the side window. "I'm sorry. I'm so sorry."

"Me too."

As they rounded the shore of Lake Merritt, a man-made lake in the city's downtown, the Alameda County Courthouse came into view.

She parked at the first available street spot she could find. She turned to Tomas.

"Please don't fight me on this."

"What are we doing?"

"It's on the second floor."

"This is where we got our marriage license."

Before exiting the car, Naomi clasped Tomas's hands tightly, wrapping hers around his.

"I remember everything, Tomas. And I don't want to talk right now. Let's just do this. That is my ask."

"This is crazy. You're angry, of course you are, but this—this is crazy."

Naomi stared at him with a cold anger and precision he had never seen.

"Two days ago I was happy."

DAY 11

STANDING IN THE window of Macy's, glue gun in hand, Naomi heard her phone ring again. When she worked, she left her cell in a corner of the window where it wouldn't be too near the grime or glue or the possibility of falling from her pocket. She had friends—Maya came to mind—who cracked their teeth in their sleep, and now used mouth guards. She didn't. She prided herself on keeping her stress level manageable enough so that she wouldn't break teeth when she slept. But his relentless calling, on top of what he had done? He couldn't be so dense as to not understand what it means to give someone space.

She would speak to him. Briefly. There would be no cracked teeth on his account.

Tomas was shocked when he heard Naomi pick up the call. Persistence wins the day. It felt like calling in to a radio station to win a prize when you were a kid, when radio stations still gave away concert tickets, cash, and the like. Just. Keep. Dialing. And maybe one day, maybe just once, you'll be Caller Number Ten.

"Hi Tomas."

"Nomes. Hi. How are you?"

"Busy. At work."

"I know. I just, well, I called."

"Yes, I'm very aware."

"So, hey, look, I know I've said I'm sorry, and I know words are just words. But I really think—if you are okay with it—"

"Tomas—"

"But you won't be able to see it, to know what I mean and how I feel, unless we're around each other more. Maybe we could meet for coffee some day?"

"Tomas?"

"Yes?"

"I picked up the phone now because I can't turn it off. I may get work calls, calls from family or friends, who knows."

"Yes."

"I want space from you. I don't want to think about you right now. I don't want to meet for coffee. You know how I feel. I put it in writing on official paper."

"Well that paper won't mean anything for like a hundred and seventy days."

"Tomas?"

"Yeah?"

"Please listen carefully. If I want to be in any contact with you, I know how to find you. I am talking to you as a courtesy now to let you know that if I see your ID come up on my phone again, I will block your number. This would make me feel even worse about myself and about us. It's middle-school bullshit, but you need to respect my boundaries."

Tomas took a moment to absorb her words.

"Okay, so I won't call or text you."

"Correct."

"Unless you call or text me."

"Right."

"Okay."

"I'm going to hang up now, Tomas."

"I love you, Naomi."

The line clicked off. Tomas was hyperventilating. Letters. Handwritten letters. She hadn't banned that yet. He would begin the letter-writing campaign as soon as his hands stopped shaking. He was calling from their car (he did not want Billy overhearing this conversation). He couldn't go back to the office. Not just yet. He had to compose himself. He had to quiet his racing mind. He would have to force himself to do something, anything, to keep from jumping out of his skin.

Wait. The library.

The library. Tomas would turn his attention to the UC Berkeley Library Annex Competition. As ubiquitously advised by Marivel, and vigorously seconded by Abbie, he now took seven attentive breaths. Breathe in through the nose for five seconds, hold for six seconds, and exhale through the mouth for seven seconds. The 5-6-7 method. Mindful breathing was shown to calm racing thoughts, to calm the body—at least that's what Abbie and Marivel had always said. After seven breaths, he did feel the world slowing, just a bit.

Yes, the prestigious competition to expand UC Berkeley's archival library. This was the kind of project that jump-started elite careers. The kind of thing that got you published and noticed. Tomas was able to quiet his mind just enough to reflect for a moment. Maybe, pushed into a corner, bereft, the ground wrenched from beneath his feet, a spark of true latent genius would show itself. Be forced to. Something that would dwarf the treehouse in imaginative scope and scale. Maybe the exorbitant price of his sin would come with a tiny consolation: it might at least uncover a hidden wellspring of creativity that could only be seen by those with the vision of the desperate. Maybe, for Tomas Araeta, this was the only way to see Schopenhauer's invisible target. The quote was in the hardbound copy of *The Collected Essays of Schopenhauer* his father had gifted him upon his high school graduation. The cranky old German philosopher wrote, "talent hits a target no one else can hit; genius hits a target no one else can see." At the time, like any "gift" from his father, Tomas took it to be backhanded criticism, the establishment of a bar he could never reach.

Maybe now, though, lost, unmoored, an idea, a conceit, a form, that would be something other than nice and *good* and workable, would emerge. Maybe even the ability to see the invisible target. When his obituary was written, would anyone say, "Tomas Araeta replaced cabinetry and light fixtures in nice single-family homes?" This was no legacy. He had no legacy. Right now his legacy was a broken marriage, the wounding of a beautiful, kind, woman, and a waiting-list number for an international adoption that he had just stubbed out like a cigarette butt.

He would stop at the warehouse first. Yes, he would let Billy see him, see how normal and perhaps even excited he was about the library. At Studio Araeta he grabbed his roll of translucent orange sketch paper—something of an affectation in the days of iPads, but a good many architects still preferred graphite on paper to those digital Etch A Sketches.

Billy had rap blaring—Bruiser Wolf—when Tomas entered.

"Hey," said Billy.

"Hi," said Tomas curtly. Billy took Tomas's tone to mean he was annoyed at the volume level.

"The music isn't too loud," said Billy prophylactically. "The jewelry hippie is still asleep, and the hermit dude didn't say anything—which means he likes it. If you're not complaining, it's liking."

"I'm on my way out. Think I am gonna take a crack at the Library Annex."

"You serious?"

"Why not?"

"Well, hey, swing for the fences I guess."

"Right."

Tomas was slightly irritated, but that was unfair. What had he shown Billy to make him think that he would throw his hat in such an exalted ring? The competition would undoubtedly have several local and international starchitects throwing their hats in as well.

"It's an open competition, and we're good."

Billy relented, shrugged, nodded.

"Okay."

Tomas grabbed his roll of trace.

"Time to get inspired."

"He's here and gone like the wind. Mercurial. Unpredictable."

God damn Billy. It was comforting to have that constant in his life, the snarky, entitled Gen Zer who treated Tomas like he was granting him a papal dispensation by deigning to work for him.

"I like the sound of that. Mercurial. Yeah."

"So hey, not to be a buzzkill, I'm just the messenger, but Cole Partridge called for you. Twice."

The pang of nausea and adrenaline hit Tomas like a bullet train. Billy turned back to his work. Tomas had told him what happened—he'd find out sooner or later, and the air mattress Tomas had brought into the office was a dead giveaway, anyway.

"Aren't you gonna say 'I told you so,'" Tomas asked Billy when he first told him.

"Nah. It's putting a hat on a hat. I wasn't a hundred percent sure—you're lying skills are decent-ish—but I kinda thought you might have banged her on that site visit you did solo."

"Well you were right. I did. And now I'm paying for it," Tomas had said, indicating the air mattress.

"Yeah. You are." It was the first time Tomas had heard what he thought was a judgmental tone in Billy's voice. But he seemed to hear judgment everywhere these days. The whooshing air brakes of a bus conveyed the harshest judgment to his ear.

Tomas sat at his desk, took a deep centering breath, took eleven of them, and began to look. He double-checked the texts, voicemails, and missed calls on his phone. Nothing. Nothing from Naomi, Cole Partridge, or Marie Partridge.

Perhaps Billy had it wrong for once. Perhaps Tomas's fear and guilty conscience were just spinning him in the wrong direction. Maybe the man was just calling about a bill. It was usually the men who called with questions about money, wanting a detailed accounting of where the hours had gone. Men wanted drawings and models. They didn't understand that hundreds and thousands of dollars might be spent on nothing more than daydreaming, nothing that could yet be expressed on paper or cut out of balsa wood.

He would call the man back, of course he would. He was a client. And after the call he would leave for the library, take in the site, start thinking about a solution, an inspired solution, one that, hopefully, would surprise even him. And, maybe, just maybe, surprise Naomi. Something that would show her that he had reflected deeply on *all* aspects of his life, and was able to make adjustments, was able to change. This was the wisest thing to do, and, in a way, the only thing to do. He couldn't—he wouldn't—call her. He would compose letters when he was in the right frame of mind. Forcing them would be a bad idea. They, too, would have to be pitch perfect.

He must find purpose and distraction in this competition. If he didn't, what did he have left?

Wait. *His work email.* How stupid. He was so distracted and trying so hard not to appear panicky in front of Billy that he had checked his personal email, not his work email.

The first three emails were from songbirdM@gmail.com. Songbird. A joke Marie had made about her last name when she first gave Tomas her contact info.

"Hey, I took Partridge as my last name. I think I have the right to dress it up." Tomas had found this so inexpressibly charming at the time. Now he wanted to claw her eyes out, and his own as well—like a mad crow. He scanned the rest of his inbox. After three emails from her, he saw two from c.partridge@PLPartners.com. He skipped reading hers. The subject line from Cole Partridge read simply, *From Cole Partridge.*

He clicked on it first. The note read,

If you attempt to contact my wife again, I will contact yours. I expect a full refund for every invoice we've paid. You are shit.

There was no subject line on the second email. It read,

You will deal with this. You have my number.

"Dude, what did you think?"

"Huh?"

Billy's voice sounded small and tinny, like it came from a distant hallway.

"That song—'Memory Tracer' by Auragraph—everyone says it sounds like something from your generation."

"Oh . . . I dunno . . . it's trash." Tomas couldn't remember the song Billy was referring to, or even whether and when they'd had such a conversation. It could have been, as it actually was, four minutes ago. Billy framed his smile with a pair of mocking thumbs up, a standard response to anything negative—or positive—Tomas said. Tomas clicked on Marie's emails. The first read:

He found our texts.

The second read:

He's a little crazy right now. He might come by your office.

The third read:

I'm sorry. This is all so fucked up.

Good god, she hadn't erased her texts? Was she as much of an idiot as him? Clearly. Had she saved them so she could reread the little notes, a chance to savor and relive the illicit excitement and ego stroke of the moment? Did she confess, did she not build a lockbox, or was she simply caught? In short, was she behaving as terribly as him?

It didn't matter. He had made a choice. The consequences and fallout would be what they would be. Jesus, how would he tell Billy that Cole Partridge had found out and that the project had vanished? Or worse, that Cole Partridge might show up and make some kind of scene? This was a cracked windshield, the initial impact radiating out a fine spider web of problems that demanded lies, obfuscation, avoidance, maybe even honesty, but would inevitably shatter into a thousand pieces.

And the concerns about the Partridges, work, Billy, were nothing compared to what had already happened with Naomi.

The office phone rang. Billy picked up, cupped the mouthpiece, turned down the volume and said to Tomas,

"It's Cole Partridge again. He sounds, uh, less than stoked."

Instinctively Tomas wanted not to take the call, but he knew this would only send his anxiety spiraling. He had the good sense to know that *wondering* about what Cole Partridge might do or say next was far scarier than taking the blow now. Tomas turned up Billy's awful music and walked into the warehouse's makeshift corridor near the bathroom. This might be his only chance to prevent Cole Partridge from walking into the office or even knocking on the front door of his home. He and Naomi had had the Partridges over to dinner to celebrate the beginning of the project. The man knew where he lived.

"Hello," Tomas said, in his best approximation of unremarkable calm.

"Why haven't you responded to my emails?" asked Cole Partridge.

"I just saw them, not five minutes ago."

"Did you start it?"

"What?"

"Did you take the initiative? Did you seduce my wife?"

The anger, the tremble in Cole's voice, pierced Tomas. He could hear Claire babbling in the background. Obviously Cole was at home. He pictured Marie in the next room, the femme fatale's face streaked with tears. His only option, his only desire, was de-escalation and accountability.

"Yes. I did."

"I don't want this!" Claire whined and pleaded.

"Daddy will be there in a minute!" Tomas heard Cole yell back. So Marie wasn't at home. Christ. No doubt they had fought, and it had been ugly enough for her to leave the home. Tomas felt sicker than he had since Naomi took him to the courthouse.

"You've destroyed another man's family. That is the kind of person you are. Should I do the same?"

"Please. This is my fault. I didn't mean—"

"Coward."

"My wife knows already."

"I feel sorry for her. I hope she leaves you. I'll make sure she does. You are a selfish asshole."

Cole hung up. Tomas grabbed the roll of orange trace and walked slowly, numbly toward the service elevator doors.

"All good?" asked Billy.

"Mmm hmm."

Tomas wandered out of the warehouse.

Someone honked. It took Tomas a moment to register that the driver behind him meant him. For a fleeting second, he wondered if it was Cole Partridge. It wasn't. Tomas looked at his speedometer: he was holding a steady twenty miles per hour. He hadn't noticed how slowly he had been driving, had barely noticed that he was driving at all.

He took a needless right turn down a narrow residential street to get away from the cars behind him, away from the drivers who had the luxury, no, who *deserved* the luxury, of getting annoyed over nothing more world-shattering than a slow driver in front of them. Tomas had forfeited that—and so much more—the moment he accepted a bite of chocolate from Marie Partridge.

What a perverse circus! A moment that had given him such a charge, had made him feel alive and desired and good about himself—genius acknowledged, charm appreciated—had turned poisonous on him so quickly. What a glaring blind spot! How weak and foolish he had been!

Destroyed another man's life. Cole Partridge was right. This is who Tomas Araeta Jr. was. Naomi was right to file immediately for divorce, his father was right to understand his son's squandered potential, Billy was right to wonder what business Tomas had in entertaining the idea of submitting to a marquee competition.

Tomas was parked now, listening to the calm news voices of

National Public Radio. Again the pendulum swung wildly: Tomas grew angry. Hadn't he once heard that something like 50 percent of married men cheat? Even if he was a bit off, even if it was, say 30 to 35 percent, he was just a regular screw-up of a guy. And of course the great men seemed to do such things without a pang of remorse, without consequence. If there were consequences, the greats saw them as gnats to be swatted away. Maybe they *were* sociopaths. Maybe they lacked the genes for compassion and shame. Maybe genius stole from our other emotional capacities to feed its voracious appetite. My god, he didn't murder anyone, he didn't hit a child, his gifts for Naomi were always specific and thoughtful (a scarf with little elephants on it—her favorite creatures in the world—came to mind, as did an afternoon of pedal-boating on Lake Merritt several years ago—he now made a note to himself to take her back to the lake at some point), he paid Billy for all the hours he wrote down, even though Lord knows there had to be a good chunk of padding in there. He was a mensch, a fallible mensch. Was that a crime?

His thoughts, his resolve, crystallized. Yes, he would still enter the library competition, but he had another flash. A means to *direct* action to repair the marriage. How did Naomi's mother work through leaving her husband? Therapy. What did her partner do for a living? *Therapy.* Had Naomi seen a therapist for whatever issues she may have had? She told Tomas she had tried once or twice, but hadn't found the right fit, but what mattered was, she had *tried*. The idea was not a nonstarter. Had he gone to therapy? No. Not yet. Probably should.

But the headline here was: he had to get Naomi to show up for therapy. She had to give him this much. Surely Marivel, whose vocation was getting people to talk to each other when they least wanted to, would get through to her, would advocate for at least trying therapy. Her life's work, her very belief in the worth of what she did, surely would trump one awkward pleading phone call from Tomas, even ten years of aversion to him. This was about *Naomi.* This would be for *her.* And Marivel was the dominant personality.

Abbie was a fence-sitter, a wishy-washy diplomat. The slightest push from Marivel and she, too, would advocate for therapy. My god, the woman had left her husband when she came out as gay—if anybody understood the value and need for talking with a neutral referee present, it would be Abigail.

One session. That's all he needed. Just get Naomi's toe in the door and he would do the rest. He could fix this. Tomas drove, hunched forward, hands grasping the wheel tightly, another mile to the library site.

It was a small, Mission-style building in need of expansion. It was understated and sweet and much loved by everyone in Berkeley. A large arched window looked from a reading room out onto the street. The walls were sixteen inches thick, the windows inset, creating a sense of depth, shadow, heft. The terra-cotta barrel tiles of the roof were thick and slightly irregular, revealing the hands that made them.

Next door was a parking lot that the university had bought, and this is where the expansion was to be.

What was the right thing to do here? A drastic contrast, as I. M. Pei had done with his glass and steel pyramid smack dab in the courtyard of the stately old Louvre? It was bold, unapologetic, and somehow, it worked. It was that rarest of artistic feats: the juxtaposition of unlike elements which, through some kind of mystical alchemy, succeeded in making each individual element more compelling than it was alone. It was like that mashup Billy had once forced him to listen to—Led Zeppelin's "Immigrant Song" mashed up with Snoop Dogg's "Drop It Like It's Hot." Tomas had said those actual words—"Ohmygod, this is actually better than either song alone"—when the mashup had come up on Billy's playlist. It had been Billy's hour to choose the music.

Tomas kept looking at the precious little jewel of a building.

Of course a convincing case could also be made for a demure addition that "quoted" the original building but made no attempt to compete with it. A stark building, with little ornament, set back on the parking lot, clearly taking a deferential stance, but with details, perhaps—an inset window, the massing of the original, a terra cotta tile roof or black iron handrail—showing reverence for the original. This was a respectable and appropriate middle ground option.

Tomas despaired.

The muddling middle. Exactly who he was. Abbie would approve of this inoffensive approach. His father would shake his head in disappointment. His own mother would approve, smiling wanly through a haze of whatever meds and wine were soothing her at the moment. Even without mother's little helpers, June Araeta would probably nod vigorously if her son took a dump in the parking lot and called it a day. Marivel would call him a "douchebox" even if he had bested Pei's pyramid.

And Naomi?

She wouldn't care about the building. A building is a container. It is nothing without people to experience joy, sadness, boredom—in it. Yes, of course, she would strive to make it the kind of container where people would feel comfortable enough to be themselves, she would strive for beauty, of course, but in the hierarchy of what's important in life? A life with a partner. Trust. The desire to bring a child into your home and love it and raise it, to do your best not to hurt those close to you. And if you still have any energy left? Of course, go out there and be the designer you want to be, find your voice. But, really, first get your shit together, Tomas Araeta Jr.

Tomas tried to shake off the miserable thoughts.

There was a third path: at the main library of the UC Berkeley campus, the architects, for that addition, had gone as deferential as one could: 80 percent of their addition was sixty feet *underground*. A few skylights, echoing the slope and detail of the original neoclassical building's roof line, poked out from the ground, looking more like decorative entry urns than the signposts of an addition that contained fifty-two *miles* of new bookshelves. And that solution worked as elegantly for the main library as the pyramid did for the Louvre.

It preserved a wonderful open green space in front of the library, opening up a view of the grand neoclassical facade that had been obstructed by unremarkable wooden temporary buildings erected in the 1940s, temporary buildings that had stood for over fifty years, now blessedly razed. One could now see the library as it was meant to be seen—at a distance—where the viewer could appreciate its grandeur, the way it sat authoritatively on the ground.

The architects of that addition, Esherick, Homsey, Dodge, & Davis of San Francisco, approached the project without preconception, with an open mind, and came to *understand* what was needed there—a chance to showcase the original, to give it breathing room, and had completely subsumed their egos to do the right thing. They went invisible, and while, in matters artistic, it could be argued that there were no right or wrong answers, this was, in fact, the right approach, the best approach. Screw subjectivity. They had done right by the original building. They had emptied their minds and egos—only with such open hearts could they find their way to the perfect solution.

What was the right thing to do for *this* library annex expansion? Go underground, too? Should Tomas propose an addition that was barely visible? One that was unequivocal in its modesty? Or one that screamed, "I'm here!"

Or was there yet a fourth way? A new building, different in style, but separated from the old by, say, a glass bridge or corridor? Where had Tomas seen that before? Christ, where *hadn't* he seen that before?

He hadn't a fresh or interesting idea in his head. Every architect had his or her influences, of course, there were no more magical new form givers, again with the exception of Gehry and possibly Hadid, but he was no Gehry or Hadid. He was just a hack without a spine who had no strong gut instinct about what he wanted to do here. The only recent thing he had done with any conviction was, how did Cole Partridge put it, "ruin another man's family." *That* he had spine enough to do.

He suddenly became conscious of pedestrians walking past him. Had they noticed the man with the roll of sketch paper in his lap, his 2B pencil in hand hovering impotently over it?

The session. The therapy session. That was the answer. Everything hinged on this crucial first step toward showing Naomi how deeply he regretted what he had done, how he *did* want to work on the relationship, not out of fear, but out of love.

He no longer would worry about appearing too eager, too desperate, too needy. This wasn't the time to "play it cool" or play it any way. If he was a needy mess, let Naomi see it. She knew him well enough to see beyond whatever jittery or sad or ecstatic mood he happened to be in at the moment.

Asking her to go. That was his next *real* project. Really the only one that mattered. He couldn't risk a phone call or text. She might block him before he could get enough information out. Marivel was a bad idea. Going through any kind of gatekeeper was stupid: he had no control over what they might actually do or say, or not do or say. His assumption that she would push Naomi toward at least one therapy session with him was just that—an assumption.

No, there was only one correct solution, just as there had been for the campus library—he would have to ambush Naomi at work, where she couldn't slam a door in his face. It would be his only shot, the only face-to-face time he could steal. And there it was again. The anger. It surged. Seventeen years of a shared life and she would not even entertain the idea of a coffee, of one conversation? Well, she had the leverage, didn't she? Tomas hated that he thought of their relationship, at least now, today, in terms of a power dynamic. That word, *leverage*, belonged to the worlds of business or politics, not love.

He wanted to talk about what had happened three years ago at the Redwood Room of the Clift Hotel, wanted to spit the memory back in her face. It came to him now with sharp clarity.

He, Naomi, and their dear friends, another solid couple, Maya and Omar, were there, at the Redwood, celebrating.

"It totally reminded me of Donkey Kong, only about a thousand times better," said Omar.

"Well yeah, dumbass, it had real puppies instead of little digital Italians," opined Maya.

Omar, Maya, Naomi and Tomas were nearing the end of their second round of cocktails.

"Just like, the cool exposed gears and pulleys and whatnots," asked Omar, "like, how did you get the puppies to not be afraid of the noise and the platforms and stuff?"

"Because she can think like a puppy. And what do puppies like?" asked Tomas.

"To eat and shit," answered Omar.

"*Pea-nut but-ter*, dumbass," said Tomas, overenunciating each syllable.

"You can't call him a dumbass," interjected Maya. "He's my boyfriend. I can call him a dumbass, but you can't."

"Right, sorry—peanut butter . . . moron."

"Ohmygod, this drink is so fucking good," slurred Naomi, enjoying listening to the others celebrate her first window display for Macy's—a triumphant Donkey Kong inspired vision with little elevator platforms operated by batteries and bike chains that allowed the puppies to ride up and disembark on little platforms where peanut butter treats awaited. Donkey Kong was the inspiration, but even if you were not familiar with the video game . . .

"Shit IS Santa's workshop. Busy little elf machines doing shit to make kids happy," said Omar.

"What is this?" asked Naomi, holding up her coupe glass.

"It's a French 75, and we're all about to have four more," said Tomas, standing to go to the bar in the Redwood Room of the Clift hotel, an elegant, high-ceilinged bar. The interior was decorated with large reproductions of Gustav Klimt's gold leaf adorned paintings of female figures, but the real reason Naomi had chosen to celebrate here was the "big chair." Outside the bar, in a corner of the lobby off the front desk, sat a giant chair that looked like it came from the set of a Tim Burton movie. You had to jump or get an assist from friends to climb onto the seat, and, once seated, you looked like an elf who had found his way to a furniture showroom for giants. Four people could easily fit for the all-important funny photo. It was silly, but after three French 75s, Omar, Maya, Tomas and Naomi had asked a hotel staff person to take a bunch of pictures of them, legs dangling, sitting on the chair.

Naomi had pregamed a bit with Garrett and the staff at Macy's—she was happily buzzed when Tomas picked her up from work—and why not?—the display window was a hit. Garrett had bought the champagne, and Tomas had wisely continued the theme with the French 75s, a mix of champagne and gin, and God knows what else.

"I love this song!" Naomi yelled as Tomas headed for the bar to order more drinks. The DJ was playing "Groove Is in the Heart" by Dee-Lite, an irresistible club standard. Wedding DJ material to be sure, but it always worked. It was like playing Prince or Michael Jackson. It was a no-brainer. Everyone loved it. Certain musicians, Jackson among them, regardless of the salacious details of their personal lives and deaths, were in the pantheon.

The bar was busy.

"It's my birthday."

Tomas turned to see a very pretty woman in a slinky blue-sequined dress standing next to him. The left shoestring strap of her dress kept falling off her shoulder and she kept pushing it back up. She sounded a little less drunk than Naomi.

"Happy birthday."

"How old do you think I am?"

"That's a horrible question, a trick question," yelled Tomas over the other voices competing for the bartender's attention. "So, I would say . . . twenty . . . six?"

"It's the big three-oh, but I think I could pass for twenty-six," she said.

"See? So I didn't really go completely fake-ass cheesy."

She glanced back at a group of friends, five other young women, sitting on a curved velvet banquette. They smiled back at her.

"Wait, it's your birthday, shouldn't *they* be up here waiting in line to get you drinks?"

"Ohmygod, you're right. These shoes are killing me. Fuck them!"

Tomas glanced at Naomi, who had "forced" Omar and Maya to get up and dance at their table. The birthday girl pulled off one shoe, then the next.

"Sometimes fashion is worth the pain," said Tomas, looking at the height of the girl's heel and the pinch at the toes.

"You like them?"

"They look great."

"You look great, too," said the girl. Tomas was wearing stovepipe slacks and a maroon velvet blazer with thin lapels for the occasion. "You wanna come sit with me and my friends?" she asked. Tomas opened his mouth, and it took him a moment to stumble through a sentence.

"Yeah. I think, hang on, lemme just let my friends know."

"My friends think you're cute, too, I can tell."

"Well, then I like your friends already," said Tomas.

Tomas left his place in line and returned to Naomi, Omar, and Maya.

"Mission unaccomplished bro?" asked Omar, seeing Tomas empty handed.

Naomi was sitting, resting her head on Maya's shoulder.

"I'll get them—I'm just—gonna do a selfie at the Big Chair with Nomes."

"We already did," she protested. "It was a pain getting up there."

"Hey, it's why we came here," said Tomas.

"Where's my drink?" Naomi demanded.

"Gonna get it in a sec. C'mon. Just a few angles I wanna get that we missed."

Tomas gently tugged at Naomi's arm. She stood and, wrapping her arm around his for support, followed him to the lobby, but there were two people sitting on the Big Chair, and another party of three waiting their turn.

"Oh forget it, c'mon, let's go back," said Naomi.

"Nomes, hey, question."

"Yup."

"There's a girl at the bar, pretty sure she's hitting on me, haven't gotten her first name and definitely don't want her last, but, she's cute, and, well, would it be okay if I gave her my number?"

Naomi stood up straighter, shaking off the alcohol as best she could.

"You brought me to the chair to ask if you could hit on some girl?"

"Well. Yeah. You always said I just had to ask, and we could talk."

"No! No fucking way. You had your chance. I gave you a ton of time."

"But you said, after the wedding, if either of us has a feeling, a desire, we could always talk to each other. That nothing was off limits."

"No. God, you can't try to fuck some girl. I mean, we're out tonight *for me*, at least that's what I thought."

"We are. And this is just to offer a number. Nothing would be tonight, but I just, I'm getting that vibe from her—"

"Fuck you. Get me my drink and try not to ruin the rest of the night. God."

"So new rule: we don't talk about difficult things?"

"Just shut up."

Naomi left, swaying a bit as she headed back to the Redwood Room. She turned and called back to him.

"C'mon! I said get the drinks." Naomi scanned the room, caught sight of the group of six cute girls sitting at the banquette, who seemed to be looking their way. "Don't ever ask me another stupid question, Tomas. Grow up." Naomi watched as Tomas approached the girls and spoke to the one wearing a clingy blue sequined dress and no shoes. After a moment, the girl nodded and paid him no more mind.

Tomas went to the bar and returned with four French 75s.

"Don't spill, friend, I want every drop you're paying for," said Maya. Tomas knelt carefully to place the four drinks on their table.

"What'd you say?" asked Naomi, as she took a sip of her drink.

"That I was with friends who I couldn't leave."

Omar and Maya looked confused.

"What are you talking about?" asked Omar.

"Prince Classy here was hitting on that girl in the sequins," said Naomi. "He wanted to ask me if it was okay to fuck her."

"Hey, asking first—it *is* the classy thing to do," joked Omar.

"Serious?" asked Maya.

"Why do you think he took me to the big chair?" asked Naomi.

"Oh," said Omar, realizing Naomi wasn't kidding.

"Wow," said Maya, her accusatory, disgusted tone unmistakable.

"We've talked about this. Ask Naomi," said Tomas.

"I'm going to enjoy the rest of my drink, and if you could sorta say nothing for like a long time? That would be awesome," added Naomi. Tomas obliged her. New Order's "Blue Monday" came on, and Naomi jumped up, grabbed Maya's hand and pulled her into another little two-woman dance party.

"What the hell was that? Everything okay?" Omar asked Tomas.

"Not really. But, yeah, it's fine," said Tomas curtly.

Watching Naomi drunkenly dance with Maya, Tomas wondered if she would remember what happened, would remember their conversation, tomorrow morning. He felt unfairly humiliated. He wondered if he would have the guts to bring it up tomorrow, to confront her on what she had always asked: that they come to each other with "taboo" wishes first, so they could talk things over like grown-ups. Sexual adventure was at the top of the list. Naomi had said, more than once, to never be afraid to ask, to talk, to be vulnerable and honest, about whatever was on their minds. They had agreed, had silently lauded themselves for their modernity and maturity. They wouldn't sneak around and lie or harbor resentment. They would talk.

The next morning Naomi raved about the French 75s and bitterly complained about her hangover.

She said nothing of the girl in the sequin dress.

Neither did Tomas.

Of course he wouldn't—couldn't—bring that up now, three years later.

A less volatile thought occurred to him. The papers! The divorce papers. Yes, he had the perfect pretext. He would be dropping off the divorce papers he had received at the courthouse. Here was the perfect reason to see her in person. Give her the damn signed papers she wanted, *then* ask her about therapy. This was good, this was smart. He would arrive with an olive branch, then ask for just one chance at talking in a room together, no expectations.

At least that is what he told himself.

DAY 13

FROM THE BROAD SIDEWALKS OF UNION SQUARE all Tomas could see of the Macy's display windows was butcher paper. Tomas wasn't even sure if Naomi had come to work. She could be spending time with her mom, with a friend, loitering in a park, who knows. Part of him did not want her to be there—that would mean she was getting on with normal life, getting on without him. But, for him, whether she was there or not, not doing something was not an option. He calmed himself. He could keep coming back if she wasn't there, he could also scour favorite restaurants, cruise by coffee houses and bars they knew, could easily stake out their own home, Abigail and Marivel's home. Indeed, he had options.

The work ambush was merely Plan A.

Tomas entered the store and was briefly flummoxed: however one accessed the display windows from inside wasn't obvious. He would have to ask if she was in. Should he just say a friend or customer had stopped by? No, that was silly. He had been there once or twice before. He could be recognized. He would say Tomas was there for her. Here, in a public setting, she would have to come out and say hi, if for no other reason than the fear that he might cause a scene if she didn't.

He asked a clerk for Naomi Curran and soon Garrett appeared. They had met before—Tomas and Naomi had gone to lunch with him when Tomas had come to the city to meet another client. They chatted over soup and salad at a nearby eatery, and both had enthusiastically and loudly agreed on how talented Naomi was, nearly competing for who could praise her more floridly. "At night, when the sun goes down and the store lights come up? She embarrasses the stars," said Tomas. "God is not supposed to give from both hands," agreed Garret, clarifying he meant her visual talent as well as her intelligence—he didn't want Tomas to misconstrue—that is to say, understand correctly—that he meant her beauty alongside her intelligence. Naomi was mortified, asked them gently to stop talking about her in her presence. Naomi Curran did not handle attention or compliments well. Especially not of the purple prose variety.

Tomas spotted Garrett walking his way.

"Garrett, hi, Tomas, Naomi's husband, we met once."

"Ah, the lucky man, yes, of course I remember. Lunch. I'll let her know you're here."

Tomas could read nothing in Garrett's words or body language. Had she told him? No, why would she. Why air one's dirty laundry at work?

Less than a minute later Naomi appeared. She wore black tights, sneakers without socks, and a blue T-shirt. Her hair was pulled back with a simple hairband. She looked great. Tired but great. Her cheeks were flushed—Tomas guessed either from physical work or warm air inside the window box. They were now both standing between the perfume and jewelry departments. Tomas was smiling.

"You came to my work."

"I did."

She gave the words a moment, then said, "What can I do for you, Tomas?"

"Actually, I've got something for *you*—here." He handed her a manila envelope and she peeked inside.

"I already filed. You could've just put this in the mail."

"I know. But I also did want to talk to you."

"I don't feel like talking, and I'm at work."

"Not some big thing, just a quick question."

Naomi looked around cursorily, to demonstrate to Tomas that she was fully aware he had deliberately chosen a "safe" public setting with strangers around, a place where the chances of her causing a scene or sprinting away had been minimized.

"This is a cheap shot, Tomas. Nowhere near the worst thing you've done, but a cheap shot for sure."

"I don't mean we talk *here*. Some place quiet. One therapy session. What do you say? That's all I wanted to ask. No expectations."

"I want to get this behind me and move on. Picking at the scab—it's not even a scab yet—won't help."

"I didn't say it would. But is it not possible that one session might actually *help* with the moving-on process?"

"You can't talk me into changing my mind, Tomas. Please, please understand that."

Tomas noticed Garrett trying not to be noticed as he watched them from the perfume counter. He was fit for his age, which couldn't have been more than, say, forty-five. Khakis, a plaid shirt. Boring stuff, but it fit well. His hair, too, was handsomely cut. Short back and sides. Nothing too mannered or too young. What was he thinking, the vulture? He clearly had nothing to do at the perfume counter. She must've told him.

"We've spent seventeen years of our lives together," said Tomas. "We're going our separate ways. What's the big deal with spending one more hour together? I mean, ten years from now, isn't it possible you might think, 'well, we even tried therapy and that didn't work?' This is just due diligence, Nomes."

"You're the one who should have future regret issues. You're the one who needs to do some due diligence. My regrets are present, *very, very* present."

Garrett's annoying presence somehow bolstered Tomas's confidence.

"You've heard my idea. Think about it. Even if it's just to cuss at me to my face like you might not be able to cuss here in cosmetics . . . think about it."

"I'm going back to work, Tomas."

She turned to leave, Tomas caught Garrett glancing their way again with that pathetic little look, trying not to seem so obviously gleeful—and suddenly, unable to stop himself, Tomas blurted out, "The only thing I fucked was an *idea*. Can you not see that?"

"Fuck you!" Naomi's loud outburst caught Tomas off guard. Others—shoppers, employees—looked their way. So much for a safe, neutral setting. Garrett pretended he didn't hear, the fit little fucker, but Tomas could see the satisfaction on his face. Oh, how he surely would console Naomi later.

"You're an asshole," she added, her voice only a notch quieter.

Jesus, my one shot, and I just torched it, thought Tomas. I had to bring up the *idea* thing. I was halfway home. She hadn't said no yet. A fluttery panic rose in his stomach.

She walked up to him, her voice quiet now, but still sharp as a razor. "You're deluded. 'Fucked an idea?' You need to know how messed up that is. The chances I agree to a session are slim and none—either way you need to leave right now." She shook her head in disgust. "Someone else *should* hear that trash." Tomas said nothing, did not quite understand what had just happened. Best not to question it. Just be grateful. He discerned a very unlikely "maybe," and that was a win.

"Leave, before slim turns to none."

Tomas did as he was told.

Naomi turned and left, too, wanting to scream, but having the control to bank it for the therapist's office if she ultimately decided to air their laundry out properly, coherently before a credentialed neutral. On his way out, Naomi caught sight of Tomas making a point of veering over to Garrett, shaking his hand vigorously.

What an ass.

DAY 31

NAOMI PEELED OFF A SCAB OF BURNED CHEESE, popped it in her mouth. Marivel was eating and wiping the grease off her phone as she texted, then eating some more, then texting some more, then wiping some more. Abigail looked at her daughter expectantly.

"Good, Mom. Really good."

Her mom made an excellent grilled cheese sandwich.

"Marivel," said Abbie, prompting her partner.

"You've dumped him for good, yes?" asked Marivel.

"I think so," said Naomi.

"Don't think. Do."

"This is not what we talked about!" said Abbie, shooting daggers at Marivel. Marivel stopped eating and wiping. She exhaled and frowned.

"I think it's a lousy idea, but if you want to give it a shot, and I think you shouldn't, I've got a guy," said Marivel.

"Hear that, Mom?"

"I did," answered Abbie coolly, "and I say why not. Who cares if it's a lousy idea. It's an hour. If it helps you in any way, great. If not, then it's only an hour—no, fifty-five minutes—wasted. I don't see a downside," added Abigail as she flipped over another piece of bread in the hot pan.

"But you see an upside?"

"You can shame him in front of a stranger."

Did her mother really just say that? Had she body swapped

with Marivel? Naomi glanced at Marivel, arms now crossed, who begrudgingly shrugged concession to Abbie's point.

"Who's the guy?" asked Naomi.

"Okay," said Marivel, brushing a foot back and forth across the floor. "The guy's name is Oscar Riordan. One of the only therapists I know who doesn't have an agenda."

"But you're all supposed to be open, right, neutral, no agenda—I mean, not you, of course, but everyone else?"

"Man, are you joking? Some people I know push reconciliation no matter how bad the relationship is; some seem to listen, but they're just trying not to forget the cat litter they're supposed to buy on the way home. Some don't know it, but they have a bias against men, or women, or queers, or whatever."

"Everybody sit."

Abigail brought more sandwiches to the table, and they dug in.

"This guy Oscar, though, I met him at a continuing education seminar. He's like blank. I mean, like, are those dead-fish eyes or like, super smart, y'know? But yeah, hundred percent, he's really thoughtful."

"Wait. So, thoughtful or dead-fish eyes?"

"Both. Like a great batter. Like Ken Griffey Jr.—Sosa and Big Mack stole the home run race from him with those fucking 'roids. Griffey would've won, man. And you? You're Griffey. Tomas is a 'roid guy. Dump him."

"I think you've made your point, Marivel," said Abbie.

Marivel defiantly bit into her sandwich.

"Getting paid to be a blank, huh?" said Naomi. "Maybe I'm in the wrong line of work."

"He sounds like you might like him," said Abigail. "Marivel," she said again, her needling tone unmistakable.

"Fine," said Marivel, putting her sandwich down. "I go to him. And I hate therapists."

Primed by Tomas's little one-act play between the perfume and jewelry departments, that's all Naomi needed to hear.

DAY 29

"**YOU LOOK LIKE SHIT.** Shittier than usual," remarked Billy, without looking at Tomas. "You all right?"

"Super."

Billy swiveled his chair to look at his boss.

"Yes?" asked Tomas, hearing Billy's chair wheels squeak.

"That air mattress and the whore baths in the sink and the baggy eyes. I mean, you're super, yeah?"

Tomas now swiveled his chair to face Billy. He did look like shit. His hair was disheveled, but not in a cool party-boy-bedhead way, just in a sloppy "I-stuck-my-head-under-the-sink-tap-for-a-few-seconds" way. His eyes were red, irritated. A sheen of oil coated his forehead.

"It'll pass."

"Cool. While you're waiting for 'it' to pass, a little deodorant would be good, too."

"I use deodorant. Every day."

"Aah, okay, must be me."

"Just do your work, man."

"Yup."

A ring at the warehouse door. They both had access to the front door camera on their phones.

"Shit. Sorry. Should I leave?" asked Billy.

"No, it's okay."

They could both see the security camera image of Cole and

Marie Partridge on their phones.

"*Can* I leave?"

"Stay. Just for a minute. 'Other People's Drama'—the best kind, right?"

The weeks of not sleeping, of constantly checking his texts and emails for anything from Naomi, had taken their toll. Tomas slurred a bit, his eyelids drooped, as if he had been drinking. He buzzed the Partridges in. A minute later they entered the studio via the service elevator. Marie led, followed by Cole. He wasn't pushing her from behind, or touching her in any way, but one could feel him invisibly shoving her along.

"Tomas, Billy, so good to see you both," said Cole.

Billy quick glanced at Tomas.

"Hi Cole. Marie," replied Tomas.

Marie said nothing. Her eyes were swollen. She had been crying. Cole took note of the air mattress in the corner.

"Getting the most for your rent?" he asked. Tomas didn't respond. Cole looked at Billy. "Who sleeps on that?"

"I do," said Tomas. Cole still glanced skeptically at Billy.

"I hate air mattresses. I hate camping."

"So did she catch you, or did you tell her?" asked Cole.

"She caught me."

"Of course. Even if she didn't, I'm sure you don't have it in you to get ahead of the problem."

Tomas said nothing.

"Mr. Partridge, did you want to have some time alone with Tomas?"

"No. Actually, I'm very glad you're here, Billy."

"Hey man, no live-shooter shit or anything like that, cool? My parents would be wrecked."

Cole laughed out loud. Tomas just stood there, rocking slightly back and forth on his feet.

"Please just say what you came to say." Marie's words were so soft as to almost be inaudible.

"Oh, *sorry babe*. You got it. So—when are we seeing the next round of drawings for the Treehouse?"

Billy glanced at Tomas, who did not know what to think.

"I've refunded all your billings," said Tomas.

"Money," said Cole flatly.

"As you requested."

"Guess I have to spell everything out. Should I have explicitly *requested* that you not fuck my wife?" Tomas cast his eyes down. He felt lightheaded. Cole turned to Marie. "Babe, I thought it was in our marriage vows, but should I have been more explicit about asking you not to fuck other people, too?"

Marie said nothing.

"Really? Nothing?"

"I'm sorry," mumbled Marie.

"Oh, right, shit, I almost forgot, you apologized. So we're all good there. So, yeah, we're moving forward with Marie's dream kitchen—happy wife, happy life, right?—so when do we see more drawings?"

"I can get back into it in the next day or two," said Tomas.

"Oh, sorry again, clarification." Cole turned to Billy, who shot Tomas a quick *You shoulda let me go when I asked* look. "Not him," said Cole, indicating Tomas, but addressing Billy. "He's a lying piece of shit. But I'm sure you can execute his design. In fact, I'm paying you double his hourly, and Tomas, you will accommodate Billy's schedule so that he can give proper focus to our dream kitchen."

"Hey, look, it's Tomas's idea, and I really don't think I'm the guy—"

"I think you are. Tomas thinks you are, or he wouldn't have hired you. This is the last time you will have to see me. You have carte blanche. Marie can tell you what she does or doesn't like, but we are going forward with this, and—I've looked into it—short of inept architecture students, nobody wants to execute another firm's design, one without their authorship, especially one small enough that the billable hours aren't worth the effort."

"Please just do it, Billy," pleaded Marie, tears in her eyes. "It's best for Claire, for our family."

"Think about it Billy. I have to get to work, and Marie has to do whatever it is she does to fill her time." They were about to leave. Cole turned back. "Do I need to check in with Naomi to make sure she knows?"

"She knows," said Tomas.

"That air mattress isn't a prop, sir," added Billy.

"It's Cole, not sir. Take care."

The Partridges left. Tomas stood, dazed, still rocking lightly side to side.

"I think you should sit, man, you look like you're going to faint."

"Huh?"

Billy physically moved Tomas into his chair.

"Well that was an unfunny shit show," said Billy. "Fuck."

"Do their kitchen," said Tomas.

"No way, man, that's a mine field."

"It's a great opportunity. My name won't be on it. It'll be all yours. It's just a schematic right now. You can make something way better out of it than what I've started with."

"The guy's a psycho."

"His behavior is completely understandable. Have you not watched a movie in your life? He didn't yell, he didn't throw a punch, he obviously didn't shoot anybody. All things considered, he's handling this ridiculously well."

"Well, yeah, he's a hedge-fund guy. He's probably got ten mistresses stashed all over the globe, for Chrissake. He just doesn't like it when *his* wife stepped out. It's the rich-dude double standard."

"Did you hear what she was saying underneath what she was saying?"

"Hey, mystic dude, I'm kind of a literalist. What I heard was 'please do it. It's good for the family,' whatever that's supposed to mean."

"He's punishing her. He's making her live with this kitchen—this reminder of what she did—to spite her."

"Wow—super awesome pep talk for me to take the job."

"What she didn't say was that he would probably leave her, separate the family, maybe go after custody of Claire, I don't know, if he couldn't enjoy this punishment."

"That's a fucked-up guess." Billy thought for a moment. "Shit you're probably right."

"Just do a great job, collect four times what I could pay you after my overhead, and make it yours, and maybe keep a family intact while you're at it." Billy thought about it, pinching at the tip of his nose over and over, one of his "I'm thinking" tells.

"This is a little warehouse, not even good snacks included, now doubling as your apartment—what *overhead*?" For the first time in a long time, Tomas smiled, just a bit.

"So you'll do it?"

"Yeah. I'm not gonna be a homewrecker."

"Thanks."

Tomas swiveled his chair away from Billy.

"Boss?"

Tomas swiveled back around.

"Can I ask you a question?"

"You've never asked me before if you could ask a question before asking it."

"I talked to my folks about what happened—"

"You did?"

"Well, yeah, I mean, it's juicy, plus they don't really know you." Tomas didn't have the energy, perhaps not even the desire, to scold his employee about boundaries.

"Okay. What's the question?"

"Well, they asked me something, and I had no clue what the answer was." Tomas looked at him impatiently. Billy continued. "Why do you want to get back together?"

"What do you mean?"

"You were obviously unhappy. Why not just call it, move on?"

"Because I love her."

"Okay."

"That was *the* most unconvincing 'okay' I've ever heard."

"Well, my mom had a friend whose husband strayed, and he actually *didn't* want to get back together. The wife wanted to do therapy and the whole nine and fix everything, but he wasn't into it. He just wanted out."

"Well I want back in."

"Right. Because you *love her*."

"What I did was shit. Inexcusable. But that's my baggage. I love Naomi, and all that matters to me now, *really matters,* is getting her back."

"Dumb question?"

"Another one?"

"Okay, so how do you *know* you love her and want to get her back?"

Tomas said nothing a moment. This was no dumb question. This went to the heart of the matter. He claims he loves his wife, yet he hurt her terribly. Maybe he did want to leave her. Maybe something unconscious was screaming in his ear to move on. Tomas had thought through all this, and now thought about it again. No. He wasn't trying to blow up the relationship. He wanted Naomi back. The pain and the unknown that would come with separation—seventeen years fading into nothing, the division of assets, the effect on family and mutual friends, Jesus, the baby they wanted to adopt!—all of it terrible.

But trying to avoid all that wasn't the reason he wanted to get back together with Naomi Curran.

"Love is love, Billy. It's the reason we buy nice cars and cologne," said Tomas. Billy stared at him.

"That sounds like lust."

Tomas slowly nodded concession to Billy's point as he rubbed his tired eyes. "All I know is this, Billy: I'm happier with her than without her. In fact, I feel ill without her."

"I guess I buy that." Billy swiveled his chair back around.

DAY 92

TOMAS BOUGHT A ROLL OF GRAY DUCT TAPE from the hardware store and got back in the car. He noticed the white scuffs on the low edge of the front bumper, thin long strips of paint which had most likely been scraped off by a street curb or parking block. He was sure it hadn't been him, and even though he was the one who used the care most often, it used to irritate him that Naomi swore it couldn't have been her.

"I drive like an anxious grandma," she protested.

"Right. Anxious grandmas don't even know when they've scraped the curb, they're so anxious," he replied. But in the end, neither cared enough about the old Hyundai's appearance to do anything about the scratches. The Hyundai was not Richard Meier's Douglas house or Adolf Loos's Steiner house. A scuff or two didn't ruin it.

DAY 59

NAOMI PUT DOWN THE HOT GLUE GUN and sat cross legged looking at what she tentatively was calling the "crystal garden." She shut her eyes and counted to thirty before opening them. Bits of Styrofoam clung to her skin, her clothes. She wiped her forehead. Nothing was quite right yet, but it wasn't quite wrong, either. Once she was settled on the forms in Styrofoam, she would move on to frosted pieces of acrylic she could cut and glue and light from within. Like the old builders' saying had it, measure twice, cut once.

"Rock candy, King Kong size."

"Huh?"

"Just what came to mind. Close?"

Garrett had quietly entered the display window, cupping his chin lightly with one hand, looking over Naomi's mockup.

"'Rock candy,'" repeated Naomi. "I like that. Better than 'crystal garden.' Less New Agey."

"Yours if you want it."

Naomi stood up, blew off a piece of Styrofoam that had been clinging to her upper lip.

"Wow," said Garrett, "we both get paid, but only one of us is breaking a sweat."

"I've always been a sweater."

"There's a dumb dad joke in there somewhere, I just don't know what it is."

Naomi flashed a tiny smile but had nothing more to say.

"Hey, just, not my business of course, but you mentioned it after he left so, is it inappropriate for me to ask how you're doing?"

"Let me ask HR."

"Sorry, really, I—I was just hoping you're okay."

She could see Garrett was genuinely taken aback.

"Guess my humor can sometimes be a little too deadpan."

"Oh. Of course. Sorry."

"I'm okay. Ish. Work helps. Time helps."

"Yeah."

Garret had broached the subject he wanted to broach but hadn't thought through a segue out of it.

"So, yeah, rock candy garden. I like it," said Naomi.

She could feel the finished project: bouquets of wild rock candy flowers jutting this way and that. At night, the only light would emanate from within the glowing crystals. Naomi had already imagined standing outside and anonymously watching the wonder in the eyes of passersby, mostly the kids, for whom this would be a magical landscape, similar to some of the vintage rides at Disneyland she had seen or remembered from online pictures—she had missed Adventure Thru Inner Space, wherein one shrunk to the size of an atom and was surrounded by "giant" snow flakes, but she had seen the pictures online, and had wished, for a moment, that she had been twenty years older.

"Have you been to Disneyland?" asked Garrett. Naomi took a moment to make sure to answer without excess enthusiasm or shock that he had just read her mind.

"Do I have a soul and a couple hundred bucks to waste? Of course I've been."

"Ah, well, it was probably torn down by the time you got there, but your work reminds me of Adventure Thru Inner Space."

She looked back at him blankly.

"Right. Of course you wouldn't know it. Well, the idea was you would shrink until, say, a snowflake was giant to you—they had these beautiful snowflakes, different colors, that you would pass by in one of those little egg-shaped chairs. At the end of the ride you'd see a giant eye and realize a man was peering at you through a microscope. That's how small you were. One of my favorite rides, but they tore it down."

"Sounds like a big mistake," said Naomi.

"The day my childhood died," said Garrett.

"I'm sorry for your loss."

Before she knew what was happening, she was playfully touching his shoulder to "console" him. For a second he said nothing, then made a show of craning his neck and looking around at the rough crystals Naomi was forming.

"Well, looks like you found my childhood," he added.

She had to stop. She didn't want to lead the poor man on. Okay, she didn't want to fan her own growing affection for him, either. She knew she had to stop sending leading, or even just ambiguous, signals. Ambiguity invited interpretation, and she knew from the tone of Garrett's voice—the sincerity, the admiration—exactly how he would interpret her niceties. The shoulder touch. What the hell was that? Why not, though? What was wrong with a little flirtation? Yes, Garrett was her boss, and it might be inappropriate, but Jesus Christ, her husband fucked a client's wife. Whatever little boundaries she might cross were nothing compared to those he had violently traversed.

"We should just sneak out the back, grab a quick Southwest flight, and play hooky at Disneyland."

"That sounds ideal," said Garrett, his voice a little higher now.

"I still love Pirates and the Haunted Mansion," said Naomi.

"The smell of the damp grotto in Pirates? Talk about childhood."

"You in?" she asked.

"A hundred percent."

Yes, a little casual, playful banter—the thing she no longer had with Tomas. And what of it? She wanted to say, "You do know I will never go to HR with some weird complaint about a little flirtation," but she would never shine a light on this, not just to not worry Garrett, but for her own sake, to not spoil a slightly charged, yet innocent moment.

"When the puppies have peed themselves dry and New Year's Eve is in the rearview mirror," she added by way of conclusion.

"Done and done."

The tone of her voice. He felt relief. She had provided his offramp. This really *was* just a little banter. God how he wanted her.

"How about your work, Garrett—love, tolerate, despise?"

"Oh tolerate for sure. Maybe moments of hate, sure, but tolerate."

"Not bad, actually. Most of my friends hate their jobs full time."

"And you?"

"I thought it showed," said Naomi.

"It does." Garret then added, "I hate you."

"Fair," replied Naomi.

"I don't know what self-help podcast you've been listening to, but let me know what it is," said Garrett.

Damn, he *was* cute.

"*Not Ruining Your Own Life for Dummies*," she said.

"I don't know anybody who's not their own worst enemy," said Garrett.

"You sound like Tomas," she said. Instantly she regretted the comment. She had broken the spell, had ripped apart the sweet gossamer moment. She tried for a quick recovery. "Time never vanishes for you at work?" she asked.

"Sometimes." He was looking right in her eyes, imploring her to understand that right now—here in this cramped little window box—time *was* vanishing for him.

Shit. She had lost control of the rudder on this one, lost control of herself.

"Back to the daily grind, then. This rock candy garden isn't gonna grow itself," she said, turning away from him. He smelled good, too.

Not cologne. Just soap and a recent shower. Garrett knew, too, he had better go. And he did. Besides, so many things are better left to the imagination. Reality rarely has a fighting chance.

DAY 88

TOMAS MADE AN UNPLANNED STOP at a liquor store on the way to Dr. Riordan's office. As their appointment time drew near, he felt himself tensing. This was his last shot—apologies; flowers; cleaning; pestering her; leaving her alone; writing letters; not writing letters; not apologizing; not cleaning; not sending flowers—nothing had worked. Marivel must've somehow convinced Naomi not to back out. Whatever. It didn't matter. She'd agreed to one session. That's all that mattered. All he wanted to do, *had to do*, was get this one right, and thought a quick whiskey and ginger would steady his nerves. He sat in their car, opened the $3 airplane-size single shot of Jack he'd bought, poured out some ginger ale from a green plastic bottle onto the pavement, poured in the whiskey, and made himself a drink.

After a few minutes, he felt himself coming into game form. Not too needy, not too stiff, not too loose, not too flippant. About as Goldilocks, he figured, as one could be, heading into a ridiculously fraught therapy session, a session that was his last best chance at stopping the bleeding, at least getting a tourniquet on this damn thing.

He parked on the street outside Riordan's office. The building itself Tomas had passed many times. It was on MacArthur Boulevard, half a mile from their home. It was an unremarkable two-story brick building with a carved wooden sign that listed the occupants. There were two MFTs, one DDS, one yoga studio, and a CPA.

His muscles and bones now a little softened by the alcohol—

the second airplane bottle was a superb call—Tomas was struck by the wooden sign. Saving relationships was just one white-collar job among many. People also came here to have their teeth cleaned, their taxes prepared, their bodies stretched. When Riordan retired or found a better lease elsewhere, would the other tenants have to carve a new sign? Or was that on the landlord? Maybe another therapist would move in. It comforted Tomas to think that he and Naomi were probably just one of perhaps ten couples Dr. Riordan might see that day. How else could he pay for an office? And how on earth could he keep it all straight? How would he not confuse the details of one couple's problems with another? He probably *did* confuse them sometimes—that's how common and pedestrian his and Naomi's "problem" was. Entirely solvable. Riordan probably had a mental playbook—some canned, but effective solution to an unapproved one-night stand.

Regardless of whatever Riordan's approach might turn out to be, Tomas was happy. Naomi had agreed to this. Everything else was a detail. Another thought bolstered him even more: the referral most likely came from Marivel, so Naomi must be feeling like the playing field was tilted her way. Plus it was tilted anyway—Tomas was the one who fucked up. He genuinely regretted what he had done. Time to take his punches so they could move on.

Naomi was already sitting in the waiting room when he entered the office. Tomas took great heart in this. Normally he was the annoyingly punctual one. He would be the one waiting with car keys in hand while Naomi still looked for her eyeglasses before they went to the movies. For years Tomas had suggested they get a little basket that would live on the kitchen counter where Naomi's glasses should go whenever she took them off. Just develop that muscle memory. But she never got around to it. Whenever she would ask him "Have you seen my glasses?" he would quietly seethe. Why didn't she just use a basket? Well, no matter. Today was today, and here she was, early, obviously eager to jump into the session.

"I already pressed the button." Naomi barely looked up from the magazine she wasn't reading anyway. There were two small old fashioned metal lever switches on the wall next to the name plates of the two MFTs, Dr. Riordan, PhD, MFT, and a P. Felling, MFT.

"At least we got the guy with the PhD," said Tomas. Naomi said nothing. "Thanks for coming." Again Naomi didn't reply. "I really appreciate it."

"Maybe let's save the talking for in there."

Yes, fair. That was the whole point of this, wasn't it? Tomas shook off the slight sense of worry that had started to cut into his two-drink buzz upon hearing Naomi's maddeningly restrained voice.

The door opened and out stepped Dr. Riordan, a small, thin, bird-like man. He looked at Tomas and Naomi with a conciliatory smile.

"Naomi? Tomas?"

They nodded.

"Come in."

Right. The two sets of doors in the same door frame. Tomas had remembered that from the one and only time he visited Marivel's office, when he was dropping something off for her at Abbie's request. Tomas looked at the two doors sandwiched together.

"This way people out here won't hear me screaming and crying in there?"

"Something like that," answered Dr. Riordan with a gentle smile, in a way that indicated Tomas wasn't the first patient to make light of the aural privacy arrangement.

"Glad one of us can joke," said Naomi.

"Well, if I don't joke a little, I *will* cry, and no one wants to see that," replied Tomas, looking at Riordan for another approving smile, but finding just a blank expression.

"Wouldn't be the worst thing," said Naomi. They stepped into the office.

"Why don't you both take a seat on the couch?" Dr. Riordan gently shut the double doors and indicated a worn leather couch topped with a faded, thin quilt over the back. Tissues on the table. Always tissues on the table. The office was what Tomas had expected: a bit messy, cluttered, comfortable. This was a good start. Maybe Marivel was on his—no—*their* side—and wasn't throwing him to the lions. Of course not. Why would she? These stakes were real. Helping Naomi heal, in whatever form that might take, was paramount, and surely trumped any ill will she had toward him. Tomas waited for Naomi to sit, then sat down, too. Dr. Riordan sat opposite them in a cheap wheeled office chair.

"So," said Dr. Riordan, as he brushed his knees with his hands, "why are we here?"

"Simple," said Naomi, with that same awful tone—that firm, cold tremor in her voice. "He cheated on me. With one of his clients. He fucked her during what was supposed to be a work meeting." Riordan nodded slowly, his face expressionless. "I knew something was wrong that night, I called him on it, and he said he was preoccupied with our baby—I mean, we're in . . . we *were* in the process of adopting. So right away he lied about it and used our future child—*our child*—as cover."

Tomas sat frozen on the couch. The two-drink buzz had vanished entirely. He just hadn't heard anyone describe his actions so succinctly, so accurately. Don't lose it, don't lose it. Let her talk. She's in the room, that's what matters. You got her to show up. Do not say anything thoughtlessly. Don't be cute. Don't be defensive. Don't . . . just don't.

"And you're very hurt by this," said Riordan. For a moment Tomas thought, *What was your PhD in, stating the obvious?*

"Yes! Of course she's hurt. Is that even a question?" Tomas couldn't help himself, and actually felt a flicker of pride at having jumped to Naomi's defense without calculation. The first words he instinctively uttered were to validate her pain. He just blurted this shit out. Good. So far, so good.

"No. Not so much a question," said Riordan. "More a confirmation. There's often a huge gap between what someone says and what we hear. I like to make sure I'm understanding what someone is saying correctly." After a pause, he continued, "But Naomi, what you just said, why don't you look at him, not me, and tell him how you feel?"

She turned to Tomas, shifting her whole body to face his, straightened her posture and said, again, with a repressed tremble, as if she was fighting back the urge to scream herself raw: "You said you, quote, 'fucked an idea.'" She glanced at Riordan, as if to make sure he heard—and understood—what she just said. "What does that even *mean*? What bullshit rationalization is that? 'I fucked an idea'? How could you do this, Tomas? Guys still hit on me. If I so much as blinked at Garrett, he'd fuck me in the middle of a showroom window! He's sweet, he's kind of attractive. But you know what? I don't and won't do that. I thought we were *building something* together. Yes, we promised each other for better or worse, all that shit, but what matters—or what mattered *to me*—is that we were going to go through this journey *together*."

Tomas's mental constructs collapsed. She was so articulate, so clear, and so right—that he was left speechless. Fucked an idea? The shame he felt shook him to the core. Using their child as cover? An even more horrid sin. If he'd had a moment, nothing about what she said—except perhaps for the part about Garrett being kind of attractive—should've come as a surprise. But it was more than that. It was the contorted facial expression and the sound of her voice, an icy contempt and pain he had never seen or heard before, that left him numb and reeling and sick.

Naomi spoke again. "All you had to do was talk to me first, you know that. I might have said 'no way.' But you didn't even have the balls to do that. I feel like a fool. I feel like I've wasted seventeen years of my life. Wasted my youth."

"Those are a lot of strong feelings, Tomas." Fucking Dr. Obvious. Thank God for him. Thank God someone not named Naomi was speaking. "I wonder what you're thinking."

Tomas thought for a few seconds before opening his mouth. Naomi reached for the tissue box. "I . . . I made a mistake." If he was about to say more, Naomi jumped back in, even more vituperative than before.

"A mistake is mixing colors and whites in the wash—it's not putting your penis in another woman's vagina." Naomi, per Dr. Riordan's instructions, looked Tomas directly in the eye as she said this.

"Tomas, it seemed you wanted to say more?"

"I don't think I have much of a thought right now. She's right. I guess, I just—I want to rewind the clock. I want things to go back to normal."

"*This* is your great insight? This is why you schemed to get me in here today? I already knew you wouldn't have any kind of explanation that would change my mind, but 'I want to rewind the clock'? You sound like a fucking twelve-year-old."

"When you say 'normal' Tomas, what do you mean by that?" Again, God bless Dr. Riordan. He was actually cooling the room down, buying Tomas a few more precious seconds to either hang or save himself.

"I want to come home and have dinner and make fun of our bad cooking and watch our shows and talk about not getting too excited about the baby."

Naomi turned to Dr. Riordan.

"He wants to come home to mommy. Him. It's about him wanting to feel all snug and comfy again." The spleen in her voice was gone. Only a deep, sad resignation remained—at what was lost, at what had been irreparably compromised. Tomas was paralyzed. If there was a right foot to put forward, he had no idea what it was.

"How do you feel about what Naomi just said?" asked Riordan. Tomas didn't know what to say, so he just said what he felt.

"I do want to come home, I do want us to be together. But I would call it intimacy, not coming home to mommy. And of course I'm sorry. But I don't even know how to apologize. Saying 'I'm sorry' isn't even in the same fucking ballpark as having sex with another woman. It's like trying to fix a leg that just got torn off with a band-aid."

"Do you agree with that, Naomi?"

"It's probably the only thing I do agree with." Naomi exhaled, took a moment. Tomas wasn't crying, but his eyes were filled with tears, and he looked dazed. This evoked no sympathy in Naomi, only a spike in disgust.

"He's supposed to be a man, a grown-up. Being a grown-up means making hard decisions. He wanted it both ways, and, I'm sorry, but you know that he's crying because he got caught, not because he feels bad."

"That's not true."

"Bullshit."

"Why do you not believe Tomas when he says it isn't true?" asked Riordan carefully.

"He lied to me the night it happened. His first impulse wasn't regret; it was to lie."

"Tomas, do you feel what Naomi says is true, that your feelings come from being caught, not from the hurt you've caused her?"

"I scrambled that night. I panicked. Yes, I tried to squirm out of it. I lied to see if I could convince her I didn't cheat. But that was months ago. What I feel now—the pain—is about what I did to her, to us, it's not about that moment."

"Before I even saw that disgusting text, you were nice and made a nice meal and talked about the baby. I felt close to you."

Tomas quickly grabbed a tissue and handed it to her. She dabbed at her eyes.

"And I see now it was all bullshit. You just felt a little guilty—maybe—but bottom line, you thought you were home free. And the thing I can never know, and it's one of the reasons I'm divorcing you, is that I will never know whether you would've seen her again if I didn't find out. Or if every time you were nice to me, it's because there were others. When a guy admits to cheating once, that means there's at least a dozen other times he's not telling you about—"

"That's fucking bullshit! This was my first and only." The anger in Tomas's voice caught Naomi, and Tomas, off guard. Riordan had no comment, no visible reaction at the shift in Tomas's tone.

"Okay. Fine. Let's say this was your first and only. What I am saying, though, is this: now I know the real character of the man I married. And I hate it. I can't believe you had it in you to do this. After I encouraged you to share anything that bothered you, anything you felt."

"I did. I tried. Once."

Naomi looked confused.

"At the Redwood Room. Maya and Omar were there."

"Are you kidding? When we were celebrating my window? That—I was drunk—that doesn't even count. I don't even remember what you said, just that your eyes were all over some bitch in a blue dress."

"I'm sorry, I'm lost. Can the two of you give me some context?"

"I can," said Tomas, feeling both nervous and righteous. He looked at Naomi, who looked at him as if he were covered in fish entrails on a hot day. "Since you just said you couldn't remember. We promised ourselves that we would come to each other if we had desires about anything—time alone, other sexual partners, drug experimentation, whatever—and talk about stuff before we did it."

"Right. Exactly. *Before* we did it," say Naomi with some sanctimony in her voice.

"Well, I did. I asked you if it was okay to get her number before I did anything, and you basically said, 'Fuck you. You aren't gonna be with anyone else.' You said that." Naomi glanced at Riordan, then Tomas.

"It was my night to celebrate. Read the damn room, Tomas."

"I can see there's something to unpack here," offered Dr. Riordan, "but I also feel we might be getting sidetracked—if it's okay with the two of you, let's tackle the present before we tackle the past." He paused before adding, "First fires first."

"Okay, sure, fine," replied Tomas. He leaned forward, legs splayed, dropped his head, then turned toward Naomi, looking up plaintively at her.

"First fires first," said Naomi quietly.

"I'm just saying," said Tomas cautiously, with measurement, "nobody's perfect, I screwed up—badly—but I don't think the last seventeen years were a waste. Lots of people are in our boat. Are you gonna tell me that every couple that's seen Marivel—that none of them haven't been able to repair the damage, maybe even make things better?"

Naomi gave his words consideration, slowly started nodding her head, and, after a few more seconds, shared her thoughts.

"I'm sorry, I'm done here," said Naomi crisply. "Tomas, congratulations, you actually succeeded in making things worse by dragging me to therapy. And by the way, Marivel thought this idea was shit. But my mom put the crybaby thumbscrews to her. Maybe threatened no yoni play time, who knows."

"You're doing it again."

"What?" she snapped back.

"Bailing when the conversation gets hard. Don't say 'let's have hard talks' if you don't actually want to."

"Fuck you!" said Naomi.

Tomas—just for an instant—felt calm.

"Naomi," asked Riordan, "what is it that has caused you to want to end our session? Specifically." Tears suddenly rolled down her cheeks.

"Look, all I know is I can't stand the pain. I just want it to end."

"I promise nothing like this will ever happen again," blurted out Tomas. "I swear. I didn't do this *to you*, I did it for—well, because I had issues."

"*Had?* You think you should have won the goddamn Pritzker Prize or something by now, and when you feel down about it, I have to deal with your moods. Until—now—you tried another approach: feeling good by fucking someone else. Someone who called you a 'genius.' Are you that susceptible? What happens the next time you're feeling needy or down? Why should I believe you won't fuck someone else, stick a needle in your arm, or snap at me for no good reason? Should I just start calling you 'genius' every day?"

Tomas was reeling, but he was able to gather himself.

"How can I prove to you that I have changed, that all the stuff you just said is stuff I now see in myself, and am working on?"

"You can't."

"Then you've set up an impossible ask for me! Be a better man, Tomas, but there's no way you can prove it to me."

"Because I don't know what that looks like. And if I did know, I wouldn't tell you anyway, because feeding you the answer—I'd know you'd just be doing or saying what I want you to do or say. And that's not good enough."

"Fine. I'm not asking for the answer, I'm asking that you—there's a reason for this waiting period—judge me with as much of an open mind as you can. But how can you if you won't even see me?"

"Let's back up for just a moment," said Riordan. "Tomas you said before that you 'promised' not to do this again." Tomas nodded eagerly. "I'm not a fan of 'promises,'" Riordan continued. "In my experience, promises are most often made in a panicked moment."

Naomi nodded vigorously.

"Tomas, consider this: the only thing you promise Naomi is that you will be honest with her about whatever you're thinking or feeling going forward. It's what she asked of you originally, if I'm understanding correctly."

"Absolutely. Of course." Thank God Riordan had put some decent words in his mouth. Tomas had the good sense not to bring up the Redwood Room again. "And Naomi, perhaps you promise to give Tomas the opportunity to speak with you about these feelings."

"*Going forward?*" said Naomi. She stood up and looked at Riordan. "Why the hell are you so focused on what *Tomas* promises or not? He could promise to comb his hair or cure cancer and I wouldn't care. Have you not heard what I've been saying?"

"I have. And the thing that strikes me is that, even though you are carrying an unbelievable amount of pain, you are in this room talking. It seems to me just as possible that you would not have come into this room, or that you would say nothing while here, or say something completely different. I wonder why you did agree—and my sense is that Tomas initiated—please correct me if I'm wrong."

After a moment, Naomi sat back down.

"Why am I here? That is an excellent question. I wanted to see how he would react face to face when I told him how I felt. I want him to hurt. For the *right* reasons. I'm tired of thinking about this, and I guess I was hoping that by vomiting it all out I might think about it less. I don't know why I'm here. I want you to see how shitty he was, I mean, maybe that sounds petty—"

"Tomas, does any of that sound petty to you?" Riordan interrupted. Tomas mumbled, "No."

"Sorry, Naomi, please continue."

"And part of me wanted to test myself. I know what I want, which is to make the best of the rest of my life despite what he did to me. And I wanted to see if you, or Tomas, or anybody, could—not talk me out of it—but at least show me something I hadn't considered." Riordan nodded and leaned back in his chair. "Nothing to say?" Naomi asked Tomas. He did have something to say, but he spoke into the air, as if he was musing aloud, alone.

"Jesus, I need therapy."

"Great! We agree!" Naomi stood up again, her body language now spry and perky. "Dr. Riordan, nice to meet you."

"Tomas, before Naomi leaves, is there anything else you'd like to say?"

The man had just bought him one more swing of the bat. He had to hit a home run. Anything short would be disastrous. But he had nothing. He tried to think of some of the ideas he had prepped in his mind before walking in the room, but it was all a panicked scramble. *Breathe. Just one breath. And think. Not about what she wants to hear—because you've obviously shit the bed there—but be honest, and hope you connect with that little ball flying toward you at a hundred miles per hour.*

"Naomi, you deserve so much better, you deserve not to have these feelings. Seeing you like this kills me. Yes, for me, and how I feel, but also and mostly for you. I feel like, like, you're a beautiful child, and for the first time, another child hurt you, and you don't understand hurt. You're just confused and sad. I've kicked us out of the garden of Eden. But you still deserve to be there. I took that away." To his surprise, and really, to Riordan's as well, she stayed a moment longer, her shoulders slumping just a bit. "If nothing else, whatever you decide about us—if I can do anything to lessen your pain—sure, divorce, if that's the best way—let me know. But will you 'let me know?'"

That was it. His best swing. He had said exactly what he wanted to say.

"Tomas, I believe you feel bad about what you did. I do. And not just because you got caught. I know it's not that simple, and I know there are things in our relationship that I should've been working on, too. I'm not perfect, and you're not perfect, and no one is, but this is one area—my heart, my capacity to enjoy life—that I can't compromise on. You've poisoned it . . . yeah, Eden is about right, only I didn't give you the apple, you gave it to me. And now the only thing I care about is figuring out how to feel the fuck better."

She was going to leave the room. That much was plain.

"We have so much good together, so much love, and history" said Tomas, "wonderful history—that, if we both want to try, and maybe it'll be a bitch for a while, but I just believe that if we both try, we can come back from this. Even if we can't be exactly like we were before, we can get to a good, maybe even a really good, place. It's worth the fight. I guess that's what I want to say. It's worth the fight."

After a few seconds, Naomi exhaled deeply. Tomas was sure he could see her body slumping a bit, relaxing. Maybe he *had* just hit the ball out of the park.

"I guess I just have a few red lines," said Naomi. "It's just who I am. There aren't many. But you crossed one. I have to *want* to grind through this with you, and for us, and I just don't. I'm sorry."

Tomas glanced desperately at Riordan.

"What I've heard here today—and please correct me if I've misunderstood—is that you, Tomas, want to stay in the relationship for a variety of reasons, and you believe that it can be repaired to a standard both you and Naomi would be happy with. And you, Naomi, feel like Tomas hurt you in a way that can not be repaired to your satisfaction."

"Yes," said Naomi quietly.

Tomas had to shove aside the shock of Riordan, in his opinion, taking the side of catastrophe, and say something, anything.

"You feel what you feel, and I feel what I feel. And it's different. Of course, just like Dr. Riordan just said. But there's . . . there's another piece here. We haven't even talked about it yet." Tomas glanced at Riordan, who smiled benevolently beyond both him and Naomi. "And that's *time*. That's the X-factor. I feel like . . . I don't know if it'll be a good or bad thing, more time, I just know—for me—I still have hope. I do. I just do."

"I'm sorry. I don't."

She stood up, walked around Dr. Riordan, and shut the two doors quietly behind her.

Time—the thing he had seized upon as their savior, the *deus ex machina* in this drama—those precious 180 days—had abandoned Tomas, betrayed him. Tomas felt nauseous. The old chestnut of indifference, not hate, being the real opposite of love, was true. She didn't want to put in the work. She was already moving past him. Tomas looked at Riordan.

"Dr. Riordan, tell me you've seen couples in our spot—*this* completely hopeless—who have still managed to patch it up?"

"I have."

Tomas hesitated a moment before asking the next question. He longed for the answer as much as he dreaded it.

"Well, first impressions are a big deal: what do you think our chances are?"

"You both were here. That is something. Many couples don't even get to a first visit. Predicting is best left to fortune tellers, and I'm not a fortune teller. But where there's still love, there's still hope. That is one constant I have noticed."

Tomas nodded absently. "Actually, one more question. If I really loved her, how could I have done what I did?"

"That's your homework. But you wouldn't be the first. That cliché about hurting those closest to us earned its stripes as a cliché." Tomas heard Dr. Riordan's words, but was now feeling an uncomfortable lightheadedness, a spike in his heart rate, a sense of disorientation. "And if one or both of you doesn't feel that love, then I would suggest putting your energy into letting go of pain and guilt and anger and moving forward individually."

Tomas hated Riordan's even-handed observations. But what he really hated was that he didn't understand, for himself, at this moment, what *love* was. The basic question Billy had asked. Who am I? Why do I do anything that I do? Am I just reacting to stimuli in the world and careening this way and that without a shred of intentionality? Have I ever taken a long moment to attempt to learn about myself in any meaningful way?

He was spinning. The disorientation. He was going through life with no more thought, perhaps less, than a rat in a maze.

"Thank you for seeing us," he said mechanically. He stood and shook the doctor's hand.

"Another constant?" added Riordan. Tomas lifted his eyes.

"This story has many chapters, and the ending hasn't yet been written."

"Is that what you tell people when it's hopeless?"

"It's what I tell everyone *because it's the truth*. You might divorce, you might talk in two weeks, two months, two years, or never again. You might reconcile and discover intimacies you never knew existed.

You might not. The anger may take years to subside on one or both of your parts. I don't know. And—if I had to say—neither do you or Naomi. The rest of the story is yet to be written, and you two are its coauthors."

Tomas nodded blankly and slowly wandered out of the office.

In the street, the bright sunlight assaulted Tomas. He squinted. The sound of people chatting, of cars driving by, was obscene. People ran errands, chatted on their cell phones, went in and out of a nearby post office. For them nothing had changed.

And why should it? We are all essentially selfish, unable to see further than the end of our own noses. Time was no longer his ally. It was his enemy.

This lack of intentionality, of reflection, in how he led his life, was despicable. No more. Tomas became resolute: he *would* write the next chapter, would carve it not in wood, but in stone, clearly and confidently and with complete intention—like Michelangelo.

Tomas slammed the car door shut. It was hot inside. He felt a bead of sweat run down his neck. He tried to call Naomi. It went straight to voicemail. He could've turned the engine over and turned on the air conditioner. It didn't occur to him. What did occur to him he couldn't stop. The crack in the dam had given way. The surface guilt and shame he had experienced for eighty-eight days was nothing. Not until he saw Naomi in Riordan's office did the layers of howling selfhatred become deafening. The dam was bursting. Time would not leave him alone. The memories—good, bad, mundane—came flooding.

Exhausted after a long day at work, Naomi, while giving him a hand job, her stroking arm propped up with her free arm, the palm of her free hand cupping the stroking arm by the elbow, Tomas said, half jokingly, half seriously, "Can you at least fake some enthusiasm?"

"My arm gets tired. If you came a little faster . . ."

"Well, that bored stare and propped arm aren't gonna help."

"Oh, god, baby, baby, your cock is so huge, ohmygod, I'm so wet right now,"

"You don't mean it."

"Well, of course not," said Naomi. "Do you think porn stars mean it when they say that kind of stuff?"

"No, but it's their job, and the viewer agrees to suspend disbelief from the beginning."

Naomi shifted her supporting arm. Tomas was losing his erection.

"Look what you did!" he said.

"If I can't be my honest self—I'm a little tired tonight—and I'm not good at pretending to be into it," she said as she continued stroking his softening cock. "What should I do?"

"Well, I dunno, just smile a little maybe?" he asked. There was a fragility in his voice.

She smiled and said, "I'm tired and you're annoying, but it makes me happy to see you happy." She gave him a quick kiss on the mouth. As she pulled away he craned his neck and kissed her deeply. Thirty seconds later his cum was running down her fingers. She wiped herself off with a tissue, then jumped up to wash her hands.

"Is my jizz so toxic?"

"I love your jizz, hon, but it's hard for me to sleep when I can smell it. You use mouthwash after you eat my pussy."

"That's totally different. That's literally right under my nose, and it's a stronger smell."

"Napoleon—"

This was not the first time Naomi had brought up Josephine.

"I know Napoleon asked Josephine not to bathe for days so he could smell and taste her funk, but in those days, they also had bugs living in their wigs."

"You're welcome, Tomas."

She returned from the bathroom and climbed into bed. He spooned her, hugged her tight, and warmly whispered, "Thank you, babe."

★ ★ ★

"How did I not know they had a Rothko here? In *Oakland*?"

"It's been here," said Naomi. "We've walked by it. Did you not read the little placard thingy?" The Oakland Museum of California did indeed have a Rothko in its permanent collection. 'Untitled 1947.' You don't remember? You called it 'Kidney beans on canvas.'"

Tomas didn't remember. The painting did not look like a classic Rothko. Of course it could take an artist years, decades, to find their voice, develop their vocabulary—consider Wright and Gehry as they approached seventy—and now that Naomi had pointed it out, yes, one could see Rothko groping his way with these floating maroon kidney beans toward the hovering rectangles that would one day define him.

"I like it," added Naomi." It's . . . playful . . . as 'playful' as Rothko's gonna get."

"Yeah, but you can definitely see why there's no bench in front of it."

"Okay, but if they did put a bench in front of it, would you like it more?"

Tomas gave the question some thought, then burst out laughing.

"Man. It's sad to admit. But yeah, Nomes. I would!"

Tomas stared again at the painting, then glanced sideways at Naomi, his shoulders dropping a bit. "If someone put a bench in front of an artfully arranged dog turd, I'd probably say it was genius."

"Wait. So do you like it or not?" asked Naomi.

Tomas contemplated.

"I like what it represents."

"Ohmygod, that is the most hedgy, uncommitted, fence sitting trash answer ever."

"*Ever?* Oh c'mon, I've had worse."

"Probably."

"It's not the orange and blue painting at MOMA. It's just not. I can say *that* with, like, eighty-eight percent confidence."

"Okay, well orange and blue is bench-worthy, I agree."

Whoever in museums was in charge of selecting which works of art *deserved* a contemplation bench, most had decided that Rothko's mature paintings deserved more than a fifteen second passing glance, more than someone merely checking a box on their list of "masterpieces," snapping a pic, and moving on.

Oh the philistines who said of Rothko, "my kid could paint that!"

No. They couldn't. The choice of color, the feathering of the borders, the proportion of the rectangles. If the phrase "deceptively simple" hadn't already been coined, Rothko's work would have birthed it.

"But God, Naomi, you're right. I don't even know if I like it or not. If you ever find my actual opinions, please return them to me."

"Ooof, big ask, my friend."

"Ceviche. Can I get you some excellent taco-truck ceviche?"

"You truly must have misplaced your mind if you have to ask that."

They left the museum and headed for the green taco truck parked half a mile north along the street that wrapped around Lake Merritt. As they sat on a battered picnic table outside the truck, digging their chips into the ceviche, Tomas said, "The more I think about it, the more I'm pretty sure I like that Rothko."

Naomi laughed, a few bits of shrimp landing on Tomas's face.

"You don't have to camp it up with a spit take, babe, I know I'm lost."

"This is why the machine barely works," Tomas said as he watched Naomi load a spaghetti encrusted plate into the dish washer. "We're asking too much of it."

"Well, if I'm gonna basically wash every dish before I put it in, then why have a dishwasher at all?"

Tomas answered, not by countering Naomi, but by loading the rest of the dishes himself. He rinsed and scraped, leaving just a few streaks of orange grease here and there. It was a rule instilled in him by his mother. "Unless you do it yourself, you have no right to criticize."

As Tomas continued scraping and loading the dishes, Naomi, watching, observing, standing next him, one hand planted on a hip, said, "Happy now?"

"You preclean the room when we stay in motels," said Tomas.

"That's different. An overworked maid is about to come in to whatever mess we leave."

"But why 'sorta' straighten the sheets at all, when she's gonna have to take them off and wash them anyway?"

"I don't want to have this conversation. I'm tired. I don't want to bicker."

"We're not bickering. I just don't get the maid thing. We always tip."

"Not the point. I'm going to bed."

Okay. She was in a mood. Tomas bit his tongue and finished loading the dishwasher.

Naomi and Tomas lay on the couch side by side. She lazily stretched out her left arm over his stomach, a gesture which meant, "please scratch." Tomas happily obliged and gently raked her arm with his fingernails as they watched *The Great British Bakeoff*, a show in which contestants vie to be the best baker in their group. What distinguishes it from other reality competition shows is its lack of mean spiritedness, and the beautiful establishing shots of English fields with low stone walls, endless green pastures and flowers.

He kissed her forehead and inhaled deeply. She squeezed her body against his a little tighter.

Tomas's whole body was vibrating. He was sobbing. He was in

no state to drive. He dropped the seat back, didn't want strangers to see him crying. At some point he startled awake. It was 7:23 p.m. He was disoriented. It took him a moment to realize he had dozed off and was still parked in front of Dr. Riordan's office.

DAY 89

NOT HAVING SLEPT, BACK AND CALVES ACHY, forehead warm, Tomas got up from his air mattress and slipped out of Studio Araeta before Billy arrived. He left a Post-it note for his sole employee: "sick today." He grabbed a sour-smelling towel from the bathroom and drove to a park in the shadow of the MacArthur Maze freeway interchange. He spent the next ten hours lying on the towel, occasionally sitting up to watch young mothers and fathers playing with their kids on the swing set and monkey bars.

DAY 93

TOMAS DROVE WEST FROM OAKLAND across the Bay Bridge—an underrated masterpiece of engineering, proportion and curve. Had the Golden Gate Bridge not existed, the Bay Bridge would surely be the engineering marvel on postcards in the tourist shops. He felt like he had grit in his eyes and a headache he couldn't quite locate. He continued onto Highway 101, and soon, the Golden Gate Bridge loomed large and beautiful. For a moment it disappeared on the curved approach that led through a grove of cypress trees in the Presidio before coming back into view.

Even the toll booths were exquisitely designed in the art deco style. Some anonymous state engineer probably detailed them, and that little booth, no bigger than an outhouse, was more beautiful than anything Tomas had ever designed or would ever design. He thought of his sketches for the library—garbage, derivative, mediocre—just like their author.

He crossed the Golden Gate and slowed at its northern end, looking for the popular vista point turnoff. He and Naomi had taken friends from out of town here a handful of times. It was a must for tourists. Tomas and Naomi didn't mind. It was the kind of thing they would regret not doing if they moved and had just taken it for granted and never bothered visiting because it was so close. The view back from the vista point toward the east bay hills was stunning.

He parked in the vista point lot and sat in the car for a few minutes, returning to his "Another Day" playlist, named after This Mortal Coil's cover of the sorrowful masterpiece by English folk singer Roy Harper. It was just after three in the afternoon and the sky was overcast.

He stepped out of the car and walked along the bridge's pedestrian path. There weren't many tourists walking across the bridge on this gray weekday. He found himself trying to appear "normal," but knew there were many surveillance cameras on the bridge, and that if he lingered too long, or paced back and forth, or behaved in any way that could be construed as odd, some local law enforcement officer might want to speak with him.

He looked over the bridge's edge at the beginning of the cantilevered span—the bridge was a gentle arc, so here, at this point, he was closer to the water than if he had been at the middle. Below him were rocks and several ramshackle outbuildings. He walked twenty or thirty feet further, until he was over open water. It didn't look as far down as he expected it would. And once you climbed the railing, which was only forty-eight inches tall, there was a structural girder below that, and below the girder, nothing. Just 220 feet of air.

DAY 92

AH, BUT WHAT IF A BODY WAS NEVER FOUND? Here was a problem. No doubt the life insurance company would fight Naomi tooth and nail on this—claiming he had run off with another woman perhaps, or just run off, cold feet at the prospect of fatherhood—and, given what had happened with Marie Partridge, they would have a compelling argument, and Naomi wasn't the type to jump into a legal conflict anyway.

"I hate conflict," she had said more than once. "Makes my stomach hurt." Marivel would certainly push for the payout, as would her father, her mother would just fret, but in the end, Tomas couldn't take the risk that Naomi wouldn't see a penny. At least he was three years past the two-year suicide exclusion on his life insurance policy. That much he hadn't screwed up.

All of this Tomas pondered in his office as he sat opposite Billy. He felt he had to put in some time at the office today. He wasn't sure why. Why would Billy care if he called in sick for three days, four days, a week?

"Don't get me sick," was all Billy said when Tomas told him he thought he had the flu.

"I'm not contagious anymore."

"You don't know that, and I get really bitchy and cranky when I get sick."

"I'm fine."

And then it came to him—the solution—so simple, so elegant. Duct tape.

Once he thought of it, it seemed like there could never have been any other option, like it was always there, waiting to be discovered, the Pietà stuck inside a block of marble. This idea—the duct tape—was brilliant, perhaps *this* was his true first flash of genius. He shook his head and smiled. Architecture wasn't the vehicle by which his genius would express itself! Suicide was. The plan, like any great parti, was both thoughtful and simple. It was in the execution of the parti when, for once, he would show that he was more than just a cocktail napkin sketch artist. He would duct tape his driver's license to the concrete walkway before he jumped. Simple. Any camera or bystander could vouch that yes, it was him, Tomas Araeta, who leaped off the bridge, the man matching the license.

But that was only part of the execution of the idea. He would also duct tape his passport and a credit card to his thigh to connect him to the driver's license left behind in case a camera was not functioning or a witness's memory became unreliable. The driver's license should be enough, but he only had one chance at this project, so he had to nail it. Redundancy. Belt and braces, as the Brits put it. The impact on the water could rip the passport and credit card out of a pocket easily, so he would have to wrap them tight to his leg with several revolutions of duct tape. For a moment the thought of the hair on his leg being torn out made him wince, then he smiled. He doubted his corpse would mind this DIY wax job.

The insurance company couldn't fight that. They might try, but the proof that it was he, Tomas Araeta, who took his own life, would be irrefutable.

As he walked back toward their car from the bridge railing, he couldn't say exactly why he was crying: it wasn't that he would be leaving behind the all-consuming pain and self-hatred for the emptiness of no consciousness. That was the *blessing* of it all, the carrot to chase. It was so many other things. He wasn't abandoning a specific child yet, just a number on an adoption list. His parents had another child, a well-adjusted child, his sister Clarissa. And Clarissa and her partner Andre had a child of their own—his baby niece Jasmine—so they already had a grandkid to dote on.

So what was it?

It was simple, really. Death was the only way to escape himself. But it wasn't a purely selfish decision: the shame, the guilt, the shock, this depression, whatever you wanted to call the feeling—was so all-enveloping that Tomas knew he would be of no use to anyone. He was a mediocrity through and through. As a man, an architect, a husband, a son, a person, he was just taking up space. Naomi was the vase, he was the chamber pot, and the world didn't need another chamber pot.

And what had he done? He had chipped that beautiful vase. He was punching far above his weight class, and had hurt a great person, a truly great person. Fine, he may not have been the first to have loved and hurt the most important person in his life, as Riordan said, but he was a bucket of character flaws, that's it. He could not point to one admirable, one decent quality, in himself. The best he could come up with was that he didn't torture animals, he wasn't a serial killer, and he wasn't rude to strangers.

What a lovely epitaph.

Why couldn't it all be simpler? If only a drunk driver or falling tree would take him out? There's a difference between wanting pain to stop, and wanting to die, but that difference had been shrinking for Tomas with every passing day. Yes, a tragic car accident or freak lightning storm would be great. If he had any dignity left, it would be preserved. Financial matters regarding Naomi would be cut and dried. But relying on being killed by a drunk driver when you most wanted it was the least reliable of his options. No, he had to stick with the basic plan.

He was certain that living would bring more pain to the people around him than dying. Certainly it would bring more to him, and what kind of life would that be for others? He had to make the pain stop. It was incessant and intolerable, and pain is so isolating that it only aggravates those around us. Nobody wants to be around a depressed, hurting creature. It's enervating. You can't take away their pain, you can't turn a mediocrity into something special. And then you oscillate between frustration and guilt for being short and impatient. No, his pain would cast a gray veil over the lives of others, and that wasn't right. The brief moments of euphoria he *had* experienced in the last three months were unconscious, desperate attempts by his body and mind to trick him out of doing the sensible thing.

They were chimeras.

Death would be an abrupt shock, of course, and it would be hard for those around him—*at first*—but that would pass, and in time he would just be a fading memory. Naomi would move on, her parents might express sadness, his own father had nothing but contempt for him, and his mother was a broken woman anyway. Clarissa had her own life to lead. A handful of friends would be shocked, yes, but on balance, he was doing everyone a favor.

DAY 93

HE HAD PARKED IN AN ISOLATED CORNER of the vista lot—two or three cars had come and gone in the time since he returned from the bridge—no one had taken particular notice of him.

He sat in the car. He turned off his playlist and instead turned on the radio to FM—KFOG—and a song he detested was playing. But he was tired of how well satellite radio and Spotify knew his taste. He was an algorithm. We all are. The thought both irked him and confirmed what he already knew: he was not special. At least KFOG might surprise him a little, might play, who knows, a Cheap Trick song followed by the Eagles, Aretha Franklin, or the Dandy Warhols.

His bowels began to churn violently. It was time.

Tomas took out his wallet, removed his driver's license and a credit card, and put the wallet in his front pants pocket. He lowered his pants, placed his passport against his inner right thigh, and wrapped the gray duct tape around it half a dozen times. On his left thigh, he did the same with a credit card. This was a bit of last-minute inspiration: separating the credit card from the passport, taping them on separate legs, just in case one of them somehow *was* torn off. The way the president and vice president are kept separate in times of crisis. There was simply no way he could not be identified.

He felt bad that he would have to traumatize a stranger, but it was necessary. He ran through it again in his mind. He would stop at the early part of the span, over the rocks and outbuildings, where there was less chance of his body floating out to sea. First he would tape his driver's license to the concrete walkway, all four sides of it, like a frame. He pictured it. He would stand back up, wait for some poor sonofabitch who happened to be strolling in his direction. When they were within, say, thirty feet of him, close enough to hear him but too far to intervene physically, he would yell at them, something like "My license is taped down!" or "I am Tomas Araeta Jr." Then he would jump.

There was one caveat: no traumatizing children. He would wait to tape down his driver's license until he saw a witness who was older than, say, twenty-five, with no children nearby. This was the decent thing to do.

A brilliant parti executed perfectly.

For a moment he stopped rehearsing the plan in his head and snapped back into the present. One car was leaving the vista lot as two more pulled in. A couple with a baby in a stroller made their way to the bridge. She seemed annoyed. Tomas guessed it was one of those days where she just felt her partner hadn't pulled his weight taking care of their child.

Wait. Had anybody seen him lower his pants in the car, seen him noiselessly crying? He patted his legs—the passport and credit card were still there, like tumors, taped securely. His heart started to heave. He wished he had a few sleeping pills to calm himself. Time was his enemy. He had to act.

A voice pierced the ever-tightening spiral of his anxiety. The radio. It came from the radio. It was Evo Korman spitting out gravel and power pop defiance.

"Blistered Eye." The Pill Splitters' masterpiece. Oh, how fitting! The song was the one place other than oblivion he could tolerate—*the past*. Where everything was still possible, and he hadn't hurt the person he cared most about in the world, and he still believed in his own potential. The passion and optimism and energy of youth and young love. Unfiltered. Un-second-guessed. That's where he wanted to be. But he couldn't go back. Those days, that person—were gone. He *was* making the right decision. He would wait for this song, his anthem, the soundtrack of his youth, to end, and then he would conclude matters.

Two minutes and forty-eight seconds later, his heart was still racing, but now he willed himself to see the song as a positive omen, as validation for his decision. His bowels stopped churning. The urgency to defecate was no longer there. Like Evo sang, "Let me disintegrate, don't let me hesitate."

Tomas reached for the door handle.

"Kinda sad about what's happening with Evo Korman." It was the KFOG DJ. FM radio still had live DJs and they were still allowed to indulge in unscripted chatter. "Did you all catch the crazy story that the punk rock icon is now living out of his van in Pacoima, down in SoCal? A woman named Vivian Rios lets him park in front of her house. Reports from Fogheads say people have reached out to help him, but he won't talk to anyone. Doesn't look so good, they say. So sad. But Fogheads, he was great once, was he not?"

Tomas stared at the radio. What was this nonsense?

Living out of his van? Did Tomas hear that right? Evo Korman, a man whose genius rivaled that of Calatrava, Wright, Mies, and eclipsed that of any second-tier singer who may have had twenty hits crack the Top Ten, but all of them forgettable in time, was *living out of a van? Doesn't look so good?* Was he sick? Mental issues? Physical issues? There wasn't a critic or layman alive with an iota of taste who didn't recognize Evo and The Pill Splitters as being a seminal influence on any aspiring musician with functioning ears and a healthy contempt for convention. The Pill Splitters were like the Stooges or the Velvet Underground or The Sex Pistols—commercial failures who sold maybe just a few thousand records in their time, but everyone who bought those records started their own band. Evo was father to a generation of musicians that would not have existed had they not heard The Pill Splitters or been to one of their live shows. Ten, fifty, one hundred years from now, their work would be vindicated and celebrated, while countless bands with shelves full of Grammy Awards would end up in history's dustbin, appropriately dismissed and forgotten. He hated the morons who dismissed them as a "one-hit college radio wonder." *Evo living out of a van? Not looking well?* A man like Evo Korman didn't belong in a suburban home, of course, but he deserved a decent place to shit and shower. Especially if he was ill. Did he have friends? Did he want friends? Was he lonely? Was he *dying?* The DJ blathered on. Tomas was no longer listening. In a few minutes, he too, just another mediocrity, would—appropriately—end up in history's dustbin.

DAY 40

AFTER SHE READ THE SHORT LETTER FROM TOMAS—she knew it was a mistake to open it, she had ignored almost all of the other envelopes with his handwriting—Naomi sat for a while, unfocused, angry.

If there's anything I can do to lessen the hurt, please let me know. I can vanish, I can see you, I can write more, I can write less—I admit I am lost—just know I want to help if I can. I can't sit still, but I don't know how to help. If there is any way, please let me know.

The poor baby can't sit still? Feeling a little antsy and distracted, is he? It's all just bait for her to reach out to the shitbird. Even telling him to fuck off thirteen ways to Sunday would require telling him, *communicating with him* in some way, to fuck off thirteen ways to Sunday. Naomi sat with her inchoate thoughts. She had to move. Movement, walking. A tonic not just from the book of Marivel, but from just about any therapist, from the quick pill prescribers to the long-haul talkers.

She walked to her mom's, a good forty-five-minute trek, hoping to find no one home. She passed the cute stores and restaurants of upscale College Avenue in Oakland's Rockridge neighborhood on the way. She forced herself to look in shop windows, glance at posted menus—she and Tomas loved A Cote for special occasions, for the purple and black of the interior, for the excellent tapas and sherries, for the crowded intimacy of the tables. She took note of people passing on the sidewalk. Change the scenery. Force her eyes to take in different stimuli. But everyone annoyed her—the overheard laugh, how someone blew their nose, how they talked to themselves. It was all disgusting. At a café with outdoor tables she heard someone chewing loudly and fought the urge to lunge at them and stab them in the throat with a fork. The rutting pigs. She just wanted to lie on her mom's couch, talk to no one, sob, laugh, go numb, whatever might come. Just in a different place. Barring a last-minute cancellation, Marivel kept fairly regular office hours, and Abigail was a realtor in a ridiculous market. Surely she'd be gone on showings.

To her great relief, neither Abigail nor Marivel's cars were in the driveway.

She had never felt this kind of misanthropy before, and it depleted her. She was exercising a muscle she never knew she had, and certainly wasn't happy to discover.

She lay on the couch, stared at the ceiling. The images came unbidden. She thought again of the smile and lust that must've been in Tomas's eyes as he entered Marie Partridge. She thought of the men who hit on her to this day—on the subway, in bars, cafés—and how that was enough of an ego stroke for her. "Sport flirting," Maya had once called it. She and Tomas had talked about its value—a little fun flirting with a stranger after a drink or two wasn't just tolerated, it was encouraged between them.

"Till death do us part is a long time," Naomi had once said. "Nothing wrong with warming up the engine."

"Totally," replied Tomas.

"I don't even actually flirt with Garrett at work, but the very way I stand, my awful horsey laugh, just sends him into a tizzy."

"Can't blame the man."

"I mean, let's agree not to lead anybody on, unless that's what we agree to, but a little sport flirting here and there is healthy."

They once planned to meet at Radio bar in downtown Oakland, described by Naomi as "an art deco haunted house dive bar with a touch of chinoiserie," and somebody had offered to buy Naomi a drink as she waited for Tomas to arrive from work, and she accepted. She was flirting with the young man when Tomas entered the dark red and black bar. Without blinking, she introduced Tomas as her husband. The young man stammered through a hello. She knew he had seen her wedding band, and probably thought well, she's alone, so who am I to assume the ring means anything? After Tomas asked his name, the young man pretended to see a friend at the other end of the bar and slunk away while she and Tomas had a good laugh at his blushing expense.

Alone, on her mother's couch, a thought came to her: why wasn't she enough for Tomas? They had talked about understanding if he, or she, felt the need to have another sexual partner, and that honest disclosure of feeling before action was the way to go, but now she questioned whether she really believed that. Was the notion she had of being a cool, modern couple who might not be exclusive what she really wanted? Was she lying to herself about the whole idea, or just the particulars of its execution? She probed her thoughts. Lust? Fine. A little boredom? Fine. A little variety? Okay. Lack of intimacy between them? Probably not. Distance, falling out of love? No. Being emotionally intimate with the other person? Absolutely not.

Why am I not enough? I'm a total catch. But—of all the women he could've chosen—she absolutely would've advised him against choosing a married mother who was also a client. Too messy. Was it in the marital bed? The kitchen? The living room floor? Were they fully undressed, or had it been an urgent half-dressed quickie?

Fuck it. She *should* be enough. Garrett would give his left arm for a date with her. Lots of guys would. She was a kind, funny, smart, pretty woman. What impossible everything was Tomas looking for? If she had just called him "genius" once an hour, would none of this had happened? Was his ego that fragile? Did he have no internal metric for valuing himself? What void was he trying to fill? What temporary fix was he seeking? And why was he looking for it *elsewhere?* He could—and should—have come to her. Was her love not validation enough? She appreciated his love and support, both spoken and unspoken. But she also knew who she was without him, and a change in the weather, a kind or mean word, something she couldn't control, wouldn't shake her to the core. But goddammit, why did he have to look somewhere else for whatever it was he needed?

DAY 93

A SUDDEN TAP AGAINST THE DRIVER'S SIDE WINDOW startled Tomas. It was a man wearing khaki pants, a holstered gun, and a heavy black windbreaker with a patch on the shoulder—*Golden Gate Bridge*—clearly the man patrolled the bridge for any "problems." Tomas quickly glanced down at his own pants—they were pulled up, thank God, but unzipped, but the ranger could not see this.

Tomas turned down the radio, unrolled the window, said nothing.

"You okay?" asked the ranger.

"Yeah. Fine."

"Saw you walking up and down the bridge."

"Right."

"Taking in the view?"

"It's gorgeous."

The ranger's eyes were scanning Tomas's face, like some bit of software, checking his smile against what his eyes revealed, the posture of the shoulders, the flush of his skin.

"Mind if I take a quick look inside?"

"No."

A moment passed.

"You'll need to step out, please."

Tomas stepped out. With his flashlight, the ranger looked carefully under the seats, in the glove box. He found a piece of paper in the back seat, crumpled. He pulled it into the gray light of the afternoon and stretched it as flat as he could. Some kind of sketch of a building.

"You an artist?" asked the ranger.

"No. An architect."

"Ah," answered the ranger, as if this single word quieted his hunch that Tomas might—*might*—be a jumper. "Sorry to bother you. You have a good day." The ranger tipped his hat before leaving. Tipped his hat! This man just walked straight out of central casting, thought Tomas. And he had beaten him. Tomas had beaten the suicide detective.

The ranger hadn't found a crumpled suicide note because there was no note to find. Tomas had thought of composing a note to Naomi and his family, but what was there to say? How many ways could he say he was sorry? How could he convince Naomi it really was an idea he had fucked? He couldn't. It sounded as lame and pitiful to him now as it did to her. What was there to say about his issues which affected her, but which stemmed from his own disappointed sense of self? His dissatisfaction with his creative life, the squandered potential that, in this moment, Tomas began to doubt he ever had, was something poor Naomi was all too familiar with, and she could fill the rest of the family in on the whole business with Partridge.

Tomas didn't even have it in him to write a decent goodbye note. All for the good. Let his action speak. It would be a succinct, apt last chapter—as far as his role was concerned—in this story.

Something felt tight around his thighs. The tape. The passport. The credit card.

There was a thought he couldn't shake. Evo Korman was living in a van and showering in a woman's home—Vivian Rios was her name, wasn't that it? What had happened to this man, someone who Tomas deemed worthy of inclusion in his pantheon? A generational talent. A man touched by the gods. "Blistered Eye" was as profound as the *actual* Pantheon itself in Rome.

A heretical thought entered Tomas's mind: was it not better, at least *easier*, in the end, to be a mediocrity who plugs along, lives an unremarkable middle-class life, with its artisanal cheeses and Restoration Hardware oil-rubbed bronze cabinet knobs and TV series binging, than to have tasted greatness, and to no longer have it? You can't miss what you don't know. Was he actually in a better position than Evo Korman? The man who created "Blistered Eye" had never again equaled those two minutes and forty-eight seconds of genius. Was Tomas's mediocrity not a curse, but—not a blessing, certainly—but perhaps a kinder fate?

Torture isn't mediocrity, thought Tomas. Torture is knowing firsthand the difference between mediocrity and greatness.

Christ, what was keeping Evo from sticking a gun in his mouth and pulling the trigger? Was he not tormented day and night, like the ache of a rotting tooth, by the awareness that he, for a moment, had achieved what so few do? Or was he happy inside that van? Did Tomas have it all wrong? Was Tomas's imagination failing him again? Was Evo just fine, and not tortured by knowing he had it in him, at least once, to create something of lasting beauty?

One way or another, Tomas had to know. "Blistered Eye." Maybe that song wasn't—as he thought a few minutes ago—the punctuation mark of the last miserable three months, maybe it was the preamble, the prelude, to the future, or at any rate, *a* future. Was this song, this blurb on the radio, some kind of beginning? Had Evo Korman figured it out? A great man like that must have some insight, at least some thoughts, on the great existential questions we have been given enough brainpower to ask, but not enough to answer satisfactorily. What a cruel time to exist! thought Tomas. Better to be a primate concerned only with eating, shitting, and fucking, or to be whatever we might be in a hundred thousand more years, when, perhaps, a satisfying, universal understanding of ourselves would be plain to all.

Or maybe he was just a self-absorbed navel gazer who deserved to be miserable.

Another thought intruded.

What if the next tidbit of news about Evo Korman was that his decomposing body was found in that van, bloated and reeking?

Tomas didn't know what he would do when he got there, or even exactly why he needed to do this, but he knew he would have to find Evo Korman. That was it. He had to help him. What form that help would take, Tomas did not know yet, but the underlying impulse was there.

The ranger had read him correctly: he would not end his life, at least not today, not now. There was some work to be done first. And that work was finding Evo Korman. Tomas pulled hard on the duct tape to free his passport and credit card. It hurt, but he thanked God or his parents or evolution or whoever had blessed him with fairly hairless thighs.

Okay, next steps: his family, Billy, maybe even Naomi, might worry at his absence. He would send out a brief text blast. He typed:

"Will be out of town for a few days. Out of cell range. Everything is fine." He hit send, set his phone down on the passenger seat, and pulled out of the vista parking lot.

DAY 62

THAT HE SEEMED NOT TO BE AWARE of how cute he was made Garrett Turner all the cuter. From the things he knew firsthand—Adventure Thru Inner Space—other reference points, he had to be fifty, fifty-five. My god Black men aged well. It also didn't hurt that he carried himself with a certain modest confidence, if the contradiction held. Naomi enjoyed their sport flirting—but she still had to be, if not cautious, then intentional and thoughtful. Cute or not, self aware or not, men at the midcentury mark like Garrett walked a razor's edge. Enough of them had hit on her for Naomi to know. They were like dying animals in their death throes. They were kicking and spasming and lashing out at any remotely attractive female. They felt their age creeping up on them—the shrinking muscle mass, the rising tide of gray hair, the loosening of the skin—and with it the inevitable feeling of becoming sexually irrelevant. Women would soon begin to look *through* them. So yes, even though she didn't want to have to measure every damn syllable and every physical gesture around Garrett, and even though he had always been nothing but a respectful gentleman, he was at that age.

After her parents divorced—that is, when Abigail, age thirty-eight, had come out of the closet and left her father Bruce when he was forty-six—she remembered him telling her about one particularly awful eHarmony date, where, over dessert, his date had told him that while he was a witty man who seemed "nice," she didn't want to lead him on, and said the chemistry just wasn't there for her. She'd further added that he was "a little old" for her, but she was "just being real," and then, seeing the hurt in his eyes, added that she hoped one day that he would thank her for her candor because "no one wants to be bullshitted."

Naomi was horrified when Bruce told her the story. "If I had been there, Bruce?" she said, "that woman would've left the restaurant with oyster forks sticking out of her eyes."

Her father merely replied, "It only stung because I do feel a little old sometimes. To women. God I wish your mom had found herself ten years earlier."

"Bruce, you're still a total catch." During the separation, for no reason she could discern other than that her father was out of his mind for a few weeks, he'd asked that she call him "Bruce." She did, and it made him laugh. From then on he was "Bruce."

He smiled—the distinguished crow's feet around his eyes. The prominence of his cheekbones when he smiled.

"I am a catch, aren't I?"

She nodded. The bitch. With this high handed "no one wants to be bullshitted" nonsense. If a man as decent and attractive as her father could feel old and undesired, so could anyone. That's what had put Naomi on high alert for that last gasp—that moment just before a man gives in and accepts that his best shot at physical affection is playing with a grandchild.

When Garrett returned with their coffees, Naomi felt happy. It may have had something to do with his lack of desperate floundering—if he did believe he was standing at the edge of sexual irrelevance, he hid it damn well—and the melting whipped cream on top of her mocha always improved everything. She quickly slurped it before it completely dissolved.

"I can really see it now, the rock candy thing," said Garrett.

"That's pretty impressive, since all I've done since you left is tear half of it down."

"Yeah, I dunno, but something good is happening. I can tell."
He was right. She was close. They both knew it.

DAY 95

ALONG THE WESTERN STRETCH OF GLENOAKS BOULEVARD in Southern California, there are very few, if any, "oak" trees left, and there is no "glen" in sight. It is a flat, barren stretch, the hottest part of Los Angeles County—the San Fernando Valley—peppered with a mix of ethnic supermarkets, dollar stores, discount department stores, warehouses, very good Salvadoran and Mexican restaurants, car repair shops, closed storefronts with cracked asphalt parking lots behind cyclone fences, and the occasional chicken or goat strutting in a front yard. Pacoima is one of several cities along Glenoaks Boulevard. West of Burbank, Glendale, and Pasadena, Pacoima is a quiet, blue-collar neighborhood, where the commercial, the industrial, and the residential are separated by no more than a building or intersection. It is hard to imagine current zoning laws allowing such unlikely neighbors to sit cheek by jowl.

The air itself is parched here, the afternoon sun unforgiving.

Head east on I-5 and one can feel the median income climbing as you pass through Sylmar, Pacoima, Arleta, Vega, Burbank, and finally into Glendale and Pasadena, where older, Whiter generations in middle-class homes live alongside large and growing prosperous Asian and Armenian communities.

From Glendale it is a short fifteen-minute drive around Griffith Park into Hollywood and Los Angeles proper. The Walk of Fame, the

Capitol Records building, Melrose Avenue, the bars, the clubs, the hip cafés, the loud shops. If there is no traffic, which one might experience at 3 a.m. on a Monday morning, Pacoima, a mere forty-five minutes from Hollywood, seems to belong to a different universe.

It had taken Tomas only twenty minutes and two search engines to locate an address for Amos and Vivian Rios. The Rios family lived on Dewey Street, which runs parallel to, and very near, Interstate 5. One can hear the constant sound of freeway traffic from their block. As his phone's GPS led him down Dewey Street, Tomas wondered if the sharp pain of the affair might still dull a bit over the next three months, might turn into a white noise hum—like the freeway—that Naomi could stomach. It all depended, he supposed, on whether, as the days went on, she would think, too, of any of the good, or ruminate only on the bad. Tomas was all too aware of human negativity bias—our innate tendency to focus on the negative and dismiss the positive. He knew that the odds were not in his favor.

But he couldn't think of what to do now, right now, besides finding Evo. Trying to hurry Naomi in any direction was like trying to hold water in your hands.

Up ahead he saw a faded baby-blue van parked on the street. His phone told him he was nine hundred feet from his destination.

DAY 94

NAOMI'S PHONE RANG. She was home, the home she and Tomas owned—she was fighting hard not to let him ruin their beautiful home for her. She tried to conjure memories and images of the good years and let go of the black bile of the last three months. She was lying on the couch, watching *My Man Godfrey*, a 1936 screwball comedy that she had watched at least a dozen times. She was getting tired. It was her comfort food, and she was hoping it would put her to sleep. She reached for her phone, but it only rang once. She saw the missed caller ID—Tomas.

She was no longer tired.

What did he want? What was he thinking? She had shut down communication months ago. But the temptation! The curiosity. Surely he hadn't called her by accident. What did he want to say? She *could* call back—she had the pretext—the missed call. She could say she called back in case it was some dire emergency. She didn't initiate the call, that was the point. Her excuse was baked in. She had nothing more she wanted to say to him at this exact moment, but what was on *his* mind? And why did he chicken out? One ring and gone. He had honored her request to have no more contact—he'd finally done something right—yet for some reason, tonight, this specific night, he couldn't help himself and he'd called. Why?

Well, whatever. It was all silly speculation.

She put the phone down and turned back to the movie. But she could not focus on the razor-sharp dialogue and chemistry between William Powell and Carole Lombard. Her mind raced. She looked again at the missed call log on her phone. The call came in at 11:13 p.m. She now game-theoried what he might have intended. Her first instinct was that Tomas had drunk-dialed her, then panicked and chickened out. Or had he thought of a new way to apologize? Was it a change in content, or merely in style? If he was drunk, maybe he just wanted to call and say hi, chat about anything, ask her how her day was. Was he hoping for a truce, if only for five minutes, just to pretend things were "normal" for a moment?

Something else ate at her. Not the question of whether he had pulled away and become indifferent over the last three months—the experience in Riordan's office proved he was anything but indifferent—but that *she* was not indifferent. This stupid rumination. Why am I thinking so much about this ridiculous missed call? It may have been a butt-dial, and here she was, wondering pointlessly and painfully about it. She knew better. She knew the difference between things over which she had agency in her life, and things she didn't. Tomas perhaps sitting on his phone was something she did not have agency over. What could she say with certainty? The call was aborted. And yet she couldn't stop herself from speculating. Was he calling to say he had made peace with her decision to divorce? That her wishes had finally sunk in? What was his hope here?

Or was this just a stunt? Had he deliberately hung up to see if she would take the bait? She thought of an old boyfriend, Anthony, who, before they started dating, wouldn't text and ask her out. Instead he'd text her something odd—like a close-up photo of a tree stump, or the words "why do people have to gargle so loudly?" Random bits. It worked. She would respond with a "thumbs up" to the tree stump or "Right?" to the gargling. He confessed on their first date that he did this to protect himself. If he directly asked a girl out, she could say yes or no, or, worst of all, not respond. This way, even if the girl wasn't that interested, or didn't like him, he had not put himself out there with any vulnerability. It was just some silly trial balloon to see if a girl would respond at all. At the time Naomi thought it was childish and brilliant and cowardly. She hadn't yet seen that approach. Now she wondered if Tomas had just floated up his version of that trial balloon.

She turned back to *My Man Godfrey* but was still too distracted to pay attention. Who cares why he dialed her number? Could be a million reasons, and the fact that butt-dial was an entirely plausible explanation? She had to shake off this feeling.

But she couldn't.

DAY 95

NINE HUNDRED FEET UNTIL 3306 DEWEY STREET, the Rios home. After spotting the baby-blue van, perhaps *the* van, Tomas took a moment to look around him. Many of the homes on this block of Dewey Street had cyclone fences, four or five feet tall, to keep people off lawns and make it known that most owners did not appreciate solicitations. These were the fences Tomas remembered from childhood playgrounds: gray metal, a drop clasp at the gate, hot to the touch as a frying pan in summer, skin-peelingly cold in winter.

Taking his hands out of his pockets, he approached the Rios home, trying not to look like he was casing the neighborhood. He double-checked the address. There was no cyclone fence at 3306.

He was now just feet from the van. Tomas was not an expert on cars, but the van appeared to be a '70s model Ford with a convex bubble window toward the rear and square windows on the rear double doors. A small metal emblem told him the model was Econoline. Tomas felt a certain relief that the van looked more like a sad, worn '70s party mobile than what he and Naomi called a "rapey van." Rapey vans were typically matte beige or gray, with no side windows. One hubcap was missing on the blue van. There was a long rusting crease above the driver's side rear wheel, an unrepaired sideswipe.

Was he really looking at the vehicle and home of the man who had written "Blistered Eye," "Plastic Empire," "Stain," and other masterpieces? "Blistered Eye" was clearly the first among equals, but those three songs alone guaranteed Evo a spot among the immortals. They were the aural equivalent of standing in the nave of Chartres Cathedral, the balcony of Fallingwater, or the galleries of the Kimbell Museum.

A few bumper stickers dotted the van's rear bumper and doors, ranging from the Dead Boys (in Tomas's mind, given to Evo by the Dead Boys themselves) to Katrina and the Waves (ironic? sincere? both? Katrina and the Waves *had* bumper stickers?) to Megadeth (who Tomas knew The Pill Splitters had once opened for and been roundly booed, but who refused to leave the stage, and concluded their show by Evo stripping naked and bowing unctuously to the crowd before being hit in the head by a beer bottle).

This was obviously Evo Korman's van.

At the Megadeth show, Evo had picked up the largest, bloodiest shard he could find and gently tossed it underhand back to the angry fan who threw the bottle. A two-inch scar around Evo's temple was a reminder of the moment. Tomas only knew all this because he had seen a cell-phone clip of the show online. Tomas never forgot the sight of Evo giggling as the crowd of tough guy metal heads parted in fear of being touched by Evo's blood when he lobbed more pieces of the bottle back toward them. Evo then hopped off the stage to hug them, but they cleared an instant circle around the bloody front man.

There stood Evo, alone, nude, encircled, a steady trickle of blood running down his temple and onto his skinny chest.

"I hope you enjoyed the show," Evo had said to the crowd. "I enjoyed you."

There the shaky video ended, glitched out on an image of Evo smiling and staring at the crowd with the patience and benevolence of . . . a calm priest? That's what always came to Tomas's mind. A young priest with a forgiving, black sense of humor. The obvious comparisons to Iggy Pop and Jonathan Richman and Jello Biafra and Ian Curtis had become tiresome. Evo was a different kind of guru.

And after a tiny handful of the world's occupants became aware of Evo—including Perry Farrell, Scott Weiland, Richard Patrick—they had all borrowed from him in their physical and vocal mannerisms, but, captivating though they could be, they weren't Evo Korman. Salieri to Mozart. Borromini to Bernini.

"He's not here right now."

Tomas turned away from the van to find a heavyset woman, probably in her late fifties, but possibly in her seventies, standing a few feet away looking at him. The extra weight took the wrinkles out of her face. He had seen older Latino men with gorgeous shocks of black hair, combed back with pomade, and beautiful Black women who he could not believe were the same age as his mother.

"Oh, he's not?" said Tomas.

"He doesn't like to give autographs."

"I'm not here for an autograph."

"Oh, you're a friend." The woman's voice perked up.

"No. Not really. I just, want to help."

"I see." She sounded a little let down. Tomas got the sick feeling that she was being too diplomatic to let him know that dozens of people had probably already dropped by to "help" Evo Korman.

"You must be Vivian Rios?"

"Oh. He's coming."

Tomas turned to see a rail-thin man, chiseled nose and cheekbones, iconic forehead scar, walking down the street wearing earmuff style headphones—fully insulated from the world. Tomas shouldn't have been shocked at Evo's appearance. Although it had been twenty years since he had followed the man's every utterance, parsed the words and body language and, of course, songs of this rock god as if he were a bona fide oracle, Evo looked shockingly small and fragile. A delicate bird with thin glass bones.

He wore skinny black jeans (skinny black jeans were all too common and trendy, but for decades Evo had worn nothing else—they were no fad for him), sandals, and a dirty white T-shirt. The sandals seemed off, but Tomas supposed a true rock god doesn't go by the playbook, he invents it.

His hair, all gray, was crudely shaven— it looked like the man had shaved it himself and just missed patches here and there. The bones of his wrists, especially, were knobby and prominent, as were the veins crisscrossing his hands.

"Evo" was the first word out of Tomas's mouth. Evo didn't respond. The headphones. Tomas wondered what Evo Korman would be listening to in 2023. Surely someone of his prolific talent and curiosity wouldn't become stagnant. He would be like a Stan Ridgway, or Danny Elfman or Laurie Anderson or Stewart Copeland or Mark Mothersbaugh—evolving, stretching the limits of their genres, composing soundtracks, listening to bands and sounds that Tomas's inelastic mind wouldn't even consider. Perhaps he was creating strange ambient noise poems, like Brian Eno after Roxy Music; or maybe he had taken on the role of the elder statesman and was mentoring a new band Tomas had never heard of—after all, it was Ray Manzarek of the Doors who had produced X's first two records, *Los Angeles* and *Wild Gift*. It was Mick Jones of The Clash who went on to produce The Libertines' masterpiece, *Up the Bracket*. And, of course, it was the kickass cyclone named Joan Jett of The Runaways and Joan Jett and the Blackhearts who had produced The Germs' legendary *GI* record. Debbie Harry of Blondie had appeared in films—all she had to do was stare into the lens, no smile, and she stole her scenes. These were all fitting and worthy second chapters.

"Mr. Korman, hello!" called out Tomas, this time loud enough for Evo to hear. And even if he hadn't heard, Tomas was also now waving his right hand—but keeping it low, in front of his chest—trying to tamp down what he obviously was, and what Evo Korman and Mrs. Rios plainly saw: an overaged fanboy.

Tomas glanced behind him. Mrs. Rios had turned to go back into her house.

Evo took off his headphones, stared at Tomas.

"Evo Korman," said Tomas.

"Okay."

"Hi. I'm Tomas Araeta. I'm a very big fan, and I just wanted to say hi, really."

"You just did. So, mission accomplished." Evo walked past Tomas toward the driver's side door of the van.

"Evo—Mr. Korman—do you have a minute?"

"Didn't Lalla tell you? I don't do autographs."

"Lalla?"

"Mrs. Rios."

"I don't want an autograph."

"Good. And I don't want to hear about how 'Blistered Eye' changed your life, either."

Tomas stopped for a second. Okay, so clearly he wasn't the first. But the universe—fate—something in him he couldn't even understand had taken him from the Golden Gate Bridge to this street in Pacoima and put him face to face with Evo Korman.

"What about how it's *kept* changing my life, even up to about three days ago?"

"I broke up The Pill Splitters eleven years ago. Should have done it sooner."

"Well, are you counting the reunion show in 2017?"

The bile seemed to rise in Evo.

"Ah, I see, a *real* fan. You probably call yourself 'a completist.' I hate completists. So fucking uptight." Evo climbed into the van, but Tomas instinctively grabbed the edge of the metal door, preventing Evo from closing it.

"I heard on the radio you were living here, and I wanted to meet you."

"Again, mission accomplished. You can let go of the door now."

Tomas did as told. Evo put his headphones back on and was about to slam the door shut.

"What are you listening to?" yelled Tomas.

"Nothing. I just like the quiet."

Evo slammed the door shut.

DAY 29

BRUCE LIVED IN ALBUQUERQUE, remarried with a second family. Naomi's two stepbrothers were grown and gone. It was now just Bruce and his wife Angela and their three Pomeranians. Bruce and Naomi spoke half a dozen times a year, and once every other year or so a rendezvous was planned. The two would meet in some place they called "exotic"—Eugene, Des Moines, Winnetka.

"Just pick a spot on the map and we'll go," Bruce had said the first year after he and Abigail separated. It was an adventure. Naomi admired how he had handled the separation, how he had the most cheerful disposition of anyone she knew. Before dialing, she chided herself for not calling him more often. She loved their time together. She loved *him*. Why didn't she call more? Maybe he just seemed less needy than her mom. But she knew he loved her to pieces. Just because he was happy didn't mean he didn't want to see his daughter more.

There is no substitute for the love of your child, no matter how well you are doing.

"Pick a spot and we'll go," even if that spot was no more glamorous than Plano, Texas. He never pushed or pulled.

She found "Bruce" in her contacts and dialed.

"Bubble, good morning."

"Hi Bruce."

"Whoa. Didn't like that sound. Nope, not at all. Let's try again."

"What's your schedule like these days? Should we pick a spot?"

"Know what? I've actually been thinking about trying to find the ocean some time. Should we go hunt for jellyfish in . . . I'm thinking... thinking, oh, Baton Rouge? Or lobster hunting in Maryland?"

"Yes!"

This was it. After the initial shock of his wife coming out had quieted a bit—that is to say, after she had acted on what he had intuited somewhere deep down to be true but never admitted to himself—what had he done? Yes, asked his daughter to call him Bruce. Beyond that? For the first six months or so he was depressed, angry, withdrawn. Then what happened? He'd exhaled. He relaxed. He gave up trying to hold water in his hands. He met his daughter in odd cities on a lark. He became happy again, happier than Naomi remembered him being for most of her childhood, and this from a man who'd been constitutionally happy to begin with.

Divorce wasn't inherently bad. That was some left-over bullshit from, well, most religions, but Bruce and Abigail had proved that the question isn't whether divorce is right or wrong, but whether it's right or wrong *for you*. Yes, they were a relatively "easy" proof of concept—she was gay—but the point stood.

Bruce was a successful businessman. He owned three Don Pacos mid-market Mexican restaurants. When local Hispanics asked him who "Don Paco" was, Bruce apologized profusely and said that Paco was the Spanish translation of Bruce, and if it wasn't, well, he just kind of always liked the name Paco. And who didn't like the honorific of "don?" The locals didn't care. His posole was superb.

"I was dead set on Provo this year, Dad, but you got me with jellyfish."

"We can absolutely do Provo some time. Just not on a Sunday. Utah's a dry state on Sundays. Discovered that the hard way when I was looking for my afternoon gimlet in Logan."

"No one should suffer like that."

"Need you to tell me what's really going on, Bubble. I can hear it. This is not the kind of suspense I like."

Tears rolled down Naomi's cheek and she wiped her nose.

"Did you just wipe your nose?" asked Bruce in a panic. "I heard something!"

"Yup."

"Shit. Talk to me."

"He cheated on me."

Bruce said nothing for three or four seconds. Then he spoke.

"Are you in Oakland?"

"Yeah."

"See you tomorrow, Bubble."

He hung up. He actually hung up on her without saying goodbye or asking if she *wanted* him to come. Even she thought the urgency and gravity in his voice—all of it blessedly sincere—was overblown. God, how she loved this man.

When Naomi had just finished architectural grad school she'd toyed with the idea of opening a sock store—a store that would carry all manner of sock you couldn't find elsewhere (socks with little tractors on them, socks with glitter moons on them, thigh-high socks with oval cutouts, socks with tiny rubber treads on them in chic patterns, socks with patterns of socks on them)—and that would just cover the first display rack you'd find. He'd had an immediate response to the idea of his daughter throwing away seven years of architecture school to open a sock store:

"Can I tell you the secret to succeeding in business—any business?" he said. "Hire good managers. And take them to a nice dinner once in a while. Tell them, literally say to them, 'I really appreciate you.' Nobody likes a praise miser. Don't assume they know how much you value them."

She'd decided not to open the sock store, but it's no wonder his posole was considered the best in town. They were made with the love and respect that radiated outward from the big Don Paco himself.

DAY 95

AFTER SHUTTING THE DOOR IN TOMAS'S FACE, Evo disappeared into the back of the van. Tomas was invigorated. A polite, diffident Evo Korman would be a neutered Evo Korman, an unnatural Evo Korman.

Tomas gently knocked on the Rios's door frame. Lalla opened the inner door, leaving the screen door shut. Tomas smiled at her through the metal mesh.

"Hello again. Does he really shower here every day?"

"Yes."

"Has he done that already today?"

Lalla shook her head.

"Okay, thank you."

Well, that was simple. Tomas would just wait the man out. In his back seat he had an old paper copy of Thomas Mann's picaresque novel, *Confessions of Felix Krull, Confidence Man,* Mann's unfinished last work. Unfinished it may have been, but, for Tomas, it was perfect. And an astonishing choice. Thomas Mann, the literary giant, the Nobel Laureate, the great man behind *Death In Venice, Buddenbrooks,* and *Magic Mountain,* had turned to a breezy novel about a young man seducing and conning women when he was seventy-nine. The book was incomplete only because Mann died while writing it. Had Mann just decided in his later years, "Hell, enough with the grave and the 'important,' I want to write something *fun*"?

This is what the greats do—follow their own heartbeat. And to do that, they actually have to *listen* to their own heartbeat. They have to know themselves profoundly. And they have to not care what others think. So very simple to say, so very difficult to do.

After an hour or so of reading, Tomas took a break. His stomach was rumbling. There was the question of lunch. What if he left for food at *precisely* the time Evo went to take his shower? Or, what if Tomas had it backward? What if Evo could see Tomas sitting in his car, and was waiting Tomas out?

There was only one safe move, short of not eating.

Again Tomas knocked on the Rios door. Lalla didn't look too surprised to see him.

"Mrs. Rios, hi. I'm Tomas Araeta. I have a favor to ask, and if you're not comfortable with it, I will not bother you again."

She was listening.

"Can I purchase some food from you?"

"Excuse me?"

Tomas couldn't place her accent, not exactly. South American, maybe, Mexican? Is Mexico part of South America? He realized he didn't know.

"I think I have something to offer Evo, and I know he doesn't want to see people, and maybe he's thinking I'll just leave, so if I could buy some food from you, I could eat it in my car, and then, when he leaves his van, I could attempt to talk to him again."

"In such cases he has asked that I call the police."

"Have you had to?"

"Twice. And some days he doesn't leave the van at all, so I don't know if you would see him anyway." Tomas had already braced himself. He knew that the brief euphoria he felt upon setting out on this trip to help Evo might fade, along with any chance he had at persuasion by enthusiasm, so he had to do *something* while he still had any optimism and energy left. But he hadn't yet come up with what that something would be. He was waiting for inspiration, hoping that being here, seeing the great man in person, would provide the answer. It hadn't yet, but that was okay. He had just made first contact. He didn't know how he would help Evo. He just knew he had to. But soon.

"Is that a fruit tree? I don't know much about plants."

Tomas was looking at a small tree with decorative circular brick trim around its base, separating grass from soil.

"Apricot."

Tomas nodded.

"Mrs. Rios, I could do some yard work for you. I'm bad, but not terrible, with a lawnmower, clippers, whatever. And I'll put in the effort no matter the outcome. It's hot out."

"Are you insulting my garden?"

"No, no. The opposite. I want to see it kept as you have it. It's just, you've been patient, tolerant—" She smiled thinly, letting him know that he had been lucky that she had put up with him this long, but that he better conclude his business soon. "I'm guessing me here to see Evo Korman probably just seems weird, but it would mean the world to me, and I just want to do something for you since I'm asking something of you—your trust and patience. And food." He threw on his best understated smile, trying to keep the needy unctuousness to a minimum.

She looked at this odd creature—he was a bit older than the others who had made the trek—they had mostly been kids in their twenties who probably knew of The Pill Splitters from their parents, and decided on a bored, drunken lark that a visit to Evo Korman in Pacoima was just the thing to keep the night interesting. But she saw that here was a man, alone, older, who was trying desperately and unsuccessfully to hide some kind of hurt and hopelessness in his eyes.

"Come in. Eat. You can watch his van from the window."

Lalla unlocked the screen door and let Tomas in. The home was tidy. Immaculate lime-green carpet, not a speck of dust on the coffee table or light fixtures. The walls were full of pictures of what Tomas assumed must be kids and grandkids.

"You have a lovely family."

"They don't visit enough, but, yes, they are my family."

She prepared some cold chicken and sliced bell peppers for Tomas.

"It's just leftovers, chicken and vegetables, do you want it hot or cold?"

"Whatever you recommend."

She warmed the chicken separately, put the bell pepper slices on two plates, and brought the meal to the dining room. A lace tablecloth was covered by a thick clear plastic sheet. The tablecloth looked like an heirloom, something Tomas and Naomi might find antique browsing, and it would not be stained on Mrs. Rios's watch.

"Evo Korman called you 'Lalla.'"

"My husband gave me that nickname. It made him crazy that I never sang a real song to the kids when they were little. I would just sing, 'La la, la la la laaaaaa, la la la, la la . . .'"

"It's pretty."

"But enough is enough. He was right to be annoyed. I should've mixed up my singing a bit."

Tomas began eating.

"Do you have a family?" asked Lalla.

"No. Not yet. My wife and I are in the process of adopting."

Lalla paused a moment, briefly wondering if this was a matter of infertility or choice. "Wonderful. All children need to be loved."

"Thanks," said Tomas, taking a second bite of chicken. "This is very good."

"You said you had something to offer Mr. Evo. I'm curious. Can you tell me?"

That was the question, wasn't it? Hearing it asked aloud by another person, though, was different. Tomas racked his brain, trying to come up with something that didn't sound completely idiotic. Gushing to Evo about how much his music meant to him had gone over like a thumbtack sandwich.

"Well," said Tomas, buying a little time, "I think it's sad in a way that people don't know how important they are to other people until it's too late. Until it's practically their funeral. Like in the newspaper. These obituaries for famous people come out *the day after* the person dies. So you know they weren't just written overnight. They were probably sitting in a drawer somewhere, as the person got older or sicker, and now when they can't hear a word you say, suddenly everyone comes out of the woodwork and tells them how much they meant. And I just think that's sad. We all want to know we made a difference. That we were loved. What's wrong with telling someone while they're still alive?"

"Is he sick?" asked Lalla with uneasy concern.

"Oh. No. I mean, I don't know. I was just making the point that we all need to hear that we matter now and then. Sorry, no, he looks in great health to me. A cheeseburger wouldn't hurt, but he looks good."

This seemed to calm her.

"Obituaries. Are you a journalist?"

"Mmm hmm." Tomas lied reflexively. He wasn't sure why, just that it seemed like it's what Lalla wanted to hear.

"I hope he appreciates whatever it is you have to say to him," said Lalla.

"Where should I take these?" asked Tomas about his dishes.

"You can leave them." He noticed her looking at him with what he thought to be compassion. He wondered if his eyes were still puffy or had dark circles. He glanced at his arm—it wasn't trembling. Had it ever trembled in the last months so that the naked eye could see it? Maybe it was just a surfeit of adrenaline and shock that only he could feel.

"Why do you help him?" asked Tomas.

"Because he never asked," replied Lalla. "And he did stink. He does need the showers." They shared a smile. "I called the police on him a few times in the beginning, but we don't have restricted parking here. I keep asking for those little stickers, but never get an answer. When the police came, he would move his van up the block or to the other side of the street. They said he wasn't breaking any laws. He knew it was me calling them, because I would talk to the police on my porch when they showed up. I wanted him to see that. But I think he thought it was funny. Only time I saw him smile." She pointed to a few lanyards made of braided plastic strings on a shelf in the dining room. "He makes me those. I don't need them, but I like the colors."

"Does he have anyone—friends, family, maybe, not just strangers—who visit?"

"I don't know."

"Are you friends with him?"

"No. He's like a stray cat: I feed him; I like to see him sometimes; he comes and goes."

Tomas had noticed pictures of a much younger Lalla Rios, perhaps from the early 1970s, in a floral print dress, standing next to a handsome Latino man in a large-lapel brown suit.

"Then why do you do it—stray cats don't usually make for the greatest company."

"I'm bored. I don't like retirement. But they gave me a little pension and health insurance and said I should go."

"What did you do?"

"Secretary for the phone company. I could type ninety-six words a minute."

"I don't know exactly what counts as great typing speed, but that sounds great."

Lalla smiled. "It is great. Every executive wanted me as his assistant. For the right reasons," she clarified.

Tomas nodded, glancing again at the pictures on the wall. "Your husband was very handsome."

"He was. And kind. He passed away eight years ago."

"I can't imagine. I'm sorry, Mrs. Rios."

"Me too."

"Do your kids live nearby?"

"The closest one is in Irvine, but she's busy—she has two little ones."

Tomas nodded.

"We were married forty-three years. Amos was a good man, a good father. He was the love of my life."

Four decades plus of marriage. No doubt they had their issues, but they had stuck it out. *Happily?* It seemed that way to Tomas. What of boredom, restlessness, a sense of potential unfulfilled? Was Amos ever haunted by these things? Was Lalla? And if so, did they confide in each other? Had either of them sought comfort and validation in the wrong place?

"It sounds like you had a good marriage," ventured Tomas.

"We were happy most days. Not all, of course, but most."

"Sounds like a *very* good marriage."

"I miss him."

For a moment neither said anything.

"What's your wife's name?" asked Lalla.

"Naomi."

"That's a pretty name."

"Well, she's very pretty, inside and out."

Suddenly Tomas felt hot tears welling behind his eyes.

"Tomas and Naomi, and soon a child." Lalla now smiled, wistfully, transported back in time. "I remember when we were expecting our first child—Daniel. I was so . . . excited, nervous, but also peaceful. I wish I could be in your wife's place again."

Tomas took his plate to the kitchen to hide his tears from Lalla.

When Tomas returned, Lalla was standing, looking out the living room window. "Call me Lalla, I prefer it."

"Okay," said Tomas.

"I saw him moving. In the van. He's awake."

Tomas looked out the window at the van but saw nothing. He must've slipped into the back.

"Thank for you for inviting me in and feeding me, Lalla. I really appreciate it."

"I hope you find what you're looking for," said Lalla.

"Me too," said Tomas.

Outside, Tomas cautiously approached the van. The rear bubble window was tinted, so instead he peered in the passenger side window of Evo's van. His angle of vision didn't allow him to see into the back. He knocked on the side slide door. No response. Of course not. The headphones. He knocked louder.

He thought of leaving—what would he say to the man anyway? Maybe his lizard brain had just sent him on this four-hundred-mile trek to keep him from jumping off the bridge, to let that stupid moment pass. And it had succeeded. Maybe it was time to go.

The door slid open with a violent clang.

"What?" asked Evo.

Tomas fumbled. "So—the headphones—really, just nothing? You don't listen to music?"

Evo appraised Tomas for a moment—he obviously wasn't just another drunk kid out on some kind of scavenger hunt, and he could see something was not right with the man standing in front of him. He took off the headphones and placed them on Tomas's head like a crown of thorns. Tomas heard what sounded like . . . waves crashing . . . the sounds of the ocean. Only one side worked—the right. He felt shocked, excited, and, more than anything, honored. Evo Korman was sharing with him experimental music he liked, or perhaps that he had created himself. Tomas realized he might be bearing witness to the birth of genius. The monotonous sound continued. It really did sound like waves breaking. Tomas waited for something, anything, to change—the tempo, the introduction of instruments or vocals, another stolen bit of sound. Tomas looked at Evo.

"What is it?" he asked.

"What do you think it is?"

"Sounds like the ocean."

"Yeah, the ocean."

Tomas took off the headphones, handed them back to Evo.

"New work?"

Evo smiled, the right side of his mouth turned up slightly, the left not at all, and here, up close, Tomas could see another one of his idol's hallmarks. One of his incisors was turned at a twenty-degree angle from the other, creating a deep shadow line in the middle of his mouth. Lore had it that it was the result of a bar fight, and the best thing about it, the thing that had always impressed a not unreasonably vain person like Tomas, is that Evo had done absolutely nothing about it. And there was a time when he probably could've afforded the dental work. But no, instead he just smiled that man-child smile of his, and that gloriously crooked tooth stood out for everyone to see. Whereas Tomas combed his hair "in a thousand ways," as the old Rod Stewart song had it—when Rod was still cool, when he was still Rod the Mod—Evo didn't care. It was just one more totem, one more notch of authenticity, revealing who the man was. How many women—or—men had Evo slept with, snaggletooth and all?

"Yeah, we're called 'The Ocean.' Do you like it?"

Tomas's gut instinct was to lie to his hero, to hide his disappointment, or to force himself to find the virtue in Evo's new direction, but fuck that. Tomas couldn't lie to himself on this one. No, not this time. Not anymore. He just couldn't. An anger he didn't understand welled up in him. Evo Korman was playing soothing *New Age garbage?* What an awful second chapter! He was Evo-Fucking-Korman, for Chrissake! And so Tomas conjured something like a spine.

"No. Not really," he said quietly.

Evo laughed, grabbed Tomas's chin and shook it.

"Shit, for a minute I thought you were gonna say you liked it."

Tomas didn't know what to think.

"Did you know when Ravi Shankar was tuning his sitar at Monterey Pop, and took a little break, all the hippies applauded, like it was a fucking real song."

Tomas didn't know that, but the odd anger lingered.

"And *you* can tell the difference between a sitar being tuned and a real song?"

"Hell no, but I'm not a hippie."

Evo took back the headphones.

"It's for my ears. Tinnitus. Stood too close to too many amps one too many times. They ring all the time."

"That sounds unbelievably annoying."

Evo shrugged. "I played, I paid."

"The ocean noise helps?"

"I like waves crashing better than the hum of fluorescent lights turned to eleven."

The anger was subsiding. "I used to work in a place with fluorescent lights on all the time," said Tomas, thinking of the lights in the UC Berkeley Wurster Hall architecture studios. "We all hated it. But we kind of came to enjoy the hate."

"Hate can be great," said Evo "If I didn't have the ocean, or this track I've got of two hours of an air conditioner running, or a lot of Eno's stuff, I'd"—and here Evo made a throat-slitting gesture but did so with that inscrutable wide-eyed smile. Tomas, having peered into the Pacific Ocean only days before, did not dismiss Evo's clichéd gesture out of hand. He did not know whether the man was serious or not. But he knew what a ringing ear felt like. After seeing Motorhead live, his ears had rung for three days—it was a scratch that could not be itched—and to have it permanently?

"I'm glad you didn't—" and here Tomas aped Evo's gesture of slashing his own throat.

"What do you want?" asked Evo. "I'm busy."

"I don't know. But I was curious about what a guy like you would be listening to these days, but I . . . hey . . ." His voice trailed off as he saw Evo's eyes glaze over. "I'll be back," said Tomas. "A couple hours."

Evo watched as Tomas abruptly turned away.

DAY 30

NAOMI WAITED FOR BRUCE AT CAFÉ STRADA, a coffee house across the street from Wurster Hall, where she'd had many a late-night small mocha with extra whipped cream as a student and TA. It wasn't unheard of for a grad student to date an undergrad, but still, once they started dating, she and Tomas had instead made Café Roma their spot, another coffee house about half a mile away from the prying eyes and gossip of Strada. Gossip and prying eyes didn't bother Naomi. The only concern she'd had about dating a student was any speculation that she might grade biasedly. She didn't.

After finding out that Tomas had cheated, she had avoided both Strada and Roma. Until today. It had been four weeks. She thought Bruce's presence might help. She vowed to make new memories in old places. She had just finished slurping the whipped cream off her mocha when Bruce walked in—really closer to a trot than a walk—straight from the airport.

"If you want extra whipped cream, Bubble, just ask. I once had a customer who complained about how little salsa we served with our chips. It's so silly. All he had to do was ask for more. When I told him he could have as much as he wanted, he looked . . . disappointed. People. Fuck 'em, amirite? Gotta love 'em."

"Hi Bruce."

"I'm going to get a coffee. No I'm not. I had too much whiskey and Coke on the plane. I'm wired. Do you want me to get you more whipped cream? I'm already standing."

"No. No, I'm just glad, more than glad, you're here. Sit. Sit, sit, sit."

Bruce joined Naomi at a two-top. Naomi was picking at an upturned edge of worn Formica.

"Dad, can I make a snarky observation?"

"Always. Did you just call me 'Dad'?"

"It's actually a question I've always wanted to ask."

Bruce nodded vigorously.

"You have a freaking sixth sense about me from one sniffle, but did you really not know Mom was gay, the woman you lived with, shared a bed with?"

"You've waited twenty . . . six? years to ask me this?"

Naomi shrugged.

"Here's the real insanity: no. Good luck unpeeling that onion."

"Did you guys sleep together? I mean, besides conceiving me."

"Yeah. Not often, but yeah. I think she felt bad and wanted to do whatever she could to make me happy before she found the courage to speak her truth. I mean, let's face it, you guys can always fake it. With us, it will salute, or it won't."

"Yeah."

"Hey, about that sixth sense?" said Bruce with uncharacteristic hesitation.

"Yeah?"

"I do have it, there's no question about that, so take nothing away from my superpower, but I think I should tell you that Tomas called me two weeks ago and told me everything."

Naomi stiffened. "Told you what?"

"That he cheated on you."

"And you didn't call me immediately?"

"Absolutely not. You don't push someone to talk, someone who's just been badly hurt, until they're ready."

Naomi would think about that later. "What did he tell you—exactly?"

"That he slept with somebody, that you two would be divorcing, and that he was sorry about what he had done and everyone who was hurt by it."

"Oh," said Naomi, "I see. He was hoping that when you and I talked, he would seem like a contrite guy who did the right thing and fessed up before I told you."

"Maybe. I thought about that, of course. But how could he know you hadn't already told me when he called me? Anyway, he kept hammering that of all the people you know, he thought that I—he said I was a little like you in this situation—would know what to say to make you feel better because he couldn't."

"That's absolutely true, I'll give him that."

"Bubble?"

"Yeah?"

"I have no idea what his agenda is, and I really don't care. I liked him fine when you were together. I liked him fine because he seemed to make you happy. But if that's not the case anymore, then I hate him."

"Thank you!"

Bruce splayed open his hand, looked at his fingers, as if he had never seen them before.

"I had to pull teeth to get Mom to say a cross word about him. And Marivel, well Marivel always thought he was a phony," Naomi said.

"Do you? Think he's a phony?"

"No. I mean, he's restless about the right things, but it comes from the wrong place. I don't think he's a phony."

"But he lied to you."

"Yes, he lied."

"Well, that's the thing, isn't it?"

"Yes. I think it is. You think I should go through with the divorce?"

"I think I don't want the weight of that question on me. Way above my pay scale."

Naomi sat back in her chair, her posture stiffening again. "So now you're waffling, too?"

"No. I'm steadfast in saying that if you're not happy, you go."

"You weren't happy, and you went."

"Of course I went! My wife was gay, and I still wanted sex. I don't mean just sex, but I wanted to feel wanted."

Naomi quietly nodded.

"You said you filed?"

"Twenty-three days ago."

"So you know about the hundred and eighty days?"

"The cooling off period."

"Yeah, divorcing your mom kinda turned me into a numbers wonk."

"I'm sure it did."

"Twenty-three days ago, eh? You filed quick." Bruce mentioned it casually, observationally, without judgment—but he mentioned it.

"Is that a problem?" Jesus, thought Naomi, was Bruce now going to start preaching the false gospel of reconciliation? Of taking more time?

"Not at all. I was just curious."

"How long did you wait until after Mom came out to file?"

"I don't remember. It was more just the shock of everything. A few months, a year, maybe. I knew we couldn't go on, but I was just . . . gasping, for a while. My memory of that time is a little shaky. But I just remember that phrase, 'the cooling off period.'" Bruce didn't ask before taking a sip of her mocha. "Good. Not too sweet. Are you still under the same roof?"

"No. He moved out. Staying in the studio or wherever."

"Good. Good. You shouldn't be inconvenienced. At all."

Ah. Good. This. This was better. When Bruce said "inconvenienced," unlike Tomas, it was *appropriate*.

"But I've been mostly staying with Mom."

"How is she?"

"Good. Ya know, Mom. She and Marivel are doing good, I think."

"I'm glad to hear that. But back to you. Did *you* see it coming?"

Naomi made a snorting sound. "I don't know. Maybe I didn't want to."

"Yeah," said Bruce with downcast empathy.

"Bruce, what do I do? I mean, I look at you now, and it looks like you came out the other side fine, if not better. I'm jealous. I want that." Bruce said nothing, looking worried. "I'm not gonna hold you to it, Dad. I just want your advice."

"I know. That's why I want to actually think for once before talking."

"I don't have all day."

"Huh?"

"Joking, Dad. I'm joking."

"Right, duh. Good. Good that you're joking. That's good." He took another sip of her mocha. "Want another one?"

She shook her head. "My stomach. I get queased out. That's why I get a small."

Mouth closed, Bruce ran his tongue across his teeth. Naomi knew it meant he was thinking, really thinking.

"It's kind of what I said before. All I care about is you. And it would kill me to think that the little prick has stolen even a pinch of your bubble-ness. Be angry, yes, be pissed, but—when you can—let it go. When you're ready. You know the old saying, 'Holding a grudge is like taking poison and expecting the other guy to die'? That's my only fear. That this wound won't heal. People cheat and do shitty stuff all the time for all kinds of reasons. That's life. But you—Naomi, my daughter—I want you back to your Naomi self."

"So do I." She took her mocha back from him and, after swirling the chocolate that had sunk to the bottom to mix it with the remaining milk, finished it off.

"Do you still love him?"

"I don't know, I don't think so."

"That's an important one to ask yourself. And once you have that answer, you're only halfway home anyway."

"What do you mean?"

"Then you gotta figure out if he loves you."

Naomi was taken aback. She was certain Tomas still loved her.

But should she now probe that question, too? "It all just sounds like a lot of work."

"It does, doesn't it? Eh, screw it. I wouldn't do it. Life is short. Let's go to Little Farm, yeah? Feed some cute animals?"

The Little Farm was just that—a little working farm nearby in Berkeley's Tilden Park—where Bruce and Abigail had taken Naomi many times when she was a child. There were chickens, hogs, rabbits, goats, a few cows, and one could feed them lettuce or carrots.

"Carrots on me," replied Naomi.

DAY 95

TOMAS GOT IN THEIR CAR, drove around the corner, parked, and took out his phone. A Best Buy electronics store. There must be one within an hour of this place. These big box stores, of which the parking lots alone demanded several football fields' worth of cheap space, were often located in less populous areas like this.

Yes. There was a Best Buy about forty minutes away in Valencia.

Tomas drove to the store, asked the clerk for help finding the personal electronics department, and selected a two-hundred-dollar-pair of noise-canceling headphones, very similar to the ones Evo wore. On his way back to Dewey Street, Tomas saw a long line of people outside a restaurant called Pollo Real.

The shadows were long and the orange sun large and low when Tomas got back to 3306. He peered in the window of Evo's van. He noticed for the first time that the back of the sideview mirror was pocked, the chrome worn. He had always wondered, was this just the natural degradation of chrome, or had it been exposed to salt air, or excessive heat? There was Evo, asleep, his head tilted forward uncomfortably, headphones on, in the passenger seat. He must've chosen the passenger seat because the lack of a steering wheel afforded him a few more inches of room to bend his back and neck. But why wasn't he sleeping in the back? Could he not easily lie down? The van was big enough. Or, again, did Tomas need to drop preconceptions and empty his mind when thinking about the greats, who, after all, probably did not share the average man's need for creature comforts?

So the question arose in his mind: did Evo Korman *prefer* to sleep sitting up? It is said that the influential eighteenth-century German art historian Johann Winckelmann deliberately slept in an uncomfortable chair so that he would sleep no more than two or three hours at a stretch, thereby giving him more waking hours to work. There was so much to do and so little time that the man simply tried to create more of it. Was that what Evo Korman was trying to do? The hunched posture of his body looked painful. Surely he had a bunk or cot or sleeping bag in the back? Tomas gently knocked on the window. Evo didn't stir.

No matter. The chicken he brought from Pollo Real was getting cold. Tomas knocked on Lalla Rios's door. She saw him through the peephole and opened the door.

"He hasn't scared you away yet."

"No. Not yet."

"You are twenty feet tall."

Tomas smiled politely but was confused.

"Sorry?"

"Your shadow."

He turned, and indeed, in the waning sunlight, his shadow stretched from her porch to the asphalt of the street. Her home of course, was lengthened, too, partially covering his shadow. He appeared to be a giant looming over her house.

"The only problem is it makes buying clothes very difficult."

She laughed. He noticed a little gold glinting from her mouth. He was intrigued by people who had gold fillings—mostly older people. In his experience dentists were always trying to figure out options to hide the patchwork done on one's corroding teeth—white fillings— but when you went gold, you went big. The choice may have been a practical one for whatever special qualities gold had that were apt for dental work, but for Tomas, it was the lack of vanity, the lack of trying to hide rotting teeth, that impressed him.

"I saw a long line, so I hope that means this place is okay."

He handed her the bag from Pollo Real.

"What is this?" she asked.

"Replacement chicken." Now it was she who looked confused. "The chicken you gave me," said Tomas.

"This is silly. You didn't need to do this."

"You didn't need to feed me."

She nodded, acquiesced. She looked tired to Tomas. Much as he wanted to invite himself in, he said, "I'm exhausted. Been a long day. Take care, Lalla."

"Try to sleep. Sleep is very important."

She shut the door, and Tomas made his way back to Evo's van. No more long shadows. It was now getting dark out. For the first time, Tomas noticed there were very few streetlights on Dewey Street. He looked up and saw stars emerging. He made a point of taking a moment—perhaps fifteen seconds or so—to really look at the stars. If he could spend five minutes savoring a Rothko, letting it wash over him, surely he could and should do the same with something as moving and humbling as the night sky. In time he felt his breathing slowing, his mind and body calming.

He turned his attention back to the Econoline van. Again he peered in the window, and again found Evo asleep in the passenger seat. It's true that he could wait for the man to wake up, but what did it matter? This was Evo Korman, not a young parent trying to keep their baby on a strict sleep schedule. He rapped his knuckles against the window. Evo didn't stir. Tomas rapped again, two short loud knocks. Evo snapped his head back, and noticed, with unwanted surprise, that the man had returned. He rolled down the window.

"What?"

"Headphones. Bought you some new ones."

"What? Why?" asked Evo groggily.

"The ones you have now—only the right side works."

"I didn't ask you what was wrong with my old ones; I asked you why you bought me new ones."

"Well, I guess it kinda drove me crazy—just the one side working—so I thought it might be driving you crazy, too." Tomas craned his neck and peeked, could see that the back of the van was filled with what looked like cobbled together recording equipment.

"Look, stop trying so fucking hard. Here's the deal: I don't have any copies of the 'Blistered Eye' single to give you—I hear they sell for two grand a pop now. Go on eBay. I got no old bumper stickers, no flyers. I don't hang on to old stuff."

"I have copy number three hundred and sixty-two of 'Blistered Eye,'" Tomas replied. "I'm not here for stuff. You said your ears ring and that the headphones help. So, I thought new headphones would help. I would think helping only one ear and not both might be just as crazy making as the tinnitus itself."

Tomas had researched tinnitus on his phone. The high-pitched ringing could drive a person mad. The typical sufferer was someone exposed to prolonged loud noises: those in the military, musicians, heavy equipment operators. And sometimes it just happened as one got older. There was no cure, only feeble mitigation. If you were one of the lucky ones, you became acclimated to it, perhaps with the help of antianxiety meds and a bedside white noise machine. If you were unlucky, deep depression could set in, dropping a gray veil on your world. Some people, not many, but some, finally could take it no longer and took their own lives to silence permanently the incessant, maddening high-pitched squeal.

"Do you remember the interview you gave where you said the fame and the girls and the parties all bought you pleasure, but not happiness?"

"No, but it sounds like me," answered Evo.

"Sounds like you weren't happy then."

"Probably not. So?"

"Are you now? Happy."

"Happiness is overblown. Comes and goes. Peace of mind is where it's at."

"Do you have peace of mind?"

Evo looked at Tomas with a pinched, careworn expression. "I know it's what I *should* want." He paused. "I was sleeping."

"I'm sorry, I thought, since you were sitting up, maybe you were just resting your eyes."

Resting your eyes. When Tomas would fall asleep during one of Naomi's beloved old movies—*All About Eve, The 39 Steps, My Man Godfrey*—she'd ask, gently irritated, if he was asleep, and he would always startle awake, answering, "No, I'm just resting my eyes."

Naomi would pause the movie—say *The 39 Steps*—and ask him,

"Okay, what's the last thing you remember?" Tomas would answer truthfully—they were on the train, and the priest was looking at the brassiere salesman funny, and Naomi would catch him up on what he had missed. And he would say, matter-of-factly, "Okay, got it," and Naomi would elbow him, which he knew meant you can't "get it" without watching *all* of it, without moment-to-moment narrative context, without seeing the faces of the players, or Hitchcock's wry sense of humor played out even in the smallest of character roles.

"It's like saying you 'get' *Look Homeward Angel* by reading the Wikipedia summary," said Naomi. "There's no joy there, only desiccated bits of information."

"*Desiccated.* You trying to show off now?"

"I got a six seventy on my SAT verbal. It comes natural," said Naomi.

"Can we talk about how many times you mention your SAT verbal scores?"

"No."

She would shift and burrow and smush her head into his chest until it was comfortable and then turn the movie back on.

Evo rubbed his bloodshot eyes. "I don't want to be your friend. I don't know why you're here, and I'm not curious enough to find out, so enjoy the rest of your journey somewhere else." Evo tried to hand Tomas the headphones back, but Tomas just turned and left.

Tomas found a Value Inn two stops farther on the freeway, drank no alcohol, and tried desperately not to think of the brassiere salesman in *The 39 Steps*. Even here, four hundred miles away from a town in which no street corner, bar, or restaurant reminded him of Naomi, he struggled not to think of her, of their shared past. They *were* good together. The banal moments, the big moments, the little things, the inside jokes, the serious talk, the banter, even the sexual chemistry, were still there—the raging fire had cooled to an ember, naturally, but still radiated plenty of warmth. Tomas briefly wondered if they had moved up the adoption list, but successfully fought the urge to check his email.

He idly flipped through TV channels, thinking to himself, well, a recording studio crammed into an old Econoline van explained the lack of space to stretch out one's body and sleep in a normal position. But it just looked so excruciating. Great man though Evo was, sleeping in the front seat, stooped over, not having a bathroom for those middle of the night pees—that can't feel okay. Written accounts never mentioned whether Winckelmann had awful back or neck pain, or what affect sleep deprivation had on his mood.

The greats were the greats, but they were still trapped in mortal, achy bodies.

DAY 124

NAOMI STEPPED BACK, shut her eyes tight and silently counted to thirty before opening them again—a little trick so she could see her work fresh. She had started doing it as an undergrad in architecture school. On the night before a project was due; when the Wurster studios buzzed with nervous, exhausted energy; when students ran to and fro borrowing scraps of chip board, balsa wood, and X-Acto knife blades from each other; when they attempted to fight off exhaustion with caffeine and Adderall; when chaotic energy enveloped everything, she would step ten feet away from her desk, shut her eyes, silently count to thirty, and open them. Then she would know whether her models and drawings, after days of frantic last-minute changes, looked great, or looked like shit. She would know then whether she had four or five hours left to get it right, or whether she could go home, grab a shower, and come back for the critique refreshed.

She opened her eyes and looked at the Rock Candy Garden. Soft hues of blue and pink and red and green reflected off her skin, off the sheen of sweat on her forehead, nose, and cheeks. Had there been a shower in the Macy's bathroom, she could've taken one. She had time to spare. It was perfect. Nothing to add or subtract. A magical landscape evoking distant planets, strange formations in the American desert, and, of course, dyed crystals of sugar on a ridiculous scale.

She was happy. She was proud. She was exhausted. It was 5:06 p.m., November 23. In twenty minutes or so the butcher paper would come down and the public would see her creation for the first time.

"God that smells good," she said aloud. She turned and found Garrett holding two bags of roasted chestnuts.

"Got one for you."

"Y'know, I actually don't like chestnuts, but I like the *idea* of chestnuts."

"No one likes chestnuts," replied Garrett, chomping on one, "but it's like yams at Thanksgiving. You eat it because it's tradition. This tastes awful," he said cheerily of the chestnut. "But, y'know, scent memory."

Naomi said nothing. Her smile had flattened. She wasn't frowning, but she seemed to have left her body.

He couldn't tell what, if anything, her eyes were focused on. "Naomi?"

That smell. It *was* magical, intoxicating. Transportive. Suddenly time collapsed for Naomi. The past became present.

It was the twenty-third of November, 2022. She had just completed her second window for the store. She was inside a display window when she had noticed a section of blue painter's tape had peeled back from the butcher paper, exposing a sliver of window. From just the right angle people would be able to see into the display, and she needed another two, three minutes to adjust the giant gift boxes she had constructed from heavy cardboard and covered in bright foil—silver, red, pink, green, and patterns she had sourced from a high-end wallpaper company: paisleys, repeating fleur-de-lis, plaids—just right. Inside the boxes were the beautiful puppies—Labs, dachshunds, shepherds, bulldogs, mixes of all kinds, on unseen platforms that allowed them to crawl out of the boxes and plop down onto the "snowy" ground made of cotton and stuffing and enough glitter to make a Pride parade seem stodgy.

She stepped toward the window to put the tape back up, glanced out the six-inch-wide exposed section of glass, and jumped back in horror. She peeked again. It was worse than she first thought. Not only were Tomas and Tomas Sr. and his wife June there, but she could also make out their friends Omar and Maya, and then there was Bruce and his wife Angela, and Tomas's sister Clarissa with her husband Andre, and of course Abigail and Marivel. She quickly put the drooping butcher paper back up and secured it with more blue tape.

Had they seen her? She didn't think so. There was no way her mother or Marivel was behind this. Omar and Maya didn't have everyone's contacts, so they were out. No, her first thought had to be the correct one: Tomas had organized this little stunt, this embarrassing catastrophe. He knew—everyone who knew her knew—that she hated surprises, hated being the center of attention. Yes, it was impressive that he could herd these cats—when had he contacted Bruce? That required a flight out here. If Tomas's father was here, it meant he'd had to ask him to come, and the man never had free time. What arm twisting, what blackmail, had Tomas used?

"You ready?"

Garrett poked his head in. It was time.

"No," said Naomi reflexively.

"It's great, you know that, right?"

"No, sorry, yes of course I'm ready. I'm gonna step out. It's hot in here."

As she did, several young workers followed Garrett in and they begin taking down the butcher paper, unrolling long swaths of it, exposing the puppies, the gift boxes, the Christmas of it all. Naomi stepped out of the store and could hear the crowd oohing and aahing. Her family and friends weren't the only ones who had gathered for the annual unveiling of the Macy's display windows.

She squinted to make sure she saw what she thought she saw. Yes, Tomas Araeta, Sr. was smiling and talking to Marivel and Abigail. Abigail was beaming. Tomas tossed a silver flask he pulled from a blazer pocket to Omar, who took a healthy swig before handing it to Maya.

Clarissa's eyes sparkled in front of the pretty shiny boxes and pups. Her husband Andre was laughing. Everyone seemed, well, happy, to be getting along.

"Bubble! You're an absolute genius." Bruce was the first to spot Naomi. She was standing awkwardly at the entrance to the store, leaning against a wall. Bruce turned back to everyone and yelled again, "This is all *my* genes!"

"It's wonderful."

"The artist herself!"

"Damn, this is what you do for a job?"

"Impressive. There's just no other word for it."

"You just ruined Christmas for the rest of the world."

"This is great, and I hate Christmas, and I hate dogs."

"You did it. Again."

The voices came in a cacophony. She recognized them all individually, but they were all gushing at once, one comment overlapping the other. It just seemed like everyone was, well, freaking out. Her cheeks burned. She glanced back at the store, but realized she had no good excuse to run back inside. Tomas, smiling, eyes a little glazed, walked over to her. He took both her hands in his. She tried to pull her hands away, but he wouldn't let go.

"I'm sorry, I know you don't like this, but I made an executive decision."

"This is . . . embarrassing. Awkward. And you knew it would be. For me."

"I did."

He released her hands. She folded them across her chest.

"You've been drinking, too," she said.

"Of course. My family's here."

Maya yelled out, "Speech!"

"This isn't cute, Tomas."

He nodded. "So here's the deal," he said. "I don't care. You don't know how to take a compliment. You shrug it off, you mumble, you shit on yourself, and I don't like that. You need to *bask*. You need to let people vomit their love and praise all over you. You're fucking great, you have to know that, and I'm gonna make you know it."

"*There* you are."

Naomi and Tomas turned to see a trim middle-aged man dressed casually in well-fitting slacks, crisp white shirt, and a cashmere V-neck sweater approaching them.

"Mr. Turner," said Tomas, hoping he had remembered Garrett's last name correctly.

"Please, Garrett."

"Well—*Garrett*," said Tomas, gesturing to the group, "these are all Naomi fans."

"It's only a small group of human beings that aren't," replied Garrett. He turned to Naomi. "I'm so glad you invited your friends and family—it's special—I'm glad you decided to share the big moment."

"Actually," said Naomi, indicating Tomas, "He did this. I had no idea."

"Oh. Well. Now that's some powerhouse husbanding right there."

"If you know my wife, then you know she's not big on compliments." Garett flashed a small smile of agreement. "But this year—Garrett—I say fuck it; these people all love her. She's all kinds of talented, and she never takes the time to just enjoy being great, being Naomi."

"Agreed."

Tomas took Naomi's hand—she couldn't pull it away now that her boss was next to her, and her friends and family were all staring. Tomas led her to the group. From one of the boxes a black-and-white corgi puppy struggled to crawl over the edge before flopping onto the platform.

"Is that corgi for sale, Bubble, or do I just break the glass and take my chances?" asked Bruce.

"You might need to get in line behind me," said Marivel.

Bruce held out the bag of chestnuts he was holding to share with others. He found no takers.

"You killed it!" said Maya to Naomi. "I bow."

"It's . . . joyous. Very nice," stammered Tomas Araeta, Sr.

"That's my husband's version of gushing," added June.

"You're my joy," said Abbie.

The gushing just didn't stop. It was all a blur of hugs and praise for Naomi. Finally a loud voice cut through the swirl.

"A toast!" yelled out Tomas. In addition to his personal flask, he had stuffed a fifth of Jameson's whiskey in his back pocket—only an inch or two of it could be jammed into his jeans—yet he had somehow kept it from falling to the ground. "I'd say thank you all for coming tonight," yelled Tomas, "but—" He turned first to the window, then clasped Naomi's hand—"I know it really is *your* pleasure to be here. *Your* honor. So you're welcome." He handed the bottle to Naomi, who, after a moment's hesitation, took a swig, a big swig, a tilt-your-head-back-and-guzzle swig. Everyone cheered. She tossed the bottle of Jameson's to Bruce, who took a gulp and passed it along.

"Naomi—speech!" yelled Maya after taking her sip.

"Yes, speech!" echoed Clarissa.

"Don't hold back, Bubble!"

"Well," said Naomi, scanning the expectant faces, "If I had known you'd all be here, A) I wouldn't be here, and B) I would've worn my dress overalls." They all laughed. *This is my wife*, thought Tomas. *She's pissed, but she's so goddamn generous and gracious that she will say just the right thing at the right moment, which is a rare talent, and, bonus, it allows me to calm down now so she can punish me later, privately. That's class.*

"This isn't just the whiskey talking," said Tomas, "but mostly it's the whiskey talking, but I'm so grateful that you're all here, and I'm happy to see you all here. And it's also definitely not the whiskey talking when I say it really is our gift to have Naomi in our lives. That we're in her orbit is a gift that none of us—well, no—yes, actually, none of us—deserve, but we've somehow hit the lottery." Was he overdoing it? He decided he didn't know or care because he knew he was speaking honestly. He turned to the window. "Look at this. Naomi's been working on this thing day and night for two months. *Two months.* There is a shit ton of work on display here, but it's so damn Naomi that all we see is the joy in it."

"And the dog shit!" Omar yelled out. Everyone glanced at the window, and sure enough, a nervous little bulldog puppy was emptying its bowels on the glittery snow.

"Don't worry, we'll hose it down every few hours," said Naomi.

"I love it. Puppies are even cuter when they get the nervous shits," said Andre.

"I agree with Tomas. It's wonderful to see all of us here, together, for something this special," said Abbie.

"It's very nice," said Tomas Sr.

"Oh good lord, I really do need to teach my husband how to gush correctly," said June. "Naomi, I feel like I'm six again. This is—just well—wonderful. Magical. I can't stop smiling."

Tomas caught Marivel's glance. She nodded at him with approval. Well there was a first time for everything.

Naomi took in all their faces. They were smiling, laughing, drinking.

Tomas squeezed Naomi's hand. "I'm sorry. I just had to."

She had a rictus of a smile on her face, politely mirroring all the smiles directed her way. Under her breath she muttered to Tomas, "I'm really glad you did this. Thank you."

DAY 96

PARKED BACK ON DEWEY STREET behind Evo's van, Tomas carefully watched the clock on the dashboard of their silver Hyundai. The thought occurred to him: since when had silver become the default color of boring sedans? Never mind that. He had decided that noon was a good time to bother Evo. The digital clock blinked 12:00, and he stepped out of the car. He approached and again found Evo asleep—again in the passenger seat—head and upper body slumped forward.

God, the man looked fragile. Tomas inhaled sharply and rapped on the window—Evo startled awake. For a moment he looked at Tomas without the slightest hint of recognition. But the synapses started firing, and Evo unrolled the window.

"This wasn't charming yesterday, and it's not charming today."

"I want to show you something."

Evo ignored Tomas, exited the van, knocked on Lalla's door, and disappeared into the house. He left the van unlocked. Tomas helped himself to a look inside. The back was indeed lined with racked audio equipment, two guitar stands, a computer and equipment which Tomas couldn't identify. So it was true. Evo *was* recording songs inside this shitty old van. No wonder he didn't have room to stretch out to sleep, and of course there was no space for a small toilet or bathroom. So he was tied to Lalla Rios's home for basic private needs.

Who was this woman? Why did she accommodate him? The

kindness of strangers. It was people like Lalla Rios for whom that phrase had been invented. Was she lonely after the death of her husband and the infrequent visits of her children? Yes, she had said so. Was her connection to Evo Korman a matter of enlightened self interest—he got use of her bathroom, and she found renewed purpose in helping this man. Perhaps he made her feel less lonely?

"Sneak in my van again and you'll be pulling your teeth out of my knuckles."

"Sorry. I was curious—"

"Obviously. Can I rummage around in your car when you turn your back?"

"Actually, I wouldn't care, but I'm sorry I didn't ask. I was thinking about how to maximize your space." Evo frowned before he smiled.

"I've heard some tortured, strange lies from people about gawking at my stuff, but 'maximizing space' is by far the worst." Tomas squirmed past Evo to get out of the van. "You said you had something to show me. If it's not coffee, I'm not interested."

"Oh. Okay."

Tomas returned ten minutes later with two coffees. Through the front windshield, Tomas could see that Evo wasn't in the passenger or driver's seat. He was in the back of the van. He knocked on the back doors. Evo opened up.

"Black, no sugar—hope that's okay?"

Evo took the coffee, was about to retreat into the van and shut the doors.

"What are you working on?"

"Working on?"

"Inside."

"Same as everyone: distraction, things that keep me bemused for a minute."

"Music?"

Evo stared at Tomas. Tomas stared at him.

"When the bottle hit my head, I didn't really feel anything. The first thing I remember is the taste of my own blood when it ran into my mouth. Y'know that metallic taste. I thought of when I was a kid and used to get nosebleeds, and sometimes the blood would go down the back of my throat, and it was that same taste."

Tomas didn't realize he had been staring at Evo's beer bottle scar.

"So—Evo—I do want to show you something."

"I wanted to thank him for throwing the bottle—I was happy, bemused—but I never found out who he was."

Tomas unfolded a piece of paper with a pencil sketch on it. "I wonder if there are times when it's inconvenient to use the Rios bathroom."

"I can piss or shit anywhere. This is just nicer. But I don't need it. It could go away tomorrow, and I wouldn't care."

Tomas held out his sketch.

"I've designed this contained box—it's basically an extra compact outhouse—but it would fit in your van—I'd have to measure—and even if you didn't have a water supply, I've fitted a five-gallon tank for it. And then on top, there's no reason not to have a little bunk for sleeping. You would bump your head if you sat up, but you could stretch out."

Evo listened to Tomas, looked over the sketch.

"A toilet for a crusty old punk you once worshipped, eh?"

"Yes."

"Staggering. Any other grand projects up your sleeve?" said Evo, turning to go back into the van.

"I'm working on my marriage. I cheated. And I need to build you this toilet."

Evo turned back to face Tomas. For the first time he smiled openly, that glorious twisted tooth on full display.

"What?" asked Tomas.

"Congratulations. I'm bemused."

DAY 127

"WOW, THE WATER STINKS WAY LESS than I remember," said Maya.

"Gentrification sucks," said Naomi. "I remember, like fifteen years ago—do you remember Martin? He was in that band Bipolar Opposite?"

"Dimples and the beard, super hot?"

"Well, yeah, he was cute."

"Ohmygod, did you guys—"

"I was already dating Tomas."

Maya scowled.

"So why didn't *I* fuck him?"

"I have no idea."

"Shame on me."

"And so much less goose shit out here these days on the lawn."

"Right? The lake is so different."

Naomi had picked a day date with Maya—renting a pedal-powered fiberglass boat on Oakland's Lake Merritt. Tomas had done the same on their fourth date. It had been a sun-bleached green boat, Naomi recalled.

"Remember 'Hands in the Estuary, Torso in the Lake'?" Naomi asked of Bipolar Opposite's one song that got a little bit of local college radio air play.

"I just remember everyone saying it was true they did find a hand in the estuary *and* a torso in the lake. But they didn't match, different bodies, that was the thing, right?"

"Back then you could get a one bedroom in Oakland for eight hundred bucks," sighed Naomi.

"I miss the old days, well, in parts," said Maya.

"The hands or the torso?"

"Pa dum pum! Naomi coming in strong with the mom jokes."

"I mean, sure," said Naomi, "I'm thirty-nine, I like fancy cheese, and I don't stay in youth hostels anymore, but an occasional body part in Lake Merritt, just once in a blue moon—a hand, maybe just a finger—wouldn't be the worst." The two women said nothing for a moment. They had stopped pedaling. The boat drifted idly in the middle of the lake.

Naomi looked at her old friend, shielded her eyes from the sun, and asked, "Hey, so, not to be a buzzkill, but I'm hurting, and you haven't answered my question."

"Because I don't want to," said Maya.

"Why not?"

"Should've brought sunglasses," said Maya. She shielded her eyes, too, so she could see Naomi's face clearly.

"Because I cheated on Omar."

"*What?*"

"Yeah. I did."

"You did? You cheated on Omar? When? And why didn't you tell me? I mean, we've only talked about me and Tomas like every time I see you."

Maya could see how hurt Naomi was that she hadn't confided in her earlier.

"Shame."

Without realizing it, Naomi exhaled deeply and slowly.

"Okay," said Naomi. "So—again—you? Cheated. On Omar?"

"Five years ago," said Maya. "It lasted, like, three hookups."

"Why didn't you come to me then, or even after?"

"I told you. Shame. I was ashamed. It's not like I didn't *think* about telling you. But it would've ruined everything. The four of us were like the Four Musketeers, and we would have had this stupid elephant in the room every time we hung out. Every moment I'd be thinking, Are they thinking about what I did? Are they feeling bad for Tomas? Are they angry? Maybe you would've just ghosted me, I don't know. I was scared."

"Wait," said Naomi, "so that means you were worried—*right away*—about what our *future* get togethers would be like?"

"Yeah, it would just be hanging there."

"No, I know, but did you know—did Omar know—right away, that you would get past this and stay together?"

"Oh. I don't know. I guess, yeah, I guess I did have a gut instinct. I must have. And, far as I know, Omar didn't tell his friends, either. At least not Tomas." Maya looked to Naomi for confirmation.

"He would've told me, so no, Omar didn't tell him."

Naomi was trying to put the pieces together—trying to understand how Maya—but especially Omar—in the heat of it all, reeling from the initial sucker punch that leaves one gasping—had not just blurted it out to everyone. How they *both* worried *right away* about the future, as if they both still saw a future together, even in the raw early days.

"On bad days it still eats my ass," added Maya. "But I'm trying not to let that . . . decision . . . define me, or me and Omar. But it's work. And Omar's pretty much been a saint about it."

"So I guess you don't think I should divorce Tomas?"

"It's a fuck ton of work, that's all I can say."

"I've been hearing that a lot," said Naomi.

Maya looked apologetically at Naomi, as if she wished she had even the tiniest pearl of wisdom to impart. "Because it is." Something suddenly occurred to Maya. "Hey, remember Roger and . . . fuck, what was his girlfriend's name . . . Fiona? I wanna say Fiona."

Naomi shook her head.

"They were epic. He cheated on her left and right, like *all the time*, and they would put away a bottle of tequila before noon. Yelling, screaming, bare-knuckle shit. I remember we were in this bar once and they started fighting and she broke the door off a men's room stall to get to him. Beat his ass."

"Wow, she's living my fantasy," said Naomi.

"She'd go after his skanks, too! Beat them up. And *then* they'd make up. All lovey-dovey. And do it all over again. It's like, they were living out every country song ever."

"Now I really wish I did remember them."

"I bet they're still together," said Maya. "We sit here, at least I did, sweating every word, all eggshells and shit, and they just fucking get wasted, fight it out, start humping again, start cheating again—lather, rinse, repeat."

"Yeah, why can't we be like that?"

"Bad genes?" said Maya.

Naomi nodded slowly.

"What happened, Maya? Why did you do it?"

Maya planted her feet on her pedals, Naomi did the same on her side, and they pushed the little boat forward, no particular destination, just moving. It was a crisp, clear day. A perfect day to be on the lake.

"This is gonna sound lame, and probably super unsatisfying, but it's a weird casserole of reasons. I was bored. I felt unappreciated. I would get out of the shower naked, and he would walk past me to get to the closet, and he didn't even glance at me anymore. I was furniture. Work sucked. I mean, it's work, right? It was fine, but making change at the bank was just . . . filling time and paying rent. There were some regulars I liked talking to, and a couple coworkers I liked—one of them was the guy I stepped out with—but I wasn't really doing anything. Stephen flirted with me, and he looked at me *that way*, even with my frumpiest clothes on and puffy eyes from a hangover. And one day we were all getting drinks after work. Everyone else was yawning, time to go. But Stephen and I stayed a little longer."

"That was the first time?"

Maya nodded.

"Why didn't you break it off with Omar? Or quit your job? Why didn't you just go?"

"I should've just tried heroin or gone bungee jumping or something," said Maya.

"Yeah, but when the excitement wears off?"

"Shit, I still loved Omar. I was unhappy, but I realized I loved him. I didn't love Stephen. I had a crush. And I just—I didn't want to deal with our problems, or my problems—god, I spent months in therapy just trying to figure out which problems were *ours*, and which were *mine*—it's like a hundred and forty bucks a pop just to get to zero."

"We tried a session, but all I wanted to do was hurt him," said Naomi.

"Cool."

"What did he do when he first found out?"

"I thought he was gonna hit me, go all Fiona, y'know? He had this look in his eye—I mean, not really, that's not him—but he threw a bunch of plates around, broke some stuff, which was kind of surprising and awesome. He yelled at me, and I slept on the couch for like three months. I took my lumps. Honestly, Naomi? I think I got off easy."

"Yeah," murmured Naomi noncommittally.

"How angry are you?"

Naomi took a breath before answering. "A lot. I'm angry. And hurt. And sad."

"Well, then, to answer your question, there's hope. You still feel."

Maya wiped a beaded line of sweat from her upper lip and started peddling vigorously. Naomi didn't. She just looked at the sun glinting off the water.

"You and Omar. Fuck. Guess it really can happen to anyone."

From the pocket of her hoodie, Maya pulled out two beers she'd snuck onto the boat, popped them open.

"Bless you," smiled Naomi. "No wonder I'm friends with you."

"Even now. Now that you know?" Naomi hadn't seen the question coming. Nor had she given it any thought. Maya was keeping her voice cool and modulated, but her worry was obvious. "You're really not furious at me?"

Naomi gulped her beer.

"I'm not. I'm *not* angry at you," said Naomi, surprised at her own feelings on the matter. "I'm mostly curious. I want someone to tell me how this goes."

"Well, it's not one size fits all. But yeah, if you both still love each other, then, yeah, maybe you can get past this."

"But it's a fuck ton of work."

Maya smiled and nodded. Naomi raised her beer can and smiled back.

"Weird," said Maya. "Me and Omar always thought you guys were perfect together. I mean, you, in particular, all blissed out and sweet, so of course Omar and I already know you have another secret house somewhere with a crawl space full of corpses. 'cause there's just no way."

"I've never claimed to be perfect."

"No, but you quietly ooze it."

"No I don't."

Maya smiled.

"Okay, fine. Give me one really nasty thing you did to Tomas."

Naomi didn't like being put on the spot, and she especially didn't like having to turn the microscope inward, and she hated most of all that she felt she *should* turn it inward at this moment.

"There's lots of stuff," she said defensively, "but what just popped into my head was when I bought him this book of Julius Shulman's photography—these amazing black-and-white photos of midcentury houses—for his birthday, right up his alley. And right after he says, 'thank you,' he says something like, 'more proof that I'm not great.'" And it just went downhill from there. I was tired of his moods, y'know, tired of all his little comments. I remember he used the word 'hack.' I think he was hoping I'd say, 'No you're not,' but I didn't. And it was his birthday, a day that *should* be about him, but not in that way. And I just snapped. I said, 'You say you're a hack. I agree. But can't you be a happy hack?'"

"Ouch."

"Yeah. I know. I wanted to hit him where it would hurt the most."

"Sounds like you hit the bullseye."

"I did. I hate that I had it in me to do it."

"So—not perfect?"

Naomi smiled ruefully and shook her head.

"Hey, look," said Maya, "sure, you said some mean-ass shit to him, but he can be a pouty bitch. I mean, sure, he's funny and smart and all that, and I've seen you guys good together, but if I hear him say that guy's name again, Mize—"

"Mies van der—"

"I'll kill him. And no jury would convict."

"Get in line," said Naomi.

The two old friends raised their half empty cans again.

"Omar's not a saint because he stuck around. He's a saint because he hasn't *held this against me*. He could keep it in his back pocket and yank it out whenever he wants to hurt me. But he hasn't."

"You're right, he is a saint. Or he's just waiting for the perfect moment to cunt punt you," said Naomi, the beer settling in, making her feel a little logy in the warm sun.

"True! He might be saving it for like Christmas dinner or something, who knows?"

"Not even a little? I mean, he doesn't needle or guilt you even a little?"

"Well, yeah, in the beginning when he was crazy hurting. But after we decided to make a go of it, no. And I don't know if he talked to Jesus or Mohammed or Dr. Phil or an actually great therapist or just decided on his own, but he hasn't since. If he had, Nomes, I would've left. I told him so."

Naomi blinked, her mouth slightly agape. "Wait. You cheated, and then *you* put conditions on getting back together?"

"Had to. It would've corroded the shit out of us if I hadn't."

"Wow."

"Yeah. Wow. *That's* what makes him a saint."

Naomi shook her head in admiration and disbelief. "I'm not a saint," she said flatly. "And I'm not even sure I want to try to make it work. But I just don't know. I need to think, to *not* think, y'know?"

"Yeah. I do."

Naomi took a deep breath, then quietly mused to herself, "You and Omar. Wow."

"Yeah. Me and Omar."

Naomi nodded. Fatigue was setting in.

"Call it?"

"Yup."

They headed back to the dock to return the boat. Naomi was silent. *How can I forgive Maya and not forgive Tomas?* she asked herself. She then smiled thinking of something Tomas often said: "I love *other people's* drama, just not my own." Maybe it was just that simple, Maya didn't hurt *her*, she hurt Omar. And mazel tov that they could put it back together. But what of Naomi's principles of honesty and communication? Were her principles something she only selectively applied? Only to Tomas, not others?

Nothing felt certain.

DAY 96

"**I'M OUT OF IDEAS** to fix my marriage."

"So you decided to bother me instead," said Evo.

"Yeah. I guess."

"Lots of people out there to bother."

"I had a thought, okay a request," ventured Tomas. "Would you write a song for my wife? If I had your talent, I would do it myself. Something about how I love her. But I don't know what it is. Maybe an apology song. I don't know." Tomas paused for emphasis. "Works in the movies—guys serenading their girls."

"I don't work on commission, and I definitely don't work under pressure from other people."

"Yeah," said Tomas thoughtlessly, "guess we're both out of inspiration. It's okay, it was a ridiculous Hail Mary, anyway. I'm gonna go the hardware store." Tomas left.

Evo stood motionless, furious. Who was this little shit to lump himself in with the creator of "Blistered Eye?" He muttered to himself, mimicking Tomas. "Guess we're *both* out of inspiration." And some absurd notion about building a toilet bed? This clean-cut looking guy was seriously messed up.

Evo climbed back into his van, shut the doors, and plucked around on his 1964 Airline with some sound snippets he had been working on. A half-formed riff here, an up-tuned chord there.

Nothing was right. Within a few minutes, he dropped the guitar to the floor and turned off the computer. He took three blue 1 mg tablets of clonazepam, opened a beer, sat in the passenger seat, and went in and out of turbulent sleep.

Tomas had researched "van toilets" online. REI carried two very simple and inexpensive solutions. The Reliance Flush-N-Go retailed for $109.95 and consisted of two parts that snapped together: a seat and bowl, which were connected to a gray plastic five-gallon tank that one emptied when full. For $19.95, he could buy the Reliance Luggable Loo toilet, which was a toilet seat mounted directly to a standard five-gallon bucket. It was cute, a little cheeky, fun. But where to dump the wastewater? This was the issue. In both these designs, Evo would have to detach the base and find a suitable place to dump his waste. On Etsy Tomas found the Road Commode Composting Toilet for $325, the base of which was somehow set up to turn shit and piss into compost. At least that way Evo would be creating fertilizer. Was Evo the composting type? Maybe, maybe not. Impossible to guess.

But anybody could buy some version of a portable toilet. Tomas wanted to create something unique, something beautiful. The sample toilets he looked up all followed that old Modernist trope, *form follows function*, and were elegant enough in their simplicity, but were they *inspired*? Did they gift the user with joy in addition to functionality? That elusive quality where all the programmatic requirements of the design brief had been met, and then the designer stretched, went beyond what was asked of him or her, and made a thing of beauty and joy?

Over the next few hours Tomas puzzled over the wastewater question. There was just no way to connect a moving vehicle to a city sewer line or septic tank. It was simply contrary to the purpose of having a home on wheels—it was smashing a round peg into a square hole.

And then it struck Tomas. Stop shying away from the wastewater issue—make that problem a virtue. He liked the humor of the standard five-gallon bucket, so he ran with that. He bought PVC piping, a flat ten-gallon storage tank, metal brackets, and specialized automobile metal fleck paint—gun barrel blue glitter. He perched the five-gallon bucket on a two-step base, hoping to evoke the "throne" concept of the toilet, and then ran PVC pipe down and away from the bucket, painting it in glorious Day-Glo psychedelic colors. With metal brackets, he attached pieces of rot resistant redwood to the toilet's base and ran the wooden frame vertically up and over the toilet, so he'd have something to mount a toilet paper holder to, as well as a shelf above the sitter's head that would have bracketed "wings" that could support a futon. But he knew the colors—the reflective purples, greens, fuchsias, silvers—in a dark van, were the things that would really pop—so he added several small surface mount pill lights to the bottom of the shelf, casting light on the sitter and fleck paint.

How had he ever put Naomi's craft, interior design—the colors, the lighting—beneath his supposedly more elevated pursuit of "frozen music"? The brief for creating beautiful store display windows was, on its face, simple: get customers to stop and enter the store. But how do you *do that*? We are bombarded by alluring images designed to create desire every day. One has to distinguish oneself from the competition, from skilled designers trained in making us feel something is lacking in our lives, and that a purchasable object—be it a car or sweater—can fill that void. One must create arresting displays that are simply delightful, that leave children and the young of heart, maybe even those whose hearts are hardened, gaping at the displays, drawn into the store even if they don't want to buy a thing. And this challenge, her vocation, he had privately thought of as lightweight. Interior decorators just came in to add a light fixture or drape some fabric over the architect's already brilliant creation—putting butter on a piece of toast and acting like you're the baker. She was right to agree that he was a hack.

"What an asshole," Tomas mumbled about himself as he added

clear coat to seal the colors he had chosen to gussy up the exposed PVC piping.

Tomas had been working in the parking lot of a TJ Maxx store that hadn't survived the pandemic. He had ample space and varying sunlight to view his creation. Stepping back, he took a few snapshots of his portable toilet-bed. It looked like a large T, with angled wooden brackets to support the bed platform. An old telephone pole or crucifix, as decorated by the Merry Pranksters or Burners, came to mind. Tomas stood back and stared. He had been at it for forty-eight hours. Had slept in his car. Hadn't noticed time passing.

Without accompanying text, he sent a few pictures to Billy. He thought of sending them to Naomi as well—she had the humor and temperament to appreciate the silliness of it all—but he didn't. It was just too fraught. There were too many ways for her to interpret the photo, and he wasn't even sure she would take from them that he was apologizing for silently denigrating her work because he couldn't see past his own rapacious insecurity and ambition. Maybe she would just take it to mean that he, too, was finally admitting their relationship was in the toilet. Too fraught.

His phone buzzed. A text from Billy.

Nice throne. Now get thee to a shrink.

Tomas smiled. Clearly young master William Sugarman understood what he was doing and the spirit in which he was doing it.

Tomas disassembled the frame, loaded the pieces in his car as best he could, dizzying 4x4s painted with glittering repeating spirals and paisleys and polka dots sticking out the rear windows, and drove back to Dewey Street. The final touch was the flat ten-gallon tank that was to be mounted to the side of the van, visible to other motorists. It was a frosted white tank, semi-translucent, and Tomas had deliberately not painted it. He hoped that Evo would enjoy the idea of passing motorists seeing his waste sloshing around in a plastic tank.

Evo was not in the passenger seat of the van when Tomas returned and did not answer when Tomas knocked on the rear windows and doors. He headed up Lalla Rios's walkway and knocked on her door. She answered, smiling.

"I'm glad you're back. I thought you left for good without saying goodbye."

"You are?" asked Tomas.

"You're not like the others. He doesn't hate you. And I think you're a nice young man. Sad, very sad, but nice."

These goddamn tears! Always popping up out of nowhere. Tomas had never felt less in control of his emotions than he had since it happened. No. Not since *it happened*. Since he had chosen to cheat on his wife.

"It's hot out. I made gazpacho. Come in."

Lalla could see him glancing around for Evo.

"I don't know where he is. I don't think he does either," she added with a wry smile.

She served Tomas a glass of cold, thick gazpacho: tomato, olive oil, water, garlic, cucumber, grapes.

"This is so good, Mrs. Rios. I didn't know how hungry I was."

"I add grapes. It takes away a little of the garlic's power, but you can still taste the garlic. When Amos would come home after a day climbing the poles—he worked for the phone company, too—all he wanted was something cold and light. So I would serve him this, and a can of beer."

"Great wife."

"He deserved it. I worked in an office. We had air conditioning. I felt so bad for him when it got to be ninety, a hundred degrees out." Tomas marveled at what a good relationship looked like. And at the gazpacho he was eating.

"This is great. I mean, really great," said Tomas.

"Peasant food. We used to drink it back home. Tomas?"

He looked at her.

"Why are you crying?"

"Huh?"

"You're crying," she said. "Why?"

"I cheated on my wife," replied Tomas softly. He looked down at the pretty floral tablecloth edged with lace under plastic and wiped at the tears. He couldn't bear to look at Lalla.

"That was one of my two guesses," said Lalla.

Tomas looked up. "What was the other one?"

"That you were sick. Maybe cancer."

"Oh. Yeah. No cancer."

It was quiet and still between them for a few seconds.

"Be honest with her, and with yourself, and what is meant to happen will happen," said Lalla.

The tears flowed even harder as Tomas nodded.

"At our twenty-fifth anniversary, our kids put us on the spot, asked us how we had stayed together for twenty-five years." Tomas looked at her intently. "I just said what came to mind. It's nothing original. I said, 'the grass is always greener on the other side, but then you have to mow two lawns.'" Tomas smiled. "Too much work," added Lalla.

"What did your husband say?"

"That my kids were jerks for putting us on the spot. *Then* he said, 'When you're angry, think once, then think again, then think once more before opening your mouth.'"

"Those are both great answers. From everything you've said, I'm almost shocked that you were ever angry with each other."

"Of course we fought. It would be crazy not to. But I guess we figured out how to fight well. He did, at least. I had the temper. But when I think on it, he would take five or ten seconds to say something when we were fighting. Usually about money or who spent more time taking care of the kids."

"Nothing . . . *bigger*, than that?" asked Tomas.

"No. But that's big enough, believe me. One of our daughters, though. She did what you did." Tomas was hungry for more. "I told her same as you, 'Let it be.' Once you've done what you can, you have to step aside. Time will tell." Lalla added, "Luisa hated that advice. She said it was too vague. And she's right. It is vague. But it is the only way I know. It's how I am able to live with losing him. I hold the joy in my right hand, and the pain in my left. They're both part of me. I have to let that be." Tomas traced a finger over the lace pattern of the tablecloth.

"Thank you for being so kind to me." Lalla looked at him with compassion, worry. "Well, I got some more work to do," continued Tomas. Lalla nodded as he stood. "Thank you, Lalla." He walked toward the front door, but before he reached it, she caught his arm. He turned around and she hugged him. He lowered his head and sobbed into her shoulder. Soon the shoulder of her dress was wet.

"I'm glad I met you," said Lalla. "You try. You do what you can. And then—you let it be."

DAY 111

NAOMI LAY ON HER MOTHER'S COUCH, starting at the ceiling, discerning faces and cloud formations and tangled vines in the old hand-finished plaster. Why? Why jeopardize so much good? What was he thinking—or not thinking? Sometimes she and Tomas would surprise each other with their ravenous sexual appetites. In those moments, it was as if they both had forgotten to eat all day, hadn't thought they were hungry, and then, suddenly realized they were starving and couldn't start fucking fast enough. He would enter her impatiently, too hurried, so that she would have to hold him, slow him, and guide him in, because it could be uncomfortable. But in truth Naomi loved that he was so impatient, that, for whatever reason, he still needed to, as he put it, "fuck you bad and fuck you now."

And he knew what she liked—biting her nipples a little harder as he stroked in and out, leaning forward and kissing her while in the doggy style position, and sometimes surprising her with something she hadn't asked for, teasing her clit with his tongue, licking her then holding back until she squirmed and moaned, offering to use "any and all of my working fingers, hands, toes, nose, or other appendages or devices" (ooh the dirty talk!) if she hadn't come and he had, to help bring her to satisfaction, in a way that still involved them both. He still lusted after her. And she lusted after him, his scent, his cock. It was good. *Why* then?

Why risk so much for so little? Naomi saw a hideously disfigured face with a missing eye in the plaster.

DAY 97

EVO HAD RETURNED. It was time for Tomas to present him with his small masterwork—a pimped out van toilet—to hopefully ease the quotidian needs of the great man's life. The toilet was fine, but it was the bed platform—unnecessary though it might be—that *made* the design. The simple evocation of a crucifix or power pole elevated the concept. Was it necessary in a functional sense? No. Evo was obviously used to sleeping upright. Was it necessary in a Naomi-would-totally-approve-because-this-brings-a-little-more-humor-and-verve to the project sense? Yes.

Tomas left the toilet and its baroque PVC pipe drainage system disassembled in his car. As he approached the Econoline, he heard something. What was that sound? That was *music*. Coming from inside the van. He strained to hear it—was this some playlist, some recording Evo was listening to? No, the starts and stops, the imbalance of treble and bass, the barely audible disapproving muttering.

Evo was playing music.

Tomas didn't dare breathe. This was "the process." He was bearing witness. He could hear the tinny shadow of genius at work. A truly great man was creating. After another minute or so, not wanting to push his luck or jinx anything, Tomas turned to walk quietly back toward his car.

"What are you doing?"

Tomas looked back. The back doors of the van had been flung open. There was Evo, his face pinched, everything about him screaming irritability.

"Nothing."

"You weird little Snoopy dog. You sad, wretched creature."

Tomas looked stricken. He had spent the last two days working on a gift for Evo, and was about to give it to him, when he'd interrupted and angered the man.

Suddenly Evo burst out laughing. "I'm talking about myself, you little pimple."

"Oh," said Tomas.

"'*Oh?*' Shit, I thought *I* was inarticulate and stupid."

"I heard you playing music."

"Is that what you heard?" Evo looked past Tomas, toward the freeway and foothills. "Here's the thing, you presumptuous, greedy little idiot. You ask me to write a song like I can just pull it out of my pocket. Do you even know what you're asking?" Tomas looked down like a chastised schoolboy. "A song is a prayer you throw up into the sky and hope—*hope*—that it slaps people in the face."

"I'm sorry. It's just. 'Blistered Eye.' It's perfect."

Evo hesitated, then spoke. "I know what 'Blistered Eye' is."

All Tomas could think to say was, "Let me put that toilet in for you."

"'Both out of inspiration.' I *have* ideas, you shit, way more than you'll ever have, good or bad. So don't presume to even guess at what I'm about."

Tomas tried to ignore the comment. "This way you won't always have to park here to use Mrs. Rios's bathroom."

"That's why you think I'm here, to use her bathroom?"

Tomas had no idea what to think. "Let me just hook it up. If you don't like it, I'll take it out. I just, lemme do this one thing, and then I gotta take off anyway."

"You're a big fanboy right?"

"Yes."

"Then you know I've never been married. So you'd have a much better chance figuring your shit out at some bookstore or shrink's office than by asking me to write you a song."

"I actually didn't come to you for a song. It just happened."

"Good. Now I will make it unhappen."

"I came to you . . . I came to you, because . . . for a moment . . . I thought about . . . I was in my car . . . I thought about checking out . . . and your song came on the radio, and the DJ told the story about you . . . and I thought it was like a sign . . . that I had to come see you. Maybe help you out."

Evo looked angrily at Tomas. "Did you just tell me you thought about killing yourself because you cheated on your wife, but my song and some bullshit blurb on the radio made you think you oughta keep living because Evo Korman needs help?"

"Is that so strange?"

After a moment, Evo answered. "I don't know."

"I do think I know what's wrong with me, why I really came here."

"Well stop burying the fucking lead. You've already taken more patience out of me than I have."

"I thought I was destined to be a great man. Like you. But I'm not. I'm just a regular guy. I just wanted to die with one building, one anything, that would be *my* 'Blistered Eye.' But I don't think I'm that guy."

Evo visibly calmed. His face relaxed. "'Blistered Eye' was a miracle. And I was lucky, or talented, or stupid enough, or practiced enough, or whatever, to bring it into existence. Do you know what it's like to have 'Blistered Eye' come out of you, and never be able to recreate it again?"

"I'm sorry I asked you to write a song."

"If you're meant to make a beautiful building, it'll happen. If not, it won't. Your marriage? I dunno." Evo looked preoccupied. He had more to say. "There's a million ways to be great. A building. A song. A garden. If I thought I had any chance of holding down a decent relationship with one person, with someone who can put up with my bullshit and my moods, I might just think about trading 'Blistered Eye' for one nice night sitting in front of the TV and feeling close to someone."

"Trade it all for Netflix and chill, huh?"

"Maybe."

"We did a lot of that. Couch and TV. I fell asleep during her movies; she fell asleep during my shows."

Evo looked away from him. "Ingrate," he said. "Fool."

"Let me put that toilet together for you."

"Will it make you feel better? Will it make you feel *great*?"

"It might distract for me a few hours. Bemuse me, even."

Evo gave up a thin smile. "And after that, architect, now listen carefully: go beg and grovel and get your damn wife back."

"Wish it was that easy."

"Told you I'm the wrong guy to give advice on this shit."

Tomas nodded, then narrowed his gaze at Evo.

"Do you really like Katrina and the Waves?"

"Yeah."

DAY 112

"TEA?" ABIGAIL WALKED OUT OF THE KITCHEN holding a small tray with two cups. Naomi turned off the television—another rerun of *Ridiculousness* could wait. She turned and saw her mother holding the tray. Suddenly Naomi was filled with compassion and love for Abigail—"First Time Ever I Saw Your Face" compassion and, for once, not sorrow, but hope and eagerness for what the present moment might hold. Her mother's favorite song was Roberta Flack's masterpiece, "First Time Ever I Saw Your Face." As a child, Naomi hated it. Even if it was "good," her mom would play it three, four, five times in a row. Now the thought of it brought forth the deepest warmth from Naomi, the question, the wondering, whether her mother had been as happy in her life as she deserved to be.

"That sounds great."

Abigail brought in the chamomile tea, sat on the edge of the couch, and placed the tray gently on the coffee table. There were a few butter cookies on a small plate that matched the tray and cups. This was "the good china" Marivel's mother had left them.

"Shouldn't be too hot; I pulled it off before the boil."

Naomi nodded and sipped. "If only chamomile could fix everything." She smiled at her mom.

"If only," said Abigail. "When you were nine, chamomile tea and carrot cake fixed just about everything. You were a strange little girl—you loved chamomile, more than hot chocolate, even. And carrot cake more than chocolate cake."

"Your cream cheese frosting was catnip, Mom. The carrot cake was just a way to get it to my mouth." The two women smiled at each other. Abigail rested her hand on her daughter's knee. There were tears welling in Abigail's dark brown eyes.

"Whether I do it right or wrong, everything I do for you comes from love," said Abigail.

Naomi nodded. The sudden lump in her throat was as big as a softball.

"You're great, Mom. You're a great mom."

DAY 98

"SO. MR. ARCHITECT. I gotta move my bowels soon. You best get cracking."

Something in Evo's tone. Something different. Lighter. Brighter. Tomas looked at him. This morning he was sitting on the floor of the van, back doors open, legs dangling. He jumped up, stood, craned his neck slowly back and forth, ear-to-shoulder.

"I'll write you that love song. In one month I will meet you and your lady, and I'll play it for her."

Tomas, dumbfounded, blurted out, "I'll be right back."

He ran to their car, and, part by part, brought over the toilet and bed crucifix. Evo lay down on the grass median between street and sidewalk, watching a sweaty Tomas assemble this absurd purple, gold, pink, and silver toilet. Evo dozed off. When he woke up, he wandered off, leaving the architect to his work. By the time he returned, dusk was approaching, and Tomas was nearly finished. He was using C-brackets to attach the frosted white waste drain tank to the side of the van.

Tomas glanced at Evo, saw that he was watching him, arms crossed, his broad smile showcasing that marvelous twisted tooth.

"You're gonna put that tank up so people can see my waste products when I drive?"

Tomas nodded.

"You're all right, Mr. Architect. You're all right."

"Okay," said Tomas, wiping his sweaty, dirty hands on his jeans, "so six o'clock p.m. at 2387 Fleming Avenue, November 18." Tomas handed Evo a sheet of paper with handwritten directions on it that would get him—step-by-step, with no room for misinterpretation—from the curb in front of the Rios house to the curb in front of his and Naomi's house. Evo looked over the detailed directions, on which Tomas had added sketches of certain turn offs and lane splits.

"Cute drawing."

"Well, I don't know if you have a cell phone, and, I like sketching anyway."

"But what makes you think I actually want to leave Lalla's curb?"

Tomas took a moment, now unsure if Evo had been putting him on, if he was just being a mercurial genius. Maybe he had no intention of writing that song or delivering it to their home. Maybe it was all a false promise, some kind of test or puzzle meant to jolt Tomas, or just some cruel little diversion to chip away at boredom.

"I don't know. I just—these are just directions to our house," stammered Tomas.

"I'll write you that song, stop pissing yourself—it won't be 'Blistered Eye.'"

"I have no expectations," said Tomas.

"Yes you do. But you've bemused me, and that counts. But I do worry I'm wasting my time over a clueless dumbshit."

"You wouldn't be the first."

"Know this: maybe the song will help; maybe it won't."

"I don't care. I've got to try."

Tomas was exhausted. Suddenly he wanted to leave. To go back home. Evo was a genius, but so what? He was also a mess just like everyone else. And Tomas was tiring of him, tiring of being scolded, tiring of this whole venture to "help" him or distract himself or whatever it was he was doing.

Evo looked at Lalla Rios's front door.

"I've seen you in there. If you haven't gotten what you need inside that house, you'll never get it—not from me, or a song, or a toilet, or anything else you can dream up."

DAY 118

TOMAS STOPPED IN AT AN OLD SAN FRANCISCO HAUNT—the Owl Tree—the facade of the small corner bar was covered with the mosaic of an owl in small black-and-white tiles, the arresting figure and piercing eyes of the creature visible only at certain distances and view angles. Inside, the bar was cozy and calming, surrounding patrons in rich wood paneling, a low coffered ceiling, comfortable booths, and—ten or so years ago—the perennially mood-brightening sight of a resident Golden Lab named Gumdrop, who could always be found at the far end of the bar, splayed out on the carpet. Before the collapse of everything, he and Naomi would stop in occasionally, and, before ordering drinks, would look for Gumdrop, pet her until she or they became tired of it—well, Gumdrop never tired of it—then finally turn their attention to the bartender.

Tomas ordered two gin and tonics in quick succession and finished them in quick succession. In a few minutes he would be heading out for the annual Araeta family reunion.

"Guess Gumdrop isn't around anymore?" Tomas asked the bartender.

"Who?" said the attractive young man with tattoos, three or four beaded bracelets on each wrist, and Jesus hair.

"Ah, never mind, that was a long time ago—cheers." Tomas raised an empty glass, shook his head "no" at the bartender's interpretation that this was Tomas ordering a third G & T, and said, "Have a good night, young man." Yes, the wizened Tomas Araeta, age thirty-six, bidding a polite farewell to this pup, perhaps two years his junior.

Tomas grabbed a Lyft to the Fairmont Hotel. Inside was the destination for the annual family fete, the Laurel Court restaurant. Tomas left their car parked in the east bay, in Oakland, on a street without parking restrictions, to avoid the nightmare that is public parking in San Francisco and the potential risk of getting a DUI in the process of "enjoying" his family's company. So it was BART and Lyft. Tomas Araeta Sr. favored the Laurel Court restaurant, with its Doric columns, tall ceilings, and unimpeachable furnishings. His father's taste was a very small resentment on Tomas's list of resentments toward the man, but one that naturally occurred to him now. On the ground floor, mere steps from the Laurel, was the hotel's own Tonga Room and Hurricane Bar—a Tiki bar committed to a level of illusion and escape that Walt Disney might approve of—"rain" falling from the ceiling, tables roofed by dry grass domes, a lagoon where a band played on a raft that floated back and forth, and tables fashioned from vintage surfboards. A half-assed Tiki bar was just sad. If you were going to go Tiki, you had to go all in, to a level of fanatic detail that Mies himself would find admirable.

But fuck Mies. His buildings may have been perfect, but they weren't *fun*. The Tonga Room was.

Tomas entered the dull, tasteful rotunda of the Laurel at nine-thirty.

"Tomas!" shouted Clarissa. She ran up to him. "I didn't think you'd come."

"That makes two of us."

Clarissa sniffed the air. "Gin and tonic?"

"Ah, well that explains why I'm here!" he said, genuinely happy to see his little sister. She flung her arms around him.

"You're a jerk. Call or visit more."

"So I get a choice?"

"Jerk."

About twenty members of the Araeta clan milled about, their voices growing louder and more animated as the liquor flowed.

"Tomas!" his mother cried out. Sickening guilt filled Tomas. He lived fifty minutes away from his parents but hadn't seen June in a year.

"I haven't seen you in seventeen months!"

"But who's counting?" said Tomas. "Quality, not quantity right?" He flashed his best Araeta smile.

"You look tired."

"You, on the other hand, look radiant, Mother."

"I'm happy you're here, that's all. Where's Naomi?"

"That's why I'm tired. She's sick as a dog."

It was instinctive. The lie. His mother had been burdened enough by his father.

"Oh my god, what happened?"

"No, no, nothing like that—just a nasty flu. She was vomiting all night."

"Oh good Lord. You should march right out of here and tend to her."

He had to get out of this quickly—the lying was nauseating him.

"I should, but I heard the devilled eggs were not to be missed."

She hugged him again.

"Food and more drink for my baby boy." Tomas hated when he called her that, but he loved her, and saw her so infrequently, that he held his tongue and smiled. "*More* drink?" She said it so casually it could've been missed. She, too, clearly smelled the fortifying gin on Tomas's breath, understood it fully, on her way to leading him to the bar and buffet. He really did love June Araeta nee Goolsbee. "I have to tell you, forget the eggs, or at least eat them later. Save your fresh taste buds and hunger for the bisque—it's out of this world this year." She grabbed him by the arm and Tomas instantly stiffened. This had nothing to do with "baby boy." He always felt a little stiff when his mother put her arm through his. To him it felt like the kind of thing lovers do. When had that changed? When had his mother's affections begun to put him off? Was he twelve? Thirteen?

How often had he thought "one day she won't be here," and immediately felt a rush of guilt and sadness about how he would stiffen when she touched him. He had only very recently planned to be a father one day, and he just knew he'd be the type to hold and cuddle and blow raspberries into his child's belly, or even better, provoke them into a state of irritation bleeding into genuine anger with too much tickling. And he also imagined how devastated he'd be when his child would grow up and naturally pull away from him. When his child would resent and resist his physical affection. He took his arm out of his mother's—sensing for a split second the sadness she wouldn't express—and instead, draped it over her shoulder and pulled her in for a hug. Something he never did.

"I miss you, too, Mom." He kept his arm wrapped protectively around her shoulder as they walked. She touched the fingers of his draped hand as she led him to the elegant buffet. Tomas Araeta Sr. was busy talking to one of his brothers but had briefly acknowledged Tomas with a smile and nod. Tomas dished himself up a bowl of lobster bisque as another relative called for his mother's attention.

"Don't you dare French exit me!" she told Tomas as she left his side.

"Promise," said Tomas. Not a moment later Clarissa reappeared.

"Are you here for Dad?" Champagne flute in hand, she took notice of Tomas's eyeline.

Tomas put the bowl of unfinished bisque down. "You first, Mom second, but . . . yeah." His voice was monotone—his affect flat.

"Naomi?"

"Sick."

"You mean sick of *this*? Power to her."

"The flu."

"Hey! Don't mess with my image of your lady. Let's give her spunky mind, not a stupid virus, the muscle in this."

"Let's!" said Tomas with a sudden effusiveness matched only by the fine bubbles in the flute of champagne he took from a passing server. He and Clarissa toasted Naomi.

"To Nomes!" said Tomas.

"May she always have the good sense to ditch us!"

They clinked glasses.

"Gonna say hi to Dad."

"Eeeyup," said Clarissa.

Tomas left his little sister, heading straight for his father. It was now or never. Soon the mellowing champagne and gin buzz that might keep his teeth off edge would fade, or, if he waited, he would in all likelihood get sloppy with one flute too many.

"Dad, do you have a minute?"

Tomas Sr. swiftly turned around. God, the man's posture was irreproachable. Tomas Sr. extended his hand for a vigorous handshake. Anything more between a grown man and his father, in this room, in this time machine, would've felt wrong. Tomas Sr.'s commanding presence, at sixty-six, was impressive. Whenever Tomas had seen his father dressing at home, in his boxer shorts and tank top, his skinny, pasty legs, the sunken aging chest—the body of this great man decaying—it shocked him. His father, clean shaven, in a suit or surgical scrubs, was a force with which to be reckoned. Vulnerable, half naked, he was just a man on the far side of middle age.

"Of course," answered Tomas Araeta Sr.

Tomas led his father to a corner of the large room where two heavy oak chairs faced each other at an angle, a round marble coffee table between them.

"What's wrong?" asked Tomas Sr.

"What do you mean?"

"We're sitting here. At your request. And, well, I'd like to flatter myself that there may be a touch of father's intuition at work."

"There is," Tomas said.

A server swept by and gently put down two apricot brandies on the table. When had Tomas Sr. ordered such specific drinks for them? God the man was good.

"Thank you," said Tomas Sr. to the pretty server who looked to be in her twenties. Tomas wasn't sure whether it actually happened or whether it was a matter of what English soccer commentators called *persistent infringement*, but he could've sworn that his father—with his eyes alone—had just flirted with the younger server.

"What happened?" asked Tomas Sr. after taking a sip of the sweet liqueur.

Tomas was relieved that his father made no small talk about his son's career, his own career, the health of any Araeta in particular, or his daughter-in-law's absence. Tomas Araeta Sr.'s time was precious even here in this "relaxed" social setting.

"I made a mistake, Dad," said Tomas, mindlessly swirling the amber brandy.

Tomas Sr. took another sip of his. "Has she filed for divorce?"

"Yes. Immediately, actually."

"Probably just a rash, visceral response," offered Tomas Sr.

"In part, yes. But, no, Dad, she gave me a side exit years ago, knowing I'm an insecure, egotistical mess, so when I messed up, all she had to do was press the eject button she had installed years ago."

Tomas Sr. gave his son's words some consideration. "I never gave her intelligence its due. Shame on me." For once Tomas didn't resentfully wonder where *his* "due" was. "Do you think she's serious?"

"She wants to sell the house. First time she's called me in months."

Tomas waited for his father's condescending glance letting him know how foolish it was for either of them to let go of precious Bay Area real estate over something as inconsequential as infidelity.

"I'm sorry, Tomas. It's not easy." Tomas Sr. reached over and squeezed his son's shoulder. Tomas froze. It took him a moment to relax and let himself feel the gentle strength of the surgeon's hand. "It won't be easy, but you will both get through this, whatever the outcome. And I can tell you that you may think you know the outcome, but you don't."

"Therapist said the same thing."

"You two are in therapy?" asked Tomas Sr. hopefully.

"Once. It's the most I could get her to agree to."

"I see."

"Dad, I remember when I was in second grade, you moved out for a couple weeks. You and Mom had been arguing for days. Was that because of a mistake?" Tomas Sr. stared at his wife as he answered. Still lithe and graceful in her movements, June swept through the crowd. She made people feel like they mattered. A superpower of his mom's that both Araeta men admired.

"Yes, it was."

"How did you fix it?"

Tomas felt no need to bring up the other affairs he knew had occurred as he became a teen and could sense such things. And maybe—no surely—there had been affairs prior as well, but, for Tomas, age nine, this was the one that felt graver than the others.

"Do you want to remain married?" asked Tomas Sr., now looking his son in the eye.

"I do."

Tomas Sr. nodded, giving his son the respect and trust that he had thought through the answer to this all-important question.

"I don't know that we ever really did fix it."

"You and Mom are still together. You seem, okay."

"Happy enough, you mean?"

"Yeah, happy enough, or you've reached some kind of détente—look at her, she doesn't *look* miserable."

"Never does."

Tomas Sr. again took in the sight of his wife as she lowered her head to speak with a cousin. The two women chatted conspiratorially.

"But I don't know how she really feels, not day to day," said Tomas Sr. "We interact. We're polite. We cohabitate successfully. And I think we weren't the worst coparents. Sometimes we even laugh. For whatever reason, you and Clarissa, the lifestyle, the reaction of others, fear of the unknown—your mother didn't leave me."

"Did you apologize?"

"Of course." And here, God knows why, Tomas Sr. added two words. "Every time."

"Did she forgive you?"

"She said she did." He took another sip of his brandy. "She never deserved any of it."

"No she didn't. I hated you for it."

"Probably still do," added Tomas Sr., glancing at his son with a rueful smile.

"Yes."

Tomas Sr. nodded, continued.

"I said the right things—I think—and I meant them, and she responded as generously as I could hope."

"I still can't tell whether either of you is happy."

"There's a scar there, Tomas. For both of us. Some days we notice it more than others. Some days, rarely, but some days, I believe we both don't notice it at all."

"But—overall—you're at least . . . *content* together, right? I wanna hear there's hope Dad."

Tomas Sr. exhaled, took a moment.

"We have made our peace with it, Tomas."

"Okay. Fine. Peace." Tomas paused before adding, "And happiness?"

Tomas Sr. tilted his head side to side.

"Yes. In moments. Yes."

Tomas took in his father's words. If Naomi decided to take him back, would "moments" of happiness be enough? Would either of them be "content?" How much compromise is too much?

"Naomi is a better person that I am. I'm sick to death that I chipped away at that."

"That's something I think about every day."

Both men said nothing for a few moments. Tomas looked again at his father.

"How did you get Mom to take you back—besides whatever her fears were?"

"Oh, I don't know," said Tomas, Sr., his voice rising as if someone had asked him how he picked the quickest line in the supermarket. "Not exactly—and, of course, I'm too afraid to ask." He looked at his son with an open smile. "Don't want her reconsidering now," he said. "My libido has quieted a bit. I'm just grateful she's still here."

Tomas had never heard such candor from his father. *Informal.* That was it. He had never heard his father speak so informally, so, well, conversationally.

"I do know time helped," said Tomas Sr.

"Don't have much of that, Dad. In sixty-two days the divorce will be final."

"And valium."

"What?"

"When things were at their worst, I insisted we split a valium, have a glass of wine, and talk until we were sick of talking."

"*Valium?*"

"If nothing else, it kept us from yelling for a few minutes and waking the two of you up."

"Did it work?"

"It's just a tool, but yes, it helped. But you and Naomi don't talk?"

"We sorta tried, in the beginning, and the one disastrous session with the therapist," said Tomas, defeat in every syllable he spoke.

"Adulthood is a trial, Tomas. A hateful trial."

"Now I see you why you gave me the Schopenhauer book when I was a kid. You two would've gotten along like a house on fire. The bitter bitch fest would have been epic."

"Probably. But he's mostly right about most things. Please tell me I'm not telling you anything you haven't already realized. You grow up, you make hard choices, and you can't know whether you're making the right choice. Some other philosopher—not Schopenhauer I believe—said, 'life is lived forward, but only understood backward.'"

"Great."

"When I watch your mother sleep, when I hear her laugh, I still care, I still get excited. No other woman has had that effect on me. Just look at her."

June was still chatting with her cousin, resting her fingertips gently on her own sternum. Tomas Sr. looked right into his son's eyes.

"Do you still love Naomi?"

"Yes."

"Then keep fighting." Tomas Sr. reached into his inside blazer pocket. "When I'm desperate and out of options, I go with honesty. And this." He pulled out an orange prescription bottle, tapped ten small blue circular pills into Tomas's hand.

"Valium?"

"Clonazepam. Antianxiety. For acute moments. It'll have the same effect. Good luck."

Tomas stared at the little blue pills before pocketing them. At that same moment, but in far less posh surroundings, another accomplished man in his sixties was taking two of the same pills with a gulp of beer. Tomas Sr. finished the last of his apricot brandy.

"Shall we rejoin the party?"

Tomas nodded and stood up. His father followed him back to the rotunda. Tomas smiled to himself at the thought that the great Tomas Araeta, MD, chief of pediatric neurosurgery at UCSF, didn't just have a prescription bottle in a medicine cabinet at home for his issues—he carried one *on his person*. The great man was prone to fits of anxiety so overwhelming he needed immediate relief on occasion. One could only hope just not before cutting open a child's head.

Tomas tapped his mother on the shoulder. She turned.

"Hi Elizabeth," said Tomas to his mother's cousin.

"Is it the lighting in here or are you getting even more handsome?" she asked.

"I think it's actually the alcohol."

Both women smiled.

"Mom, no French exit tonight. I just want to say goodbye."

"And that you'll call or visit more often?"

"Words out of my mouth."

He hugged her, lowered his head, and whispered into her ear, "I love you, Mom."

"You too, baby boy."

Tomas turned to leave and found his sister—or rather she found him—and was clearly waiting for the debrief.

"Well?" asked Clarissa.

"I knew there'd come a day when I would want to talk to him, Rissa; I just didn't think it would be during my lifetime."

DAY 136

NAOMI WALKED INTO CAFÉ STRADA. She was thrilled that Bruce had, unannounced—except for a text seven hours ago—again decided to pop over to her corner of California. She spotted him at a table and immediately slowed her gait. Wait. No.

Bruce waved enthusiastically for Naomi to join him at a table.

"First mocha's on me," he yelled across the room.

Naomi flashed a false smile, then approached.

"If this is some kind of weird intervention, just don't." Naomi looked at Bruce, then her mother, who was sitting opposite him.

"Hi honey," said Abigail meekly.

"Sit, sit. You standing there is making us nervous," said Bruce.

"You both being here—*together*—is making me far *more* nervous. I know you guys are good now—kumbaya and all . . . but, why? I've talked this to death with each of you."

"I wanted to compare notes with your mom, see what she was thinking."

"Honey, please sit."

Naomi relented, sat down.

"So you two went behind my back to talk about . . . what?"

"Two parents talking about their child is not going behind your back, Bubble," said Bruce, in a troublingly earnest tone. Then he added cheerfully, "Get you a mocha?"

"No."

Naomi looked angrily at Abigail.

"This wasn't my idea. Your father insisted I come."

"That I believe," said Naomi. "You're nothing if not a champion fence sitter."

Bruce and Abigail spoke over each other.

"That's not very nice."

"It's one of my worst flaws."

"Okay, forget the coffee," added Bruce, again in that earnest tone. "Yes, I wanted your mom to be here, and no, we didn't go 'behind your back.' We had a private conversation, and, we felt from our own experience, that we might have something to offer. 'Reality test' as the shrinks say, but actually not in reality. I'm confused. Anyway, I'm not in love with your mom, but—*part of me*—loves her."

"And I love your dad—in my way."

"Well I couldn't be more tickled that the two of you 'love each other' with some kind of weird asterisks there."

Bruce and Abigail said nothing, then Bruce spoke up. "We want to help you let go of anger, to get where we are—individually, no kumbaya—but in hopefully less time."

"Okay. This already does feel like you're ramping up to excuse Tomas because of your own weird past."

"No," said Abigail with a resolution that surprised her daughter. "It means we compared notes, and we have a thought experiment for you."

"How generous of you."

"You're cheesed, we see that, so let's just jump in," said Bruce.

"By all means," responded Naomi.

"Okay. So. Flip it around. If you cheated on him, would you want him to forgive you—and—would you want to try to make it work again?"

"I knew you were defending him!"

"Call it what you like," said Bruce, "but it was one of the ways that helped me let go of the anger I felt toward Mom."

"Does it really hurt anything to walk through the question?" asked Abigail.

Naomi shook her head and summoned her most contemptuous glare, but privately she admitted to herself that she was surprised she hadn't gone through this exercise on her own.

"Oh God, stop holding hands. You're laying it on a little thick."

Bruce and Abigail let go of each other's hands and instead spent their nervous energy noisily sipping their near empty cups of tea and coffee. The premise of the thought experiment was flawed, thought Naomi. She wouldn't cheat in the first place. Of that she was certain. But if she did, would she want him to forgive her? Naomi next spoke with the slow deliberation of a finalist at the National Spelling Bee.

"A) I wouldn't do what he did; I just wouldn't, and B) If I did do it, and the reason I cheated was fixable, and I didn't think he would keep it in his back pocket as a dagger, I might. I might get back together."

"Okay," said Bruce. "Let's put garden variety lust to the side just for a second. Just for a second. If the main issue is—and here correct me if I'm botching your thoughts—is his insecurity and need for a ridiculous amount of validation, does that fall—for you, only for you—under *fixable*?"

Naomi turned to her mother.

"Anything to add before I continue with this fun 'thought experiment'?"

"Marivel knows much more about this than I do—I think your father should've asked her to come here today instead of me."

"Mom?"

"Yes?"

"Marivel isn't here. Can you, Abigail Rendeski, form your own opinion on whether you could have forgiven Dad if he had cheated on you—not even the gay thing—just cheated."

Abigail wasn't flop sweating, at least not externally.

"I think it depends on whether you think people can change or not."

"I think," said Naomi, "some people can change. But I'd wonder if they're straining every second to be that 'changed person,' and that their old self is just under the surface, and the slightest bit of pressure will explode whatever changes you've convinced yourself they've made. I mean, they say you can't change a zebra's stripes for a reason, right?"

"Okay," said Bruce, matter of fact. "So you wouldn't want him to forgive you—because your stripes are permanent, unchangeable."

"Well, I—I'm not bragging, or maybe I am—but I think I'm the type of person who *could change* if it meant improving the relationship or myself, and, *at the same time*, do it without losing my stripes. I'd still be me, just, hopefully, a better version of me."

"Your father feels—" Bruce shot Abigail a disapproving glance.

"We both feel," said Bruce.

"Yes," Abbie corrected herself. "We both wonder, rather—we think we sensed something in you that made us think you might still have real feelings for Tomas."

"Of course I have feelings for Tomas! Duh. Obviously. What a stupid comment! I loved him! He was the most important person in my life."

Bruce puffed his cheeks, then exhaled.

"Yeah, I guess our 'insights' suck," he said. "And they're stupid. Definitely stupid." Bruce turned to Abigail. "Well, I think our fine work here is done."

"No—no, no, no, no," said Naomi. "We're not done. Now, here's a question for you two: how do *you guys* feel about Tomas? Can *you* forgive him. That's *my* thought experiment."

"I've said it before, Bubble. If your life is better without him, he goes. If it's better with him, even after what he did, then he stays. My scale for forgiving or not forgiving him is how you're doing. Right now he's a placeholder to me. He could be a charcoal briquette or Spiderman or a can of Spam. Again, is your life better with the charcoal or Spam in it, or better without?"

"And you?" Naomi turned toward her mother.

"I just feel like you hate everything I say."

"That's not true. Don't pout. Just tell me what you think."

"Okay. I will. Your father forgiving me was like lifting an anvil off my chest. To this day, I still can breathe a little easier."

"And," added Bruce, "I eventually figured out that holding that anger was only hurting *me*. I imagined your mom in bed with other women—what they did, the expression on your mom's face—and it ate at me." Naomi's ears were pricked. Here was something she fully understood.

"So—what did you do to fix that?"

"I stopped daydreaming about Mom in bed with other women."

"That simple, eh?"

"That simple," said Bruce.

"Big difference here, though. Mom being gay wasn't fixable," said Naomi. "In an okay way. Again, it was a shitshow when it happened, but there wasn't a bad guy, not really. Just a—and I don't mean this judgy, Mom—a wishy-washy woman who hadn't admitted to herself who she was."

Her parents said nothing. She looked at each of them in turn.

"Okay, so *you* stopped daydreaming, and *you* took an anvil off your chest—I gather you both can forgive Tomas?"

Again they said nothing.

"Right. Okay, so you can. Thanks."

"Broken record here," said Bruce, "It's all about what he means for you."

"And letting go of the anger doesn't mean you're taking him back. It just means you're letting go of anger," said Abigail. Naomi inhaled deeply and sighed.

"It's all a big ask. I'd have to make peace not just with his penis being in another woman's vagina, but that he lied to me about it. How can I know that he really, deep down, has changed, or whether he's just being on best behavior for a few months?"

"Can I be maddeningly vague?" asked Bruce.

"That's Mom's thing."

"*You're* the expert here," continued Bruce, "not Marivel or anyone else. There is no ruler, no test. You'll know in your gut and heart if he's really changed."

"I just think I still sense love there," said Abbie, "and it's so hard to find, and maybe it really is beyond repair, but I don't know. And you're right. What you said before—that I did nothing wrong, but Tomas did—it *is* different; it's not apples to apples."

Naomi opened her mouth to quiz her mother on the specifics of the love she claimed she still sensed between her and Tomas.

"Well, let's not say you did *nothing* wrong, Abbie," said Bruce. "I was devastated. You *did* sleep with Margaret when we were still married; you told me that."

"It's not cheating if I'm gay; we agreed on that!"

"Of course it's still cheating! We did not agree. You were having your cake and eating it too—doesn't matter if it was cock or pussy cake."

"Oh, so now you're revising your opinions."

"You misinterpreted, badly misinterpreted, my feelings, but please, do not ever say 'I did nothing wrong!'"

"I knew it. I knew you still hated me! I knew I shouldn't have come today!"

"Guys, please! Inside voices," said Naomi, taking note of the other patrons glancing their way.

"You could've come to me *first*," said Bruce, "broken it off, and *then* munched pussy. That would've been the noble way to go."

"I was a mess!"

"Are a mess!"

"And you're a liar. You never really forgave me. You're not all 'I'm at peace about it.'"

"I one hundred percent forgave you. I'm just saying, don't say you did nothing wrong. Ever heard of a little thing called *accountability*?"

"And you're a saint?"

"No, but I kept my junk in my pants."

"Oh, should I get on my knees and thank you?"

"Mom. Dad." Naomi's voice was cold, firm.

They looked up at her, noticed other patrons pretending to look at their books or laptops as they snickered and waited to hear more. Bruce grabbed Abigail's hand, stroked it brusquely.

"We are fine! Arguing is normal and healthy."

"I wish you had told me earlier how you really felt," said Abbie.

"Yeah, and I wish you had told me you were gay before I proposed." She yanked her hand from his.

"No relitigating," said Abbie. "Marivel says, once something is addressed, do not relitigate!"

"It's not relitigating if one of us never admitted to their crimes." Naomi stood up.

"I'm leaving now. I hope you two have a lovely afternoon."

"Stay. C'mon, let's get you that mocha," pleaded Bruce. "We never get time together, just the three of us."

"I can't imagine why," Naomi replied. As she left, she could hear her mother whispering loudly to Bruce, "I told you you should have brought Marivel instead of me."

"How can you think you didn't cheat?"

"I had a condition."

"Being gay is not a 'condition.'"

"You're happy—you have a nice life."

"No thanks to you."

Naomi, wide eyed, shook her head as the café door closed behind her. A block away, waiting for a car to pass to cross the street, she found herself asking a question: 'I genuinely believe *I* can change—can Tomas?'

DAY 122

"**HOW MANY OF YOUR LICENSING EXAMS** have you taken?" asked Tomas.

Tomas had been looking over Billy's drawings for the Partridge treehouse. It was no longer his project, of course, but he was curious. The basic concept was still there, but Billy had articulated it—in proportion and detail—in ways that surprised Tomas. The texturing of the cantilevered room, the relationship of the kitchen area to the new interior stair, the placement of the stair itself. Billy had made significant changes.

It felt good to be back in the office. Not great, but good. Like returning to your own bed after vacation. Most people would rather stay in Venice or Phuket or Nairobi another week or two, but there was comfort in the familiar.

"Um, three, and I failed two," Billy answered, "but I'm gonna retake those when the mood feels *right*, and then I'll do the other four—again—mood dependent."

"Okay."

"Yeah. Never been a great tester. I also hate board games with ticking clocks and buzzers. I use the pause button a lot when I watch *Jeopardy*."

"Someone your age watches *Jeopardy*?"

"When I want to feel smart. And when I wanna feel *really* smart,

I watch *Celebrity Jep*, because that's when they toss out nothing but softballs. I mean, not to humble puff, but celebrities are all morons. I totally destroyed the guy from *Loopholes*."

"Thought: if you don't go out on your own at some point, and I still think you should, by the way, or even if you do, but before you do, would you ever want to become a partner in Studio Araeta?"

Billy shot Tomas a cock-eyed glance.

"IRS trouble? Credit card debt?"

"No. Well?"

Billy still waited for the other shoe to drop. It didn't. Tomas had made the decision to offer Billy partnership on the drive back from Pacoima. These latest drawings only confirmed his instincts, the feeling he'd had when he first looked at Billy's portfolio: Billy had talents he didn't; they complemented each other. And on top of that, Tomas liked Billy.

"I don't have the money to buy in. My parents run a fish and chips shop. Who still eats fish and chips? I don't even think they still eat that shit in England anymore."

"You ever hear of sweat equity?"

"Yeah. It was on celebrity Jeopardy."

"Billy, I had a sketch, an idea, for the treehouse. You improved it, you made the proportions work when it came time for turning an idea into a possible building, you made changes that a blind man could see are good. We don't suck together. Why not activate our wonder twin powers?"

"Will you pay for all my haircuts?"

"Yes."

"And we'll figure out the details of my sweat later?"

"Absolutely. More questions?"

Billy absentmindedly pinched the tip of his nose over and over.

"Y'know, it may take me a while, but I will pass those stupid tests."

"I'm sure you will, but even if you don't, I have the stamp, we have the talent—done."

"Well, shit," said Billy, affecting a Southern drawl. "Bring it in, old man." Billy got out of his chair, leaned down, and hugged Tomas while he was still sitting in his.

For the second time in four months, well, the first escapade with Evo being questionable as to whether it was of any value to the man, Tomas felt he had done right by someone.

"Okay, I know this is the honeymoon," Billy said, "and I hate to wreck the moment, but if we don't get the library, will you still want to partner up?"

"An architect without a point of view isn't an architect. I have a point of view. Sorta. You have a point of view. Clearly. I think we bring different things to the table."

"Okay, so is that some kind of weird yes?"

"Yes. That's a yes. I'd like you to be my partner."

"My mom and dad'll be stoked. Especially the sweat thing. They'd much prefer I pay for stuff with sweat than money."

"Smart parents."

DAY 136

"**I THINK I'VE GOT A NEW LEAD.** It's a small job," said Billy.

"That was fast."

"I'm a partner now. Gotta make rain, right? Okay, it's basically tearing down a detached piece-of-shit garage and putting up an ADU. Honestly, they could just buy a prefab 'small house,' but it's a solid 'maybe.'" Much as he tried, Billy was unsuccessful in downplaying his excitement.

"Talk to me," said Tomas.

"Okay," said Billy, "let's just put it out there: nepotism. My mom's got this friend, Diana, and her husband's mom is gonna move in with them, and they want to do a good cottage, and they have some coin, so my mom asked me if we wanted to do it."

"Billy, that's great news. Congratulations. Well done." A feeling came over Tomas. Something he hadn't felt before. What was it? Pride. It *was* pride. Fatherly pride. The pride of a mentor. Billy shrugged, still playing it cool, modest, and suddenly Tomas wanted nothing more in the world than to correct that.

"Billy, I wouldn't care if it was a pity commission from your mom herself after she found out you had stage 4 cancer—she's trusting you because you are talented. Too much money is at stake with making a building. You *have* to believe in the designer, no matter what the connection. Again, please listen carefully: *congratulations.*"

"Hey man, I know I'm good. Don't need you to gild the lily there, buddy."

"Then it's settled. This is your project. You design it, you take the meetings, you supervise construction."

"You sure? I'm already doing Partridge on the side to keep us from being murdered or whatnot."

"I'm taking the library seriously, Billy. I have to. I need to give it my everything."

They both turned away from each other and went back to work. Tomas had settled on a rough concept for the competition. But not before working up half a dozen cocktail napkin ideas and really turning them over in his mind first. That much he had finally learned from his former TA, Naomi Curran. But *this* was the sketch: "the kite." Tomas couldn't help that he latched onto pithy little images: treehouse; wave; kite, whatever it might be. The original building would be the body of the kite, and his adjacent addition would be its colorful tails. He would expertly imitate a handful of key facade details from original building, but that was it. The multiple tails would then grasp the new addition—a distorted and, at points, deflated oval, clad in titanium.

This was it. This was his idea. And he loved it. Yes a striking contrast—but with literal, physical connection—not like Pei's pyramid. These were two unlike pieces grasping each other. He could come up with arguments as to why this made programmatic sense, site specific sense, and so on, but it also passed the most important test of all: it made Tomas smile. He daydreamed that Naomi would feel the same way about it.

"It's not shit." Tomas didn't realize Billy had gotten up from his chair to look over his shoulder at his sketches. Tomas was shocked. Billy didn't just gush like that.

"Thanks. It's just an idea, it needs a lot of refinement, but it's what we're doing."

"Go maestro, make your magic," said Billy—sardonically to

Tomas's ear (thank God being offered partnership hadn't changed him) before returning to his desk.

At that moment Naomi returned from work to find a box of stargazer lilies delivered on their porch. She contemplated throwing them in the green bin, or giving them to her mom and Marivel, or to someone at work. But what had the lilies done wrong?

She read the small card that came with the flowers:

Thinking of you—Tomas

She took the flowers inside, trimmed the stems, put them in a blue and white vase they had bought in Budapest on their postgraduation Eurail trip, and dumped in the packet of plant food. She arranged them just a bit, making them fuller, and put them on the dining room table. They *were* beautiful, and other people might not love stargazer lilies the way she did.

DAY 137

NAOMI RECEIVED THE NEWS with some ambivalence. Garrett had called. Macy's was sufficiently happy with her window displays that they were offering her a full-time contract as an in-house "design consultant." On the prosaic level of putting dollars in her pocket, she knew exactly how to take the news: with relief, gratitude, and pride. Stability. This would be a job, not just a gig. As to what this meant for her relationship with Garrett, she did not know what to think. Had he lobbied to get her this job? Was he being truthful when he said the "Star Chamber" on the upper floors was simply impressed by her and asked him to offer her the position? Did any of that even matter? Who cares whether Garrett pushed for this or not? Who cares whether he was as attracted to her as, well, she was to him? She'd earned it. He was her liaison to the brass. If he thought she had the chops for this job, it was his *job* to push.

But there was another consideration.

What did she want to do with her time, *her life*, right now? She was still waiting for a further response from Love Without Limits. She hadn't heard back yet from Cecilia about her prospects as a single mother. That was the marquee feature here. Yes. Exactly. Right. Yes. What was she thinking? Speculating about how she got a job offer was irrelevant, a sideshow. Caring for a vulnerable human being, a child, was the main event. Everything else was a detail, even the thing she had asked Tomas over to discuss.

All this she was contemplating when Tomas knocked on the door.

She opened it, and there he stood, a resigned, muted smile on his face. He seemed much more relaxed than when she last saw him—at Riordan's office. Was he finally accepting the consequences of his actions? Was he finally realizing that she was right, that limping around on three flat tires was no way to live?

"Hi," he said.

"Hi."

"I wanted to talk to you, too."

"Okay," replied Naomi, "But first we do have to talk about selling the house."

For whatever reason—the calming effect of the clonazepam he had taken half an hour ago, the silver bullet he knew was coming in the form of a personally delivered love song by Evo Korman, or just time passing—he didn't scream.

"You still want to sell the house?" he repeated back. The question wasn't asked in a hostile manner. It was neutral parroting for confirmation. She had texted him about it three weeks ago.

"I do."

"You don't want to try to buy me out or vice versa? I mean, your dad—"

"Would do it in a heartbeat. But, Tomas, I don't want to live here. I've had five months to think about it. This was our house, and I loved it. But now everything just makes me sad. I've been trying, really trying, to let that go. But I'm struggling."

"Where would you live?"

"An apartment. I looked. I think I could manage a studio or one bedroom."

"We—I mean, either of us alone—probably won't ever to be able to buy again in this market."

"I know. But my emotional well-being is more important right now. Can you understand that?"

Tears welled in Tomas's eyes, but he wasn't crying.

"I'm not asking you this in the heat of the moment. I know how good we had it. But for me to move on, I need not to be in here."

Tomas said nothing.

"I'm sure you know this already, Tomas, but either of us can force a sale. And I really don't want to go down that road."

Tomas's eyes suddenly cleared; he stood up straight.

"Okay."

"Okay what?"

"It's not what I want, but I'd only want it anyway if you wanted it, too. So yes. We sell."

Naomi had been sure this was the hill on which he would make his last stand, a line he would not let her cross without an ugly fight. If he gave up on this, it meant she had won. She had finally gotten through to him. He had finally seen that it was time to move on.

"Well, we're both here," continued Tomas. "Should we talk about picking a realtor, how we stage it, all that stuff?"

How we stage it? Naomi's mind spun. This was too easy. A moment ago there were tears in his eyes. Now he wanted to talk about the *particulars* of selling? He was too smart for psychological games, or Trojan horse ploys, or any silly nonsense like that. He had to be. Or he had to know she would see right through it.

"I'm guessing," he continued, "for a place this size, painting, staging costs—fifteen to twenty thousand."

Naomi nodded.

"I can ask my dad," said Tomas. "We'll pay him back after the sale."

Again Naomi nodded. "It might be more," she said. "Who knows what the termite report will say."

Tomas crossed his arms, cocked his head toward Naomi, smiled and shook his head.

"What?" said Naomi.

"This is crazy. I'm an architect, you're a designer, it would be pretty lame if we couldn't figure out ourselves how to make this place look great. We can stage it ourselves."

"You okay?"

"What do you mean?"

"You seem really . . . chill, mellow or something."

"Well, at this moment that's how I feel."

"So . . . what?" she said, skepticism bubbling up, "you want to talk about paint colors, landscaping, granite countertops?"

"Sure, but—just to jump in on one thing you said—I'm very on the fence about granite. It's the most expensive thing we can put in here, but I feel like the trend is a month or two from being over. Like chalkboard-faced Sub Zero fridges and pressed tin ceilings were a couple years back. I think we paint in and out, fix up the landscaping—not gorilla hair—a nice lawn, succulent accents, maybe, but I'm pretty lost about how not to eat up, say, *only* five grand on the kitchen and bathroom, but make them look better. Why don't you do all that stuff, and I'll use some of my contractor contacts for stuff like dry rot, electrical upgrades, the invisible boring shit."

"I'm not married to granite," said Naomi. She stood up from the couch, unsure of what to do with her body.

"Hey, you're fixing up the interior. If you like granite, then granite it is. And once we're done? We just sit back and watch the ridiculous bidding war. Thoughts?"

She couldn't string together another thought about the house. Her mind was still processing Tomas's sanguine demeanor.

"You said you had something you wanted to talk about, too?"

As she looked at him, she placed her hands on her hips—god her hips looked good, even in drawstring sweats, with a little skin exposed between the top hem and the bottom of her T-shirt.

"Oh," he said, trying to refocus.

Christ, he was so taken aback by her talk of selling the house he had almost forgotten what he was going to say.

That easygoing smile. It was driving her nuts. How was he pulling it off? He looked like a cute schoolboy.

Tomas was shocked—not unpleasantly—to find part of himself stirring. His libido had vanished in the last five months. He had masturbated only three times, and those times were just perfunctory exercises to make sure the equipment still worked. Now, standing in front of his soon-to-be ex-wife, the stirring intensifying, he thought he had better do something before he embarrassed himself. He sat down on the couch.

"So, let's hear it," said Naomi, still standing.

Tomas lifted a cheek and pulled out *Man's Search For Meaning* from his back pocket. "Permit me to read."

She sat down in a worn club chair opposite him. They had found the chair, its stubby legs bearing the chew scars of the previous owner's dog, at the Laney College flea market, one of their first purchases as a couple.

"*He who has a why to live for can bear with almost any how.*"

Tomas, triumphant, looked at Naomi.

"That's it?"

"That's it," he said, smiling. She looked at him blankly.

"*Man's Search for Meaning*," he continued. "My dad gave it to me. And the author, Viktor Frankl—the guy survived the Holocaust—says that our biggest problem in life is not money or sex or fear of death and all that, it's about finding something meaningful in your life. The line I read is a Nietzsche quote. Frankl mentions it a bunch in the book."

"I read the book in high school, Tomas. Every kid had to. Can't believe you didn't."

Tomas went on. He seemed unperturbed by the irritation in Naomi's voice. "There's a lot of stuff in there about meeting your suffering with class," said Tomas, "I think that's why Dad gave it to me."

"Okay. So what's your 'why?'"

"Huh?"

"The 'why to live for.' Your big mind-blowing quote. What's your 'why'?"

Tomas snapped out of whatever slow-motion reverie he was in. He knew this was *the question*. He had been expecting some form of it ever since he'd cheated. And he had thought through it many times. It was, in a sense, the homework given to him by Riordan. If I love my wife, how could I cheat on her? That question bled into a bigger one: what *was* his why in life? Was there any through line? Was there any theme he could detect common to architecture, to searching out Evo Korman, to cheating with Marie Partridge, to loving and resenting his mother, to worshipping one band but not the other, to hating his father, to enjoying a baseball game in person, to going to museums with Naomi, to loving Naomi, to everything he had done in life? Or did he just blow this way and that with the prevailing winds? Was there no particular theme to his life, and was that okay? Was he trying to attach a theme or structure or storyline to human nature, *his* nature—which inherently might not have one? It was all too much. But the edges of a thought had occurred to him many times, so why not just say it?

"Connection," he said. "To people. When I feel alone, when I miss you, or miss Mom, or miss Rissa, or even Billy, I don't feel good. And that's on me. There's nothing stopping me from connecting."

"So I should forgive you because I miss you?" she snapped.

"You miss me?"

The words just came out.

"You know what I mean."

"No. I don't. You need to tell me."

Tomas somehow felt he had already blown it. It probably already sounded to Naomi like he was using "connection" as a reason to forgive. But that's not what he meant. This wasn't "I fucked an idea," this was different. Hell, he might as well plow on now.

"Okay, architecture, Nomes. I envy and admire the greats because their work connects with people. It transports them. And I know that I don't have that talent yet, and maybe never will. Marie Partridge blew some smoke up my ass, and it felt so good, I slept with her." He paused, wanting to give Naomi space to react, but she said nothing. "And that's where I go off the rails. I realized I don't just want connection; I want someone to pat me on the head and say, 'Good boy.' But that's crazy because it's out of my hands. If I spend my life waiting for someone else to tell me I'm worthwhile, I'm screwed. I can't control that."

Tomas kept speaking, but it was almost as if he were alone in the room, giving himself a lecture. "It screwed up my priorities. The most important connection—the most important *person*—in my life, is you. And it turns out I'm a walking cliché. I took you for granted. I treated you like furniture—sometimes. I met somebody, well, two people, that's a story for a different time, and one of them, who happens to be a great, said he would've traded it all for what we had on our most boring day together. And the other person. Well, she's just some amazingly kind creature who knows how to be a good partner, and who picked a good partner. I got the picking a partner down pat—nailed it, in fact, but the rest. Christ." Tomas lowered his head and shook it. "Man, it's like, there's no happiness I can't turn into misery."

"Do you need *me*—or just *somebody*—to make you feel worthwhile?"

"No. Just you. And ideally, not even you. Ideally, I'm good with myself. I've changed—I have—but why should you believe me?" Tomas looked down at his hands in his lap. Every guy who cheats says they can change, but do they really? Maybe. More importantly, did *Naomi* think he could change?

"I'm sad, too, Tomas. Not just angry. I loved you, we built a life, and that—for me—is gone. I'm sad about it every day. I miss our old life—every day. I believe everything you just said, but you're only half of us."

Well there it was. They were done. Tomas suddenly realized that this moment—hard as it was, was a moment between them that'd had some honesty and vulnerability to it—and might not happen ever again.

"Hey, any of my old beer left in the fridge?" asked Tomas.

"Probably."

"Do you mind?"

"No."

Tomas retrieved a beer, poured half of it in a glass and returned to the living room. From his pocket he fished out a blue tablet and held it up.

"Can I throw out an idea?"

"What is that?"

"A chill pill. Clonazepam. Literally, it chills you out. My dad gave it to me. So very low likelihood of fentanyl in it."

"Is that why you're so mellow right now?"

"Probably. Took one an hour ago. But this is the thing. I'm not here just because I'm a little high—my dad, when he and Mom were having problems, so I guess every day basically—they would split a valium, have a glass of wine, and just talk."

"Does your dad know about what happened?"

"Yeah, that's why he gave me the clonazepam. And the book."

"Don't think I wanna take any pill, Tomas."

"Right. I know how you feel about even baby aspirin, but seriously, this is like a little minivacation from the shit storm. You will not regret it. Everything unclenches. Just for a little while. I tested it before tonight. You might be just a little groggy and forgetful for a few minutes after, but there's no hangover, and I did want to say a few other things to you, but I didn't think I'd have the courage to say them, or that you'd be okay with hearing them, without a little help."

Unclenching for a moment did sound tempting to Naomi. Was this a cucumber martini in pill form?

"If nothing else," continued Tomas, "you will feel a little floaty and relaxed for a few hours."

Naomi again studied Tomas's mien. He really did seem serene, quiet. "Okay. I'll try half."

He split the blue pill in two, handed her half. She swallowed it, then gulped from the short glass of beer he poured for her. They sat in silence for a moment.

"It takes about ten minutes to kick in. So—how would you stage this place?"

Naomi swiveled her head to and fro, scrunched her nose and replied, "I hate to say it, eggshell latte and high gloss white for the trim."

"Oof. Bland."

"I know. Totally unobjectionable. Uh, small place, so small furniture. A few baroque framed 'crazy' mirrors to let folks know it's a little 'rock 'n' roll.' Plus mirrors will make the place feel a little bigger, blah, blah, blah."

"Straight up the middle, huh?"

"For the masses? Yup." Naomi took another sip—she could feel her muscles begin to liquefy, just a bit, her face slacken. "A nice Chagall or Cezanne print, probably. Maybe go nuts with just one wall—slate blue or something."

"An accent wall!" chirped Tomas. "Accent wall. Accent wall. It sounds funny—well, anything sounds funny if you say it enough. Credenza, credenza, creden—"

"If it was us, I was gonna stencil something for the nursery—probably gilt gold or copper over eggplant or a deep orange—balloons, bunnies, trees, something—but I wouldn't do that for strangers. Too much."

Tomas tilted his head back and stared at the ceiling, letting it wash over him that she had just, unprompted, brought up the adoption. Their shared "office" was going to be the nursery for their child who would've been—what, now fifteen? Nine?—who knows, on the list. But that she brought it up at all. Must be the clonazepam talking. "Maybe maroon for the front door—maroon and au lait, who can object?" added Naomi.

"Wait, au lait, not *latte*?"

They both laughed. He reached for his glass of beer and the two toasted.

"So—what else is on your mind, Tomas Araeta?"

"Oh man, and I was just beginning to chill."

Naomi held up her glass, smiled, her eyelids drooping just a little. "You brought it up. Man, this stuff is *great*."

"Dr. Tomas Areata Sr. coming through."

He opened another beer, poured her half.

"You remember The Pill Splitters?"

"Duh. I think I introduced you to them."

"No way. Other way around."

"Please, you're high."

"So are you."

"I definitely told you about them. You freaked out when I played 'Blistered Eye' in studio the first time."

Tomas smiled, shrugged.

"I met Evo Korman a month or two ago. That was the other story I wanted to tell you."

"Really?"

"Yeah. He's living in a van parked in front of this house outside LA."

"How'd you find him?"

"There was a story on the radio."

"Oh. Wait—*why* did you find him? To get an autograph or something?"

"No—"

"Wait! I know. He's a 'bona fide genius,' and you wanted to see if some of him would rub off on you."

She chuckled, so did he.

"Fair. Very fair. But no. I mean, not in the end."

"Bullshit. But anyway . . . is that the big thing you wanted to tell me, that you stalked a recluse singer from twenty years ago?"

"I wanted to help him. The story about him living alone in a van made me think he was miserable and maybe needed help."

"Noble." Her sarcasm wasn't razor sharp at this moment. With the clonazepam settling it, it was more like a butter knife.

"I couldn't tell whether he was miserable or happy or just okay—I mean, I don't know, hard to tell—he didn't want any help, that's for sure. Maybe he's happy, shit, I don't know." Tomas gulped more beer.

"'Blistered Eye' *is* a great song," said Naomi.

"Yeah. It is. I was floundering, Nomes. Stupid. I don't know what the hell I was doing finding him. *Stalking* him."

"Worse ways to flounder, I guess."

"You know I'll find 'em."

They shared a bittersweet smile.

"He looked at me with a buttload of disgust when I told him about us lying on the couch and watching TV, like creating 'Blistered Eye' was nothing compared to creating a relationship. He made me feel lower than dogshit. 'Ingrate,' he called me."

Naomi said nothing.

"And this woman who let him come into her home, Lalla Rios, well, I know this is gonna sound all overromanticized and shit, but she was the wise one in this picture. She's a grandma, she's lived, her husband passed eight years ago. She doesn't sugarcoat it, but she sees everything, the big picture, and well, she just bottom-lined it: she told me do what I can, and then let it be. That's it. That's everything."

"Sounds like the trip wasn't a total boondoggle," said Naomi, her voice soft and sweet.

Impulse overtook Tomas, impulse tempered by sorrow.

"Can I hold your hand for a moment?"

Naomi didn't object. She was feeling generous and expansive. Perhaps it was the clonazepam, forcing open an actual clenched fist. Naomi had always thought, and it came again to her now, that if you look closely enough, there are no boundaries between us and anything else: another person, a table, anything. With a powerful enough microscope, edges blur, and with an even more powerful microscope, matter—stuff—is mostly empty space. So Naomi allowed the blurred feeling to take over and opened her hand to Tomas's. They had been a hand-holding couple—walking to the movies, running errands. Nothing special—just a habit. And now she realized how much she missed the habit.

"Holding hands can be as hot as sex." She'd told this to Tomas once. He agreed. He had called it "electric foreplay," and he meant it. They both felt it could be as intimate as the act itself. He held her hand now, and she could see, in profile, as he stared forward, that there were tears welling in his eyes. She exhaled, still holding his hand, and said, "Tomas, I don't think you did what you did to hurt me, but I am so sad thinking that whatever is missing in your life, I am not enough."

Tomas nodded.

"I thought we had it all, or at least as much as any one couple deserves to have," she added.

"I've always wondered," said Tomas, "about people who get married a second or third or fourth time, y'know. You can't go back to that idealistic *till death do us part* place anymore because you know better. So what are they thinking?" He turned to face Naomi.

There were tears in her eyes now, too.

"Either they're somehow able to forget and go back to that place, or they change their expectations of what marriage looks like," she said softly.

"Expectations," snorted Tomas with disgust. "I'm not Mies, I'm not Evo Korman, I'm not anything other than what I am. And that's okay. And I figured it out five months and twelve days too late." Tears ran down Naomi's cheeks. Tomas reached over, caught one with his finger. "I'm going to go now, Nomes, because if I stay another moment, I'm going to lean over and kiss you."

He stood up, still holding her hand, and she remained sitting. Neither let go.

"Thirsty Thursdays," said Naomi.

It was Thursday, November 17.

"Thirsty Thursdays" was their nickname for having cocktails at home during the pandemic. Sometimes with their "bubble" of friends, sometimes just the two of them. They also enjoyed the occasional Tipsy Tuesday or Wet Wednesday.

"Thirsty Thursdays," repeated Tomas.

He gently pulled her arm, and she stood up. He put his nose into her neck and inhaled deeply.

"I miss Thirsty Thursdays," he mumbled. "I miss you."

The world's boundaries blurred. Their internal microscopes saw that there was no distinction between one and the other. They held each other a moment. She felt his growing stiffness just above her mons pubis. Some distinctions, some differences, were not incompatible with the oceanic oneness that was beginning to drown them. Her heart fluttered a beat thinking that mere layers of clothing separated them. Embarrassed, realizing she might feel him against her, he pulled away. She pulled his lower back in forcefully and whispered to him,

"I want you inside me."

They both dissolved—not a gentle melting, but a furious congress. He couldn't wait for her to slide off her panties. She pulled him, and he pushed her, into the bedroom, where he grasped the crotch of her panties and moved them to the side, his socks still on, and quickly entered her. He was certain he would cum within seconds, but he didn't. Once he felt her warmth, her opening up to him, he slowed down to savor every millisecond, every millimeter as he slowly, haltingly, went deeper. He knew from her short, sharp breaths that she felt a tinge of pleasurable pain, and he took it slow, as her body opened to him. After he entered her fully for the first time—life's ultimate one-drink buzz—he thrust slowly for a while, then pulled out and held himself at the tip of her labia, and slid in, a millimeter at a time, teasing her, teasing himself—and time collapsed. He was here, now, united with his wife. He wanted to consume her. He pulled out, scooted down, and caressed her with his tongue, before jumping to her breasts, swirling his tongue around her nipples, trying to swallow her entire breast, his mouth agape.

He returned with his mouth to that wonderful welcoming wet warmth between her legs, and she stiffened and held his head just so—making sure he didn't move a fraction of an inch. A few short breaths later she shuddered and told him to stop. He flicked her clit gently a few more times with his tongue, and she gasped with each touch. The sensitivity was unbearable. They both giggled. He looked at her flushed cheeks—that beautiful shade of pink. He gave her a moment for the sensitivity to subside, and, seeing in her eyes that she was ready for him, he entered her again.

"Harder, faster," she murmured. And he banged away like a stupid, rutting animal. He loved that sound—his thighs and testicles slapping against her backside. She spread her legs wide and held her feet. She did this sometimes and it turned him on even more. Like a sixth gear he never knew existed. "Come inside me," she said. Soon he felt that wonderful rumbling ache shoot from his lower back around his waist to his groin, and he came. The spasms came in ecstatic waves.

They said nothing afterward, just lay on their backs, with their legs draped over each other, eyes closed, breathing slowing. Finally she mumbled,

"Why can't things be normal again?" before nodding off.

"They can be," he replied softly, but she didn't respond. She was deep in sleep aided by alcohol and clonazepam and the release of orgasm. Tomas remained awake another half hour, savoring the loosening of a taut coil of anguish. He admired his wife's—they wouldn't be "exes" for another forty-three days—body's profile in the half light, the gentle curves, and, like all men facing catastrophe, offered up silent promises of better behavior to a god he otherwise didn't believe in.

DAY 138

TOMAS STARTLED AWAKE before daybreak. He immediately checked for Naomi, and, to his delight, found she was still there, still breathing deeply, still asleep, her face placid. He silently chided himself with a little smile—life wasn't like fiction—you didn't always wake up to find your wounded partner gone. Last night *had* happened. They had felt, well, as she herself put it, "normal." Time. What had his father said about time? Time the healer. Time and narcotics.

We are each of us not so unique and special, thought Tomas with content, calm detachment. Some experiences are universal and have universal and common trajectories and solutions. God knows Tomas Araeta Sr. wasn't the kind of weak man to ever duct tape a passport to his thigh, but he did know a thing or two about life. Tomas conceded the clonazepam and beer had given him and Naomi just enough breathing space to lower their guards, to be present and enjoy the moment. To remember what it was like. Tomas hoped he would one day be the kind of father who would support and encourage his child without planting the seed of impossible expectations. His father, a great man in his field, had seemed to make some kind of peace with his decisions and the toll they exacted, but Tomas would not be his father.

Tomas thought of other fathers, thought bitterly of the Great Man view of history espoused at school. The implication was simple: if you can't be Frank Lloyd Wright or Palladio or Hadid or any of the other luminaries whose work we are anointing, then you are a hopeless mediocrity, a bastard child, and best of luck to you. It had ruined him. Because he was *capable* of ruination. It was the natural price of one of his manifold character flaws—an inborn, inflated egoism—that would always leave him feeling inadequate. His father, of course, had implicitly, and sometimes explicitly, expressed disappointment in his son, which, upon further reflection, Tomas decided was, in fact, another way of saying you will never be a great man.

The Great Man lens was toxic bullshit. He was done with it. The pantheon would have to be razed.

Tomas would stop unfavorably comparing himself to anyone, and channel that energy into appreciating and savoring the blessings that had been bestowed upon him, most especially, Naomi. Tomas and Naomi would live their lives looking through the correct end of the telescope from now on. Life was to be lived forward, not backward. Forget backward. Again, just another avenue to misery, another chance to compare yourself to the perfect and the impossible. Fuck the Monday morning quarterbacks. They weren't on the field for a reason.

Well, there was only one thing left to do.

Get coffee and eat.

He and Naomi enjoyed Peet's dark roast anything, and he would check to see if there were any bagels in the house. If not, he could run to the store. Naomi stirred a bit as Tomas turned to get out of bed. He stopped, then continued, moving slowly and fluidly so as not to wake her.

Naomi was wide awake, but she didn't want Tomas to know it. She needed time. Time to compose her words. What she really wanted was for him was to leave the house and not return. She didn't want to have to explain what she now thought must be obvious to him. He couldn't be that stupid or deluded. They both were hurting, they got high, and for a moment, in their weakness, inhaling the fumes of good memories, and raw animal lust, they had some fun together. A hookup is what it was. A hookup isn't a shameful thing.

People crave sex and they have it. As long as expectations are more or less in alignment—i.e., no one is expecting a marriage proposal, or the forgetting and forgiving of a ruptured trust—everything is fine.

And Tomas had seemed sincere about staging the house, about realizing that he had to come to terms with his own baggage. He really seemed to have made a few breakthroughs, some real changes, so that he surely understood the nature of last night: a hookup and a nice way to close things out. This was silly. She wasn't going to feign sleep and wait forever for him to disappear. As he made coffee, she jumped out of bed, threw on jeans and a T-shirt and entered their living room.

"Well," said Tomas, "we have two options. We make do with wheat toast, or under great protest, I go to Noah's and get some fresh bagels. Your call."

"Toast is fine."

Not the kind of clipped answer Tomas was hoping for—not the soft tone of last night—but there were still a few eggshells to sidestep, so he didn't want to read too much into the fact that she hadn't said the kind of thing she normally would say, something like, "Too easy. You're supposed to ask me to go to Noah's, I say I don't want to leave the warm house, that I really don't care, that butter fixes everything, and you go instead, but I remind you that you can't be a petty martyr about it."

He smiled wide at her as he brought her coffee.

"Thanks."

"You're welcome," said Tomas, with mock formality. Saying thank you and you're welcome were not part of their old chitchat. "You sure about toast?" he asked. "I can get bagels, and I promise I'll do it with only minimal pouting."

"You are a charming bastard," said Naomi.

Better. There. The thaw. It was coming. Tomas could feel it. The minefield of eggshells was thinning out moment by moment.

"So," ventured Tomas, "I'm gonna be the first to go out on a limb and say last night was pretty spectacular. There. I said it."

"Sometimes it's good to scratch an itch," replied Naomi.

"Yeah, that whole thing my grandmother used to say about not scratching mosquito bites, that's garbage. The scratch is so worth the worse itch later, right?"

Naomi nodded and sipped her coffee.

"So I think I've got us the perfect realtor," said Naomi. "Her name is Leticia Owens, you met her, a friend of Mom's, she knows the neighborhood up and down. We should meet her about the asking price, timing, no granite, or maybe yes granite, all that stuff."

Okay, thought Tomas, *just keep your cool. She needs a little more time, a little more convincing. Don't push. You just slept together; you're having coffee. You're talking. Where were you two months ago? This is huge progress. Don't get greedy. Maybe she just wants to save a little face and not cave in all at once. Or she still has doubts. Whatever. Just stick with what you can be sure of. Don't spiral. Don't speculate. Don't ruminate. Be cool. Be Evo Korman. Be Lalla Rios. Because what you* do *know is that any reasonable jury would find that there was no denying the electricity of last night, and not just the electricity, but the comfort, the relaxation, the ease.*

"Okay, well, let's set it up and talk to her."

Naomi smiled. For the first time that morning. A genuine smile. She hugged Tomas, impulsively, quickly.

"Thank you."

"Hey, I haven't agreed to pick up the bagels *yet*," said Tomas.

"No, I'm serious. I thought you might be weird about last night. You're changing, and that's great. I'm happy to see it. It'll serve you in the best way. I don't want to get all schmaltzy and talk about silver linings, but I think you are kinda growing, and I'm kinda not in a hundred percent pain all the time anymore." Even as Tomas uttered the next words, he regretted them. He could see the oncoming train but could do nothing to jump out of the way.

"You really still want to go through with it?"

"Well, yes. You just said—"

The train was inches away.

"Yeah, no, I know, but I thought—I don't know if you remember, but you said last night you wished things could be normal."

"That's true. I do, Tomas, I wish they could be."

Her voice was even, agonizingly even. He threw himself in front of the train.

"Well, I know my radar can suck, but last night, and I even thought this morning, things were feeling pretty damn normal, no?"

"Tomas, last night was great. And I'm not gonna say it was a mistake. It wasn't. It was the perfect note to go out on. *Now* the last memory of our marriage won't be completely sour."

Tomas couldn't believe his ears. He tried to sound calm, but he knew he didn't.

"Naomi, you just said it, I'm changing—and I am. People get past things!"

"And I said I'm happy that you're growing, Tomas."

That fucking neutrality! This calm and cool bullshit!

"Naomi, are you really saying we can't get past this? One very bad day against seventeen pretty damn good years, and that's what's going to define us?"

"I'm not saying we can't get past this; I'm saying—last night was great—but I'm not there yet. And I'm not sure what 'there' actually looks like. Can we just say—right now—we had a wonderful time?" Inwardly Tomas reeled a moment before taking in her words, taking them in thoughtfully. She was right. Exes have unexpected sex all the time as they sputter toward a breakup. Enjoy it for what it was. She was right.

"Yeah," said Tomas. "We had a wonderful time." Naomi sensed a mixture of deflation and acceptance in his voice. And he smiled, and she knew—bittersweet and melancholy as it all was—that his acceptance was genuine.

Maybe he hadn't just thrown himself in front of the train.

DAY 150

"DUDE, YOU MIGHT WANT TO GET A HAIRCUT and brush your teeth," said Billy.

"I brushed my teeth yesterday, and my hair looks on point."

"Send me the link to whatever funhouse mirror you just bought. You might at least want to consider a little more manscaping than your usual metrosexual self a.k.a. I'm reminding you the photographer moved their appointment to tomorrow at three a.k.a. I'm now a partner and don't want your '*disheveled, but not disheveled in a cool rock 'n' roll or absent-minded professor way*' vibe to be part of our first portrait image in the big leagues."

Billy frowned. He had just dropped the word "photographer" and his normally thirsty business partner still didn't seem intrigued. What the fuck?

Billy handed Tomas a page he had printed out.

"Guess this makes it all officially official, sensei."

It was a press release. Studio Araeta was one of five final contenders for the library expansion project.

"Congratulations, dude," said Billy. "Well done."

Tomas had been shocked when he first got the call—not an email—a call, from the head of the selection committee a week ago. Not just for the obvious reason—Studio Araeta had no pedigree or reputation. Competitions like this were usually won by the likes of a Tom

Wright, or Morphosis, or Odile Decq, and until this moment Studio Araeta had no signature style. He and Billy didn't even have a model building studio with which to craft the kind of models that respectable architecture offices had at their disposal, where one described a design to a computer, which in turn told a series of automated knives how to carve wood or blocks of Styrofoam into gorgeous, sexy models with sinewy curves no human hand could render.

Studio Araeta wasn't on anyone's radar. Until now.

He and Billy had put together their model in a style that could fairly be called analog to the digital of the age, with glue and chipboard. He knew the other four firms by their work and reputation—two of them were a bit derivative of Gehry and his rough seas of erupting, overlapping waves, but he and Billy had stuck to a series of interlocking and overlapping and disjointed planes—"the cascade," they had nicknamed the design. Tomas had jettisoned "the kite" in a fit of . . . well, he had just jettisoned it.

And indeed the facade looked like a bureau where half the shelves were pulled out to varying degrees. Steps. The type of "steps" one might find on the face of a cliff—irregularly spaced. That's what they had gone for, a sense of loose, organic ascension, and that's what they described in the brief text accompanying their model and conceptual drawings. "Climbing toward wisdom through that venerated pastime, reading."

When Tomas first presented the rethink to Billy, he said, "It's whimsical, and I hate that word." Tomas couldn't tell whether his partner was skewering or praising the design, or both.

"You like it?" Tomas asked Billy.

"That's what I just said."

"Mmm."

"'*Mmm*'? Guess you're saving your enthusiasm for later."

Tomas didn't reply.

Later was now, a day before the photographer would arrive, a week after their idea had been validated by the outside world, and still Billy waited for Tomas's eruption of well-earned braggadocio.

Tomas had spent that morning driving over the Golden Gate Bridge. It was something he needed to do. He stopped at the vista parking lot on the northeastern side. He walked to the spot where, nearly a month ago, he'd peered at the rocks and lone shack dotting the shoreline 220 feet below. Never figured out what that shack actually was.

DAY 151

NAOMI LOOKED AT HERSELF once more in the mirror. She truly was one of the few people who looked good in yellow, even mustard yellow, of which her vintage dress had a generous splash.

She looked approvingly at her exposed upper arms. They didn't sag, not just yet, anyway. She had been blessed by good genes. She didn't work out beyond walking to the store or coffee shop and had never lifted a dumbbell or climbed on a Peloton or elliptical machine in her life. Well, that needed to be clarified. She did "exercise" when the mood struck her—walking, stretching, doing push-ups and sit-ups on a mat in the living room—but she abhorred gym rats. She pitied them. She walked past gyms with their large plate glass windows facing the street. *How sad,* she'd think. Clearly the designers of gyms would not have built giant picture windows if their clientele didn't want to be seen working out. But they all looked so intense and unhappy, fighting time and gravity, putting themselves on garish display. It reeked of desperation and conceitedness to Naomi.

She held up her right arm and shook it—she wasn't toned like, say, Michelle Obama, but she was fit and looked great. *Who am I kidding,* she thought, *I'm as vain as any gym rat.* But she smiled at the thought. We're all just trying. We're all messes. We're all a farrago of contradiction and hypocrisy.

Her knees were lovely. She hadn't thought about them until Tomas told her they occasionally gave him an erection.

"I even looked up 'knee porn,' but honestly? Your knees were hotter," he once told her. "Trade you dick pics for knee shots?"

"Sure, and thank you, but instead of dick pics, how about a selfie of you holding a sponge in front of a clean rack of dishes? Or you digging a fence post?"

He'd pointed out they already had a fence at the house, and she rolled her eyes. "It's not about the fence post. Just dig a hole and get sweaty!"

He playfully bit and kissed her knees, sometimes, it seemed, mechanically, out of habit, but sometimes to send a clear signal that he wanted sex. He never tired of her knees. She had to give him that.

As for Garrett? She knew that she could show up to dinner tonight in a burlap sack, knees fully covered, and he'd still be appreciative. But why not enjoy the sexiness and animal vigor of youth while she still had some left?

Before leaving to meet him, she again recapped his behavior to herself. They had had coffees together often. Most every day she worked. And he had made no effort to trash Tomas or move in quick when she was especially vulnerable, even or perhaps especially after Tomas ambushed her at work and everyone understood exactly what had happened. He had been a gentleman. And he had been—well, one never truly knows—but he had always been honest with her.

She had chosen A Cote, a tapas restaurant and bar in Oakland's Rockridge Neighborhood, not far from where her mother lived. The street on which the restaurant stood, College Avenue, terminated at CCAC, the local college of the arts and crafts. Architect Jim Jennings had designed the CCAC sculpture building, a Miesian rectangular box composed of white square I-beam frames filled with glass block. She and Tomas hated glass block genuinely and appreciated it ironically—it was such a sad little bit of flair in '80s movies and homes. A splash of glass block on the kitchen or bathroom wall just wasn't enough. You had to go all in, you had to commit, you couldn't *dabble* in glass block. And in the hands of someone like Jennings, it could look great. Jennings wasn't one of Tomas's "great men," though. He was merely "good, very good." Naomi shook her head, realizing she was echoing Tomas's thinking. The sculpture building was *fine*, it was great, but what mattered were the students and teachers inside. Was the building conducive to what *they* were trying to achieve?

"Jesus," mumbled Naomi to herself disapprovingly as she sipped her chardonnay at the bar. She had consciously chosen A Cote, a restaurant she and Tomas had frequented a handful of times, in the hope of making new, untainted memories, or at a minimum, in the hope of overcoming her lingering avoidance of "their" spots which she had every damn right to still enjoy without him.

"Sorry I'm late. I'd like to say traffic was a bitch, but it wasn't. I just panicked over picking out the right shirt."

Naomi turned to see Garrett smiling. He wore a blue shirt and blue tie, black slacks—a hint of his goth past coming out. But the overall impression was that of stylish high school teacher. He looked great, thought Naomi. No more thinking about Tomas, or great men, or the correct use of glass block.

"No problem, I was just contemplating—and actually solving—some of the world's pressing problems over this glass of wine. It's a habit of mine."

"You look great," said Garrett. "And if you can knock off some of our existential problems while you're at it, well, power to you, and thank you from the rest of us. What did you solve this evening?"

"There's too much toothpaste in the world. I can't decide anymore. Some of them promise to whiten your teeth—I mean, each brand has at least four variations of whitening, which really stumps me—or do I go with the one that focuses on breath, or fixing your enamel, or being sensitive to your gums. Too much choice is *not good*. Give me A or B to pick from—then I can feel empowered, like I get to choose, but when I have forty-five choices? I get paralyzed."

"This *is* troubling," said Garrett. "When I was a kid, it was Crest or Colgate."

"And it's part of the reasons other countries hate us. As if we're running out of real problems, we make forty-five toothpastes."

"My dentist says I don't floss well enough. Even when I have no cavities. Why can't she compliment me once in a while? 'No cavities this visit. Nice job, Garrett. Your gums aren't bleeding too bad.' How painful would that be?"

"Sounds like you need to change dentists, or stop flossing so well."

A server approached Naomi now that "the friend" she was waiting for had arrived.

"Thanks for inviting me. I love the vibe of this place," said Garrett.

Naomi quickly finished the last of her wine, put the glass back on the counter with an unintentionally heavy clang, and they left to take their seats at a table. They ordered half a dozen tapas dishes from the menu. In the conversational lull after his first sip of wine, before any food arrived, Garrett showed a pursed, guarded smile and said,

"This will sound totally presumptuous, but I need to say it."

"Ooh, now you've got my attention."

"Oh, so you've just been faking it all this time?"

"Yeah. Was I doing a good job?"

"Oscar worthy."

He flashed a smile before his more serious demeanor returned.

"When the paperwork goes through for you to be our in-house designer, I will be your boss again. That paperwork hasn't gone through yet, and probably won't for another two or three weeks, maybe a month."

Naomi nodded and took another big sip of wine from her fresh glass.

"So right now we're just friends," said Naomi lightly, "and there is no underlying work-related power imbalance."

"Right. But there is a ticking clock. And it would be wrong of me—well, I don't know about wrong—because we both are aware of your upcoming employment—but, for me, at least, I just feel I have to freaking buzzkill everything and blurt it out at the top of our ... *date?*"

"Oh it's a date. And I can do a little basic math, too. So right now if I leaned across this table and kissed you, there would be no messy work complications."

The sultry way she said it. A tone he had never heard from her. She looked stunning. Her super cute vintage dress revealed a tasteful amount of cleavage and no more. He thought he could smell her clean, fresh skin clear across the table. And he thought he must look like an anxious, dumbstruck, thirteen-year-old boy. Or worse, a sad fifty-five-year-old man yearning, sniffing, at youth.

She leaned forward and kissed him on the mouth. A light, long kiss, slow. She pulled back and smiled. *Is he blushing?* she thought. *How cute!* Their second glasses of wine were settling in nicely. Poor thing couldn't even speak. She was the first to say something after the kiss.

"Nicer even than I imagined."

"Me, too."

The earth had shifted. Their relationship was now different. Their conversation through dinner continued normally—but neither would remember what they talked about, the clever rejoinders each would try to make to impress the other. What they both did know was that everything was funneling toward the end of the meal and the decision on what to do next.

She lived ten minutes away.

Garrett lived in San Francisco.

Would she ask him to stay the night? Or better if he just went home after they slept together at her place? Or they could go to his place, and she could Uber back? The logistics could be played by ear. Those were inconsequential details. The check would arrive soon. And then a niggling thought whispered to her. She didn't want to hear it, thought she was above it, above playing any kind of games, but she couldn't quell the little voice in her head.

I can't wait to tell Tomas.

She wanted him to know that she had been on a date—with a kind, appreciative man who wasn't a complete stranger on his best behavior. She had worked with him side by side for months, had seen him in a prosaic environment, where neither had been on their best behavior. They had spent time together when she was preoccupied and he was bored, and through all this, he didn't seem to have Tomas's "great man" baggage. We all have baggage, of course, that's a given, but not everyone carries around the kind of baggage that can hobble a relationship, and those who do, some of them surely face down their demons before acting on them.

She pulled out her purse to get her wallet.

"No, please, let me get it."

"I invited. My treat," she said, putting her card on the bill tray.

"Next time? I mean, if there is a next time."

She nodded. After she got her card back, they stepped outside the restaurant.

"I'm stuffed. Not 'I couldn't eat another bit of calamari stuffed,' but stuffed," she said.

"Same. Also more of whatever those croquettes were."

"They had cheese—what else is there to know?"

"Absolutely nothing."

"Excuse us."

They didn't realize they had been blocking the door. With a few "sorrys," they stepped aside to let another couple through.

"So, do you want to get a drink or something?" asked Garrett. Bless his heart, he was still looking shy and tentative. As to Naomi's heart? It was pounding. The feelings that washed over her—nausea, anger, pride, attraction—she could scarcely describe them all. He wasn't just cute, he was handsome. At least in the moonlight after two glasses of wine. And he was reasonably funny and not too quiet or too chatty.

And then she spoke.

"Garrett, I do like you, and I'm afraid I'd like you more after tonight, and then we would be working together in a few weeks, and then it would be weird."

It was both a lie and the truth. If she wanted to have a little fun tonight and maybe for a few more dates and let it go at that, she knew he would be fine with it. The question was, would *she* be fine with it?

"Oh. Of course," he replied. He couldn't hide the confusion and disappointment in his voice. He knew beforehand that this could be an outcome, but he really had hoped that maybe they could enjoy a three-week vacation together. That's why he'd made a point of bringing up future work early. It was the right thing to do. But, depending on her expectations, it could backfire.

Then again, the kiss over the table? What was that all about?

"I'm sorry," said Naomi.

"I just—I wished you hadn't kissed me, y'know. Now I'll know what I'm missing."

His voice, his attitude—some of the accommodation and politeness had vanished. There was a crisp edge there. He was upset. He wanted her, and she had denied him, had teased him.

"I suck," she said. "You're right, and I'm sorry."

She hugged him.

"I'll drop you off. Did you drive or take BART?" he asked coolly.

"No. I need to walk. I need to forget about how I just treated you."

"I had a lovely time." He hugged her back curtly, his smile as tight and guarded as a bank guard's, and left.

Fuck Tomas! This was his fault! It had been five months. Garrett was a great guy. Good ole Tomas, all feeling better about things now that he understood his issues. Good for fucking Tomas. Wonderful, enlightened Tomas.

She needed a drink. A stiff one. She made an SOS phone call—not a text—to Maya. Maya was there in twenty minutes. Naomi was waiting for her at McNally's, an Irish bar up the block from A Cote. The bartender was a white-haired man in his sixties who wore a short black apron, didn't smile, didn't try to charm anyone. Naomi's kind of bartender.

She was drinking a Maker's and Coke—a basic tool to get the job done. She was surprised at how fast she downed it. She barely felt its effects. She ordered another. Half an hour later she and Maya were finishing another round. Still Naomi didn't feel all that tipsy.

"Did you *want* to fuck him?"

"I thought I did. I mean, I *did*, but then this little stupid voice, y'know, I hated that part of me wanted to do it to get revenge on Tomas."

"A revenge fuck is classic. Time tested. But does he know Garrett? How would he have found out?"

"I would've told him. That's the whole point."

Maya nodded. It made *some* sense.

"What?" asked Naomi.

"But then you wouldn't have it over him. You'd be in the mud with him."

Naomi swirled the melting ice in her glass a moment.

"God," she said, "you're right. Guess I'm glad I backed out with Garrett. He's too nice of a guy anyway."

"Yeah," said Maya, her mind drifting to her next thought. "Anyway, like you said, you're divorcing—power plays can only work if you're still together."

And if they did get back together, Maya was absolutely right: she *couldn't* hold it over him. It would damage both of them. No less corrosive, perhaps, than what Tomas had done. Just a slower, colder burn. Now a more invasive thought came to mind. She was sitting in a bar with a philanderer, a cheater. She had asked a cheater to join her, because, well, because she liked Maya, and felt she'd understand. She could forgive Maya. As had Omar. Did she and Tomas not have a foundation at least as sound as Maya and Omar? Naomi's head spun.

"We slept together, me and Tomas."

"Oh," said Maya, with a surprised, greedy smile, "Do tell."

"It was nice."

"*Nice?*"

"Okay, it was really nice. Close. Comfortable. I needed a good fucking."

"Make-up sex—another classic."

"It wasn't make-up sex."

"Then what was it?"

"A moment."

"C'mon, you were married ten years."

Naomi looked at Maya, her eyes clear despite the liquor.

"I don't ever want to be hurt like this again. I don't want to feel like a fool."

"Oh man, you and Omar should talk—he word-for-worded you on that."

"Me and Omar and all the other thousands."

"Yeah."

"I wish I could be him. I wish we could be you guys."

"We're not perfect. We're just trying."

"It really was a nice moment," Naomi mumbled to herself.

DAY 161

"SHE'S BEAUTIFUL."

"Eh, all babies are."

"Not really. I've seen a ton that look like confused old men."

"You're biased. And you damn well better be." Tomas and Clarissa were in the kitchen of her apartment, chairs arranged in adoration of "Baby Jasmine," eleven months old. Clarissa and Tomas watched in wide-eyed admiration as Jasmine, with an unsteady hand, picked up a Cheerio from a scattered pile on her highchair table, and brought it to her mouth.

"Who's gonna be a better uncle from now on?" asked Tomas in a baby voice.

"Oh don't worry, Andre and I have massive heavy-lifting plans for you when she's a bit older. Babysitting, T-ball, you still don't cook, right?"

"Pasta, toast, bagels. I survive."

"Fine. Homework help, pushing her on the swing. Um. I'm tired, I'll think of more."

Tomas smiled and nodded.

"What's wrong big brother?"

"Besides the shitshow I just told you about?"

"Yeah. Besides that."

"Well," said Tomas, "do you remember, when we were kids, that one day . . . I didn't want to play chess with you . . ." The words now came haltingly. "But I said yes because Mom kept nagging me. It was raining out, just a shit day. We were bored and getting on each other's nerves . . . and I finally said yes, but mostly because I really wanted to beat you badly. Humiliate you."

"And?" said Clarissa, picking up a few Cheerios Jasmine had thrown overboard. Tomas didn't understand. His sister seemed unbothered.

"I let you win for a while, then I slammed the door on you. Checkmate. And I called you an idiot."

Clarissa cupped her mouth, hiding it from Jasmine, and in a hard mocking whisper, said, "You fucking asshole!"

"I'm serious, Rissa."

"Oh. Okay," she said, trying now to appear to take her brother seriously. "Um, no I don't remember that particular day, but you never wanted to play with me. I was four years younger than you. Why would you?"

"You don't remember that chess game?"

"Honestly, Tomas, I don't. Also: why are you apologizing for a twenty-five-year-old chess game when we were kids?"

"Because I was cruel to you. You were my baby sister, and I was calculating and cruel to you. Clarissa, *you cried*."

"Of course I cried. You were 'calculating and cruel' to me!" she chirped cheerfully. "Hey, if you're in Twelve Step or something and doing the apology tour, you can tell me."

"No, probably should be, but I'm not."

Tomas helped Jasmine pick up two Cheerios at once.

"Booze, sex, opiates, gambling, tell me, it's okay," Clarissa said.

Tomas shook his head.

She could see his pain. "Hey." He looked at her. "What's up?" she said, now genuinely concerned.

Tomas wiped at tears. "I'm just, it's no fun realizing you're not a good person."

"Everything seems black right now. I get it. What you did was shitty. But as your sister, I would take the stand and swear that you're a good person, no more or less"—again she cupped her mouth—"f-ed up, than the rest of us."

"Thanks." He awkwardly patted her hand. "You and Andre good?"

"Yeah. We are."

Tomas nodded.

"Good. I'm glad."

Clarissa could see Tomas wanted more, could see he was trying not to look plaintive, but was doing a poor job of it.

"We work on it, Tomas. He gets on my nerves, I get on his, we can be frosty, bitchy, nasty, but overall? We're more happy than not."

"That's the secret, huh? fifty-one percent happiness?"

"No secret. Just love and work, I guess. I don't believe in 'the One.' I mean, there's eight billion of us right now. What if my 'One' was herding yak in Nepal or something? I'd never meet him. And I just don't think God or whatever would be that cruel."

"That would be pretty messed up."

"I believe in the lower case, little 'o' one, y'know? You meet someone, you fall in love, and then the real work starts."

"Sounds romantic."

"Shut up, you calculating and cruel jerk."

Tomas shrugged and smiled.

"Andre and I have talked about it. I could rattle off a hundred things about him I don't like, and I'm a thousand percent sure he could do the same. But what's the point? We love each other. The 'one' is the person you decide is worth all the aggravation and hard times and all the rest of it, and still you love them, and still you want to spend—god this sounds crazy—the rest of your life with them."

"Yeah," said Tomas. For a moment they both just stared at Baby Jasmine, watching her eat her Cheerios. "Shit, Clarissa, when did you get so wise? I'm supposed to be the big brother giving you advice."

"I learned from you."

"What did you learn from me?" asked Tomas hopefully.

"How to play chess."

Tomas took his sister's hand, squeezed it, and wouldn't let go. Baby Jasmine successfully brought another Cheerio to her mouth.

DAY 151

"JUST A NICE MOMENT, HUH?" said Maya. "You're full of shit. But I'll let that slide because we need to *dig in*. Spe-ci-fics. This is a sex story. I need more."

"We talked—we were meeting about selling the house—at least that's what I thought. We drank, we took some clonazepam, and it happened."

"Oh. Okay, so he borderline roofied you. Interesting. And?"

Naomi caught the bartender's attention and gestured for another.

"Oh god, Maya, sometimes I think maybe I do want to work on this. I miss his body, his voice, our trips to the museums, our time watching TV on the couch, his humor. Christ, even his neediness doesn't bug me right now." There were tears in Naomi's eyes. "Thank God I didn't sleep with Garrett." Maya softened—lurid curiosity turned to tenderness—she was careful not to interrupt Naomi. "How did Omar forgive you? Tell me again."

"Honestly? I think he came to a place where he realized—felt in his heart and gut—that there is no such thing as a perfect person, and that, whatever my imperfections are, we had enough good, and that we both were flawed enough, that we could do this."

Naomi nodded before continuing. "And other days I think I *don't* want to work on this."

"He probably had those days, too. Frankly, I'm glad he didn't share them with me. But we love each other. I guess that's real important."

"Omar really is a saint."

"No he's not. And thank God. I don't need that kind of pressure."

"I'm not a saint."

"Do you *want* to be?"

Naomi gave the question some thought.

"No. Tomas sees it. I can be moody—not Tomas level moody—but I can be. And I can be aloof, or I won't say what bothers me, or just whatever."

"Or you do say it and you call him a hack. But who cares? Bottom line: you're admitting to being human, got it."

Naomi slowly nodded. She suddenly felt exhausted. Her elbow slipped off the edge of the bar.

"Honey, I think we better get you home."

"Yeah," mumbled Naomi. "I miss him."

DAY 172

NAOMI HADN'T YET CALLED THE REALTOR.

"I hate myself for letting my anger toward him drive me out of our home."

Abbie and Marivel spoke over each other.

"Stay angry, change the locks, just don't move out!"

"I know you'll make your own memories. New memories. Beautiful memories."

"His sorry ass is dumped. Story over."

"Bruce and I will buy him out," added Abigail.

Abigail and Marivel were on speaker phone. Naomi was in the second bedroom—their shared office, their future nursery—not cleaning anything out, just looking, just tidying up things. Nothing really.

"Thanks," said Naomi, sounding neither convinced nor unconvinced. "At first I thought it would just be this house of horrors—and of course I know all the practical reasons not to move when you actually have property in the bay—and I'm a hundred percent weighing that, too, but my emotional state, my gut, my heart, I mean, what's the good of staying here just because I could maybe manage it financially, if it creates some kind of depression-anxiety sinkhole, y'know?"

"We do," said Marivel. "He's the sinkhole."

"We love you to pieces," added Abigail. "Should I call Bruce?"

"Give me a sec. It's just, this is what I'm thinking right now.

Y'know, 'hasten slowly' and all that."

"Okay. Marinate a little, whatever, then buy his ass out and kick him to the curb," said Marivel.

"It's weird. In eight days it'll all be over."

"Right. Good," said Marivel.

After she hung up, Naomi walked through the house. Down the hallway, she poked her head in the bathroom, then she walked into their bedroom, then the living room, the dining room, which was really just a nook off the kitchen. She stood in the kitchen. Crisp fall sunlight streamed in through a window.

She would stay in the house.

She would make a home for herself and her child.

Only eight days left. She would need to tell Tomas about her change in plans. But what if he didn't agree? What if he tried to insist on a sale, or force one? What if he demanded to stay in the house, and got his father to attempt to buy her out at some ridiculously high price?

But she wasn't anxious. Not really. The questions passed through her mind, they did, but something about Tomas the last few times they interacted—he did seem different—and if he really went down the road of pettiness, vindictiveness, obstinacy—well, then her radar was well and truly broken, and he *was* a defective human being, and she should just be thrilled to get out of the relationship.

She took a deep breath and walked through her thoughts again more slowly. Eight days. She would need to call him soon. Her phone rang. "Tomas" came up on the caller ID. Good lord, was the man psychic?

"Hi," she answered.

"Hey," said Tomas. "Do you have a second?"

"Sure. What's up?"

"Sorry, I meant a second in person. Can I meet you at the house Thursday at six? And I one hundred percent promise it's not about the house—it's just I'm expecting something to arrive there, kind of a big surprise, and it's meant for both of us . . . and it's . . . well you might get a kick out of it."

"Okay," she answered, with trepidation. "And I also wanted to talk to you about something. About the house."

"Yes, of course. Well, I'll see you then."

He sounded like he was in a rush.

DAY 176

TOMAS ARRIVED AT FIVE-THIRTY. In four days the divorce would be finalized. He was, technically, breathing, but only just. He was half an hour early. He needed to burn through some of this adrenaline. He thought of what he could do for Naomi. Buy more flowers? Walk to the Mexican bakery on Fruitvale and buy her wedding cookies, one of her favorite sweets? Show up with wine? Throw out some more quotes from philosophers? Seek out others to confess to?

Nothing felt right, and then it dawned on him. Nothing felt right because it was all too late. He had heard that professional coaches don't coach on game day. It's the weeks and months of practice and memorizing plays before the game that counted. By the time game day arrived, the player either knew what to do, knew what split-second decisions to make, all of it with an open, empty alertness, or not.

So the question was, how had Tomas done in the last six months as the coach of their future? He drove a block away, parked the car again, and just walked around *that* block. He would just circle the block until six o'clock arrived. And he *did* have a last-minute surprise change to the starting lineup: Evo's love song. Due in thirty minutes. Delivered by the man in person. Would it matter to Naomi? Maybe, maybe not. Well, his work was done. He had tried to show his contrition and save the marriage in the only ways he knew how. No more coaching.

It was 5:58 pm. Game time.

He knocked on the door. Naomi answered quickly. She wore sky blue capri pants, black flats, and a worn black T-shirt, her hair pulled back in a ponytail. Hula hoop. That was the first thing that came to Tomas's mind. In that outfit, hair pulled back, she should be shimmying with a hula hoop. He knew it was just a simple work outfit. One that happened to beg for a hula hoop.

"I forgot that one of us actually *works* for a living," said Tomas.

"Oh forgive me. Should I change for the 'big surprise?'" asked Naomi. Tomas was surprised not to hear sarcasm, but rather playfulness, in her voice.

"No, no, no—you look great. I was just saying, again—wait, did I ask you how your day was?"

"Okay. Good, actually. Nearly done with the display. Ready for another sunny California Christmas."

"Mmmm."

After a few moments, Naomi said, "You know you're welcome to sit down."

"Huh? I'm good." Tomas glanced at his watch—6:09 p.m. He immediately realized that just because he was counting on Evo to show at exactly six o'clock, it might not happen. Evo could be in traffic. He could be driving from another state all together. He could've abandoned his promise the second Tomas left Pcoima. If he showed up in the next three hours, say, it would be a miracle.

"Or stand and shift nervously from foot to foot, whatever feels right," said Naomi.

"Can I put on some music?"

"Like I said, whatever feels right."

She seemed so placid. Tomas had no idea what she was thinking.

Tomas put on Joanna Brouk's instrumental piece, "The Space Between." It was very pretty, calming and melancholy. Something Evo had mentioned in passing.

"Feeling funereal?" asked Naomi.

"No. Just finally giving the new age thing a try, I guess. I know I used to shit on anything having to do with crystals or tinkling wind chimes—but yeah, y'know, trying to open my mind, wait for ten minutes, and *then* be a judgmental dick about everything."

Naomi's heart, too, was pounding.

It was 6:16 pm.

She could see how antsy Tomas was, had no idea what he was expecting and was getting tired of feeling antsy herself.

"Hey, can we talk about something as we wait for whatever it is we're waiting for?"

"Yeah, duh, sorry, totally forgot." Tomas sat down.

"So I've been thinking. I don't think I want to sell the house. I want to try to buy out your half." She didn't pause, didn't want to give him a chance to say anything until she could present her pitch fully. "We can get three appraisals—you pick all the appraisers if you want—and I will get the cash together and buy you out. I thought I didn't want to be in this house any longer, but—glory be to the wisdom of the cooling off period, that *was* some founding fathers' level of foresight, like you said—I think I do, and, well, I'd like you to consider this."

She had thought about, but then rejected, the notion of telling Tomas right away about how she still planned to go forward with the adoption and wanted the house to be a home for her child. She just wanted to float the notion of a buyout, focus on one shock at a time.

"Sure. Whatever you want to do," said Tomas. He seemed distracted to Naomi, still fidgety, looking out the window.

Had he really just caved? So easily? Not even a pinched frown? She needed to hear it one more time.

"Great. So you're good with getting the appraisals, me buying you out, setting this in motion . . . soon?"

He turned to her, sensed her apprehension.

"Yeah, Naomi, you can buy me out."

"Okay. Thank you."

He looked at her warmly.

"What?"

"You are a genuinely good person. You've never been mean to me; you've never needled me about stuff—needling is my lane. You've been mad at me, of course, but you don't do things to hurt people. Shit, how did none of that rub off on me in seventeen years?"

Naomi knew he was being "charming," but she also knew there was a gulf of difference between someone who is being charming because they have an agenda, and someone who is being charming because they've just said something painfully real to themselves, and can't help but dial it back, juxtapose it, with something a little glib—but with some truth in it, too—so as not to be "too heavy," even when it was perfectly appropriate to be heavy. And was there an aspect of fishing for a compliment here? Yes. Tomas was needy in that way, but of all his character flaws, or quirks, if one is feeling generous, being self-deprecating to prompt a compensatory compliment was hardly the worst.

Naomi replied, "It's true. How *did* my goodness not rub off on you?" She wanted to add, jokingly, "Except for that business about 'hack,'" but the thought of what she had said made her flinch inwardly.

"Maybe—*maybe*," said Tomas, "I'll have enough buyout money from the house to pay the army of therapists I'll need to figure out how you didn't rub off on me."

"You're also great, Tomas. We're all selfish sometimes."

"You're just being polite," said Tomas. "Name two selfish traits you have. Real ones."

"I love my mom, but I can be snappy and impatient with her."

"What? No! It'd be weird if you weren't. Everyone's parents are irritating. I love my mom to pieces when I'm not with her. When I visit, she irks me. And my dad, well, I can't stand him, but I can't cut him out completely, either. But—okay—I'll count it. Impatience with parents. Next."

"I pick my nose when I drive sometimes."

"Nose picking? *Really?* That's flaw number two? That's like those job interviews where people say, 'My greatest weakness is I work too hard.'"

"Well you're the one who put me on the spot."

Where the hell was Evo? What else better did *he* have to do? The longer he lingered here with Naomi the more likely he was to say or do something to cement her decision to divorce, a decision which she had probably already made. *Probably?* No. Certainly. She would be buying him out of the house. Duh. *Did you not just hear what you agreed to, idiot?*

"I lied to you."

"Hmm?" Tomas asked.

"After the Redwood Room."

"What do you mean?"

"Well, I pretended I didn't remember the next morning because I was mad at myself for being jealous, and I had always preached to you about 'just talk to me,' and you did, and I shot you down rudely, and, well, I'm sorry."

"That's okay."

"That's it? '*That's okay.*'"

"Yeah, my timing was bad, and I didn't know the next morning whether you did—or didn't—remember, what happened. Not until you talked about it later. The whole thing was weird."

"But we should have talked *more* about it," said Naomi.

"Guess we both chickened out."

They shared a compassionate, unguarded glance—yes, they should've talked about it more. But that was a long time ago.

"How's work been? I mean, y'know, really," asked Tomas.

"Well. Actually, I've been offered a permanent job as Macy's interior designer."

"Jesus Christ, I've been sitting here for ninety minutes, and you bury the lead like that? That's fucking fantastic! Very well done, Naomi Curran. And much deserved."

"Thanks, yeah, I didn't even know they had the position."

"Maybe they didn't have the position. Maybe they invented it for you. Are you happy about it?"

Naomi thought about it for a moment.

"Actually, yeah, I am. I mean, you know how it is—you hear 'permanent job' or 'promotion' and you knee-jerk a 'yes,' and you feel excited, but sometimes you don't even know if you want the job. It's like, I would never want to be manager of an interior design firm, critiquing other people's work, hiring, firing, crap like that. That's a promotion I *wouldn't* want. Anyway, I'll just be a one-woman band, and I'm pretty sure they trust me enough by now to give me the level of freedom I need. So yeah, I'm happy about it."

Tomas impulsively hugged her, then quickly broke off the hug, took a step back.

"Well, that's . . . that's great."

"And you?"

"Good. Good. I made Billy a partner."

"The little shit you were always complaining about? *That* Billy?"

Tomas sheepishly shrugged.

"Yeah."

"That's wonderful! You were always happiest when you came through the door and vented about what an ungrateful, entitled brat he was."

"And even worse than being ungrateful and entitled?"

"I'm listening."

"He's talented. Like, he's good. *Very* good. I need him more than I don't need him, and I'm afraid of him leaving, so . . . we're partners. Yay."

"I like this for you. Kinda buried the lead a bit yourself there, Tomas Araeta."

"Not really. But my actual lead . . . well, it doesn't really matter. I've enjoyed talking to you." It was nearly eight. Evo could show up at midnight two years from now for all he knew, and what was the point anyway, Naomi would buy him out, move on with her life, and that was fine.

"Me too," said Naomi. "It's been nice."

"You know I hate that word—*nice*—but tonight? I feel the same. It's the right word."

Naomi nodded. As much as he wanted this moment, this easygoing feeling with Naomi, to last an eternity, he did not want to wear out his welcome.

"Anyway, I'm gonna call it."

"Oh. Okay." Did she sound a little disappointed? It flashed across Tomas's mind to propose sharing another clonazepam and beer, but he was so tired, and, if this "nice" feeling just kept going, eventually it would become torture. The more comfortable he became with Naomi, the more painful the separation would be. They could even sleep together again—the muscle memory of good chemistry—and it would just be one more thing to say goodbye to. Tomas wanted more and knew that a starving man would only have his appetite awakened by a nibble, that his stomach would begin to eat itself if he couldn't have a full meal.

"So you take point on this?" said Tomas.

"Huh?"

"The buyout. Just let me know what to do, what you're thinking, and when to do it."

"Sure. Well, congrats again on promoting Billy."

"Same to you on your promotion. I'm glad."

Tomas stood up from the couch where they had been sitting next to each other and headed for the door. He turned around.

"Please be happy again," he said.

She said nothing, just looked at her husband, as he left their home.

Naomi was going to call Bruce right away to talk about the specifics of the buyout, but realized she didn't feel like talking to anybody. She put on the song Tomas had played, "The Space Between," lay on the couch, and began to cry.

DAY 177

NAOMI PASSED THROUGH THE GATES of Mountain View Cemetery, a hillside cemetery in Oakland, where she and Tomas had strolled and picnicked occasionally, where he had proposed marriage the second time, and where, sometimes, she would go alone, find a hill with dappled shade, and lie down to read or just close her eyes. She found a comfortable spot in between obelisks on Millionaire's Row, lay down on a blanket she had brought, spent a few moments letting the breathtaking view of the East Bay wash over her, and then opened Thomas Wolfe's *Look Homeward Angel* to a random page and started reading. She had read the book half a dozen times. It didn't matter where she jumped in. Every sentence, every passage, was a jewel. The way the man described food? The way he made you crave a slab of bacon? Uncanny. Today she opened to the passage, "Each moment is the fruit of forty thousand years. The minute-winning days, like flies, buzz home to death, and every moment is a window on all time." And there was something especially comforting about reading in a cemetery for Naomi, knowing how fleeting life was, and that this was okay, it was nothing to kick against. And, for months, she had been kicking, cursing the "wasted" years, with Tomas Araeta Jr.

But today, and for the last few weeks, she had stopped kicking.

They weren't all wasted. He was right about that. There had been good years, many of them. And just yesterday, he had said yes to the buyout. By any metric, today was a good day. She *could* hold the good and the bad in the same hand, at the same time.

She needed to be here, needed to remind herself that every moldering skeleton on this hillside had at one point been a living, feeling human being, had been heartbroken, had been elated, had been bored. And they were now gone, and one day she would be, too.

It was all so comforting.

She felt the same way when standing before the ocean. The indifferent waves rolling in and out over millennia. They didn't care about whether your husband had fucked a client, whether, on occasion, you drank a little too much, whether you had made out with your best friend Maya's boyfriend in college and hadn't been caught. It just didn't matter. The waves didn't care. They just kept coming.

"Good book?" said a voice. Naomi turned and looked behind her to find a stooped, white-haired man wearing a tam and a heavy sweater and using a retractable metal walking stick. "I'm nosy. I tried to look over your shoulder, but my eyes aren't what they used to be."

"One of my favorites," said Naomi to the old gentleman. *Look Homeward Angel.*

The old man nodded. "Never was a big reader myself. My wife—she's buried two hills over—she read everything she could get her hands on."

"I like her already," said Naomi.

"I come here to talk to her."

"That's very sweet," said Naomi.

"I wasn't a good husband," said the man. "I tried. Now when I come she forgives me." He paused. "At least that's what I think I hear. Maybe it's just the wind. Well, you have a good day."

"You too," said Naomi, and she watched the old man walk down the paved path and find himself a comfortable bench on which to gaze out at the bay, maybe hear his wife's whispers in the breeze.

DAY 178

"I'M SO GLAD YOU ASKED ME TO LUNCH," said Abigail. That one word: *so*. Her mother couldn't help herself. The emphasis her mother laid on it, how she stretched it out, how those two letters normally strangled and smothered Naomi. Today they didn't.

Naomi met her mother for lunch at a mobile Indian chaat shack parked at the foot of the UC campus. The shack was a precursor to the upscale, ethnic food trucks that now dotted most farmers' markets in most cities and college towns. The chaat shack had been there since Naomi was a student and TA—a "portable" trailer on two wheels that hadn't been moved in over a decade. A makeshift awning and some plastic furniture and—the sweetest touch of all to Naomi—a large square of AstroTurf lined with fake potted flowers—defined an outdoor dining space.

"Try the samosas, Mom. They're amazing. Tasty but somehow not dripping with grease."

"Why don't you order for us both—I'm famished."

Still—*still!*—her mother's needy deference didn't annoy.

"I know I've been short and difficult during all this," said Naomi. "But now that it's almost over, I want you to know I appreciate you—even if you do sit on the fence and fret yourself to pieces most of the time."

"Well, I am who I am, honey. With something as important as

this, I had to tread very carefully."

"I know."

"You look good. How do you feel?"

"Getting there. Bit by bit."

"Years. It can take years to get back to something that feels like normal."

"I actually think I'm a little ahead of schedule on that."

"Oh? Wonderful."

They sat and waited for their number to be called. From her pocket Naomi pulled out a folded piece of paper.

"Remember how we went with Shakespeare's 'Sonnet 116' for our wedding vows?"

"How can I forget? It's one of the loveliest descriptions of love I've ever heard."

"Tomas and I both hated it." Abigail smiled apologetically. "I mean, it *is* beautiful, the Bard is the Bard, but we actually wrote a draft of our vows ourselves, but kinda chickened out at the last minute, thinking they weren't romantic enough." Taking note of Naomi unfolding the piece of paper, Abigail ventured, "Will you be sharing them with me?"

"No, Mom, I just took them out of my pocket to pique your curiosity. Of course. I found them the other day in our office when I was cleaning some stuff out." Naomi unfolded the sheet of college rule paper and began reading.

"Dearly beloved—hang on—"

"No, no, I'll get it!" Their number had been called. Abbie didn't want to do anything to interrupt the momentum—the *desire*—of her daughter to share something so tantalizing as the first draft of her wedding vows. If she needed to sneeze or pee, she would've held it. Abbie quickly brought back their samosas in two red baskets lined with checkered wax paper.

"You were saying, honey?"

"So here's what we wrote:

Dearly beloved, we are gathered here today to celebrate—or at least shrug and acknowledge—that Dick and Jane have decided that they're a little bit lonely, a little bit tired of dating, and would prefer reliable companionship to a life alone. They like each other well enough, and don't get on each other's nerves too much, and their sex life—well, it's not perfect, but when they do have sex, and it's once or twice a month these days, they enjoy the closeness of it. And besides, as we get older, sex will be less important (we hope!) than having someone to raise a child with, to take care of the house with, to help us manage finances, to take us to doctor's appointments when our eyesight fails and our hands shake, to put together a nice celebration of life—with a slide show and kick-ass background music—when we die. So let's be clear: we're good friends, sometimes we even both want sex at the same time, and really, at the end of the day, on this spinning rock, we love each other, and that's amazing. There's no other word for it. Well, there might be, but we like this one. So—Dick and Jane—may your life together be amazing!"

Naomi looked up at her mom. Abigail was stunned.

"It's . . . wonderful, wonderful," was all her mother could manage.

"We should've gone with it. Fuck. We were as wise as we would ever be, and we didn't even know it."

"I—that was beautiful. But Dick and Jane, like the old comic books? Before your time."

"Actually, Tomas was making a reference to a Gil Scott-Heron song—also before our time—but a timeless song, so there's that—but 'the eyesight failing and we love each other, and that's amazing' was all me. I was even gonna put something in there about serenely wiping each other's asses when we got old, but Tomas thought it was too much. He was right. No one serenely wipes anyone else's ass."

"The whole thing is so . . . you two. Why didn't you use this instead of the sonnet?"

"We thought it might sound negative."

"Well. It does," blurted out Abigail. "But in a good way. It just feels like it's all about realistic expectations and cherishing the little things."

Naomi dropped her head, shook it.

"Fuck me. We really should've used it. Goddammit."

"Can I have a copy?"

"Sure." Naomi looked back up at Abigail. "You know, Mom, I actually—how can I say it. I can handle the memories. I have some good ones, a lot of them, and I really believe that those aren't fake, that he wasn't fake. It's like, we had a ten-year marriage, with nine good years, and one shit one. Maybe just one shit month. And at first I thought the one erased the nine, but I kinda think—I wanna think—that's not true. I think Tomas loved me, maybe still loves me, but that he has a problem I can't solve. And I am worried to death wondering whether he can really, actually, truly solve it, even if he swears up and down it's solved."

Abigail smiled. It was a selfish smile. Here she'd found affirmation for her own marriage to Bruce, affirmation for the good things in her relationship with Naomi's father, in the prism through which her daughter was now viewing the end of her own marriage.

"Honey, I think it's wonderful that you can see it that way. Your father, bless his heart, I think he's been able to see that I was confused, but that I loved him, and that becoming who I really was didn't diminish the good years . . . well, we had you, and even if all the years were terrible, that alone was worth everything, the good and the bad."

"'Man is not affected by things, but by his thoughts about things.'"

"Hmm?"

"Something from a little coffee table book you got me. Years ago."

"'At the end of the day, on this . . . rock?'"

"Spinning rock."

"'. . . *on this spinning rock, we love each other.*' The Bard doesn't have much on you."

Naomi was going to say something about blindly biased mothers comparing their children favorably to Shakespeare, but she didn't.

DAY 179

TOMAS INSTINCTIVELY USED HIS OLD KEY to open the front door. He couldn't see Naomi, but he heard her rummaging around in the office. "Nomes?" he called out.

"Back here."

He realized he hadn't knocked.

"Sorry, I just let myself in."

Tomas didn't know what to do with his body. Should he follow her voice to what was to have been their future nursery? Should he just stand like a moron in the living room and wait, as he was now doing? What, on this penultimate day, should he do? What did he *want* to do? Scream? Throttle her neck? Run out of their and never stop running? Move to Fiji? Why had she asked him over *at all*? She had to know it could only hurt him. And she wasn't like that.

He sat on the couch. Moments later, she emerged. She was holding a large black boom box with built-in cassette player.

"Wow, haven't seen that in a minute," said Tomas.

"Remember why we got it?" asked Naomi.

"Of course. Halloween. I was Ad-Rock; you were Mike D."

"If Omar and Maya had thrown their usual costume party that year, I'm pretty sure we would've won."

"Not a doubt in my mind." Tomas tried to conceal in his voice the deep ache he felt. She was obviously beginning to clear stuff out, things like the boom box, which she felt was "his," not hers or theirs. The thought of the division of personal items, who would get which set of dishes, which pieces of furniture, and the thing he dreaded most, the division of photos they had deemed "print worthy," began to slowly shatter Tomas. This must be why she had asked him over. To start splitting stuff up. In his sightline was a picture of Naomi "holding up" the Leaning Tower of Pisa when they had tripped through Italy. They had seen other tourists do it. If you stand in just the right spot, and hold your hand just so, it appears to the camera that you are keeping the tower from falling.

Suddenly it occurred to Tomas he might not want *any* of those photos. The pain of what he had lost might be too great. He understood now how people could leave intimate family photographs in thrift shops.

Naomi lifted the boom box to her shoulder and said, "I remember thinking, it wasn't as heavy as you'd think. Like it was a stage prop."

"And I remember thinking, as long as it rattles car windows, it's a good one."

Naomi opened the battery compartment.

"Oof. Still have six D batteries in here. I hope it's not rusted out."

Tomas was touched. Whatever Naomi was feeling, that she wanted to turn on the old machine felt like she wanted—if only for a few seconds—to bask in memories of better times. He remembered that they had found the boombox not in a nice antique shop, but at a local Goodwill.

She turned the power on and immediately a blast of radio static assaulted their ears.

"Guess it works."

"Oh yeah, that's a window rattler for sure," said Tomas.

Naomi wore a red bandanna and a plaid men's button up short sleeve from the early '60's with a small button-down collar, and jeans.

"Rosie," said Tomas.

"Keeps the sweat out of my eyes."

She flashed a tiny smile. Rosie the Riveter. What Tomas always called her when she wore the red bandanna. He wanted to tell her how cute she looked in her boyish outfit, her cheeks reddened by whatever work or cleaning she had been doing. But nothing felt right. Everything felt like grasping.

"Hang on."

She vanished again into the second bedroom and came back moments later, holding a padded shipping envelope. It was open. She pulled out a cassette tape.

"I'm guessing we bought... Cyndi Lauper? Digital Underground? Seals and Crofts before 'yacht rock' was even a thing?" asked Tomas of the cassette tape.

"This showed up a few hours ago."

She tossed him the tape.

Tomas could see that the writing on the original label had been whited out and, in an unsteady hand, someone had written "Thomas" on it.

Evo. He hadn't flaked—yes, he hadn't *shown up*—but he hadn't flaked, either. He had arrived in his own way. There was no return address on the envelope, but Tomas could see the envelope was postmarked Lansing, Michigan.

"What is it?" asked Naomi.

"Well, if it's what I think it is, let's just play it."

Tomas put the cassette in, shut the small plastic door, and sat the boombox on the living room coffee table. Naomi joined him on the sofa. They both just stared at it for a moment, Tomas glanced at her, she at him, then Tomas pressed *play*.

For three seconds all they heard was the hiss of a blank tape, and then an unmistakable voice.

"Do I speak now?" Another second passed. "Hello Tomas, this is Lalla. Lalla Rios. There was a story I wanted to tell you before you left, but I couldn't remember it. But I remember now. I think I told you I met Amos at the phone company. He was a lineman—he called himself a 'pole monkey'—which I thought was funny. We met when a customer called to complain that his phone didn't work, and also that he had seen someone working on the pole outside his house, but that nothing was fixed. I told him he had called the wrong number, that there was a different phone number for repair, that I was accounts payable, and then he said a bad word, and I told him that wasn't helpful, and right away he said he was sorry. Then I asked him, 'If your phone doesn't work, how can you call me right now?' He laughed so hard I started laughing, and then he told me he was five blocks away at a friend's house. Anyway, sorry, I'm probably talking too long. I told the man I would personally make sure a good technician would come to his house soon. I had never done that, I didn't even have the permission to do that, but when he laughed like that, I had to do something. I went to the dock where all the repair trucks are, and the first man I saw was Amos Rios. I asked him if he could go fix the man's phone line, and right away he said yes. Two days later he took me to a nice Italian restaurant for dinner. Okay, I promise I will tell the story now. Every month in the office someone would be called 'employee of the month,' and they would put their picture up in the hallway, and we would stop fifteen minutes early—always on a Friday—to have cake and punch. I remember thinking maybe one day I would get this award, but after working there for two years, I realized the award meant nothing. The company just went through the department employees and when it was your turn, you got one. By the time I retired, I had eleven of them. It was silly, but it still felt nice. Even the cake and punch with my coworkers. It was nice to talk to them for a few minutes about things that had nothing to do with work. Well, after Amos and I had been dating about four months, it was my turn to get Employee of the Month again. I told him how everyone got it. He told me I deserved it anyway. And then on that Friday, I knew it was time for my cake and punch. But when I stepped into the hallway, it was so many people I couldn't believe it. Amos had gotten every lineman who wasn't on a service call to show up, and even people from Operations, and also friends who didn't work at the phone company. Our regular friends. I heard a popping noise. Amos had brought a bottle of champagne. We never had champagne. It was against company policy, but my boss, Mr. Mason, was a very nice man, and I looked at him. I was scared I was in trouble, but all he did was nod, and we all had champagne that day. I told Amos never to do that again. He ignored what I said. All he said was, 'You deserve more than this every day.' That was the day I knew we would be together forever."

Tomas turned to glance at Naomi. Tears were streaming down her face. For a moment, he was taken aback, but quickly realized, why shouldn't she be crying? She, too, deserved more every day. She, too, deserved an Amos to appreciate her properly. Impulsively Tomas said, "I hope you find an Amos one day." Another voice spoke from the tape, another inimitable voice.

"Your toilet bed works. I didn't think it would. People give me looks when they realize it's my shit and piss they're looking at it. That bemuses me. I pump the brakes so it really sloshes around in there."

Then nothing. The hiss took over again, but after a few more moments . . .

"You can probably guess I left Lalla's house. I'll miss her. One of the only people I've ever missed. Your toilet took away my excuse for being with her. So screw you for that. But—fuck it—it was time to go anyway."

Evo cleared his throat loudly—as if he was expectorating a lung—before spitting. Tomas and Naomi turned to each other and grimaced. And then that voice, like shards of glass, returned.

"So I wrote a few lines—not a full song—you ask too much. But your fucking little sob story, you stray mutt, that pasty little look in your eye? You wanted me to write a love song? I can't write about what I don't know. What's your lady's name . . . Emerald? Shit, can't remember now, not important—but I do know what it's like to hurt people, or make them go into a trance for three or four minutes, but

I don't know what the two of you felt. Well, correction. I had a dog when I was a kid. Bozo, a dachshund. I loved Bozo. This isn't a song, but here's a few lines."

Tomas glanced again at Naomi. The tears had stopped. She stared into space. He took her hand in his. She let him.

Evo plucked his guitar in a manner Tomas had never heard before from the man—a kind of slow Flamenco, where each note had its breathing space. Evo plucked faster and faster and soon he was playing a rhythmic drone, no longer Flamenco—harder, uglier, relentless. And then that uncanny voice, a strange alloy of exhaustion and the animal drive to keep on. "*Give me your hand and I just might live; give me your hand and I might pull you in. Run away, drown with me. My claw is a dandelion. One breath from you and a million blades float away.*"

Evo abruptly stopped singing and playing.

"Not thrilled with it, but there you go. Live your lives. I hate most people. But the ones I don't hate, when I'm in their orbit, that's the only place I am. I see everything at once. I'd walk through glass for those moments."

Tomas and Naomi heard a quiet click. Evo had stopped recording. They sat in silence, staring at the mute boom box, listening to the hiss. Naomi reached to turn it off.

"That was . . . unexpected."

"Yeah," said Tomas.

"Sounds like he didn't completely hate you," said Naomi, consciously adding a little cheer to her voice.

"I guess not."

"But he's not the headliner, is he?"

"No. He's not."

"Did you get what you needed from Lalla?"

"If I didn't, I really do need to find a reliable Mexican veterinarian to get me a jug of pentobarbital."

Naomi smiled.

"Funny," said Tomas. "I thought you asked me over to talk about the house. I was sure Evo had flaked." Naomi got up, went to the dining room table, and brought back a piece of paper that had been folded in three—obviously a letter taken from an envelope.

Saying nothing, she handed it to Tomas.

He immediately recognized the letterhead—"Love Without Borders." He knew from general life experience that a physical letter rather than an email signaled importance. A monetary check. A summons. A death in the family. There would also be a duplicate email, there probably already had been, but he realized he had stopped receiving them for several weeks, despite how close he and Naomi were to the head of the line.

He read the letter. It informed Naomi Curran, and Naomi Curran alone, that they had received the requested change in her application, and that she—as a single parent—was found still to be an eligible and desirable candidate. More than that, it was time. Tomas read the last few lines several times.

We will expect you at 9:00 a.m. on December 12. Your stay will be a week. Final documentation will be processed, and you and Jorge will return to your home together.

Tomas reread the brief letter several times.

"Jorge. It's a beautiful name," he said.

There it was. She had gone forward with the biggest decision in their life. She had changed her status to single parent, the agency had approved the change, and in three weeks, she would go to Bolivia, and return with a baby son.

And in one day, tomorrow, their divorce would be finalized.

"Congratulations," said Tomas. He took her hand again and squeezed it. "You'll be a great mom. A freakin' all star."

"Thank you." She'd had no idea how he would react to the news.

"I want you to have as much joy in your life as you can, Nomes, moments of whatever Evo was talking about, whatever Lalla actually felt. I am deeply sorry that my selfishness cut into that—I saw expressions on your face and looks in your eyes that will haunt me the rest of my days. I wish I could undo it all. But I can't. But if there's anything I can do—house stuff, whatever—just let me know."

"Okay. Thank you. There is something—"

"I know. It's tomorrow."

She nodded.

"I have to go to work after, so meet me on the steps at nine o'clock?"

"I'll be there at eight fifty-nine," he said.

She nodded, he gave her hand a quick reassuring squeeze, stood up, and walked toward the door.

"You're really not gonna mention the library project?"

Tomas turned around, confusion written large on his face.

"Huh?"

"Billy told me."

"Billy? How—he doesn't know how to—"

"He called the store, the general number, until he got to me. Kid's a pest."

"Lord you have no idea."

"When will you hear back?"

"In a few weeks."

"You're on the short list for the kind of project that could launch you into the stratosphere. Were you just not gonna tell me?"

"I mean, I'm sure at some point I would've said something," said Tomas listlessly.

"What's going on? You should be doing cartwheels or something."

"I feel good about it. Of course. It's great."

"Could you try to sound a little less convincing?"

"Huzzah and rah rah and all that."

"I said less convincing, not snarky."

"I know I sound like an entitled dickhole. I guess it isn't front and center for me right now. Anyway, you have no reason to believe me, but I finally got what I thought I wanted, and it's *fine*, it's even great and all, but it's not cheeseburgers or a good Old Fashioned or orgasm great. And it certainly isn't *you* great."

"Can't you just savor something for once? Bask for . . . I dunno, twenty seconds?"

"I'm basking now."

Naomi said nothing.

"I'm not Mies. Or Wright. Or Hadid. Or anyone else. I'm not Evo Korman, I'm not Lalla Rios. They are the great ones, and I'll always love their work, but I'm me. And that's fine enough. And when I close my eyes and all the noise dies down and everything else falls away—I see only you. And I remember only us."

She nodded slowly, without emotion.

He spoke again. "Tomorrow 8:59."

Again she nodded.

He left. Naomi stayed on the couch, reached forward, and rewound the cassette in the boom box.

DAY 180

NAOMI ARRIVED AT THE SUBWAY STOP nearest the Alameda County Courthouse at eight-thirty. She had checked the BART schedule and could have taken a later train that would have put her at the courthouse closer to nine, but she didn't want to risk a late train, or any other delay. It was a brisk, cool, day. Dots of sunlight flickered off Lake Merritt. The steady sound of morning traffic around the lake was punctuated by the occasional squawk of geese. The pedal boats were all moored.

When she arrived at the courthouse, she saw that Tomas was already sitting midway up the flight of stone steps. He stood when he saw Naomi.

She quickened her pace.

"Hi." She carried a manila folder in her hand.

"Hi."

"Ready?"

"Yeah," he replied.

She trotted up the steps, quickly, passing him. He picked up his pace in turn. She turned back and saw the crown of his head as he hurried. She was breathing heavily. She slowed down. There was no reason to race. It was 8:43. The clerk's office wouldn't open for another seventeen minutes. They would have to loiter somewhere anyway.

She stopped at the top of the steps. Tomas glanced up, saw her standing.

"You okay?" asked Tomas.

Tomas could see her breathing heavily, her chest moving up and down.

"Oh, god, Tomas, I'm either about to make the best decision of my life, or a huge mistake."

Tomas said nothing. He had made an uneasy peace with their separation and divorce. More than that, he felt he had foregone the right to say anything more on the subject. He had already tried everything his feeble imagination could conjure. Now it was time to honor Naomi's request. He did not want to corrupt her decision-making process in any way. He did not want even the smallest dandelion's spore worth of responsibility in what she had decided.

"Tomas, I am still hurting, and may be for I don't know how long, but I love you. I can't shake that. It makes me nuts. People do shitty things and can be forgiven. But this is big, and my head says, 'Don't get in a car that is sputtering and might not be fixable.' But I remember the funny and sweet you, and I know how bad you feel. And maybe we can get there again."

Tomas's breath came in short, sharp jabs.

"Why are you frowning?" asked Naomi, a hint of confusion in her voice.

"Am I? I didn't realize."

"Tomas, I can't promise anything. I'm bringing a baby into my life. I can bring a partner into my life at some point and that's okay. But what I *do not want*—what I can't imagine forgiving myself for—is bringing someone in who that baby will come to know and feel safe with and love, and then yanking you out of their life."

You? Did Tomas hear that right? "You? You mean me?"

Naomi nodded. "A hundred and eighty days, Tomas. I still need time. I need to focus on Jorge. I want to see you. I want you to visit now and again. I don't want to just be roommates, but I'm scared right now to be anything more. I need time. Can you just be yourself, the Tomas I loved, and wait, and be here—or not—on my terms, for a hundred and eighty more days? Obviously I'll understand if you say no—I know I'm asking you to wait in a stuck elevator. But there is a scar. And I think I can live with it. I think I want to be with you. I do. If you really believe all the things you've told me in the last six months, if you can be at peace just being Tomas Araeta, I can—and want—to live with that person. But I'm scared. I know I'm putting you on probation, but I just need time."

Tomas said nothing, just listened.

"I'm sorry, I imagined this moment going a thousand different ways, and I know there's some dumb clock in front of us. And if you can't answer now—"

"Naomi," interrupted Tomas.

She stopped, listened.

"One hundred and eighty days. Limbo, elevators, traffic on the 580, whatever you want to call it. I'm in."

"Marivel won't like it," said Naomi, sounding almost genuinely fearful.

"Be weird if she did!"

Naomi slowly stepped down the seven steps separating them. They were nearly eye to eye.

"I'm probably gonna ask you this a hundred more times, and be thinking about it when I'm not asking you," said Naomi, "but are you really at peace about everything?"

"*Everything?* Oh god no. Didn't you just say you loved *some* parts of the old me? I thought we would just cherry pick *those* parts."

She smiled and laughed but needed him to say something else. He needed to say it, too.

"I'm not a zombie, Nomes, and I don't think that's what you want. I'll still be a moody pill, but I have a wonderful partner who I will turn to on the dark days, the great days, the boring days, the days in between. And whatever she needs, I hope she knows—and *wants*—to come to me, too, and in my own way, maybe perfectly, maybe not, probably most times off the mark, I'll at least try. Always. I love you.

But talk is cheap. I love caramel and Julius Shulman's photos of the Koenig house, too. All I can do is show you who I am."

"One hundred and eighty days?" asked Naomi.

Tomas wrapped his arms gently around her waist.

"One hundred and eighty days."

ACKNOWLEDGMENTS

I DON'T KNOW HOW TO WRITE an adequate or complete Acknowledgments section. I believe that every person we meet, every encounter we have, informs how we see the world, how we pursue the things we find joyful and meaningful. Writing a book, cooking, gardening, watching TV, playing with your kids, staring at the clouds. Whatever form our passions take, all of it is colored by our connection to people, however fleeting or deep. So I do want to thank everyone I've ever met, but I'm pretty sure that sounds pretentious and insane.

So I'll try to be a little more specific.

As for writing this book, I'd like to thank two people who I met in my late teens, whose unorthodox and opinionated and funny and fearless worldviews profoundly influenced me and my writing: Rick Howell and Kayle Hilliard. They are one of a kind, and my life is richer for knowing them.

I'd like to thank Liam Callanan for reading an early draft of the novel and giving me invaluable global and specific feedback.

I owe a debt as well to Justin Lin, who for twenty years has helped me be tougher on myself when it comes to editing the written word.

So many others have directly or indirectly informed this book: Rafael Botello, Travis Foss, Semone Clark, Robert Consing, Lisa Carter, Raymond Consing, Bill Halfon, Jonathan Jaffe, Gabriel Botello, James Carter, Jeff Briggs, Linda Howell, Alfredo Botello Sr.,

Murray Silverstein, Greg Daniels, Kelsey Burt, Iiad Mamikunian, Denise Rene, and others, many others.

And, of course, without Koehler Books there would be no book. My team has been a true pleasure to work with: acquisitions editor Greg Fields for his passion and close reading, publisher John Koehler for caring enough to create a personal relationship and shepherd me through the process, my in-the-trenches editor Becky Hilliker for making the kinds of suggestions now that will hopefully save me from crushing embarrassment later, and graphic artist Danielle Koehler, who fully understood the tone and intention of the book and captured it visually. They all helped make the process of turning a Word document into a novel a collaborative pleasure.

Thanks everyone.

www.ingramcontent.com/pod-product-compliance
Lightning Source LLC
LaVergne TN
LVHW041655060526
838201LV00043B/447